UNNATURAL
CREATURES

BOOKS BY NEIL GAIMAN FROM BLOOMSBURY

NOVELS

Fortunately, the Milk . . .
The Graveyard Book
Odd and the Frost Giants
Coraline

SHORT STORIES

M is for Magic

PICTURE BOOKS

Illustrated by Dave McKean
Crazy Hair
The Day I Swapped My Dad for Two Goldfish
The Wolves in the Walls

Illustrated by Charles Vess
Instructions
Blueberry Girl

Illustrated by Gris Grimly
The Dangerous Alphabet

Illustrated by Adam Rex
Chu's Day

GRAPHIC NOVELS

Illustrated by Dave McKean
Signal to Noise
The Tragical Comedy or Comical Tragedy of Mr Punch
MirrorMask

Illustrated by P. Craig Russell
Coraline

THE MUSEUM OF
UNNATURAL
HISTORY PRESENTS

UNNATURAL
CREATURES

STORIES SELECTED BY

NEIL GAIMAN

WITH MARIA DAHVANA HEADLEY
ILLUSTRATED BY BRIONY MORROW-CRIBBS

a number of stories featuring

UNNATURAL CREATURES

along with several other creatures who are either unlikely,

impossible, or do not exist at all.

BLOOMSBURY
LONDON NEW DELHI NEW YORK SYDNEY

Bloomsbury Publishing, London, New Delhi, New York and Sydney

First published in Great Britain in June 2013 by Bloomsbury Publishing Plc
50 Bedford Square, London WC1B 3DP

First published in the United States by HarperCollins Publishers
10 East 53rd Street, New York NY10022

This paperback edition first published in February 2014

Printed in Great Britain by CPI Group (UK) Ltd, Croydon CR0 4YY

1 3 5 7 9 10 8 6 4 2

For Bigfoot, for the time travelers, for the pirates, for the robots, for any boring people (who obviously aren't actually secret agents in boring disguise), for people in space rockets, and for our mothers
—N.G.

INTRODUCTION

WHEN I WAS A BOY, the best place in the world was in London, a short walk from South Kensington Station. It was an ornate building, made of colored bricks, and it had—and come to think of it, still has—gargoyles all over the roof: pterodactyls and saber-toothed tigers. There was a *Tyrannosaurus rex* skeleton in the lobby, and a stuffed replica of a dodo in a dusty case. There were things in bottles that had once been alive, and things in glass boxes that were alive no longer, sorted and catalogued and pinned.

It was called the Natural History Museum. In the same building was the Geological Museum, with meteorites and diamonds and strange and glorious minerals, and just around the corner was the Science Museum, where I could test my hearing, and rejoice in how much higher than an adult I could hear.

It was the best place in the world that I could actually visit.

I was convinced that the Natural History Museum was missing only one thing: a unicorn. Well, a unicorn *and* a dragon. Also it was missing werewolves. (Why was there nothing about werewolves in the Natural History Museum? I wanted to know about werewolves.) There were vampire bats, but none of the better-dressed vampires on display, and no mermaids at all, not one—I looked—and as for griffins or manticores, they were completely out.

(I was never surprised that they did not have a phoenix on display. There is only one phoenix at a time, of course, and while the Natural History Museum was filled with dead things, the phoenix is always alive.)

I liked huge stone-skeleton dinosaurs and dusty impossible animals in glass cases. I liked living, breathing animals, and preferred them when they weren't pets: I loved encountering a hedgehog or a snake or a badger or the tiny frogs that, one day every spring, came hopping up from the pond across the road and turned the garden into something that seemed to be moving.

I liked real animals. But I liked the animals who existed in a more shadowy way even more than I liked the ones who hopped or slithered or wandered into my real life, because they were impossible, because they might or might not exist, because simply thinking about them made the world a more magical place.

I loved my monsters.

Where there is a monster, the wise American poet Ogden Nash told us, *there is a miracle.*

I wished I could visit a Museum of Unnatural History, but, even so, I was glad there wasn't one. Werewolves were wonderful because they could be anything, I knew. If someone actually caught a werewolf, or a dragon, if they tamed a manticore or stabled a unicorn, put them in bottles, dissected them, then they could only be one thing, and they would no longer live in the shadowy places between the things I knew and the world of the impossible, which was, I was certain, the only place that mattered.

There was no such museum, not then. But I knew how to visit the creatures who would never be sighted in the zoos or the museum or the woods. They were waiting for me in books and in stories, after all, hiding inside the twenty-six characters and a handful of punctuation marks. These letters and words, when placed in the right order, would conjure all manner of exotic beasts and people from the shadows, would reveal the motives and minds of insects and of cats. They were spells, spelled with words to make worlds, waiting for me, in the pages of books.

The link between animals and words goes way back. (Did you know that our letter A began its life as a drawing of the upside-down head of a bull? The two bits at the bottom that the A stands on, those were originally horns. The pointy top bit was its face and nose.)

The book you are holding, with its werewolves and mysterious things in chests, with its dangerous inksplats and its beasts and snakegods, its sunbird, its unicorns and mermaids and even its beautiful Death, exists to help take care of the current Museum of Unnatural History.

The Museum of Unnatural History is a real place; you can visit it. It is part of the mysterious and shadowy organization that has brought us Pirate Stores and Superhero Supply Stores while at the same time spreading literacy by supporting, hosting, and teaching a number of writing programs for kids, along with providing a place where they can do homework, not to mention attend workshops.

By buying this book, you are supporting 826 DC and literacy, and I am grateful, and Dave Eggers, who cofounded the whole 826 movement, is grateful, and the kids who attend 826 DC are grateful too. Probably some of the griffins and mermaids, who are, as far as we know, not in the museum, are also grateful, but of this, as of so many things, we cannot be certain.

Neil Gaiman
September 2012

PS: An introduction is not an acknowledgments page. Lots of people have donated their time and their stories to make this book a reality, and I am grateful to all of them, to all the authors in this book and to everyone who has helped. But I want to embarrass my coeditor, Maria Dahvana Headley, by thanking her here by name. Maria is not just an excellent writer, but she is also an organized powerhouse and is the only reason that this book is coming out on time without lots and lots of blank pages in it. Thank you, Maria.

TABLE OF CREATURES

UNNATURAL CREATURES

1

GAHAN WILSON is a cartoonist. He draws things that scare me. Sometimes he writes stories too. In this story, with a somewhat unpronounceable title (you'll see why), he combines writing and drawing with terrifying results, to show us a most unnatural creature indeed.

One morning, beside the eggs and toast, there's a dark spot on the tablecloth, and where it came from, no one knows. The only certainty is that the moment one stops looking at it, it moves. And as it moves, it grows. . . .

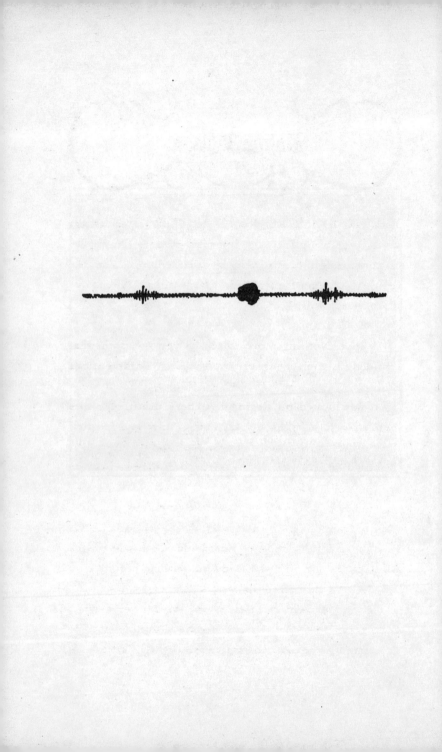

by
Gahan Wilson

THE FIRST TIME REGINALD ARCHER saw the thing, it was, in its simplicity, absolute. It owned not the slightest complication or involvement. It lacked the tiniest, the remotest, the most insignificant trace of embellishment. It looked like this:

A spot. Nothing more. Black, as you see, somewhat lopsided, as you see—an unprepossessing, unpretentious spot.

It was located on Reginald Archer's dazzlingly white linen tablecloth, on his breakfast table, three and one half inches from the side of his eggcup. Reginald Archer was in the act of opening the egg in the eggcup when he saw the spot.

He paused and frowned. Reginald Archer was a bachelor, had been one for his full forty-three years, and he was fond of a smoothly running household. Things like black spots on table linens displeased him, perhaps beyond reason. He rang the bell to summon his butler, Faulks.

That worthy entered and, seeing the dark expression upon his master's face, approached his side with caution. He cleared his throat, bowed ever so slightly, just exactly

the right amount of bow, and, following the direction of his master's thin, pale, pointing finger, observed, in his turn, the spot.

"What," asked Archer, "is *this* doing here?"

Faulks, after a moment's solemn consideration, owned he had no idea how the spot had come to be there, apologized profusely for its presence, and promised its imminent and permanent removal. Archer stood, the egg left untasted in its cup, his appetite quite gone, and left the room.

It was Archer's habit to retire every morning to his study and there tend to any little chores of correspondence and finance which had accumulated. His approach to this, as to everything else, was precise to the point of being ritualistic; he liked to arrange his days in reliable, predictable patterns. He had seated himself at his desk, a lovely affair of lustrous mahogany, and was reaching for the mail which had been tidily stacked for his perusal, when, on the green blotter which entirely covered the desk's working surface, he saw:

He paled, I do not exaggerate, and rang once more for his butler. There was a pause, a longer pause than would usually have occurred, before the trustworthy Faulks responded to his master's summons. The butler's face bore a recognizable confusion.

"The spot, sir—" Faulks began, but Archer cut him short.

"Bother the spot," he snapped, indicating the offense on the blotter. "What is *this*?"

Faulks peered at the in bafflement.

"I do not know, sir," he said. "I have never seen anything quite like it."

"Nor have I," said Archer. "Nor do I wish to see its likes again. Have it removed."

Faulks began to carefully take away the blotter, sliding it out from the leather corner grips which held it to the desk, as Archer watched him icily. Then, for the first time, Archer noticed his elderly servant's very odd expression. He recalled Faulks's discontinued comment.

"What is it you were trying to tell me, then?" he asked.

The butler glanced up at him, hesitated, and then spoke.

"It's about the spot, sir," he said. "The one on the tablecloth. I went to look at it, after you had left, sir, and I cannot understand it, sir—it was *gone*!"

"Gone?" asked Archer.

"Gone," said Faulks.

The butler glanced down at the blotter, which he now held before him, and started.

"And so is *this*, sir!" he gasped, and, turning round the blotter, revealed it to be innocent of the slightest trace of a

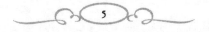

Conscious, now, that something very much out of the ordinary was afoot, Archer gazed thoughtfully into space. Faulks, watching, observed the gaze suddenly harden into focus.

"Look over there, Faulks," said Archer, in a quiet tone. "Over yonder, at the wall."

Faulks did as he was told, wondering at his master's instructions. Then comprehension dawned, for there, on the wallpaper, directly under an indifferent seascape, was:

Archer stood, and the two men crossed the room.

"What can it be, sir?" asked Faulks.

"I can't imagine," said Archer.

He turned to speak, but when he saw his butler's eyes move to his, he looked quickly back at the wall. Too late— the ⟍ was gone.

"It needs constant observation," Archer murmured, then, aloud: "Look for it, Faulks. Look for it. And when you see it, *don't take your eyes from it for a second*!"

They walked about the room in an intensive search. They had not been at it for more than a moment when Faulks gave an exclamation.

"Here, sir!" he cried. "On the windowsill!"

Archer hurried to his side and saw:

"Don't let it out of your sight!" he hissed.

As the butler stood, transfixed and gaping, his master chewed furiously at the knuckles of his left hand. Whatever the thing was, it must be taken care of, and promptly. He would not allow such continued disruption in his house.

But how to get rid of it? He shifted to the knuckles of his other hand and thought. The thing had—he hated to

admit it, but there it was—*supernatural* overtones. Perhaps it was some beastly sort of ghost.

He shoved both hands, together with their attendant knuckles, into his pants pockets. It showed the extreme state of his agitation, for he loathed nothing more than unsightly bulges in a well-cut suit. Who would know about this sort of thing? Who could possibly handle it?

It came to him in a flash: Sir Harry Mandifer! Of course! He'd known Sir Harry back at school, only plain Harry, then, of course, and now they shared several clubs. Harry had taken to writing, made a good thing of it, and now, with piles of money to play with, he'd taken to spiritualism, become, perhaps, the top authority in the field. Sir Harry was just the man! If *only* he could persuade him.

His face set in grimly determined lines, Archer marched to his telephone and dialed Sir Harry's number. It was not so easy to get through to him as it had been in the old days. Now there were secretaries, suspicious and secretive. But he was known, that made all the difference, and soon he and Sir Harry were together on the line. After the customary greetings and small talk, Archer brought the conversation around to the business at hand. Crisply, economically, he described the morning's events. Could Sir Harry find it possible to come? He fancied that time might be an important factor. Sir Harry would! Archer thanked him with all the warmth his somewhat constricted personality would allow, and, with a heartfelt sigh of relief, put back the receiver.

He had barely done it when he heard Faulks give a small cry of despair. He turned to see the old fellow wringing his hands in abject misery.

"I just blinked, sir!" he quavered. "Only blinked!"

It had been enough. A fraction of a second unwatched, and the ▟▜▙ was gone from the sill.

Resignedly, they once again took up the search.

Sir Harry Mandifer settled back comfortably in the cushioned seat of his limousine and congratulated himself on settling the business of Marston Rectory the night before. It would not have done to leave that dangerous affair in the lurch, but the bones of the Mewing Nun had been found at last, and now she would rest peacefully in a consecrated grave. No more would headless children decorate the Cornish landscape, no more would the nights resound with mothers' lamentations. He had done his job, done it well, and now he was free to investigate what sounded a perfectly charming mystery.

Contentedly, the large man lit a cigar and watched the streets go sliding by. Delicious that a man as cautiously organized as poor old Archer should find himself confronted with something so outrageous. It only showed you that the tidiest lives have nothing but quicksand for a base. The snuggest haven's full of trapdoors and sliding panels, unsuspected attics and suddenly discovered rooms. Why should the careful Archer find himself exempt? And he hadn't.

The limousine drifted to a gentle stop before Archer's house and Mandifer, emerging from his car, gazed up at the

building with pleasure. It was a gracious Georgian structure which had been in Archer's family since the time of its
construction. Mandifer mounted its steps and was about to
apply himself to its knocker when the door flew open and
he found himself facing a desperately agitated Faulks.

"Oh, sir," gasped the butler, speaking in piteous tones,
"I'm so glad you could come! We don't know what to make
of it, sir, and we can't hardly keep track of it, it moves so
fast!"

"There, Faulks, there," rumbled Sir Harry, moving
smoothly into the entrance with the unstoppable authority
of a great clipper ship under full sail. "It can't be as bad as
all that now, can it?"

"Oh, it can, sir, it can," said Faulks, following in Mandifer's wake down the hall. "You just can't get a *hold* on it,
sir, is what it is, and every time it's back, it's *bigger*, sir!"

"In the study, isn't it?" asked Sir Harry, opening the
door of that room and gazing inside.

He stood stock-still and his eyes widened a trifle
because the sight before him, even for one so experienced
in peculiar sights as he, was startling.

Imagine a beautiful room, exquisitely furnished,
impeccably maintained. Imagine the occupant of that room
to be a thin, tallish gentleman, dressed faultlessly, in the
best possible taste. Conceive of the whole thing, man and
room in combination, to be a flawless example of the sort of
styled perfection that only large amounts of money, filtered
through generations of confident privilege, can produce.

Now see that man on his hands and knees, in one of the room's corners, staring, bug-eyed, at the wall, and, on the wall, picture:

"Remarkable," said Sir Harry Mandifer.

"Isn't it, sir?" moaned Faulks. "Oh, isn't it?"

"I'm so glad you could come, Sir Harry," said Archer, from his crouched position in the corner. It was difficult to make out his words as he spoke them through clenched teeth.

"Forgive me for not rising, but if I take my eyes off this thing or even blink, the whole—oh, God *damn* it!"

Instantly, the

vanished from the wall. Archer gave out an explosive sigh, clapped his hands to his face, and sat back heavily on the floor.

"Don't tell me where it's got to now, Faulks," he said, "I don't want to know; I don't want to hear about it."

Faulks said nothing, only touched a trembling hand on Sir Harry's shoulder and pointed to the ceiling. There, almost directly in its center, was:

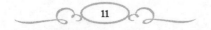

Sir Harry leaned his head close to Faulks's ear and whispered: "Keep looking at it for as long as you can, old man. Try not to let it get away. Then in his normal, conversational tone, which was a kind of cheerful roar, he spoke to Archer: "Seems you have a bit of a sticky problem here, what?"

Archer looked up grimly from between his fingers. Then, carefully, he lowered his arms and stood. He brushed himself off, made a few adjustments on his coat and tie, and spoke:

"I'm sorry, Sir Harry. I'm afraid I rather let it get the better of me."

"No such thing!" boomed Sir Harry Mandifer, clapping Archer on the back. "Besides, it's enough to rattle anyone. Gave me quite a turn, myself, and I'm used to this sort of nonsense!"

Sir Harry had developed his sturdy technique of encouragement during many a campaign in a haunted house and ghost-ridden moor, and it did not fail him now. Archer's return to self-possession was almost immediate. Satisfied at the restoration, Sir Harry looked up at the ceiling.

"You say it started as a kind of spot?" he asked, peering at the dark thing which spread above them.

"About as big as a penny," answered Archer.

"What have the stages been like, between then and now?"

"Little bits come out of it. They get bigger, and, at the

same time, other little bits come popping out, and, as if that weren't enough, the whole ghastly thing keeps *swelling*, like some damned balloon."

"Nasty," said Sir Harry.

"I'd say it's gotten to be a yard across," said Archer.

"At least."

"What do you make of it, Sir Harry?"

"It looks to me like a sort of plant."

Both the butler and Archer gaped at him. The

instantly disappeared.

"I'm sorry, sir," said the butler, stricken.

"What do you mean, *plant*?" asked Archer. "It can't be a plant, Sir Harry. It's perfectly flat, for one thing."

"Have you touched it?"

Archer sniffed.

"Not very likely," he said.

Discreetly, the butler cleared his throat.

"It's on the floor, gentlemen," he said.

The three looked down at the thing with reflectful expressions. Its longest reach was now a little over four feet. "You'll notice," said Harry, "that the texture of the carpet does not show through the blackness, therefore it's not like ink, or some other stain. It has an independent surface."

He stooped down, surprisingly graceful for a man of his size, and, pulling a pencil from his pocket, poked at the thing. The pencil went into the darkness for about a quarter of an inch, and then stopped. He jabbed at another point, this time penetrating a good, full inch.

"You see," said Sir Harry, standing. "It does have a complex kind of shape. Our eyes can perceive it only in a two-dimensional way, but the sense of touch moves it along to the third. The obvious implication of all this length, width and breadth business is that your plant's drifted in from some other dimensional set, do you see? I should imagine the original spot was its seed. Am I making myself clear on all this? Do you understand?"

Archer did not, quite, but he gave a reasonably good imitation of a man who had.

"But why did the accursed thing show up here?" he asked.

Sir Harry seemed to have the answer for that one too, but Faulks interrupted it, whatever it may have been, and we shall never know it.

"Oh, sir," he cried. "It's gone, again!"

It was, indeed. The carpet stretched unblemished under the three men's feet. They looked about the room, somewhat

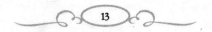

anxiously now, but could find no trace of the invader.

"Perhaps it's gone back into the dining room," said Sir Harry, but a search revealed that it had not.

"There is no reason to assume it must confine itself to the two rooms," said Sir Harry, thoughtfully chewing his lip. "Nor even to the house, itself."

Faulks, standing closer to the hallway door than the others, tottered, slightly, and emitted a strangled sound. The others turned and looked where the old man pointed. There, stretching across the striped paper of the hall across from the door was:

"This is," Archer said, in a choked voice, "*really* a bit too much, Sir Harry. Something simply must be done or the damned thing will take over the whole, bloody house!"

"Keep your eyes fixed on it, Faulks," said Sir Harry, "at all costs." He turned to Archer. "It has substance, I have proven that. It can be attacked. Have you some large cutting instrument about the place? A machete? Something like that?"

Archer pondered, then brightened, in a grim sort of way.

"I have a kris," he said.

"Get it," said Sir Harry.

Archer strode from the room, clenching and unclench-ing his hands. There was a longish pause, and then his voice called from another room:

"I can't get the blasted thing off its mounting!"

"I'll come and help," Sir Harry answered. He turned to Faulks who was pointing at the thing on the wall like some loyal bird dog. "Never falter, old man," he said. "Keep your gaze rock steady!"

The kris, an old war souvenir brought to the house by Archer's grandfather, was fixed to its display panel by a complicatedly woven arrangement of wires, and it took Sir Harry and Archer a good two minutes to get it free. They hurried back to the hall and there jarred to a halt, abso-lutely thunderstruck. The

was nowhere to be seen, but that was not the worst: the butler, Faulks, was gone! Archer and Sir Harry exchanged startled glances and then called the servant's name, again and again, with no effect whatever.

"What can it be, Sir Harry?" asked Archer. "What, in God's name, has happened?"

Sir Harry Mandifer did not reply. He grasped the kris before him, his eyes darting this way and that, and Archer, to his horror, saw that the man was trembling where he stood. Then, with a visible effort of will, Sir Harry pulled himself together and assumed, once more, his usual staunch air.

"We must find it, Archer," he said, his chin thrust out. "We must find it and we must kill it. We may not have another chance if it gets away, again!"

Sir Harry leading the way, the two men covered the ground floor, going from room to room, but found nothing. A search of the second also proved futile.

"Pray God," said Sir Harry, mounting to the floor above, "the creature has not quit the house."

Archer, now short of breath from simple fear, climbed unsteadily after.

"Perhaps it's gone back where it came from, Sir Harry," he said.

"Not now," the other answered grimly. "Not after Faulks. I think it's found it likes our little world."

"But what *is* it?" asked Archer.

"It's what I said it was—a plant," replied the large man, opening a door and peering into the room revealed. "A special kind of plant. We have them here, in our dimension."

At this point, Archer understood. Sir Harry opened

another door, and then another, with no success. There was the attic left. They went up the narrow steps, Sir Harry in the lead, his kris held high before him. Archer, by now, was barely able to drag himself along by the banister. His breath came in tiny whimpers.

"A meat eater, isn't it?" he whispered. "*Isn't* it, Sir Harry?"

Sir Harry Mandifer took his hand from the knob of the small door and turned to look down at his companion.

"That's right, Archer," he said, the door swinging open, all unnoticed, behind his back. "The thing's a carnivore."

2

I keep bees. Or at least, there are seven hives of bees in my garden. (Yes, the honey is wonderful, and yes I've been stung, but not very often.) The strangest thing about the bees and wasps in this story is that all the natural history is quite right (E. LILY YU knows her bees) but it's still, well, unnatural. Lily won the John W. Campbell Award for Best New Writer. Also, she sings in elevators.

In this story we encounter the mapmaking wasps of Yiwei and the colony of bees they see as their natural servants. . . .

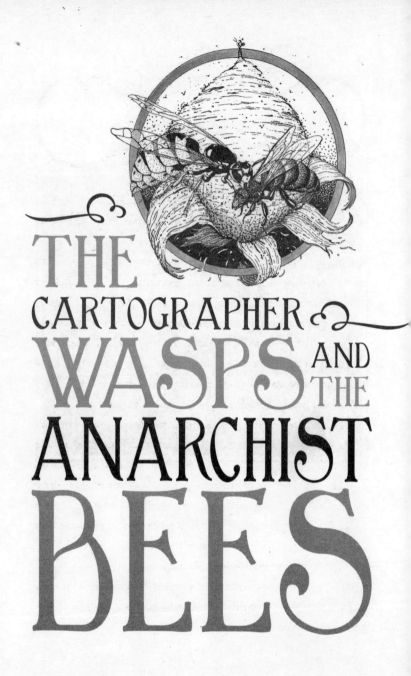

THE CARTOGRAPHER WASPS AND THE ANARCHIST BEES

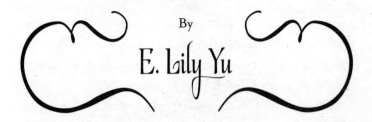

By

E. Lily Yu

FOR LONGER THAN ANYONE COULD REMEMBER, the village of Yiwei had worn, in its orchards and under its eaves, clay-colored globes of paper that hissed and fizzed with wasps. The villagers maintained an uneasy peace with their neighbors for many years, exercising inimitable tact and circumspection. But it all ended the day a boy, digging in the riverbed, found a stone whose balance and weight pleased him. With this, he thought, he could hit a sparrow in flight. There were no sparrows to be seen, but a paper ball hung low and inviting nearby. He considered it for a moment, head cocked, then aimed and threw.

Much later, after he had been plastered and soothed, his mother scalded the fallen nest until the wasps seething in the paper were dead. In this way it was discovered that the wasp nests of Yiwei, dipped in hot water, unfurled into beautifully accurate maps of provinces near and far, inked in vegetable pigments and labeled in careful Mandarin that could be distinguished beneath a microscope.

The villagers' subsequent incursions with bee veils and kettles of boiling water soon diminished the prosperous population to a handful. Commanded by a single stubborn foundress, the survivors folded a new nest in the shape of a paper boat, provisioned it with fallen apricots and squash blossoms, and launched themselves onto the river. Browsing cows and children fled the riverbanks as they drifted downstream, piping sea chanteys.

At last, forty miles south from where they had begun, their craft snagged on an upthrust stick and sank. Only one drowned in the evacuation, weighed down with the remains of an apricot. They reconvened upon a stump and looked about themselves.

"It's a good place to land," the foundress said in her sweet soprano, examining the first rough maps that the scouts brought back. There were plenty of caterpillars, oaks for ink galls, fruiting brambles, and no signs of other wasps. A colony of bees had hived in a split oak two miles away. "Once we are established we will, of course, send a delegation to collect tribute.

"We will not make the same mistakes as before. Ours is a race of explorers and scientists, cartographers and philosophers, and to rest and grow slothful is to die. Once we are established here, we will expand."

It took two weeks to complete the nurseries with their paper mobiles, and then another month to reconstruct the Great Library and fill the pigeonholes with what the oldest cartographers could remember of their lost maps. Their comings and goings did not go unnoticed. An ambassador from the beehive arrived with an ultimatum and was promptly executed; her wings were made into stained-glass windows for the council chamber, and her stinger was returned to the hive in a paper envelope. The second ambassador came with altered attitude and a proposal to divide the bees' kingdom evenly between the two governments, retaining pollen and water rights for the bees—"as an acknowledgment of the preexisting claims of a free people to the natural resources of a common territory," she hummed.

The wasps of the council were gracious and only divested the envoy of her sting. She survived just long enough to deliver her account to the hive.

The third ambassador arrived with a ball of wax on the tip of her stinger and was better received.

"You understand, we are not refugees applying for recognition of a token territorial sovereignty," the foundress said as attendants served them nectars in paper horns, "nor are we negotiating with you as equal states. Those were the assumptions of your late predecessors. They were mistaken."

"I trust I will do better," the diplomat said stiffly. She was older than the others, and the hairs of her thorax were sparse and faded.

"I do hope so."

"Unlike them, I have complete authority to speak for the hive. You have propositions for us; that is clear enough. We are prepared to listen."

"Oh, good." The foundress drained her horn and took another. "Yours is an old and highly cultured society, despite the indolence of your ruler, which we understand to be a racial rather than personal proclivity. You have laws, and traditional dances, and mathematicians, and principles, which of course we do respect."

"Your terms, please."

She smiled. "Since there is a local population of tussah moths, which we prefer for incubation, there is no need for anything so unrepublican as slavery. If you refrain from insurrection, you may keep your self-rule. But we will take a fifth of your stores in an ordinary year, and a tenth in drought years, and one of every hundred larvae."

"To eat?" Her antennae trembled with revulsion.

"Only if food is scarce. No, they will be raised among us and learn our ways and our arts, and then they will serve as officials and bureaucrats among you. It will be to your advantage, you see."

The diplomat paused for a moment, looking at nothing at all. Finally she said, "A tenth, in a good year—"

"Our terms," the foundress said, "are not negotiable."

The guards shifted among themselves, clinking the plates of their armor and shifting the gleaming points of their stings.

"I don't have a choice, do I?"

"The choice is enslavement or cooperation," the foundress said. "For your hive, I mean. You might choose something else, certainly, but they have tens of thousands to replace you with."

The diplomat bent her head. "I am old," she said. "I have served the hive all my life, in every fashion. My loyalty

is to my hive and I will do what is best for it."

"I am so very glad."

"I ask you—I beg you—to wait three or four days to impose your terms. I will be dead by then, and will not see my sisters become a servile people."

The foundress clicked her claws together. "Is the delaying of business a custom of yours? We have no such practice. You will have the honor of watching us elevate your sisters to moral and technological heights you could never imagine."

The diplomat shivered.

"Go back to your queen, my dear. Tell them the good news."

It was a crisis for the constitutional monarchy. A riot broke out in District 6, destroying the royal waxworks and toppling the mouse-bone monuments before it was brutally suppressed. The queen had to be calmed with large doses of jelly after she burst into tears on her ministers' shoulders.

"Your Majesty," said one, "it's not a matter for your concern. Be at peace."

"These are my children," she said, sniffling. "You would feel for them too, were you a mother."

"Thankfully, I am not," the minister said briskly, "so to business."

"War is out of the question," another said.

"Their forces are vastly superior."

"We outnumber them three hundred to one!"

"They are experienced fighters. Sixty of us would die for each of theirs. We might drive them away, but it would cost us most of the hive and possibly our queen—"

The queen began weeping noisily again and had to be cleaned and comforted.

"Have we any alternatives?"

There was a small silence.

"Very well, then."

The terms of the relationship were copied out, at the wasps' direction, on small paper plaques embedded in propolis and wax around the hive. As paper and ink were new substances to the bees, they jostled and touched and tasted the bills until the paper fell to pieces. The wasps sent to oversee the installation did not take this kindly. Several civilians died before it was established that the bees could not read the Yiwei dialect.

Thereafter the hive's chemists were charged with compounding pheromones complex enough to encode the terms of the treaty. These were applied to the papers, so that both species could inspect them and comprehend the relationship between the two states.

Whereas the hive before the wasp infestation had been busy but content, the bees now lived in desperation. The natural terms of their lives were cut short by the need to gather enough honey for both the hive and the wasp nest. As they traveled farther and farther afield in search of nectar, they stopped singing. They danced their findings grimly, without joy. The queen herself grew gaunt and thin from breeding replacements, and certain ministers who understood such matters began feeding royal jelly to the strongest larvae.

Meanwhile, the wasps grew sleek and strong. Cadres of scholars, cartographers, botanists, and soldiers were dispatched on the river in small floating nests caulked with beeswax and loaded with rations of honeycomb to chart the unknown lands to the south. Those who returned bore beautiful maps with towns and farms and alien populations of wasps carefully noted in blue and purple ink, and these, once studied by the foundress and her generals, were carefully filed away in the depths of the Great Library for their southern advance in the new year.

The bees adopted by the wasps were first trained to clerical tasks, but once it was determined that they could be taught to read and write, they were assigned to some of the reconnaissance missions. The brightest students, gifted at trigonometry and angles, were educated beside the cartographers themselves and proved valuable assistants. They learned not to see the thick green caterpillars led on silver chains, or the dead bees fed to the wasp brood. It was easier that way.

When the old queen died, they did not mourn.

By the sheerest of accidents, one of the bees trained as a cartographer's assistant was an anarchist. It might have been the stresses on the hive, or it might have been luck;

wherever it came from, the mutation was viable. She tucked a number of her own eggs in beeswax and wasp paper among the pigeonholes of the library and fed the larvae their milk and bread in secret. To her sons in their capped silk cradles—and they were all sons—she whispered the precepts she had developed while calculating flight paths and azimuths, that there should be no queen and no state, and that, as in the wasp nest, the males should labor and profit equally with the females. In their sleep and slow transformation they heard her teachings and instructions, and when they chewed their way out of their cells and out of the wasp nest, they made their way to the hive.

The damage to the nest was discovered, of course, but by then the anarchist was dead of old age. She had done impeccable work, her tutor sighed, looking over the filigree of her inscriptions, but the brilliant were subject to mental aberrations, were they not? He buried beneath grumblings and labors his fondness for her, which had become a grief to him and a political liability, and he never again took on any student from the hive who showed a glint of talent.

Though they had the bitter smell of the wasp nest in their hair, the anarchist's twenty sons were permitted to wander freely through the hive, as it was assumed that they were either spies or on official business. When the new queen emerged from her chamber, they joined unnoticed the other drones in the nuptial flight. Two succeeded in mating with her. Those who failed and survived spoke afterward in hushed tones of what had been done for the sake of the ideal. Before they died they took propolis and oak-apple ink and inscribed upon the lintels of the hive, in a shorthand they had developed, the story of the first anarchist and her twenty sons.

Anarchism being a heritable trait in bees, a number of the daughters of the new queen found themselves questioning the purpose of the monarchy. Two were taken by the wasps and taught to read and write. On one of their visits to the hive they spotted the history of their forefathers, and, being excellent scholars, soon figured out the translation.

They found their sisters in the hive who were unquiet in soul and whispered to them the strange knowledge they had learned among the wasps: astronomy, military strategy, the state of the world beyond the farthest flights of the bees. Hitherto educated as dancers and architects, nurses and foragers, the bees were full of a new wonder, stranger even than the first day they flew from the hive and felt the sun on their backs.

"Govern us," they said to the two wasp-taught anarchists, but they refused.

"A perfect society needs no rulers," they said. "Knowledge and authority ought to be held in common. In order to imagine a new existence, we must free ourselves from the structures of both our failed government and the unjustifiable hegemony of the wasp nests. Hear what you can hear and learn what you can learn while we remain among them. But be ready."

. . .

It was the first summer in Yiwei without the immemorial hum of the cartographer wasps. In the orchards, though their skins split with sweetness, fallen fruit lay unmolested, and children played barefoot with impunity. One of the villagers' daughters, in her third year at an agricultural college, came home in the back of a pickup truck at the end of July. She thumped her single suitcase against the gate before opening it, to scatter the chickens, then raised the latch and swung the iron aside, and was immediately wrapped in a flying hug.

Once she disentangled herself from brother and parents and liberally distributed kisses, she listened to the news she'd missed: how the cows were dying from drinking stonecutters' dust in the streams; how grain prices were falling everywhere, despite the drought; and how her brother, little fool that he was, had torn down a wasp nest and received a faceful of red and white lumps for it. One of the most detailed wasps' maps had reached the capital, she was told, and a bureaucrat had arrived in a sleek black car. But because the wasps were all dead, he could report little more than a prank, a freak, or a miracle. There were no further inquiries.

Her brother produced for her inspection the brittle, boiled bodies of several wasps in a glass jar, along with one of the smaller maps. She tickled him until he surrendered his trophies, promised him a basket of peaches in return, and let herself be fed to tautness. Then, to her family's dismay, she wrote an urgent letter to the Academy of Sciences and packed a satchel with clothes and cash. If she could find one more nest of wasps, she said, it would make their fortune and her name. But it had to be done quickly.

In the morning, before the cockerels woke and while the sky was still purple, she hopped onto her old bicycle and rode down the dusty path.

Bees do not fly at night or lie to each other, but the anarchists had learned both from the wasps. On a warm, clear evening they left the hive at last, flying west in a small, tight cloud. Around them swelled the voices of summer insects, strange and disquieting. Several miles west of the old hive and the wasp nest, in a lightning-scarred elm, the anarchists had built up a small stock of stolen honey sealed in wax and paper. They rested there for the night, in cells of clean white wax, and in the morning they arose to the building of their city.

The first business of the new colony was the laying of eggs, which a number of workers set to, and provisions for winter. One egg from the old queen, brought from the hive in an anarchist's jaws, was hatched and raised as a new mother. Uncrowned and unconcerned, she too laid mortar and wax, chewed wood to make paper, and fanned the storerooms with her wings.

The anarchists labored secretly but rapidly, drones alongside workers, because the copper taste of autumn was in the air. None had seen a winter before, but the memory of the species is subtle and long, and in their hearts, despite the summer sun, they felt an imminent darkness.

The flowers were fading in the fields. Every day the anarchists added to their coffers of warm gold and built their white walls higher. Every day the air grew a little crisper, the grass a little drier. They sang as they worked, sometimes ballads from the old hive, sometimes anthems of their own devising, and for a time they were happy. Too soon, the leaves turned flame colors and blew from the trees, and then there were no more flowers. The anarchists pressed down the lid on the last vat of honey and wondered what was coming.

Four miles away, at the first touch of cold, the wasps licked shut their paper doors and slept in a tight knot around the foundress. In both beehives, the bees huddled together, awake and watchful, warming themselves with the thrumming of their wings. The anarchists murmured comfort to each other.

"There will be more, after us. It will breed out again."

"We are only the beginning."

"There will be more."

Snow fell silently outside.

The snow was ankle-deep and the river iced over when the girl from Yiwei reached up into the empty branches of an oak tree and plucked down the paper castle of a nest. The wasps within, drowsy with cold, murmured but did not stir. In their barracks the soldiers dreamed of the unexplored south and battles in strange cities, among strange peoples, and scouts dreamed of the corpses of starved and frozen deer. The cartographers dreamed of the changes that winter would work on the landscape, the diverted creeks and dead trees they would have to note down. They did not feel the burlap bag that settled around them, nor the crunch of tires on the frozen road.

She had spent weeks tramping through the countryside, questioning beekeepers and villagers' children, peering up into trees and into hives, before she found the last wasps from Yiwei. Then she had had to wait for winter and the anesthetizing cold. But now, back in the warmth of her own room, she broke open the soft pages of the nest and pushed aside the heaps of glistening wasps until she found the foundress herself, stumbling on uncertain legs.

When it thawed, she would breed new foundresses among the village's apricot trees. The letters she received indicated a great demand for them in the capital, particularly from army generals and the captains of scientific explorations. In years to come, the village of Yiwei would be known for its delicately inscribed maps, the legends almost too small to see, and not for its barley and oats, its velvet apricots and glassy pears.

In the spring, the old beehive awoke to find the wasps gone, like a nightmare that evaporates by day. It was difficult to believe, but when not the slightest scrap of wasp paper could be found, the whole hive sang with delight.

Even the queen, who had been coached from the pupa on the details of her client state and the conditions by which she ruled, and who had felt, perhaps, more sympathy for the wasps than she should have, cleared her throat and trilled once or twice. If she did not sing so loudly or so joyously as the rest, only a few noticed, and the winter had been a hard one, anyhow.

The maps had vanished with the wasps. No more would be made. Those who had studied among the wasps began to draft memoranda and the first independent decrees of queen and council. To defend against future invasions, it was decided that a detachment of bees would fly the borders of their land and carry home reports of what they found.

It was on one of these patrols that a small hive was discovered in the fork of an elm tree. Bees lay dead and brittle around it, no identifiable queen among them. Not a trace of honey remained in the storehouse; the dark wax of its walls had been gnawed to rags. Even the brood cells had been scraped clean. But in the last intact hexagons they found, curled and capped in wax, scrawled on page after page, words of revolution. They read in silence.

Then—

"Write," one said to the other, and she did.

3

I first read this story when I was a small boy, and have never forgotten its optimism, its gentle good humor, or the relationship between the two lead characters. FRANK R. STOCKTON was an American humorist and writer, best known for his short story, "The Lady, or the Tiger?"

A lonely griffin visits a village and makes itself comfortable at the side of the Minor Canon assigned to keeping it from eating the townspeople. It insists that it will be hungry only at the equinox, but as the equinox approaches, the villagers become concerned and decide to take matters into their own hands. . . .

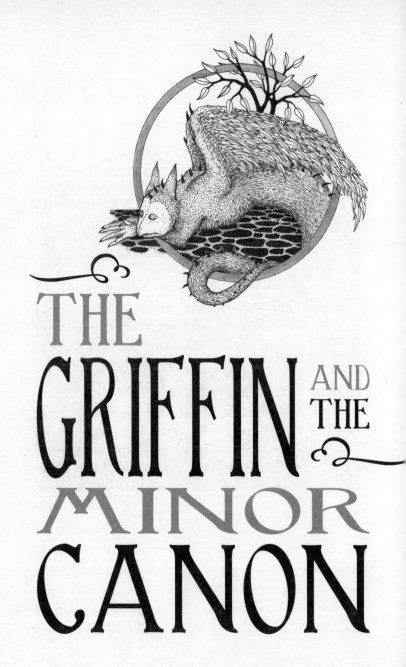

THE GRIFFIN AND THE MINOR CANON

By

Frank R. Stockton

OVER THE GREAT DOOR OF AN OLD, old church which stood in a quiet town of a far-away land there was carved in stone the figure of a large griffin. The old-time sculptor had done his work with great care, but the image he had made was not a pleasant one to look at. It had a large head, with an enormous open mouth and savage teeth; from its back arose great wings, armed with sharp hooks and prongs; it had stout legs in front, with project-ing claws, but there were no legs behind, the body running out into a long and powerful tail, finished off at the end with a barbed point. This tail was coiled up under him, the end sticking up just back of his wings.

The sculptor, or the people who had ordered this stone figure, had evidently been very much pleased with it, for little copies of it, also in stone, had been placed here and there along the sides of the church, not very far from the ground, so that people could easily look at them, and pon-der on their curious forms. There were a great many other sculptures on the outside of this church—saints, martyrs, grotesque heads of men, beasts, and birds, as well as those of other creatures which cannot be named, because nobody knows exactly what they were; but none were so curious and interesting as the great griffin over the door, and the little griffins on the sides of the church.

A long, long distance from the town, in the midst of dreadful wilds scarcely known to man, there dwelt the Griffin whose image had been put up over the church door. In some way or other, the old-time sculptor had seen him, and afterward, to the best of his memory, had copied his figure in stone. The Griffin had never known this, until, hundreds of years afterward, he heard from a bird, from a wild animal, or in some manner which it is not now easy to find out, that there was a likeness of him on the old church in the distant town. Now this Griffin had no idea how he looked. He had never seen a mirror, and the streams where he lived were so turbulent and violent that a quiet piece of water, which would reflect the image of anything looking into it, could not be found. Being, as far as could be ascertained, the very last of his race, he had never seen another griffin. Therefore it was, that, when he heard of this stone image of himself, he became very anxious to know what he looked like, and at last he determined to go to the old church, and see for himself what manner of being he was. So he started off from the dreadful wilds, and flew on and on until he came to the countries inhabited by men, where his appearance in the air created great consternation; but he alighted nowhere, keeping up a steady flight until he reached the suburbs of the town which had his image on its church. Here, late in the afternoon, he alighted in a green meadow by the side of a brook, and stretched himself on the grass to rest. His great wings were tired, for he had not made such a long flight in a century, or more.

The news of his coming spread quickly over the town, and the people, frightened nearly out of their wits by the arrival of so extraordinary a visitor, fled into their houses, and shut themselves up. The Griffin called loudly for someone to come to him, but the more he called, the more afraid the people were to show themselves. At length he saw two laborers hurrying to their homes through the fields, and in a terrible voice he commanded them to stop. Not daring to disobey, the men stood, trembling.

"What is the matter with you all?" cried the Griffin. "Is there not a man in your town who is brave enough to speak to me?"

"I think," said one of the laborers, his voice shaking so that his words could hardly be understood, "that—perhaps—the Minor Canon—would come."

"Go, call him, then!" said the Griffin; "I want to see him."

The Minor Canon, who filled a subordinate position in the church, had just finished the afternoon services, and was coming out of a side door, with three aged women who had formed the weekday congregation. He was a young man of a kind disposition, and very anxious to do good to the people of the town. Apart from his duties in the church, where he conducted services every weekday, he visited the sick and the poor, counseled and assisted persons who were in trouble, and taught a school composed entirely of the bad children in the town with whom nobody else would have anything to do. Whenever the people wanted something difficult done for them, they always went to the Minor Canon. Thus it was that the laborer thought of the young priest when he found that someone must come and speak to the Griffin.

The Minor Canon had not heard of the strange event, which was known to the whole town except himself and the three old women, and when he was informed of it, and was told that the Griffin had asked to see him, he was greatly amazed, and frightened. "Me!" he exclaimed. "He has never heard of me! What should he want with me?"

"Oh! You must go instantly!" cried the two men.

"He is very angry now because he has been kept waiting so long; and nobody knows what may happen if you don't hurry to him."

The poor Minor Canon would rather have had his hand cut off than go out to meet an angry griffin; but he felt that it was his duty to go, or it would be a woeful thing if injury should come to the people of the town because he was not brave enough to obey the summons of the Griffin.

So, pale and frightened, he started off.

"Well," said the Griffin, as soon as the young man came near, "I am glad to see that there is someone who has the courage to come to me."

The Minor Canon did not feel very courageous, but he bowed his head.

"Is this the town," said the Griffin, "where there is a

church with a likeness of myself over one of the doors?"

The Minor Canon looked at the frightful creature before him and saw that it was, without doubt, exactly like the stone image on the church. "Yes," he said, "you are right."

"Well, then," said the Griffin, "Will you take me to it? I wish very much to see it."

The Minor Canon instantly thought that if the Griffin entered the town without the people knowing what he came for, some of them would probably be frightened to death, and so he sought to gain time to prepare their minds.

"It is growing dark, now," he said, very much afraid, as he spoke, that his words might enrage the Griffin, "and objects on the front of the church cannot be seen clearly. It will be better to wait until morning, if you wish to get a good view of the stone image of yourself."

"That will suit me very well," said the Griffin. "I see you are a man of good sense. I am tired, and I will take a nap here on this soft grass, while I cool my tail in the little stream that runs near me. The end of my tail gets red-hot when I am angry or excited, and it is quite warm now. So you may go, but be sure and come early tomorrow morning, and show me the way to the church."

The Minor Canon was glad enough to take his leave, and hurried into the town. In front of the church he found a great many people assembled to hear his report of his interview with the Griffin. When they found that he had not come to spread ruin and devastation, but simply to see his stony likeness on the church, they showed neither relief nor gratification, but began to upbraid the Minor Canon for consenting to conduct the creature into the town.

"What could I do?" cried the young man. "If I should not bring him he would come himself and, perhaps, end by setting fire to the town with his red-hot tail."

Still the people were not satisfied, and a great many plans were proposed to prevent the Griffin from coming into the town. Some elderly persons urged that the young men should go out and kill him; but the young men scoffed at such a ridiculous idea. Then someone said that it would be a good thing to destroy the stone image so that the Griffin would have no excuse for entering the town; and this proposal was received with such favor that many of the people ran for hammers, chisels, and crowbars, with which to tear down and break up the stone griffin. But the Minor Canon resisted this plan with all the strength of his mind and body. He assured the people that this action would enrage the Griffin beyond measure, for it would be impossible to conceal from him that his image had been destroyed during the night. But the people were so determined to break up the stone griffin that the Minor Canon saw that there was nothing for him to do but to stay there and protect it. All night he walked up and down in front of the church door, keeping away the men who brought ladders, by which they might mount to the great stone griffin, and knock it to pieces with their hammers and crowbars. After many hours the people were obliged to give up their attempts, and went home to sleep; but the Minor Canon remained at his post till early morning, and then he hurried away to the field where he had left the Griffin.

The monster had just awakened, and rising to his forelegs and shaking himself, he said that he was ready to go into the town. The Minor Canon, therefore, walked back, the Griffin flying slowly through the air, at a short distance above the head of his guide. Not a person was to be seen in the streets, and they proceeded directly to the front of the church, where the Minor Canon pointed out the stone griffin.

The real Griffin settled down in the little square before the church and gazed earnestly at his sculptured likeness. For a long time he looked at it. First he put his head on one side, and then he put it on the other; then he shut his right eye and gazed with his left, after which he shut his left eye and gazed with his right. Then he moved a little to one side and looked at the image, and then he moved the other way. After a while he said to the Minor Canon, who had been standing by all this time:

"It is, it must be, an excellent likeness! That breadth between the eyes, that expansive forehead, those massive jaws! I feel that it must resemble me. If there is any fault to find with it, it is that the neck seems a little stiff. But that is nothing. It is an admirable likeness—admirable!"

The Griffin sat looking at his image all the morning and all the afternoon. The Minor Canon had been afraid to go away and leave him, and had hoped all through the day that he would soon be satisfied with his inspection and fly away home. But by evening the poor young man was utterly exhausted, and felt that he must eat and sleep. He frankly admitted this fact to the Griffin, and asked him if he would not like something to eat. He said this because he felt obliged in politeness to do so, but as soon as he had spoken the words, he was seized with dread lest the monster should demand half a dozen babies, or some tempting repast of that kind.

"Oh, no," said the Griffin, "I never eat between the equinoxes. At the vernal and at the autumnal equinox I take a good meal, and that lasts me for half a year. I am extremely regular in my habits, and do not think it healthful to eat at odd times. But if you need food, go and get it, and I will return to the soft grass where I slept last night and take another nap."

The next day the Griffin came again to the little square before the church, and remained there until evening, steadfastly regarding the stone griffin over the door. The Minor Canon came once or twice to look at him, and the Griffin seemed very glad to see him; but the young clergyman could not stay as he had done before, for he had many duties to perform. Nobody went to the church, but the people came to the Minor Canon's house, and anxiously asked him how long the Griffin was going to stay.

"I do not know," he answered, "but I think he will soon be satisfied with regarding his stone likeness, and then he will go away."

But the Griffin did not go away. Morning after morning he came to the church, but after a time he did not stay there all day. He seemed to have taken a great fancy to the Minor Canon, and followed him about as he pursued his various avocations. He would wait for him at the side door of the church, for the Minor Canon held services every day, morning and evening, though nobody came now. "If anyone should come," he said to himself, "I must be found at my post." When the young man came out, the Griffin would accompany him in his visits to the sick and the poor, and would often look into the windows of the schoolhouse where the Minor Canon was teaching his unruly scholars. All the other schools were closed, but the parents of the Minor Canon's scholars forced them to go to school, because they were so bad they could not endure them all day at home, griffin or no griffin. But it must be said they generally behaved very well when that great monster sat up on his tail and looked in at the schoolroom window.

When it was perceived that the Griffin showed no signs of going away, all the people who were able to do so left the town. The canons and the higher officers of the church had fled away during the first day of the Griffin's visit, leaving behind only the Minor Canon and some of the men who opened the doors and swept the church. All the citizens who could afford it shut up their houses and traveled to distant parts, and only the working people and the poor were left behind. After some days these ventured to go about and attend to their business, for if they did not work they would starve. They were getting a little used to seeing the Griffin, and having been told that he did not eat between equinoxes, they did not feel so much afraid of him as before. Day by day the Griffin became more and more attached to the Minor Canon. He kept near him a great part of the time, and often spent the night in front of the little house where the young clergyman lived alone. This strange companionship was often burdensome to the Minor Canon; but, on the other hand, he could not deny that he derived a great deal of benefit and instruction from it. The Griffin had lived for hundreds of years, and had seen much; and he told the Minor Canon many wonderful things.

"It is like reading an old book," said the young clergyman to himself; "but how many books I would have had to read before I would have found out what the Griffin has told me about the earth, the air, the water, about minerals, and metals, and growing things, and all the wonders of the world!"

Thus the summer went on, and drew toward its close. And now the people of the town began to be very much troubled again.

"It will not be long," they said, "before the autumnal equinox is here, and then that monster will want to eat. He will be dreadfully hungry, for he has taken so much exercise since his last meal. He will devour our children. Without doubt, he will eat them all. What is to be done?"

To this question no one could give an answer, but all

agreed that the Griffin must not be allowed to remain until the approaching equinox. After talking over the matter a great deal, a crowd of the people went to the Minor Canon, at a time when the Griffin was not with him.

"It is all your fault," they said, "that that monster is among us. You brought him here, and you ought to see that he goes away. It is only on your account that he stays here at all, for, although he visits his image every day, he is with you the greater part of the time. If you were not here, he would not stay. It is your duty to go away and then he will follow you, and we shall be free from the dreadful danger which hangs over us."

"Go away!" cried the Minor Canon, greatly grieved at being spoken to in such a way. "Where shall I go? If I go to some other town, shall I not take this trouble there? Have I a right to do that?"

"No," said the people, "you must not go to any other town. There is no town far enough away. You must go to the dreadful wilds where the Griffin lives; and then he will follow you and stay there."

They did not say whether or not they expected the Minor Canon to stay there also, and he did not ask them anything about it. He bowed his head, and went into his house, to think. The more he thought, the more clear it became to his mind that it was his duty to go away, and thus free the town from the presence of the Griffin.

That evening he packed a leather bag full of bread and meat, and early the next morning he set out on his journey to the dreadful wilds. It was a long, weary, and doleful journey, especially after he had gone beyond the habitations of men, but the Minor Canon kept on bravely, and never faltered. The way was longer than he had expected, and his provisions soon grew so scanty that he was obliged to eat but a little every day, but he kept up his courage, and pressed on, and, after many days of toilsome travel, he reached the dreadful wilds.

When the Griffin found that the Minor Canon had left the town he seemed sorry, but showed no disposition to go and look for him. After a few days had passed, he became much annoyed, and asked some of the people where the Minor Canon had gone. But, although the citizens had been anxious that the young clergyman should go to the dreadful wilds, thinking that the Griffin would immediately follow him, they were now afraid to mention the Minor Canon's destination, for the monster seemed angry already, and, if he should suspect their trick, he would doubtless become very much enraged. So everyone said he did not know, and the Griffin wandered about disconsolate. One morning he looked into the Minor Canon's schoolhouse, which was always empty now, and thought that it was a shame that everything should suffer on account of the young man's absence.

"It does not matter so much about the church," he said, "for nobody went there; but it is a pity about the school. I think I will teach it myself until he returns."

It was the hour for opening the school, and the Griffin went inside and pulled the rope which rang the school bell. Some of the children who heard the bell ran in to see what was the matter, supposing it to be a joke of one of their companions; but when they saw the Griffin they stood astonished, and scared.

"Go tell the other scholars," said the monster, "that school is about to open, and that if they are not all here in ten minutes, I shall come after them." In seven minutes every scholar was in place.

Never was seen such an orderly school. Not a boy or girl moved, or uttered a whisper. The Griffin climbed into the master's seat, his wide wings spread on each side of him, because he could not lean back in his chair while they stuck out behind, and his great tail coiled around in front of the desk, the barbed end sticking up, ready to tap any boy or girl who might misbehave. The Griffin now addressed the scholars, telling them that he intended to teach them while their master was away. In speaking he endeavored to imitate, as far as possible, the mild and gentle tones of the Minor Canon, but it must be admitted that in this he was not very successful. He had paid a good deal of attention to the studies of the school, and he determined not to attempt to teach them anything new, but to review them in what they had been studying; so he called up the various classes, and questioned them upon their previous lessons. The children racked their brains to remember what they had learned. They were so afraid of the Griffin's displeasure that they recited as they had never recited before. One of the boys far down in his class answered so well that the Griffin was astonished.

"I should think you would be at the head," said he. "I am sure you have never been in the habit of reciting so well. Why is this?"

"Because I did not choose to take the trouble," said the boy, trembling in his boots. He felt obliged to speak the truth, for all the children thought that the great eyes of the Griffin could see right through them, and that he would know when they told a falsehood.

"You ought to be ashamed of yourself," said the Griffin. "Go down to the very tail of the class, and if you are not at the head in two days, I shall know the reason why."

The next afternoon the boy was number one.

It was astonishing how much these children now learned of what they had been studying. It was as if they had been educated over again. The Griffin used no severity toward them, but there was a look about him which made them unwilling to go to bed until they were sure they knew their lessons for the next day.

The Griffin now thought that he ought to visit the sick and the poor; and he began to go about the town for this purpose. The effect upon the sick was miraculous. All, except those who were very ill indeed, jumped from their beds when they heard he was coming, and declared themselves quite well. To those who could not get up, he gave herbs and roots, which none of them had ever before thought of as medicines, but which the Griffin had seen used in various parts of the world; and most of them recovered. But, for all that, they afterward said that no matter what happened to them, they hoped that they should never again have such a doctor coming to their bedsides, feeling their pulses and looking at their tongues.

As for the poor, they seemed to have utterly disappeared. All those who had depended upon charity for their daily bread were now at work in some way or other; many of them offering to do odd jobs for their neighbors just for the sake of their meals, a thing which before had been seldom heard of in the town. The Griffin could find no one who needed his assistance.

The summer had now passed, and the autumnal equinox was rapidly approaching. The citizens were in a state of great alarm and anxiety. The Griffin showed no signs of going away, but seemed to have settled himself permanently among them. In a short time, the day for his semiannual meal would arrive, and then what would happen? The monster would certainly be very hungry, and would devour all their children.

Now they greatly regretted and lamented that they had sent away the Minor Canon; he was the only one on whom they could have depended in this trouble, for he could talk freely with the Griffin, and so find out what could be done. But it would not do to be inactive. Some step must be taken immediately. A meeting of the citizens was called, and two old men were appointed to go and talk to the Griffin. They were instructed to offer to prepare a splendid dinner for him on equinox day—one which would entirely satisfy his hunger. They would offer him the fattest mutton; the most tender beef, fish, and game of various sorts; and anything of the kind that he might fancy. If none of these suited, they were to mention that there was an orphan asylum in the next town.

"Anything would be better," said the citizens, "than to have our dear children devoured."

The old men went to the Griffin, but their propositions were not received with favor.

"From what I have seen of the people of this town," said the monster, "I do not think I could relish anything which was prepared by them. They appear to be all cowards, and, therefore, mean and selfish. As for eating one of them, old or young, I could not think of it for a moment. In fact, there was only one creature in the whole place for whom I could have had any appetite, and that is the Minor Canon, who has gone away. He was brave, and good, and honest, and I think I should have relished him."

"Ah," said one of the old men very politely, "in that case I wish we had not sent him to the dreadful wilds!"

"What!" cried the Griffin. "What do you mean? Explain instantly what you are talking about!"

The old man, terribly frightened at what he had said, was obliged to tell how the Minor Canon had been sent away by the people, in the hope that the Griffin might be induced to follow him.

When the monster heard this, he became furiously

angry. He dashed away from the old men and, spreading his wings, flew backward and forward over the town. He was so much excited that his tail became red-hot, and glowed like a meteor against the evening sky. When at last he settled down in the little field where he usually rested, and thrust his tail into the brook, the steam arose like a cloud, and the water of the stream ran hot through the town. The citizens were greatly frightened, and bitterly blamed the old man for telling about the Minor Canon.

"It is plain," they said, "that the Griffin intended at last to go and look for him, and we should have been saved. Now who can tell what misery you have brought upon us."

The Griffin did not remain long in the little field. As soon as his tail was cool he flew to the town hall and rang the bell. The citizens knew that they were expected to come there, and although they were afraid to go, they were still more afraid to stay away; and they crowded into the hall. The Griffin was on the platform at one end, flapping his wings and walking up and down, and the end of his tail was still so warm that it slightly scorched the boards as he dragged it after him.

When everybody who was able to come was there the Griffin stood still and addressed the meeting.

"I have had a contemptible opinion of you," he said, "ever since I discovered what cowards you are, but I had no idea that you were so ungrateful, selfish, and cruel as I now find you to be. Here was your Minor Canon, who labored day and night for your good, and thought of nothing else but how he might benefit you and make you happy; and. as soon as you imagine yourselves threatened with a danger—for well I know you are dreadfully afraid of me—you send him off, caring not whether he returns or perishes, hoping thereby to save yourselves. Now, I had conceived a great liking for that young man, and had intended, in a day or two, to go and look him up. But I have changed my mind about him. I shall go and find him, but I shall send him back here to live among you, and I intend that he shall enjoy the reward of his labor and his sacrifices. Go, some of you, to the officers of the church, who so cowardly ran away when I first came here, and tell them never to return to this town under penalty of death. And if, when your Minor Canon comes back to you, you do not bow yourselves before him, put him in the highest place among you, and serve and honor him all his life, beware of my terrible vengeance! There were only two good things in this town: the Minor Canon and the stone image of myself over your church door. One of these you have sent away, and the other I shall carry away myself."

With these words he dismissed the meeting, and it was time, for the end of his tail had become so hot that there was danger of its setting fire to the building.

The next morning, the Griffin came to the church, and tearing the stone image of himself from its fastenings over the great door, he grasped it with his powerful forelegs and flew up into the air. Then, after hovering over the town for a moment, he gave his tail an angry shake and took up his flight to the dreadful wilds. When he reached this deso-late region, he set the stone griffin upon a ledge of a rock which rose in front of the dismal cave he called his home. There the image occupied a position somewhat similar to that it had had over the church door; and the Griffin, panting with the exertion of carrying such an enormous load to so great a distance, lay down upon the ground, and regarded it with much satisfaction. When he felt somewhat rested he went to look for the Minor Canon. He found the young man, weak and half starved, lying under the shadow of a rock. After picking him up and carrying him to his cave, the Griffin flew away to a distant marsh, where he procured some roots and herbs which he well knew were strengthening and beneficial to man, though he had never tasted them himself. After eating these, the Minor Canon was greatly revived, and sat up and listened while the Grif-fin told him what had happened in the town.

"Do you know," said the monster, when he had fin-ished, "that I have had, and still have, a great liking for you?"

"I am very glad to hear it," said the Minor Canon, with his usual politeness.

"I am not at all sure that you would be," said the Grif-fin, "if you thoroughly understood the state of the case, but we will not consider that now. If some things were different, other things would be otherwise. I have been so enraged by discovering the manner in which you have been treated that I have determined that you shall at last enjoy the rewards and honors to which you are entitled. Lie down and have a good sleep, and then I will take you back to the town."

As he heard these words, a look of trouble came over the young man's face.

"You need not give yourself any anxiety," said the Griffin, "about my return to the town. I shall not remain there. Now that I have that admirable likeness of myself in front of my cave, where I can sit at my leisure, and gaze upon its noble features and magnificent proportions, I have no wish to see that abode of cowardly and selfish people."

The Minor Canon, relieved from his fears, lay back, and dropped into a doze; and when he was sound asleep the Griffin took him up, and carried him back to the town. He arrived just before daybreak, and putting the young man gently on the grass in the little field where he himself used to rest, the monster, without having been seen by any of the people, flew back to his home.

When the Minor Canon made his appearance in the morning among the citizens, the enthusiasm and cordiality with which he was received were truly wonderful. He was taken to a house which had been occupied by one of the vanished high officers of the place, and everyone was anxious to do all that could be done for his health and comfort. The people crowded into the church when he held services, so that the three old women who used to be his weekday congregation could not get to the best seats, which they had always been in the habit of taking; and the parents of the bad children determined to reform them at home, in order that he might be spared the trouble of keeping up his former school. The Minor Canon was appointed to the highest office of the old church, and before he died, he became a bishop.

During the first years after his return from the dreadful wilds, the people of the town looked up to him as a man to whom they were bound to do honor and reverence; but they often, also, looked up to the sky to see if there were any signs of the Griffin coming back. However, in the course of time, they learned to honor and reverence their former Minor Canon without the fear of being punished if they did not do so.

But they need never have been afraid of the Griffin. The autumnal equinox day came round, and the monster ate nothing. If he could not have the Minor Canon, he did not care for anything. So, lying down, with his eyes fixed upon the great stone griffin, he gradually declined, and died. It was a good thing for some people of the town that they did not know this.

If you should ever visit the old town, you would still see the little griffins on the sides of the church; but the great stone griffin that was over the door is gone.

4

I was there when NNEDI OKORAFOR won the World Fantasy Award for Best Novel for *Who Fears Death*, and cheered as loudly as anyone. She's a wonderful writer who makes her home in Chicago and has the best hair in the world.

Twelve years old, and able to speak with poisonous snakes, Ozioma's the undefeated champion of her village—despite the fact that everyone in it thinks she's a witch. One day, though, a tremendous serpent descends from the heavens, and tests even Ozioma's courage. . . .

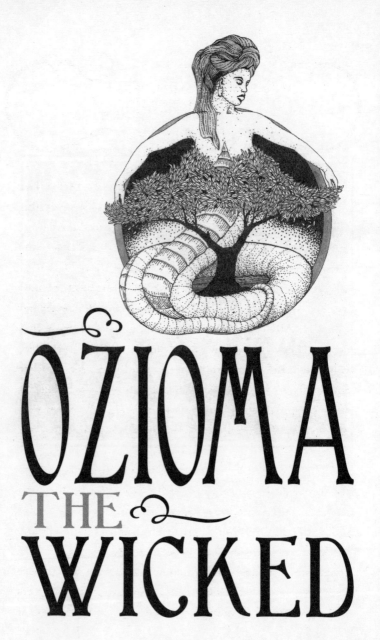

OZIOMA
THE
WICKED

By

Nnedi Okorafor

TO MOST, OZIOMA WAS A NASTY LITTLE GIRL whose pure heart had turned black two years ago, not long after her father's death. Only her mother would disagree, but her mother was a mere fourth wife to a dead yam farmer. So no one cared what her mother thought.

Now at the age of twelve, Ozioma often went for days without speaking. People stayed away from her, even her relatives. All feared what might happen to them if they crossed her. They called her witch and child sorceress, titles that were feared and disrespectfully respected in her small village of Agwotown. Of course, they only called her these powerful yet ugly names behind her back, never ever to her face. Most people wouldn't dare look deep in her dark brown eyes.

This was all because of what Ozioma could do.

You see, the people of Agwotown feared the bite of a snake far more than most Nigerians. Though the town was old, with well-built buildings and homes and a nicely controlled forest, the snakes in the area remained bold. The snakes stuck around; and for some reason, the snakes here were very, very deadly. They hid in the bushes and tall grass that surrounded homes; they safely crossed the streets at night when there were few cars and trucks; and they moved freely along the dirt paths that led through the forest to the stream.

One would be with friends, laughing and chatting, and then with a stumbly giggly sidestep find herself in the grass. Next thing she knew, a snake would be working its fangs into her ankle. Death would usually come painfully quick, especially if it was a puff adder or carpet viper. Most people in Agwotown had lost relatives, friends, classmates, and enemies to the bite of a snake. So in Agwotown, people didn't fear the dangerous roads, armed robbers, or losing their entire bank accounts to a 419 scammer. People feared snakes. And Ozioma could speak to them.

Those who had heard the story about her doing it two years ago, couldn't stop talking about it. It was this incident that they said caused her "blackened heart," for who could commune with a snake and not be corrupted? There had been a cobra in her uncle's yam garden, and it had slithered up beside him while he tended to a root. When he turned around, he was face-to-face with the brown-hooded demon, a cobra. Ozioma happened to be coming out of the house with a bottle of orange Fanta.

She hadn't spoken to anyone in two days. "She had been in one of her moods," her uncle later told the elders when they asked about the incident. It had been a month since her father had passed and people hadn't started avoiding her yet.

"No!" Ozioma shouted when she saw her uncle face-

to-face with the cobra. She dropped the drink and ran over on her long, strong legs. Thankfully, neither her uncle nor the cobra moved. Eyewitnesses said that she then knelt down and brought her face right up to the snake's face. Her uncle was shoulder to shoulder with her, frozen in terror.

"It *kissed* her lips with its tongue as she whispered to it," her uncle later told the elders with a shudder of disgust. "I was right there but I could not make out a word she spoke." The elders were equally disgusted as they listened. One even turned to the side and spat. Nevertheless, Ozioma must have said something, because the snake immediately dropped down and slithered away.

Ozioma turned to her uncle grinning with relief— grinning for the first time since her father passed. She missed her father so much. Using the ability she'd had all her life yet only shown her parents a few times was exciting. And using it to save her uncle who looked so much like her father broke the clouds surrounding her heart and let in sunshine. She loved her uncle as she loved all of her relatives, in her quiet way.

Nevertheless, her uncle did not return her grin. Instead, he surprised her with a frown that would make even the proudest flower wither. Ozioma shrank away from him, quickly got up and went home. After that, her uncle didn't speak a word to his "evil, snake-charming" niece.

Her uncle went on to tell the elders and several of his friends about what she did, making sure to describe how he'd been about to chop the snake in half before she came and conversed with the beast as if it were her best friend. Then these people told others and others told others. Soon, everyone in Agwotown knew about Ozioma and her wicked ways. Everyone said they saw it coming. A girl of a poor family without a father was a girl prone to witchcraft, they said. Nevertheless, the day the spitting cobra came down the giant kapok tree in the middle of the village, do you wonder who they turned to?

Ozioma was standing over the large pot of bubbling red stew humming to herself. Her mother was chatting with her aunt in the back. Her mp3 player was connected to some old speakers and it was playing an afrobeat song her father used to love. Outside, it was thundering and it would rain any minute, but that didn't concern her. She was cooking, something she'd loved to do since her mother showed her three years ago. Cooking made her feel in control, it made her feel grown.

She'd cut the onions with care, savored in the soft, firm perfection of the red tomatoes, shaken in a combination of thyme, red pepper, salt, and curry, and marveled at the greenness of the greens. She had brought out and cut up the half chicken that she'd salted, spiced, and baked hard and dry. So now she was humming and stirring slowly so as not to break up the baked chicken she'd added to the stew.

"Ozioma!"

Her eyes, which had been out of focus, lost in visions

of yummy food, immediately grew sharp. She blinked, noticing a classmate from school, Afam, standing at the window. Afam was one of the few who didn't call her "snake kisser." And once, he'd asked her to show him how to talk to snakes. She'd considered, but then decided against it. Sometimes snakes were tricky. They didn't always do what you asked them to do. Though they wouldn't bite her, they might bite Afam. Snakes liked to test the toughness of skin.

She frowned questioningly at Afam, now. She wasn't in the mood to speak to anyone today. She just wanted to cook.

"Come!" Afam said. He paused. "Hurry!"

It was the pause that got to Ozioma. And a feeling. She let go of the spoon and it sunk into the thick red stew. She ran out the door without bothering to put sandals on. The air was heavy and humid. It pressed at her skin.

She followed Afam up the road. Past Auntie Nwaduba's house, where Auntie Nwaduba had once slapped her for not greeting her loudly enough. Past Mr. and Mrs. Efere's house, the old couple that liked to grow flowers during rainy season and hated when Ozioma got too close to them. Mr. Efere sat on his porch in front of his tiger lilies, suspiciously watching her run by. Past her uncle's home. To the back. Through his yam garden where she'd saved him from the cobra. And finally, up the road to the center of town, the meeting place at the giant kapok tree that reached high in the sky.

Afam stopped, out of breath. "There," he said, pointing.

Then he quickly backed away and ran off, hiding behind the nearest house and peeking around its corner. Ozioma turned back to the tree just as it began to rain.

Shaped like two spiders, a large one perched upside down upon a smaller other, the thick smooth branches and roots were ideal for sitting. On days of rest, the men gathered around it to argue, converse, drink, smoke, and play cards on different branch levels.

Ozioma frowned, as thunder rumbled and lightning flashed. This was the last place anyone wanted to be during a storm. Aside from the threat of being struck, the tree was known to harbor good and evil spirits, depending on the day. Or so it was said. Today, it was clearly harboring something else. As Ozioma stood there taking in the situation, big warm droplets fell like the tears of a manatee.

It was the season where the tree dropped its seedpods. In the rain, fluffy yellow waterproof seeds bounced down like white bubbles along with the drops. Six men stood around the tree, in shorts, pants, T-shirts, and sandals. They were as motionless as the tree. Except for one. This man writhed in the red dirt, which was quickly becoming soupy like the stew she'd left to burn. The man was screaming and clawing at his eyes.

Ozioma caught the eye of her oldest brother. The son of her father's second wife, he always turned and walked the other way when he saw her coming. He stood still as a stone beside the writhing man. Ozioma didn't allow herself to look too closely at the man in pain on the ground.

She'd recognize him. She looked up at the tree and beyond it and felt her heart flip, then she felt her body flood with adrenaline. She blinked the raindrops from her eyes, sure that she couldn't be seeing what she was seeing. But she was. It was just like in the stories the local *dibia* liked to tell.

The enormous chain dangled through the heavy grey clouds between the tree's top branches. It looked black in the rain. Ozioma knew it was made of the purest, strongest iron that no blacksmith could bend. It was older than time, the ladder of the gods. And something had slithered down it.

"How many?" Ozioma asked in a low voice, addressing the man closest to her. It was Sammy, another cousin who'd stopped talking to her after the cobra incident. She was worried he wouldn't hear her over the rain but she couldn't risk speaking any louder.

"One," he whispered, water dropping from his lips as he spoke. "Very very big, o! Under the roots."

She could feel all eyes on her. Everyone wishing, hoping, praying that she would get them out of this. All these people who otherwise wouldn't see her, who refused to see her. Ozioma wished she could go back to cooking her perfect stew.

She could see the creature between a cluster of the tree's roots. Part of it, at least. She let out a slow breath. This one would take some convincing. This one was bigger than two men. It could certainly raise its forebody to her height. The better to spit its venom into her eyes. A spitting cobra. The venom would be a powerful poison that burned like acid. Its victim wouldn't die; he or she would be blind for days and then die.

Still, if it was a spitting cobra, even the other villagers knew that this kind of cobra's eyesight was poor. And if one remained very still, it couldn't differentiate a human being from a tree. This was common Agwotown knowledge. Thus as soon as this one spit in the one man's eyes, leaving him thrashing with pain in the dirt, everyone immediately knew to freeze.

Ozioma's mother once told her that when she was a baby, Ozioma used to eat dirt and play with leaves and bugs. "Maybe that's why you can speak the snakes' language. You loved to crawl on your belly, as they do." Maybe this was true. Whatever the reason, before she even saw this snake, not only did she know it was a spitting cobra, she also knew that it was not like the others.

Slowly, Ozioma crept forward. It was watching her from between the roots. It slowly slithered out. Its face was otherworldly, that of a sly old man who has lived long and quietly watched many wars and times of peace. Beads of water ran down its head and long, mighty body.

"Ozioma, what are you going to do?" her brother whispered.

"Quiet," she said. *Only when the monsters come do they remember my name,* Ozioma thought, annoyed. *Now they have fear in their eyes that I can actually see because they look at me.*

Ozioma stood there in the rain five feet from the

creature, staring into its eyes, her jean shorts and red shirt soaked through. The men around her stayed frozen with fear and self-preservation. Its eyes were golden and its body was jungle green, not the usual red brown of spitting cobras. It slowly rose up and opened its hood, which was a lighter green. Still holding itself up, it glided closer while remaining upright, something that was difficult for most cobras.

Ozioma wanted to tear out of there screaming. But it was too late. She was here. It would spit poison in her eyes before she could escape. She'd put herself here. To save her people, people who hated her. Her father would have done the same thing. He'd once faced armed robbers who'd tried to rob a market. He'd been the only one brave enough to shout at those stupid men who turned out to be teenagers too afraid to wield the machetes they'd threatened everyone with.

The rain beaded on the snake's scaly head, but not one of the tree's fruits dropped on it. When it spoke, its voice came to her as it did with every snake, a hissing sound that carried close to her ears.

Step aside. I want this tree. I like it. It is mine.

"No," she said aloud. "This is our town tree. These are my . . . relatives."

The cobra just looked at her, its face expressionless as any animal's.

I will kill you and all the human beings around me, then. They cannot stay motionless forever.

"This is my home," she said. "It's all I have. They hate

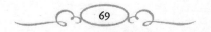

69

me and many times I hate them but I will always love them. I won't let you harm any more of them!"

She could quietly read her favorite books. She could stand alone feeling outcast as her classmates socialized nearby. She could yearn for the love of her brothers, aunts, uncles, and cousins. She could look at herself in the mirror and wish she could smile with ease. And she could cry and cry for her deceased father. But she couldn't bear the idea of seeing the people of her town killed by this beast.

The snake beast's eyes bore into her and she shuddered. But she didn't look away. It brought its face, slowly, gradually, dangerously, close to hers. Then it stared. It smelled acrid and sweet, like flowers growing in a chemical spill. It opened its mouth so she could see the fangs from which the poison shot. Ozioma was screaming inside. Her skin prickled and the rain falling on her felt like blood.

Still, Ozioma stared back.

Who are you?

"Ozioma."

Who are they?

"My people."

They hate you.

Ozioma flinched. "The fact remains."

You have no respect. Even now, you look me in the eye. Even now, you SPEAK to me. I may burn the meat of your head to jelly and force you to feel every part of it.

"W . . . why do you want our tree?"

I take what I choose. Just as I have taken that man's life.

Ozioma didn't turn around to look at the man who was probably not in pain anymore. She held the snake's stare. She had a feeling if she broke its gaze, all was lost. "But you came from the sky."

This tree reaches high. It touches the spirit realm. I want it.

They stared. How many minutes had she been standing there looking into the soul of this beast? It was still raining warm drops. She could see the men with her peripheral vision. How long could they all hold still?

You are more like me. Step aside. Let me finish them off when they can stand it no more.

"I will fight you," she insisted. But the longer she stared, the more Ozioma could feel her nerve slipping.

You have no poison.

"I have hands."

It will be a quick fight, child.

"I'm not a child," she angrily said, her resolve momentarily strengthening. "I am twelve years old and my father is dead."

The snake inched closer, its lipless maw touching Ozioma's face. Even in the warm rain, its flesh felt dry and cool.

If not a child, then a weak adult.

It gave her a sharp nudge and she couldn't help herself from stumbling back, her bare feet squelching in the mud. The creature had felt solid and heavy, a million pounds of powerful muscle and sinew from the sky. All the strength she had drained from her like spilled water. She'd broken its gaze. She'd lost. She was done for. They all were. She dug the heel of her foot in the mud, preparing to flee.

The rain began to fade. Ozioma glanced up at the sky as the deluge dwindled to drizzle. The clouds suddenly broke above the tree and even the snake looked up. The men who'd been unmoving for several minutes, took the chance to quickly scramble away. Some of them hid behind the tree, others behind houses and nearby bushes. By this time, several townspeople had gathered in these places, witnessing the whole thing.

Ozioma, however, stayed where she was. Looking, as the giant snake did, up into the break in the clouds above.

Something was spiraling through the rain like a fish through coral. She had the body of a snake, a strong feminine torso and the common face of a market woman. Ozioma fell to her knees, her mouth agape as several other people gasped and pointed and called the approaching goddess's name.

"Aida-Wedo! It's Aida-Wedo!"

"Oh my God, Ozioma has angered the goddess!"

A rainbow broke around Aida-Wedo as the rain completely stopped. The clouds rushed away like fleeing dogs at her approach. The rainbow spilled and arched over the tree.

The goddess flew to the chain, grabbed it with one hand and shimmied down to the tree's top. She wrapped her green-brown lower snake body around one of the thinnest branches as if it were the sturdiest. She leaned to the side to get a better look at Ozioma through the tree. Even her dark brown upper body moved with the power and control of a snake. Her large breasts jiggled like ocean waves.

"*This is a fine tree*," she said in a rich voice that probably carried to all the people in the area hiding, watching, and listening. She pointed at the snake beast and it immediately returned to the tree and began to ascend. Ozioma let out a relieved breath and slowly stood up.

When the beast reached Aida-Wedo, it leaned close and spoke to the goddess. Ozioma could hear it whispering, but she was too far to understand its words. The beast paused, looking back at Ozioma.

"*Ozioma Ugochukwu Mbagwu, do you know who this is?*" Aida-Wedo asked.

"No," Ozioma said.

"*This is Ekemini and he is one of* my *people.*" She laughed knowingly and the rainbow in the sky swelled, bathing everything in a marigold, tangerine, soft rose, periwinkle, and wooden green. "*And my people are powerful and rather . . . unpredictable. Do you know that you are fortunate to be alive?*"

"I didn't want it to kill anyone else," Ozioma said, hardening her voice. She motioned to the man who'd been writhing on the ground. Indeed he had stopped moving. Ozioma still couldn't see his face but it didn't matter. There was no one in her town she didn't know and who didn't know her.

The goddess said nothing as she appraised Ozioma. Ozioma stood tall. She'd just stared death in the eye for ten minutes. Even the goddess had implied it. Ozioma felt like a goddess herself. What was death? She met the goddess's stare, but then, out of respect, she looked down. Her father taught her that she should always, always, always, respect her elders. And what was older than a goddess?

"It says that it is impressed with you," Aida-Wedo said.

It has a funny way of showing it, she thought. *Was it not about to kill me?!* She said none of this, of course. It was best not to tell the goddess what she thought of the beast who'd just killed one of her tribesmen. Ozioma was still looking deferentially at the ground when she saw the first one drop into the mud. She gasped, her eye focusing on it. She bent down, picked it up and washed it in a nearby puddle. She held it to her eye. A piece of solid gold shaped just like a raindrop. In the goddess's rainbow light, it still shined its bright perfect gold. Another fell, then another. None hit Ozioma, and hundreds covered the body of the man who'd died.

The goddess ascended up the giant iron chain before the shower of solid gold drops ended. But by then, men were running around Ozioma gathering the valuable gifts into their pockets and occasionally touching Ozioma on the shoulder. Respect, awe, apology, and understanding, all wrapped up in those wordless touches. Ozioma gathered her share, too, once she was sure the snake beast and the goddess were gone.

For the next seventy-five years, not one person in the town of Agwotown was bitten by a snake. Not until a little boy named Nwokeji who could talk to eagles tempted fate. But that is another story.

5

I first encountered the bird in this story in the works of E. Nesbit. I wrote the story in the style of a remarkable American writer named R. A. Lafferty, as an eighteenth-birthday present for my daughter Holly. I hope you like it.

Lightning bugs, dolphinfish, dung beetle, unicorn flank steak . . . the intrepid members of the Epicurean Society have eaten every kind of animal. Or have they . . . ?

SUNBIRD

By
Neil Gaiman

THEY WERE A RICH AND A ROWDY BUNCH at the
Epicurean Club in those days. They certainly knew how to
party. There were five of them:

There was Augustus TwoFeathers McCoy, big enough
for three men, who ate enough for four men and who
drank enough for five. His great-grandfather had founded
the Epicurean Club with the proceeds of a tontine which
he had taken great pains, in the traditional manner, to
ensure that he had collected in full.

There was Professor Mandalay, small and twitchy and
grey as a ghost (and perhaps he was a ghost; stranger things
have happened) who drank nothing but water, and who
ate doll-portions from plates the size of saucers. Still, you
do not need the gusto for the gastronomy, and Mandalay
always got to the heart of every dish placed in front of him.

There was Virginia Boote, the food and restaurant
critic, who had once been a great beauty but was now a
grand and magnificent ruin, and who delighted in her
ruination.

There was Jackie Newhouse, the descendant (on the
left-handed route) of the great lover, gourmand, violin-
ist and duelist Giacomo Casanova. Jackie Newhouse had,

like his notorious ancestor, both broken his share of hearts and eaten his share of great dishes.

And there was Zebediah T. Crawcrustle, who was the only one of the Epicureans who was flat-out broke: he shambled in unshaven from the street when they had their meetings, with half a bottle of rotgut in a brown paper bag, hatless and coatless and, too often, partly shirtless, but he ate with more of an appetite than any of them.

Augustus TwoFeathers McCoy was talking—

"We have eaten everything that can be eaten," said Augustus TwoFeathers McCoy, and there was regret and glancing sorrow in his voice. "We have eaten vulture, mole, and fruit bat."

Mandalay consulted his notebook. "Vulture tasted like rotten pheasant. Mole tasted like carrion slug. Fruit bat tasted remarkably like sweet guinea pig."

"We have eaten kakapo, aye-aye, and giant panda—"

"Oh, that broiled panda steak," sighed Virginia Boote, her mouth watering at the memory.

"We have eaten several long-extinct species," said Augustus TwoFeathers McCoy. "We have eaten flash-frozen mammoth and Patagonian giant sloth."

"If we had but gotten the mammoth a little faster," sighed Jackie Newhouse. "I could tell why the hairy elephants went so fast, though, once people got a taste of them. I am a man of elegant pleasures, but after but one bite, I found myself thinking only of Kansas City barbecue sauce, and what the ribs on those things would be like, if they were fresh."

"Nothing wrong with being on ice for a millennium or two," said Zebediah T. Crawcrustle. He grinned. His teeth may have been crooked, but they were sharp and strong. "But for real taste you had to go for honest-to-goodness mastodon every time. Mammoth was always what people settled for, when they couldn't get mastodon."

"We've eaten squid, and giant squid, and humongous squid," said Augustus TwoFeathers McCoy. "We've eaten lemmings and Tasmanian tigers. We've eaten bowerbird and ortolan and peacock. We've eaten the dolphinfish (which is not the mammal dolphin) and the giant sea turtle and the Sumatran rhino. We've eaten everything there is to eat."

"Nonsense. There are many hundreds of things we have not yet tasted," said Professor Mandalay. "Thousands perhaps. Think of all the species of beetle there are, still untasted."

"Oh, Mandy," sighed Virginia Boote. "When you've tasted one beetle, you've tasted them all. And we all tasted several hundred species. At least the dung beetles had a real kick to them."

"No," said Jackie Newhouse, "that was the dung-beetle balls. The beetles themselves were singularly unexceptional. Still, I take your point. We have scaled the heights of gastronomy, we have plunged down into the depths of gustation. We have become cosmonauts exploring undreamed-of worlds of delectation and gourmanderie."

"True, true, true," said Augustus TwoFeathers McCoy. "There has been a meeting of the Epicureans every month

for over a hundred and fifty years, in my father's time, and my grandfather's time, and my great-grandfather's time, and now I fear that I must hang it up, for there is nothing left that we, or our predecessors in the club, have not eaten."

"I wish I had been here in the twenties," said Virginia Boote, "when they legally had man on the menu."

"Only after it had been electrocuted," said Zebediah T. Crawcrustle. "Half-fried already it was, all char and crackling. It left none of us with a taste for long pig, save for one who was already that way inclined, and he went out pretty soon after that anyway."

"Oh, Crusty, why must you pretend that you were there?" asked Virginia Boote, with a yawn. "Anyone can see you aren't that old. You can't be more than sixty, even allowing for the ravages of time and the gutter."

"Oh, they ravage pretty good," said Zebediah T. Crawcrustle. "But not as good as you'd imagine. Anyway there's a host of things we've not eaten yet."

"Name one," said Mandalay, his pencil poised precisely above his notebook.

"Well, there's Suntown Sunbird," said Zebediah T. Crawcrustle. And he grinned his crookedy grin at them, with his teeth ragged but sharp.

"I've never heard of it," said Jackie Newhouse. "You're making it up."

"I've heard of it," said Professor Mandalay. "But in another context. And besides, it is imaginary."

"Unicorns are imaginary," said Virginia Boote. "But gosh, that unicorn flank tartare was tasty. A little bit horsey, a little bit goatish, and all the better for the capers and raw quail eggs."

"There's something about Sunbirds in one of the minutes of the Epicurean Club from bygone years," said Augustus TwoFeathers McCoy. "But what it was, I can no longer remember."

"Did they say how it tasted?" asked Virginia.

"I do not believe that they did," said Augustus, with a frown. "I would need to inspect the bound proceedings, of course."

"Nah," said Zebediah T. Crawcrustle. "That's only in the charred volumes. You'll never find out about it from there."

Augustus TwoFeathers McCoy scratched his head. He really did have two feathers, which went through the knot of black hair shot with silver at the back of his head, and the feathers had once been golden, although by now they were looking kind of ordinary and yellow and ragged. He had been given them when he was a boy.

"Beetles," said Professor Mandalay. "I once calculated that, if a man such as myself were to eat six different species of beetle each day, it would take him more than twenty years to eat every beetle that has been identified. And over that twenty years enough new species of beetle might have been discovered to keep him eating for another five years. And in those five years enough beetles might have been discovered to keep him eating for another two and a half years, and so on, and so on. It is a paradox of inexhaustibility. I call it Mandalay's Beetle. You would have to enjoy eating beetles, though," he added, "or it would be a very bad thing indeed."

"Nothing wrong with eating beetles if they're the right kind of beetle," said Zebediah T. Crawcrustle. "Right now, I've got a hankering on me for lightning bugs. There's a kick from the glow of a lightning bug that might be just what I need."

"While the lightning bug or firefly (*Photinus pyralis*) is more of a beetle than it is a glowworm," said Mandalay, "they are by no stretch of the imagination edible."

"They may not be edible," said Crawcrustle. "But they'll get you into shape for the stuff that is. I think I'll roast me some. Fireflies and habanero peppers. Yum."

Virginia Boote was an eminently practical woman. She said, "Suppose we did want to eat Suntown Sunbird. Where should we start looking for it?"

Zebediah T. Crawcrustle scratched the bristling seven-day beard that was sprouting on his chin (it never grew any longer than that; seven-day beards never do). "If it was me," he told them, "I'd head down to Suntown of a noon in midsummer, and I'd find somewhere comfortable to sit—Mustapha Stroheim's coffeehouse, for example, and I'd wait for the Sunbird to come by. Then I'd catch him in the traditional manner, and cook him in the traditional manner as well."

"And what would the traditional manner of catching him be?" asked Jackie Newhouse.

"Why, the same way your famous ancestor poached quails and wood grouse," said Crawcrustle.

"There's nothing in Casanova's memoirs about poaching quail," said Jackie Newhouse.

"Your ancestor was a busy man," said Crawcrustle. "He couldn't be expected to write everything down. But he poached a good quail nonetheless."

"Dried corn and dried blueberries, soaked in whiskey," said Augustus TwoFeathers McCoy. "That's how my folk always did it."

"And that was how Casanova did it," said Crawcrustle, "although he used barley-grains mixed with raisins, and he soaked the raisins in brandy. He taught me himself."

Jackie Newhouse ignored this statement. It was easy to ignore much that Zebediah T. Crawcrustle said. Instead, Jackie Newhouse asked, "And where is Mustapha Stroheim's coffeehouse in Suntown?"

"Why, where it always is, third lane after the old market in the Suntown district, just before you reach the old drainage ditch that was once an irrigation canal, and if you find yourself in One-eye Khayam's carpet shop you have gone too far," began Crawcrustle. "But I see by the expressions of irritation upon your faces that you were expecting a less succinct, less accurate, description. Very well. It is in Suntown, and Suntown is in Cairo, in Egypt, where it always is, or almost always."

"And who will pay for an expedition to Suntown?" asked Augustus TwoFeathers McCoy. "And who will be on this expedition? I ask the question although I already know the answer, and I do not like it."

"Why, you will pay for it, Augustus, and we will all come," said Zebediah T. Crawcrustle. "You can deduct it from our Epicurean membership dues. And I shall bring my chef's apron and my cooking utensils."

Augustus knew that Crawcrustle had not paid his Epicurean Club membership in much too long a time, but the Epicurean Club would cover him; Crawcrustle had been a member of the Epicureans in Augustus's father's day. He simply said, "And when shall we leave?"

Crawcrustle fixed him with a mad old eye, and shook his head in disappointment. "Why, Augustus," he said. "We're going to Suntown, to catch the Sunbird. When else should we leave?"

"Sunday!" sang Virginia Boote. "Darlings, we'll leave on a Sunday!"

"There's hope for you yet, young lady," said Zebediah T. Crawcrustle. "We shall leave Sunday indeed. Three Sundays from now. And we shall travel to Egypt. We shall spend several days hunting and trapping the elusive Sunbird of Suntown, and, finally, we shall deal with it in the traditional way."

Professor Mandalay blinked a small grey blink. "But," he said, "I am teaching a class on Monday. On Mondays I teach mythology, on Tuesdays I teach tap dancing, and on Wednesdays, woodwork."

"Get a teaching assistant to take your course, Mandalay O Mandalay. On Monday you'll be hunting the Sunbird," said Zebediah T. Crawcrustle. "And how many other professors can say that?"

They went, one by one, to see Crawcrustle, in order to discuss the journey ahead of them, and to announce their misgivings.

Zebediah T. Crawcrustle was a man of no fixed abode. Still, there were places he could be found, if you were of a mind to find him. In the early mornings he slept in the bus terminal, where the benches were comfortable and the transport police were inclined to let him lie; in the heat of the afternoons he hung in the park by the statues of long-forgotten generals, with the dipsos and the winos and the hopheads, sharing their company and the contents of their bottles, and offering his opinion, which was, as that of an Epicurean, always considered and always respected, if not always welcomed.

Augustus TwoFeathers McCoy sought Crawcrustle out in the park; he had with him his daughter, Hollyberry NoFeathers McCoy. She was small, but she was sharp as a shark's tooth.

"You know," said Augustus, "there is something very familiar about this."

"About what?" asked Zebediah.

"All of this. The expedition to Egypt. The Sunbird. It seemed to me like I heard about it before."

Crawcrustle merely nodded. He was crunching something from a brown paper bag.

Augustus said, "I went to the bound annals of the Epicurean Club, and I looked it up. And there was what I took to be a reference to the Sunbird in the index for forty years ago, but I was unable to learn anything more than that."

"And why was that?" asked Zebediah T. Crawcrustle, swallowing noisily.

Augustus TwoFeathers McCoy sighed. "I found the relevant page in the annals," he said, "but it was burned away, and afterwards there was some great confusion in the administration of the Epicurean Club."

"You're eating lightning bugs from a paper bag," said Hollyberry NoFeathers McCoy. "I seen you doing it."

"I am indeed, little lady," said Zebediah T. Crawcrustle.

"Do you remember the days of great confusion, Crawcrustle?" asked Augustus.

"I do indeed," said Crawcrustle. "And I remember you. You were only the age that young Hollyberry is now. But there is always confusion, Augustus, and then there is no confusion. It is like the rising and the setting of the sun."

Jackie Newhouse and Professor Mandalay found Crawcrustle that evening, behind the railroad tracks. He was roasting something in a tin can, over a small charcoal fire.

"What are you roasting, Crawcrustle?" asked Jackie Newhouse.

"More charcoal," said Crawcrustle. "Cleans the blood, purifies the spirit."

There was basswood and hickory, cut up into little chunks at the bottom of the can, all black and smoking.

"And will you actually eat this charcoal, Crawcrustle?" asked Professor Mandalay.

In response, Crawcrustle licked his fingers and picked out a lump of charcoal from the can. It hissed and fizzed in his grip.

"A fine trick," said Professor Mandalay. "That's how fire-eaters do it, I believe."

Crawcrustle popped the charcoal into his mouth and crunched it between his ragged old teeth. "It is indeed," he said. "It is indeed."

Jackie Newhouse cleared his throat. "The truth of the matter is," he said, "Professor Mandalay and I have deep misgivings about the journey that lies ahead."

Zebediah merely crunched his charcoal. "Not hot enough," he said. He took a stick from the fire, and nibbled off the orange-hot tip of it. "That's good," he said.

"It's all an illusion," said Jackie Newhouse.

"Nothing of the sort," said Zebediah T. Crawcrustle primly. "It's prickly elm."

"I have extreme misgivings about all this," said Jackie Newhouse. "My ancestors and I have a finely tuned sense of personal preservation, one that has often left us shivering

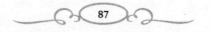

on roofs and hiding in rivers—one step away from the law, or from gentlemen with guns and legitimate grievances— and that sense of self-preservation is telling me not to go to Suntown with you."

"I am an academic," said Professor Mandalay, "and thus have no finely developed senses that would be comprehensible to anyone who has not ever needed to grade papers without actually reading the blessed things. Still, I find the whole thing remarkably suspicious. If this Sunbird is so tasty, why have I not heard of it?"

"You have, Mandy old fruit. You have," said Zebediah T. Crawcrustle.

"And I am, in addition, an expert on geographical features from Tulsa, Oklahoma, to Timbuktu," continued Professor Mandalay. "Yet I have never seen a mention in any books of a place called Suntown in Cairo."

"Seen it mentioned? Why, you've taught it," said Crawcrustle, and he doused a lump of smoking charcoal with hot pepper sauce before popping it in his mouth and chomping it down.

"I don't believe you're really eating that," said Jackie Newhouse. "But even being around the trick of it is making me uncomfortable. I think it is time that I was elsewhere."

And he left. Perhaps Professor Mandalay left with him: that man was so grey and so ghostie, it was always a toss-up whether he was there or not.

Virginia Boote tripped over Zebediah T. Crawcrustle while he rested in her doorway, in the small hours of the morning. She was returning from a restaurant she had needed to review. She got out of a taxi, tripped over Crawcrustle and went sprawling. She landed nearby. "Whee!" she said. "That was some trip, wasn't it?"

"Indeed it was, Virginia," said Zebediah T. Crawcrustle. "You would not happen to have such a thing as a box of matches on you, would you?"

"I have a book of matches on me somewhere," she said, and she began to rummage in her purse, which was very large and very brown. "Here you are."

Zebediah T. Crawcrustle was carrying a bottle of purple methylated spirits, which he proceeded to pour into a plastic cup.

"Meths?" said Virginia Boote. "Somehow you never struck me as a meths drinker, Zebby."

"Nor am I," said Crawcrustle. "Foul stuff. It rots the guts and spoils the taste buds. But I could not find any lighter fluid at this time of night."

He lit a match, then dipped it near the surface of the cup of spirits, which began to burn with a flickery light. He ate the match. Then he gargled with the flaming liquid, and blew a sheet of flame into the street, incinerating a sheet of newspaper as it blew by.

"Crusty," said Virginia Boote, "that's a good way to get yourself killed."

Zebediah T. Crawcrustle grinned through black teeth. "I don't actually drink it," he told her. "I just gargle and breathe it out."

"You're playing with fire," she warned him.

"That's how I know I'm alive," said Zebediah T. Crawcrustle.

Virginia said, "Oh, Zeb. I am excited. I am so excited. What do you think the Sunbird tastes like?"

"Richer than quail and moister than turkey, fatter than ostrich and lusher than duck," said Zebediah T. Crawcrustle. "Once eaten it's never forgotten."

"We're going to Egypt," she said. "I've never been to Egypt." Then she said, "Do you have anywhere to stay the night?"

He coughed, a small cough that rattled around in his old chest. "I'm getting too old to sleep in doorways and gutters," he said. "Still, I have my pride."

"Well," she said, looking at the man, "you could sleep on my sofa."

"It is not that I am not grateful for the offer," he said, "but there is a bench in the bus station that has my name on it."

And he pushed himself away from the wall, and tottered majestically down the street.

There really was a bench in the bus station that had his name on it. He had donated the bench to the bus station back when he was flush, and his name was attached to the back of the bench, engraved upon a small brass plaque. Zebediah T. Crawcrustle was not always poor. Sometimes he was rich, but he had difficulty in holding on to his wealth, and whenever he had become wealthy he discovered that the world frowned on rich men eating in hobo jungles at the back of the railroad, or consorting with the winos in the park, so he would fritter his wealth away as best he could. There were always little bits of it here and there that he had forgotten about, and sometimes he would forget that he did not like being rich, and then he would set out again and seek his fortune, and find it.

He had needed a shave for a week, and the hairs of his seven-day beard were starting to come through snow white.

They left for Egypt on a Sunday, the Epicureans. There were five of them there, and Hollyberry NoFeathers McCoy waved goodbye to them at the airport. It was a very small airport, which still permitted waves goodbye.

"Goodbye, Father!" called Hollyberry NoFeathers McCoy.

Augustus TwoFeathers McCoy waved back at her as they walked along the asphalt to the little prop plane, which would begin the first leg of their journey.

"It seems to me," said Augustus TwoFeathers McCoy, "that I remember, albeit dimly, a day like this long, long ago. I was a small boy, in that memory, waving goodbye. I believe it was the last time I saw my father, and I am struck once more with a sudden presentiment of doom." He waved one last time at the small child at the other end of the field, and she waved back at him.

"You waved just as enthusiastically back then," agreed

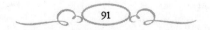

Zebediah T. Crawcrustle, "but I think she waves with slightly more aplomb."

It was true. She did.

They took a small plane and then a larger plane, then a smaller plane, a blimp, a gondola, a train, a hot-air balloon, and a rented Jeep.

They rattled through Cairo in the Jeep. They passed the old market, and they turned off on the third lane they came to (if they had continued on they would have come to a drainage ditch that was once an irrigation canal). Mustapha Stroheim himself was sitting outside in the street, sitting on an elderly wicker chair. All of the tables and chairs were on the side of the street, and it was not a particularly wide street.

"Welcome, my friends, to my *kahwa*," said Mustapha Stroheim. "Kahwa is Egyptian for 'café,' or for 'coffee-house.' Would you like tea? Or a game of dominoes?"

"We would like to be shown to our rooms," said Jackie Newhouse.

"Not me," said Zebediah T. Crawcrustle. "I'll sleep in the street. It's warm enough, and that doorstep over there looks mighty comfortable."

"I'll have coffee, please," said Augustus TwoFeathers McCoy.

"Of course."

"Do you have water?" asked Professor Mandalay.

"Who said that?" said Mustapha Stroheim. "Oh, it was you, little grey man. My mistake. When I first saw you I thought you were someone's shadow."

"I will have *shay sokkar bosta*"—said Virginia Boote—which is a glass of hot tea with the sugar on the side. "And I will play backgammon with anyone who wishes to take me on. There's not a soul in Cairo I cannot beat at backgammon, if I can remember the rules."

Augustus TwoFeathers McCoy was shown to his room. Professor Mandalay was shown to his room. Jackie Newhouse was shown to his room. This was not a lengthy procedure; they were all in the same room, after all. There was another room in the back where Virginia would sleep, and a third room for Mustapha Stroheim and his family.

"What's that you're writing?" asked Jackie Newhouse.

"It's the procedures, annals, and minutes of the Epicurean Club," said Professor Mandalay. He was writing in a large leather-bound book with a small black pen. "I have chronicled our journey here, and all the things that we have eaten on the way. I shall keep writing as we eat the Sunbird, to record for posterity all the tastes and textures, all the smells and the juices."

"Did Crawcrustle say how he was going to cook the Sunbird?" asked Jackie Newhouse.

"He did," said Augustus TwoFeathers McCoy. "He says that he will drain a beer can, so it is only a third full. And then he will add herbs and spices to the beer can. He will stand the bird up on the can, with the can in its inner cavity, and place it up on the barbecue to roast. He says it is the traditional way."

Jackie Newhouse sniffed. "It sounds suspiciously modern to me."

"Crawcrustle says it is the traditional method of cooking the Sunbird," repeated Augustus.

"Indeed I did," said Crawcrustle, coming up the stairs. It was a small building. The stairs weren't that far away, and the walls were not thick ones. "The oldest beer in the world is Egyptian beer, and they've been cooking the Sunbird with it for over five thousand years now."

"But the beer can is a relatively modern invention," said Professor Mandalay as Zebediah T. Crawcrustle came through the door. Crawcrustle was holding a cup of Turkish coffee, black as tar, which steamed like a kettle and bubbled like a tar pit.

"That coffee looks pretty hot," said Augustus Two-Feathers McCoy.

Crawcrustle knocked back the cup, draining half the contents. "Nah," he said. "Not really. And the beer can isn't really that new an invention. We used to make them out of an amalgam of copper and tin in the old days, sometimes with a little silver in there, sometimes not. It depended on the smith, and what he had to hand. You need something that would stand up to the heat. I see that you are all looking at me doubtfully. Gentlemen, consider: of course the ancient Egyptians made beer cans; where else would they have kept their beer?"

From outside the window, at the tables in the street, came a wailing, in many voices. Virginia Boote had persuaded the locals to start playing backgammon for money, and she was cleaning them out. That woman was a backgammon shark.

Out back of Mustapha Stroheim's coffeehouse there was a courtyard, containing a broken-down old barbecue, made of clay bricks and a half-melted metal grating, and an old wooden table. Crawcrustle spent the next day rebuilding the barbecue and cleaning it, oiling down the metal grille.

"That doesn't look like it's been used in forty years," said Virginia Boote. Nobody would play backgammon with her any longer, and her purse bulged with grubby piasters.

"Something like that," said Crawcrustle. "Maybe a little more. Here, Ginnie, make yourself useful. I've written a list of things I need from the market. It's mostly herbs and spices and wood chips. You can take one of the children of Mustapha Stroheim to translate for you."

"My pleasure, Crusty."

The other three members of the Epicurean Club were occupying themselves in their own way. Jackie Newhouse was making friends with many of the people of the area, who were attracted by his elegant suits and his skill at playing the violin. Augustus TwoFeathers McCoy went for long walks. Professor Mandalay spent time translating the hieroglyphics he had noticed were incised upon the clay bricks in the barbecue. He said that a foolish man might believe that they proved that the barbecue in Mustapha Stroheim's backyard was once sacred to the Sun. "But I, who am an intelligent man," he said, "see immediately that what has happened is that bricks that were once, long ago, part of a temple have, over the millennia, been reused. I doubt that these people know the value of what they have here."

"Oh, they know all right," said Zebediah T. Crawcrustle. "And these bricks weren't part of any temple. They've been right here for five thousand years, since we built the barbecue. Before that we made do with stones."

Virginia Boote returned with a filled shopping basket. "Here," she said. "Red sandalwood and patchouli, vanilla beans, lavender twigs and sage and cinnamon leaves, whole nutmegs, garlic bulbs, cloves and rosemary—everything you wanted and more."

Zebediah T. Crawcrustle grinned with delight.

"The Sunbird will be so happy," he told her.

He spent the afternoon preparing a barbecue sauce. He said it was only respectful, and besides, the Sunbird's flesh was often slightly on the dry side.

The Epicureans spent that evening sitting at the wicker tables in the street out front, while Mustapha Stroheim and his family brought them tea and coffee and hot mint drinks. Zebediah T. Crawcrustle had told them that they would be having the Sunbird of Suntown for Sunday lunch, and that they might wish to avoid food the night before, to ensure that they had an appetite.

"I have a presentiment of doom upon me," said Augustus TwoFeathers McCoy that night, in a bed that was far too small for him, before he slept. "And I fear it shall come to us with barbecue sauce."

They were all so hungry the following morning. Zebediah T. Crawcrustle had a comedic apron on, with the words KISS THE COOK written upon it in violently green letters. He had already sprinkled the brandy-soaked raisins and grain beneath the stunted avocado tree behind the house, and he was arranging the scented woods, the herbs, and the spices on the bed of charcoal. Mustapha Stroheim and his family had gone to visit relatives on the other side of Cairo.

"Does anybody have a match?" Crawcrustle asked.

Jackie Newhouse pulled out a Zippo lighter, and passed it to Crawcrustle, who lit the dried cinnamon leaves and dried laurel leaves beneath the charcoal. The smoke drifted up into the noon air.

"The cinnamon and sandalwood smoke will bring the Sunbird," said Crawcrustle.

"Bring it from where?" asked Augustus TwoFeathers McCoy.

"From the Sun," said Crawcrustle. "That's where he sleeps."

Professor Mandalay coughed discreetly. He said, "The Earth is, at its closest, ninety-one million miles from the Sun. The fastest dive by a bird ever recorded is that of the peregrine falcon, at two hundred seventy-three miles per hour. Flying at that speed, from the Sun, it would take a bird a little over thirty-eight years to reach us—if it could fly through the dark and cold and vacuum of space, of course."

"Of course," agreed Zebediah T. Crawcrustle. He shaded his eyes and squinted and looked upward. "Here it comes," he said.

It looked almost as if the bird was flying out of the Sun; but that could not have been the case. You could not look directly at the noonday Sun, after all.

First it was a silhouette, black against the Sun and against the blue sky, then the sunlight caught its feathers, and the watchers on the ground caught their breath. You have never seen anything like sunlight on the Sunbird's feathers; seeing something like that would take your breath away.

The Sunbird flapped its wide wings once, then it began to glide in ever-decreasing circles in the air above Mustapha Stroheim's coffeehouse.

The bird landed in the avocado tree. Its feathers were golden, and purple, and silver. It was smaller than a turkey, larger than a rooster, and had the long legs and high head of a heron, though its head was more like the head of an eagle.

"It is very beautiful," said Virginia Boote. "Look at the two tall feathers on its head. Aren't they lovely?"

"It is indeed quite lovely," said Professor Mandalay.

"There is something familiar about that bird's head-feathers," said Augustus TwoFeathers McCoy.

"We pluck the head feathers before we roast the bird," said Zebediah T. Crawcrustle. "It's the way it's always done."

The Sunbird perched on a branch of the avocado tree, in a patch of sun. It seemed almost as if it were glowing, gently, in the sunlight, as if its feathers were made of sunlight, iridescent with purples and greens and golds. It preened itself, extending one wing in the sunlight, then it nibbled and stroked at the wing with its beak until all the feathers were in their correct position, and oiled. Then it extended the other wing, and repeated the process. Finally, the bird emitted a contented *chirrup*, and flew the short distance from the branch to the ground.

It strutted across the dried mud, peering from side to side shortsightedly.

"Look!" said Jackie Newhouse. "It's found the grain."

"It seemed almost that it was looking for it," said Augustus TwoFeathers McCoy. "That it was expecting the grain to be there."

"That's where I always leave it," said Zebediah T. Crawcrustle.

"It's so lovely," said Virginia Boote. "But now I see it closer, I can see that it's much older than I thought. Its eyes are cloudy and its legs are shaking. But it's still lovely."

"The Bennu bird is the loveliest of birds," said Zebediah T. Crawcrustle.

Virginia Boote spoke good restaurant Egyptian, but beyond that she was all at sea. "What's a Bennu bird?" she asked. "Is that Egyptian for Sunbird?"

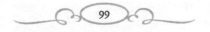

"The Bennu bird," said Professor Mandalay, "roosts in the persea tree. It has two feathers on its head. It is sometimes represented as being like a heron, and sometimes like an eagle. There is more, but it is too unlikely to bear repeating."

"It's eaten the grain and the raisins!" exclaimed Jackie Newhouse. "Now it's stumbling drunkenly from side to side—such majesty, even in its drunkenness!"

Zebediah T. Crawcrustle walked over to the Sunbird, which, with a great effort of will, was walking back and forth on the mud beneath the avocado tree, not tripping over its long legs. He stood directly in front of the bird, and then, very slowly, he bowed to it. He bent like a very old man, slowly and creakily, but still he bowed. And the Sunbird bowed back to him, then it toppled to the mud. Zebediah T. Crawcrustle picked it up reverently, and placed it in his arms, carrying it as if one would carry a child, and he took it back to the plot of land behind Mustapha Stroheim's coffeehouse, and the others followed him.

First he plucked the two majestic head feathers, and set them aside.

And then, without plucking the bird, he gutted it, and placed the guts on the smoking twigs. He put the half-filled beer can inside the body cavity, and placed the bird upon the barbecue.

"Sunbird cooks fast," warned Crawcrustle. "Get your plates ready."

The beers of the ancient Egyptians were flavored with

cardamom and coriander, for the Egyptians had no hops; their beers were rich and flavorsome and thirst quenching. You could build pyramids after drinking that beer, and sometimes people did. On the barbecue the beer steamed the inside of the Sunbird, keeping it moist. As the heat of the charcoal reached them, the feathers of the bird burned off, igniting with a flash like a magnesium flare, so bright that the Epicureans were forced to avert their eyes.

The smell of roast fowl filled the air, richer than peacock, lusher than duck. The mouths of the assembled Epicureans began to water. It seemed like it had been cooking for no time at all, but Zebediah lifted the Sunbird from the charcoal bed, and put it on the table. Then, with a carving knife, he sliced it up and placed the steaming meat on the plates. He poured a little barbecue sauce over each piece of meat. He placed the carcass directly onto the flames.

The members of the Epicurean Club sat in the back of Mustapha Stroheim's coffeehouse, sat around an elderly wooden table, and they ate with their fingers.

"Zebby, this is amazing!" said Virginia Boote, talking as she ate. "It melts in your mouth. It tastes like heaven."

"It tastes like the sun," said Augustus TwoFeathers McCoy, putting his food away as only a big man can. He had a leg in one hand, and some breast in the other. "It is the finest thing I have ever eaten, and I do not regret eating it, but I do believe that I shall miss my daughter."

"It is perfect," said Jackie Newhouse. "It tastes like love and fine music. It tastes like truth."

Professor Mandalay was scribbling in the bound annals of the Epicurean Club. He was recording his reaction to the meat of the bird, and recording the reactions of the other Epicureans, and trying not to drip on the page while he wrote, for with the hand that was not writing he was holding a wing, and, fastidiously, he was nibbling the meat off it.

"It is strange," said Jackie Newhouse, "for as I eat it, it gets hotter and hotter in my mouth and in my stomach."

"Yup. It'll do that. It's best to prepare for it ahead of time," said Zebediah T. Crawcrustle. "Eat coals and flames and lightning bugs to get used to it. Otherwise it can be a trifle hard on the system."

Zebediah T. Crawcrustle was eating the head of the bird, crunching its bones and beak in his mouth. As he ate, the bones sparked small lightnings against his teeth. He just grinned and chewed the more.

The bones of the Sunbird's carcass burned orange on the barbecue, and then they began to burn white. There was a thick heat-haze in the courtyard at the back of Mustapha Stroheim's coffeehouse, and in it everything shimmered, as if the people around the table were seeing the world through water or a dream.

"It is so good!" said Virginia Boote as she ate. "It is the best thing I have ever eaten. It tastes like my youth. It tastes like forever." She licked her fingers, then picked up the last slice of meat from her plate. "The Sunbird of Suntown," she said. "Does it have another name?"

SUNBIRD

"It is the Phoenix of Heliopolis," said Zebediah T. Crawcrustle. "It is the bird that dies in ashes and flame, and is reborn, generation after generation. It is the Bennu bird, which flew across the waters when all was dark. When its time is come it is burned on the fire of rare woods and spices and herbs, and in the ashes it is reborn, time after time, world without end."

"Fire!" exclaimed Professor Mandalay. "It feels as if my insides are burning up!" He sipped his water, but seemed no happier.

"My fingers," said Virginia Boote. "Look at my fingers." She held them up. They were glowing inside, as if lit with inner flames.

Now the air was so hot you could have baked an egg in it.

There was a spark and a sputter. The two yellow feathers in Augustus TwoFeathers McCoy's hair went up like sparklers.

"Crawcrustle," said Jackie Newhouse, aflame, "answer me truly. How long have you been eating the Phoenix?"

"A little over ten thousand years," said Zebediah. "Give or take a few thousand. It's not hard, once you master the trick of it; it's just mastering the trick of it that's hard. But this is the best Phoenix I've ever prepared. Or do I mean, 'this is the best I've ever cooked this Phoenix'?"

"The years!" said Virginia Boote. "They are burning off you!"

"They do that," admitted Zebediah. "You've got to get

used to the heat, though, before you eat it. Otherwise you can just burn away."

"Why did I not remember this?" said Augustus Two-Feathers McCoy, through the bright flames that surrounded him. "Why did I not remember that this was how my father went, and his father before him, that each of them went to Heliopolis to eat the Phoenix? And why do I only remember it now?"

"Because the years are burning off you," said Professor Mandalay. He had closed the leather book as soon as the page he had been writing on caught fire. The edges of the book were charred, but the rest of the book would be fine. "When the years burn, the memories of those years come back." He looked more solid now, through the wavering burning air, and he was smiling. None of them had ever seen Professor Mandalay smile before.

"Shall we burn away to nothing?" asked Virginia, now incandescent. "Or shall we burn back to childhood and burn back to ghosts and angels and then come forward again? It does not matter. Oh, Crusty, this is all such *fun!*"

"Perhaps," said Jackie Newhouse through the fire, "there might have been a little more vinegar in the sauce. I feel a meat like this could have dealt with something more robust." And then he was gone, leaving only an after-image.

"*Chacun à son goût,*" said Zebediah T. Crawcrustle—which is French for "each to his own taste"—and he licked his fingers and he shook his head. "Best it's ever been," he said, with enormous satisfaction.

"Goodbye, Crusty," said Virginia. She put her flame-white hand out, and held his dark hand tightly, for one moment, or perhaps for two.

And then there was nothing in the courtyard back of Mustapha Stroheim's *kahwa* (or coffeehouse) in Heliopolis (which was once the city of the Sun, and is now a suburb of Cairo), but white ash, which blew up in the momentary breeze, and settled like powdered sugar or like snow; and nobody there but a young man with dark, dark hair and even, ivory-colored teeth, wearing an apron that said KISS THE COOK.

A tiny golden-purple bird stirred in the thick bed of ashes on top of the clay bricks, as if it were waking for the first time. It made a high-pitched *peep!* and it looked directly into the Sun, as an infant looks at a parent. It stretched its wings as if to dry them, and, eventually, when it was quite ready, it flew upward, toward the Sun, and nobody watched it leave but the young man in the courtyard.

There were two long golden feathers at the young man's feet, beneath the ash that had once been a wooden table, and he gathered them up, and brushed the white ash from them and placed them, reverently, inside his jacket. Then he removed his apron, and he went upon his way.

Hollyberry TwoFeathers McCoy is a grown woman, with children of her own. There are silver hairs on her head, in there with the black, beneath the golden feathers in the bun at the back. You can see that the feathers must once have looked pretty special, but that would have been a long time ago. She is the president of the Epicurean Club—a rich and rowdy bunch—having inherited the position, many long years ago, from her father.

I hear that the Epicureans are beginning to grumble once again. They are saying that they have eaten everything.

(For HMG—a belated birthday present)

DIANA WYNNE JONES wrote stories that combined humor and magic, adventure and wisdom. She is one of my favorite writers and was one of my favorite people. I miss her. You should read her books. In this story you will encounter Chrestomanci, the enchanter who makes sure that people are not abusing their magic. He can also be found in *Charmed Life*, and several other books.

This is a story about invisible dragons, and about gods, and about a wise sage and a young man who seeks him.

THE SAGE OF THEARE

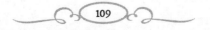

By

Diana Wynne Jones

THERE WAS A WORLD CALLED THEARE in which Heaven was very well organized. Everything was so precisely worked out that every god knew his or her exact duties, correct prayers, right times for business, utterly exact character and unmistakable place above or below other gods. This was the case from Great Zond, the King of the Gods, through every god, godlet, deity, minor deity and numen, down to the most immaterial nymph. Even the invisible dragons that lived in the rivers had their invisible lines of demarcation. The universe ran like clockwork. Mankind was not always so regular, but the gods were there to set him right. It had been like this for centuries.

So it was a breach in the very nature of things when, in the middle of the yearly Festival of Water, at which only watery deities were entitled to be present, Great Zond looked up to see Imperion, god of the sun, storming towards him down the halls of Heaven.

"Go away!" cried Zond, aghast.

But Imperion swept on, causing the watery deities gathered there to steam and hiss, and arrived in a wave of heat and warm water at the foot of Zond's high throne.

"Father!" Imperion cried urgently.

A high god like Imperion was entitled to call Zond Father. Zond did not recall whether or not he was actually Imperion's father. The origins of the gods were not quite so orderly as their present existence. But Zond knew that, son of his or not, Imperion had breached all the rules. "Abase yourself," Zond said sternly.

Imperion ignored this command, too. Perhaps this was just as well, since the floor of Heaven was awash already, and steaming. Imperion kept his flaming gaze on Zond. "Father! The Sage of Dissolution has been born!"

Zond shuddered in the clouds of hot vapor and tried to feel resigned. "It is written," he said, "a Sage shall be born who shall question everything. His questions shall bring down the exquisite order of Heaven and cast all the gods into disorder. It is also written—" Here Zond realized that Imperion had made him break the rules too. The correct procedure was for Zond to summon the god of prophecy and have that god consult the Book of Heaven. Then he realized that Imperion *was* the god of prophecy. It was one of his precisely allotted duties. Zond rounded on Imperion. "What do you mean coming and telling me? You're god of prophecy! Go and look in the Book of Heaven."

"I already have, Father," said Imperion. "I find I prophesied the coming of the Sage of Dissolution when the gods first began. It is written that the Sage shall be born and that I shall not know."

"Then," said Zond, scoring a point, "how is it you're

here telling me he *has* been born?"

"The mere fact," Imperion said, "that I can come here and interrupt the Water Festival shows that the Sage has been born. Our Dissolution has obviously begun."

There was a splash of consternation among the watery gods. They were gathered down the hall as far as they could get from Imperion, but they had all heard. Zond tried to gather his wits. What with the steam raised by Imperion and the spume of dismay thrown out by the rest, the halls of Heaven were in a state nearer chaos than he had known for millennia. Any more of this, and there would be no need for the Sage to ask questions. "Leave us," Zond said to the watery gods. "Events beyond even my control cause this Festival to be stopped. You will be informed later of any decision I make." To Zond's dismay, the watery ones hesitated—further evidence of Dissolution. "I promise," he said.

The watery ones made up their minds. They left in waves, all except one. This one was Ock, god of all oceans. Ock was equal in status to Imperion and heat did not threaten him. He stayed where he was.

Zond was not pleased. Ock, it always seemed to him, was the least orderly of the gods. He did not know his place. He was as restless and unfathomable as mankind. But, with Dissolution already begun, what could Zond do? "You have our permission to stay," he said graciously to Ock, and to Imperion: "Well, how did you know the Sage was born?"

"I was consulting the Book of Heaven on another matter," said Imperion, "and the page opened at my prophecy concerning the Sage of Dissolution. Since it said that I would not know the day and hour when the Sage was born, it followed that he has already been born, or I would not have known. The rest of the prophecy was commendably precise, however. Twenty years from now, he will start questioning Heaven. What shall we do to stop him?"

"I don't see what we can do," Zond said hopelessly. "A prophecy is a prophecy."

"But we must do something!" blazed Imperion. "I insist! I am a god of order, even more than you are. Think what would happen if the sun went inaccurate! This means more to me than anyone. I want the Sage of Dissolution found and killed before he can ask questions."

Zond was shocked. "I can't do that! If the prophecy says he has to ask questions, then he has to ask them."

Here Ock approached. "Every prophecy has a loophole," he said.

"Of course," snapped Imperion. "I can see the loophole as well as you. I'm taking advantage of the disorder caused by the birth of the Sage to ask Great Zond to kill him and overthrow the prophecy. Thus restoring order."

"Logic-chopping is not what I meant," said Ock.

The two gods faced one another. Steam from Ock suffused Imperion and then rained back on Ock, as regularly as breathing. "What did you mean, then?" said Imperion.

"The prophecy," said Ock, "does not appear to say

which world the Sage will ask his questions in. There are many other worlds. Mankind calls them if-worlds, meaning that they were once the same world as Theare, but split off and went their own way after each doubtful event in history. Each if-world has its own Heaven. There must be one world in which the gods are not as orderly as we are here. Let the Sage be put in that world. Let him ask his predestined questions there."

"Good idea!" Zond clapped his hands in relief, causing untoward tempests in all Theare. "Agreed, Imperion?"

"Yes," said Imperion. He flamed with relief. And, being unguarded, he at once became prophetic. "But I must warn you," he said, "that strange things happen when destiny is tampered with."

"Strange things maybe, but never disorderly," Zond asserted. He called the watery gods back and, with them, every god in Theare. He told them that an infant had just been born who was destined to spread Dissolution, and he ordered each one of them to search the ends of the earth for this child. ("The ends of the earth" was a legal formula. Zond did not believe that Theare was flat. But the expression had been unchanged for centuries, just like the rest of Heaven. It meant "Look everywhere.")

The whole of Heaven looked high and low. Nymphs and godlets scanned mountains, caves and woods. Household gods peered into cradles. Watery gods searched beaches, banks, and margins. The goddess of love went deeply into her records, to find who the Sage's parents might be. The invisible dragons swam to look inside barges and house-boats. Since there was a god for everything in Theare nowhere was missed, nothing was omitted. Imperion searched harder than any, blazing into every nook and crevice on one side of the world, and exhorting the moon goddess to do the same on the other side.

And nobody found the Sage. There were one or two false alarms, such as when a household goddess reported an infant that never stopped crying. This baby, she said, was driving her up the wall and if this was not Dissolution, she would like to know what was. There were also several reports of infants born with teeth, or six fingers, or such-like strangeness. But, in each case, Zond was able to prove that the child had nothing to do with Dissolution. After a month, it became clear that the infant Sage was not going to be found.

Imperion was in despair, for, as he had told Zond, order meant more to him than to any other god. He became so worried that he was actually causing the sun to lose heat. At length, the goddess of love advised him to go off and relax with a mortal woman before he brought about Dissolution himself. Imperion saw she was right. He went down to visit the human woman he had loved for some years. It was established custom for gods to love mortals. Some visited their loves in all sorts of fanciful shapes, and some had many loves at once. But Imperion was both honest and faithful. He never visited Nestara as anything but a handsome man, and he loved her devotedly. Three years ago, she had borne him a son, whom Imperion loved almost as much as he loved Nestara. Before the Sage was born to trouble him, Imperion had been trying to bend the rules of Heaven a little, to get his son approved as a god too.

The child's name was Thasper. As Imperion descended to earth, he could see Thasper digging in some sand outside Nestara's house—a beautiful child, fair-haired and blue-eyed. Imperion wondered fondly if Thasper was talking properly yet. Nestara had been worried about how slow he was learning to speak.

Imperion alighted beside his son. "Hello, Thasper. What are you digging so busily?"

Instead of answering, Thasper raised his golden head and shouted. "Mum!" he yelled. "Why does it go bright when Dad comes?"

All Imperion's pleasure vanished. Of course no one could ask questions until he had learned to speak. But it would be too cruel if his own son turned out to be the Sage of Dissolution. "Why shouldn't it go bright?" he said defensively.

Thasper scowled up at him. "I want to know. *Why* does it?"

"Perhaps because you feel happy to see me," Imperion suggested.

"I'm not happy," Thasper said. His lower lip came out. Tears filled his big blue eyes. "Why does it go bright? I want to *know*. Mum! I'm not happy!"

Nestara came racing out of the house, almost too concerned to smile at Imperion. "Thasper love, what's the matter?"

"I want to *know*!" wailed Thasper.

"What do you want to know? I've never known such an inquiring mind," Nestara said proudly to Imperion as she picked Thasper up. "That's why he was so slow talking. He wouldn't speak until he'd found out how to ask questions. And if you don't give him an exact answer, he'll cry for hours."

"When did he first start asking questions?" Imperion inquired tensely.

"About a month ago," said Nestara. This made Imperion truly miserable, but he concealed it. It was clear to him that Thasper was indeed the Sage of Dissolution and he was going to have to take him away to another world. He smiled and said, "My love, I have wonderful news for you. Thasper has been accepted as a god. Great Zond himself will have him as cupbearer."

"Oh not now!" cried Nestara. "He's so little!"

She made numerous other objections too. But, in the end, she let Imperion take Thasper. After all, what better future could there be for a child? She put Thasper into Imperion's arms with all sorts of anxious advice about what he ate and when he went to bed. Imperion kissed her good-bye, heavyhearted. He was not a god of deception. He knew he dared not see her again for fear he told her the truth.

Then, with Thasper in his arms, Imperion went up

to the middle-regions below Heaven, to look for another world.

Thasper looked down with interest at the great blue curve of the world. "Why—?" he began.

Imperion hastily enclosed him in a sphere of forgetfulness. He could not afford to let Thasper ask things here. Questions that spread Dissolution on earth would have an even more powerful effect in the middle-region. The sphere was a silver globe, neither transparent nor opaque. In it, Thasper would stay seemingly asleep, not moving and not growing, until the sphere was opened. With the child thus safe, Imperion hung the sphere from one shoulder and stepped into the next-door world.

He went from world to world. He was pleased to find there were an almost infinite number of them, for the choice proved supremely difficult. Some worlds were so disorderly that he shrank from leaving Thasper in them. In some, the gods resented Imperion's intrusion and shouted at him to be off. In others, it was mankind that was resentful. One world he came to was so rational that, to his horror, he found the gods were dead. There were many others he thought might do, until he let the spirit of prophecy blow through him, and in each case this told him that harm would come to Thasper here. But at last he found a good world. It seemed calm and elegant. The few gods there seemed civilized but casual. Indeed, Imperion was a little puzzled to find that these gods seemed to share quite a lot of their power with mankind. But mankind did not seem to abuse this power, and the spirit of prophecy assured him that, if he left Thasper here inside his sphere of forgetfulness, it would be opened by someone who would treat the boy well.

Imperion put the sphere down in a wood and sped back to Theare, heartily relieved. There, he reported what he had done to Zond, and all Heaven rejoiced. Imperion made sure that Nestara married a very rich man who gave her not only wealth and happiness but plenty of children to replace Thasper. Then, a little sadly, he went back to the ordered life of Heaven. The exquisite organization of Theare went on untroubled by Dissolution.

Seven years passed.

All that while, Thasper knew nothing and remained three years old. Then one day, the sphere of forgetfulness fell in two halves and he blinked in sunlight somewhat less golden than he had known.

"So that's what was causing all the disturbance," a tall man murmured.

"Poor little soul!" said a lady.

There was a wood around Thasper, and people standing in it looking at him, but, as far as Thasper knew, nothing had happened since he soared to the middle-region with his father. He went on with the question he had been in the middle of asking. "Why is the world round?" he said.

"Interesting question," said the tall man. "The answer usually given is because the corners wore off spinning around the sun. But it could be designed to make us end where we began."

"Sir, you'll muddle him, talking like that," said another lady. "He's only little."

"No, he's interested," said another man. "Look at him."

Thasper was indeed interested. He approved of the tall man. He was a little puzzled about where he had come from, but he supposed the tall man must have been put there because he answered questions better than Imperion. He wondered where Imperion had got to. "Why aren't you my dad?" he asked the tall man.

"Another most penetrating question," said the tall man. "Because, as far as we can find out, your father lives in another world. Tell me your name."

This was another point in the tall man's favor. Thasper never answered questions: he only asked them. But this was a command. The tall man understood Thasper. "Thasper," Thasper answered obediently.

"He's sweet!" said the first lady. "I want to adopt him." To which the other ladies gathered around most heartily agreed.

"Impossible," said the tall man. His tone was mild as milk and rock firm. The ladies were reduced to begging to be able to look after Thasper for a day, then. An hour. "No," the tall man said mildly. "He must go back at once." At which all the ladies cried out that Thasper might be in great danger in his own home. The tall man said, "I shall take care of that, of course." Then he stretched out a hand and pulled Thasper up. "Come along, Thasper."

As soon as Thasper was out of it, the two halves of the sphere vanished. One of the ladies took his other hand and he was led away, first on a jiggly ride, which he much enjoyed, and then into a huge house, where there was a very perplexing room. In this room, Thasper sat in a five-pointed star and pictures kept appearing around him. People kept shaking their heads. "No, not that world either." The tall man answered all Thasper's questions, and Thasper was too interested even to be annoyed when they would not allow him anything to eat.

"Why not?" he said.

"Because, just by being here, you are causing the world to jolt about," the tall man explained. "If you put food inside you, food is a heavy part of this world, and it might jolt you to pieces."

Soon after that, a new picture appeared. Everyone said "Ah!" and the tall man said "So it's Theare!" He looked at Thasper in a surprised way. "You must have struck someone as disorderly," he said. Then he looked at the picture again, in a lazy, careful kind of way. "No disorder," he said. "No danger. Come with me."

He took Thasper's hand again and led him into the picture. As he did so, Thasper's hair turned much darker. "A simple precaution," the tall man murmured, a little apologetically, but Thasper did not even notice. He was not aware what color his hair had been to start with, and besides, he was taken up with surprise at how fast they were going. They whizzed into a city, and stopped abruptly. It was a good house, just on the edge of a poorer district. "Here is someone who will do," the tall man said, and he knocked at the door.

A sad-looking lady opened the door.

"I beg your pardon, madam," said the tall man. "Have you by any chance lost a small boy?"

"Yes," said the lady. "But this isn't—" She blinked. "Yes it *is*!" she cried out. "Oh Thasper! How could you run off like that? Thank you so much, sir." But the tall man had gone.

The lady's name was Alina Altun, and she was so convinced that she was Thasper's mother that Thasper was soon convinced too. He settled in happily with her and her husband, who was a doctor, hardworking but not very rich. Thasper soon forgot the tall man, Imperion, and Nestara. Sometimes it did puzzle him—and his new mother too— that when she showed him off to her friends she always felt bound to say, "This is Badien, but we always call him Thasper." Thanks to the tall man, none of them ever knew that the real Badien had wandered away the day Thasper came, and fell in the river, where an invisible dragon ate him.

If Thasper had remembered the tall man, he might also have wondered why his arrival seemed to start Dr. Altun on the road to prosperity. The people in the poorer district nearby suddenly discovered what a good doctor

Dr. Altun was, and how little he charged. Alina was shortly able to afford to send Thasper to a very good school, where Thasper often exasperated his teachers by his many questions. He had, as his new mother often proudly said, a most inquiring mind. Although he learned quicker than most the Ten First Lessons and the Nine Graces of Childhood, his teachers were nevertheless often annoyed enough to snap, "Oh, go and ask an invisible dragon!" which is what people in Theare often said when they thought they were being pestered.

Thasper did, with difficulty, gradually cure himself of his habit of never answering questions. But he always preferred asking to answering. At home, he asked questions all the time: "Why does the kitchen god go and report to Heaven once a year? Is it so I can steal biscuits? Why are dragons invisible? Is there a god for everything? Why is there a god for everything? If the gods make people ill, how can Dad cure them? Why must I have a baby brother or sister?"

Alina Altun was a good mother. She most diligently answered all these questions, including the last. She told Thasper how babies were made, ending her account with, "Then, if the gods bless my womb, a baby will come." She was a devout person.

"I don't want you to be blessed!" Thasper said, resorting to a statement, which he only did when he was strongly moved.

He seemed to have no choice in the matter. By the time

he was ten years old, the gods had thought fit to bless him with two brothers and two sisters. In Thasper's opinion, they were, as blessings, very low grade. They were just too young to be any use. "Why can't they be the same age as me?" he demanded, many times. He began to bear the gods a small but definite grudge about this.

Dr. Altun continued to prosper and his earnings more than kept pace with his family. Alina employed a nursemaid, a cook, and a number of rather impermanent houseboys. It was one of these houseboys who, when Thasper was eleven, shyly presented Thasper with a folded square of paper. Wondering, Thasper unfolded it. It gave him a curious feeling to touch, as if the paper was vibrating a little in his fingers. It also gave out a very strong warning that he was not to mention it to anybody. It said:

> *Dear Thasper,*
> *Your situation is an odd one. Make sure that you call me at the moment when you come face-to-face with yourself. I shall be watching and I will come at once.*
>
> *Yrs,*
> *Chrestomanci*

Since Thasper by now had not the slightest recollection of his early life, this letter puzzled him extremely. He knew he was not supposed to tell anyone about it, but he also knew that this did not include the houseboy. With the letter in his hand, he hurried after the houseboy to the kitchen.

He was stopped at the head of the kitchen stairs by a tremendous smashing of china from below. This was followed immediately by the cook's voice raised in nonstop abuse. Thasper knew it was no good trying to go into the kitchen. The houseboy—who went by the odd name of Cat—was in the process of getting fired, like all the other houseboys before him. He had better go and wait for Cat outside the back door. Thasper looked at the letter in his hand. As he did so, his fingers tingled. The letter vanished.

"It's gone!" he exclaimed, showing by this statement how astonished he was. He never could account for what he did next. Instead of going to wait for the houseboy, he ran to the living room, intending to tell his mother about it, in spite of the warning. "Do you know what?" he began. He had invented this meaningless question so that he could tell people things and still make it into an enquiry. "Do you know what?" Alina looked up. Thasper, though he fully intended to tell her about the mysterious letter, found himself saying, "The cook's just sacked the new houseboy."

"Oh bother!" said Alina. "I shall have to find another one now."

Annoyed with himself, Thasper tried to tell her again. "Do you know what? I'm surprised the cook doesn't sack the kitchen god too."

"Hush, dear. Don't talk about the gods that way!" said the devout lady.

By this time, the houseboy had left and Thasper lost the urge to tell anyone about the letter. It remained with him as his own personal exciting secret. He thought of it as The Letter From a Person Unknown. He sometimes whispered the strange name of The Person Unknown to himself when no one could hear. But nothing ever happened, even when he said the name out loud. He gave up doing that after a while. He had other things to think about. He became fascinated by Rules, Laws, and Systems.

Rules and Systems were an important part of the life of mankind in Theare. It stood to reason, with Heaven so well organized. People codified all behavior into things like the Seven Subtle Politenesses, or the Hundred Roads to Godliness. Thasper had been taught these things from the time he was three years old. He was accustomed to hearing Alina argue the niceties of the Seventy-Two Household Laws with her friends. Now Thasper suddenly discovered for himself that all Rules made a magnificent framework for one's mind to clamber about in. He made lists of rules, and refinements on rules, and possible ways of doing the opposite of what the rules said while still keeping the rules. He invented new codes of rules. He filled books and made charts. He invented games with huge and complicated rules, and played them with his friends. Onlookers found these games both rough and muddled, but Thasper and his friends revelled in them. The best moment in any game was when somebody stopped playing and shouted, "I've thought of a new rule!"

This obsession with rules lasted until Thasper was fifteen. He was walking home from school one day, thinking over a list of rules for Twenty Fashionable Hairstyles. From this, it will be seen that Thasper was noticing girls, though none of the girls had so far seemed to notice him. And he was thinking which girl should wear which hairstyle, when his attention was caught by words chalked on the wall:

> IF RULES MAKE A FRAMEWORK FOR THE MIND TO CLIMB ABOUT IN, WHY SHOULD THE MIND NOT CLIMB RIGHT OUT, SAYS THE SAGE OF DISSOLUTION.

That same day, there was consternation again in Heaven. Zond summoned all the high gods to his throne. "The Sage of Dissolution has started to preach," he announced direfully. "Imperion, I thought you got rid of him."

"I thought I did," Imperion said. He was even more appalled than Zond. If the Sage had started to preach, it meant that Imperion had got rid of Thasper and deprived himself of Nestara quite unnecessarily. "I must have been mistaken," he admitted.

Here Ock spoke up, steaming gently. "Father Zond," he said, "may I respectfully suggest that you deal with the Sage yourself, so that there will be no mistake this time?"

"That was just what I was about to suggest," Zond said gratefully. "Are you all agreed?"

All the gods agreed. They were too used to order to do otherwise.

As for Thasper, he was staring at the chalked words, shivering to the soles of his sandals. What was this? Who was using his own private thoughts about rules? Who was this Sage of Dissolution? Thasper was ashamed. He, who was so good at asking questions, had never thought of asking this one. Why should one's mind not climb right out of the rules, after all?

He went home and asked his parents about the Sage of Dissolution. He fully expected them to know. He was quite agitated when they did not. But they had a neighbor, who sent Thasper to another neighbor, who had a friend, who, when Thasper finally found his house, said he had heard that the Sage was a clever young man who made a living by mocking the gods.

The next day, someone had washed the words off. But the day after that, a badly printed poster appeared on the same wall. **THE SAGE OF DISSOLUTION ASKS BY WHOSE ORDER IS ORDER ANYWAY?? COME TO SMALL UNCTION SUBLIME CONCERT HALL TONITE 6:30.**

At 6:20, Thasper was having supper. At 6:24, he made up his mind and left the table. At 6:32, he arrived panting at Small Unction Hall. It proved to be a small shabby building quite near where he lived. Nobody was there. As far as Thasper could gather from the grumpy caretaker, the meeting had been the night before. Thasper turned away, deeply disappointed. Who ordered the order was a question he now longed to know the answer to. It was deep. He had a notion that the man who called himself the Sage of Dissolution was truly brilliant.

By way of feeding his own disappointment, he went to school the next day by a route which took him past the Small Unction Concert Hall. It had burnt down in the night. There were only blackened brick walls left. When he got to school, a number of people were talking about it. They said it had burst into flames just before 7:00 the night before.

"Did you know," Thasper said, "that the Sage of Dissolution was there the day before yesterday?"

That was how he discovered he was not the only one interested in the Sage. Half his class were admirers of Dissolution. That, too, was when the girls deigned to notice him. "He's amazing about the gods," one girl told him. "No one ever asked questions like that before." Most of the class, however, girls and boys alike, only knew a little more than Thasper, and most of what they knew was secondhand. But a boy showed him a carefully cut out newspaper article in which a well-known scholar discussed what he called the so-called Doctrine of Dissolution. It said, longwindedly, that the Sage and his followers were rude to the gods and against all the rules. It did not tell Thasper much, but it was something. He saw, rather ruefully, that his obsession with rules had been quite wrong-headed and had, into the bargain, caused him to fall behind the rest of his class in learning of this wonderful new doctrine. He became a

Disciple of Dissolution on the spot. He joined the rest of his class in finding out all they could about the Sage. He went round with them, writing up on walls **DISSOLUTION RULES OK**.

For a long while after that, the only thing any of Thasper's class could learn of the Sage were scraps of questions chalked on walls and quickly rubbed out. **WHAT NEED OF PRAYER? WHY SHOULD THERE BE A HUNDRED ROADS TO GODLINESS, NOT MORE OR LESS? DO WE CLIMB ANYWHERE ON THE STEPS TO HEAVEN? WHAT IS PERFECTION: A PROCESS OR A STATE? WHEN WE CLIMB TO PERFECTION IS THIS A MATTER FOR THE GODS?**

Thasper obsessively wrote all these sayings down. He was obsessed again, he admitted, but this time it was in a new way. He was thinking, thinking. At first, he thought simply of clever questions to ask the Sage. He strained to find questions no one had asked before. But in the process, his mind seemed to loosen, and shortly he was thinking of how the Sage might answer his questions. He considered order and rules and Heaven, and it came to him that there was a reason behind all the brilliant questions the Sage asked. He felt light-headed with thinking.

The reason behind the Sage's questions came to him the morning he was shaving for the first time. He thought, *The gods need human beings in order to be gods!* Blinded with this revelation, Thasper stared into the mirror at his own face half covered with white foam. Without humans believing in them, gods were nothing! The order of Heaven, the rules and codes of earth, were all only there because of people! It was transcendent. As Thasper stared, the letter from the Unknown came into his mind. "Is this being face-to-face with myself?" he said. But he was not sure. And he became sure that when the time came, he would not have to wonder.

Then it came to him that the Unknown Chrestomanci was almost certainly the Sage himself. He was thrilled. The Sage was taking a special mysterious interest in one teenage boy, Thasper Altun. The vanishing letter exactly fitted the elusive Sage.

The Sage continued elusive. The next firm news of him was a newspaper report of the Celestial Gallery being struck by lightning. The roof of the building collapsed, said the report, "only seconds after the young man known as the Sage of Dissolution had delivered another of his anguished and self-doubting homilies and left the building with his disciples."

"He's not self-doubting," Thasper said to himself. "He knows about the gods. If *I* know, then *he* certainly does."

He and his classmates went on a pilgrimage to the ruined gallery. It was a better building than Small Unction Hall. It seemed the Sage was going up in the world.

Then there was enormous excitement. One of the girls found a small advertisement in a paper. The Sage was to deliver another lecture, in the huge Kingdom of Splendor

Hall. He had gone up in the world again. Thasper and his friends dressed in their best and went there in a body. But it seemed as if the time for the lecture had been printed wrong. The lecture was just over. People were streaming away from the hall, looking disappointed.

Thasper and his friends were still in the street when the hall blew up. They were lucky not to be hurt. The police said it was a bomb. Thasper and his friends helped drag injured people clear of the blazing hall. It was exciting, but it was not the Sage.

By now, Thasper knew he would never be happy until he had found the Sage. He told himself that he had to know if the reason behind the Sage's questions was the one he thought, but it was more than that. Thasper was convinced that his fate was linked to the Sage's. He was certain the Sage *wanted* Thasper to find him.

But there was now a strong rumor in school and around town that the Sage had had enough of lectures and bomb attacks. He had retired to write a book. It was to be called *Questions of Dissolution*. Rumor also had it that the Sage was in lodgings somewhere near the Road of the Four Lions.

Thasper went to the Road of the Four Lions. There he was shameless. He knocked on doors and questioned passersby. He was told several times to go and ask an invisible dragon, but he took no notice. He went on asking until someone told him that Mrs. Tunap at 403 might know. Thasper knocked at 403, with his heart thumping.

Mrs. Tunap was a rather prim lady in a green turban. "I'm afraid not, dear," she said. "I'm new here." But before Thasper's heart could sink too far, she added, "But the people before me had a lodger. A very quiet gentleman. He left just before I came."

"Did he leave an address?" Thasper asked, holding his breath.

Mrs. Tunap consulted an old envelope pinned to the wall in her hall. "It says here, 'Lodger gone to Golden Heart Square,' dear."

But in Golden Heart Square, a young gentleman who might have been the Sage had only looked at a room and gone. After that, Thasper had to go home. The Altuns were not used to teenagers and they worried about Thasper suddenly wanting to be out every evening.

Oddly enough, No. 403 Road of the Four Lions burnt down that night.

Thasper saw clearly that assassins were after the Sage as well as he was. He became more obsessed with finding him than ever. He knew he could rescue the Sage if he caught him before the assassins did. He did not blame the Sage for moving about all the time.

Move about the Sage certainly did. Rumor had him next in Partridge Pleasaunce Street. When Thasper tracked him there, he found the Sage had moved to Fauntel Square. From Fauntel Square, the Sage seemed to move to Strong Wind Boulevard, and then to a poorer house in Station

Street. There were many places after that. By this time, Thasper had developed a nose, a sixth sense, for where the Sage might be. A word, a mere hint about a quiet lodger, and Thasper was off, knocking on doors, questioning people, being told to ask an invisible dragon, and bewildering his parents by the way he kept rushing off every evening. But, no matter how quickly Thasper acted on the latest hint, the Sage had always just left. And Thasper, in most cases, was only just ahead of the assassins. Houses caught fire or blew up sometimes when he was still in the same street.

At last he was down to a very poor hint, which might or might not lead to New Unicorn Street. Thasper went there, wishing he did not have to spend all day at school. The Sage could move about as he pleased, and Thasper was tied down all day. No wonder he kept missing him. But he had high hopes of New Unicorn Street. It was the poor kind of place that the Sage had been favoring lately.

Alas for his hopes. The fat woman who opened the door laughed rudely in Thasper's face. "Don't bother me, son! Go and ask an invisible dragon!" And she slammed the door.

Thasper stood in the street, keenly humiliated. And not even a hint of where to look next. Awful suspicions rose in his mind: he was making a fool of himself; he had set himself a wild goose chase; the Sage did not exist. In order not to think of these things, he gave way to anger. "All right!" he shouted at the shut door. "I *will* ask an invisible dragon! So there!" And, carried by his anger, he ran down to the river and out across the nearest bridge.

He stopped in the middle of the bridge, leaning on the parapet, and knew he was making an utter fool of himself. There were no such things as invisible dragons. He was sure of that. But he was still in the grip of his obsession, and this was something he had set himself to do now. Even so, if there had been anyone about near the bridge, Thasper would have gone away. But it was deserted. Feeling an utter fool, he made the prayer-sign to Ock, Ruler of Oceans—for Ock was the god in charge of all things to do with water—but he made the sign secretly, down under the parapet, so there was no chance of anyone seeing. Then he said, almost in a whisper, "Is there an invisible dragon here? I've got something to ask you."

Drops of water whirled over him. Something wetly fanned his face. He heard the something whirring. He turned his face that way and saw three blots of wet in a line along the parapet, each about two feet apart and each the size of two of his hands spread out together. Odder still, water was dripping out of nowhere all along the parapet, for a distance about twice as long as Thasper was tall.

Thasper laughed uneasily. "I'm imagining a dragon," he said. "If there was a dragon, those splotches would be the places where its body rests. Water dragons have no feet. And the length of the wetness suggests I must be imagining it about eleven feet long."

"I am fourteen feet long," said a voice out of nowhere.

It was rather too near Thasper's face for comfort and blew fog at him. He drew back. "Make haste, child-of-a-god," said the voice. "What did you want to ask me?"

"I—I—I—" stammered Thasper. It was not just that he was scared. This was a body blow. It messed up utterly his notions about gods needing men to believe in them. But he pulled himself together. His voice only cracked a little as he said, "I'm looking for the Sage of Dissolution. Do you know where he is?"

The dragon laughed. It was a peculiar noise, like one of those water-warblers people make bird noises with. "I'm afraid I can't tell you precisely where the Sage is," the voice out of nowhere said. "You have to find him for yourself. Think about it, child-of-a-god. You must have noticed there's a pattern."

"Too right, there's a pattern!" Thasper said. "Everywhere he goes, I just miss him, and then the place catches fire!"

"That too," said the dragon. "But there's a pattern to his lodgings too. Look for it. That's all I can tell you, child-of-a-god. Any other questions?"

"No—for a wonder," Thasper said. "Thanks very much."

"You're welcome," said the invisible dragon. "People are always telling one another to ask us, and hardly anyone does. I'll see you again." Watery air whirled in Thasper's face. He leaned over the parapet and saw one prolonged clean splash in the river, and silver bubbles coming up. Then nothing. He was surprised to find his legs were shaking.

He steadied his knees and tramped home. He went to his room and, before he did anything else, he acted on a superstitious impulse he had not thought he had in him, and took down the household god Alina insisted he keep in a niche over his bed. He put it carefully outside in the passage. Then he got out a map of the town and some red stickers and plotted out all the places where he had just missed the Sage. The result had him dancing with excitement. The dragon was right. There was a pattern. The Sage had started in good lodgings at the better end of town. Then he had gradually moved to poorer places, but he had moved in a curve, down to the station and back towards the better part again. Now, the Altuns' house was just on the edge of the poorer part. The Sage was *coming this way*! New Unicorn Street had not been so far away. The next place should be nearer still. Thasper had only to look for a house on fire.

It was getting dark by then. Thasper threw his curtains back and leaned out of his window to look at the poorer streets. And there it was! There was a red-and-orange flicker to the left—in Harvest Moon Street, by the look of it. Thasper laughed aloud. He was actually grateful to the assassins!

He raced downstairs and out of the house. The anxious questions of parents and the yells of brothers and sisters followed him, but he slammed the door on them. Two minutes' running brought him to the scene of the fire. The street was a mad flicker of dark figures. People were piling furniture in the road. Some more people were helping a dazed woman in a crooked brown turban into a singed armchair.

"Didn't you have a lodger as well?" someone asked her anxiously.

The woman kept trying to straighten her turban. It was all she could really think of. "He didn't stay," she said. "I think he may be down at the Half Moon now."

Thasper waited for no more. He went pelting down the street. The Half Moon was an inn on the corner of the same road. Most of the people who usually drank there must have been up the street, helping rescue furniture, but there was a dim light inside, enough to show a white notice in the window. ROOMS, it said.

Thasper burst inside. The barman was on a stool by the window craning to watch the house burn. He did not look at Thasper. "Where's your lodger?" gasped Thasper. "I've got a message. Urgent."

The barman did not turn round. "Upstairs, first on the left," he said. "The roof's caught. They'll have to act quick to save the house on either side."

Thasper heard him say this as he bounded upstairs. He turned left. He gave the briefest of knocks on the door there, flung it open, and rushed in.

The room was empty. The light was on, and it showed a stark bed, a stained table with an empty mug and some sheets of paper on it, and a fireplace with a mirror over it. Beside the fireplace, another door was just swinging shut. Obviously somebody had just that moment gone through it. Thasper bounded towards that door. But he was checked, for just a second, by seeing himself in the mirror over the fireplace. He had not meant to pause. But some trick of the mirror, which was old and brown and speckled, made his reflection look for a moment a great deal older. He looked easily over twenty. He looked—

He remembered the Letter from the Unknown. This was the time. He knew it was. He was about to meet the Sage. He had only to call him. Thasper went towards the still gently swinging door. He hesitated. The Letter had said call at once. Knowing the Sage was just beyond the door, Thasper pushed it open a fraction and held it so with his fingers. He was full of doubts. He thought, *Do I really believe the gods need people? Am I so sure? What shall I say to the Sage after all?* He let the door slip shut again.

"Chrestomanci," he said, miserably.

There was a *whoosh* of displaced air behind him. It buffeted Thasper half around. He stared. A tall man was standing by the stark bed. He was a most extraordinary figure in a long black robe, with what seemed to be yellow comets embroidered on it. The inside of the robe, swirling in the air, showed yellow, with black comets on it. The tall man had a very smooth dark head, very bright dark eyes and, on his feet, what seemed to be red bedroom slippers.

"Thank goodness," said this outlandish person. "For a moment, I was afraid you would go through that door."

The voice brought memory back to Thasper. "You

brought me home through a picture when I was little," he said. "Are you Chrestomanci?"

"Yes," said the tall outlandish man. "And you are Thasper. And now we must both leave before this building catches fire."

He took hold of Thasper's arm and towed him to the door which led to the stairs. As soon as he pushed the door open, thick smoke rolled in, filled with harsh crackling. It was clear that the inn was on fire already. Chrestomanci clapped the door shut again. The smoke set both of them coughing, Chrestomanci so violently that Thasper was afraid he would choke. He pulled both of them back into the middle by the room. By now, smoke was twining up between the bare boards of the floor, causing Chrestomanci to cough again.

"This would happen just as I had gone to bed with flu!" he said, when he could speak. "Such is life. These orderly gods of yours leave us no choice." He crossed the smoking floor and pushed open the door by the fireplace.

It opened on to blank space. Thasper gave a yelp of horror.

"Precisely," coughed Chrestomanci. "You were intended to crash to your death."

"Can't we jump to the ground?" Thasper suggested. Chrestomanci shook his smooth head. "Not after they've done this to it. No. We'll have to carry the fight to them and go and visit the gods instead. Will you be kind enough to lend me your turban before we go?" Thasper stared at this odd request. "I would like to use it as a belt," Chrestomanci croaked. "The way to Heaven may be a little cold, and I only have pajamas under my dressing gown."

The striped undergarments Chrestomanci was wearing did look a little thin. Thasper slowly unwound his turban. To go before gods bareheaded was probably no worse than going in nightclothes, he supposed. Besides, he did not believe there were any gods. He handed the turban over. Chrestomanci tied the length of pale blue cloth around his black and yellow gown and seemed to feel more comfortable. "Now hang on to me," he said, "and you'll be all right." He took Thasper's arm again and walked up into the sky, dragging Thasper with him.

For a while, Thasper was too stunned to speak. He could only marvel at the way they were treading up the sky as if there were invisible stairs in it. Chrestomanci was doing it in the most matter of fact way, coughing from time to time, and shivering a little, but keeping very tight hold of Thasper nevertheless. In no time, the town was a clutter of prettily lit dolls' houses below, with two red blots where two of them were burning. The stars were unwinding about them, above and below, as they had already climbed above some of them.

"It's a long climb to Heaven," Chrestomanci observed. "Is there anything you'd like to know on the way?"

"Yes," said Thasper. "Did you say the gods were trying to kill me?"

"They are trying to eliminate the Sage of Dissolution,"

said Chrestomanci, "which they may not realize is the same thing. You see, you are the Sage."

"But I'm not!" Thasper insisted. "The Sage is a lot older than me, and he asks questions I never even thought of until I heard of him."

"Ah yes," said Chrestomanci. "I'm afraid there is an awful circularity to this. It's the fault of whoever tried to put you away as a small child. As far as I can work out, you stayed three years old for seven years—until you were making such a disturbance in our world that we had to find you and let you out. But in this world of Theare, highly organized and fixed as it is, the prophecy stated that you would begin preaching Dissolution at the age of twenty-three, or at least in this very year. Therefore the preaching had to begin this year. You did not need to appear. Did you ever speak to anyone who had actually heard the Sage preach?"

"No," said Thasper. "Come to think of it."

"Nobody did," said Chrestomanci. "You started in a small way anyway. First you wrote a book, which no one paid much heed to—"

"No, that's wrong," objected Thasper. "He-I-er, the Sage was writing a book *after* the preaching."

"But don't you see," said Chrestomanci, "because you were back in Theare by then, the facts had to try to catch you up. They did this by running backwards until it was possible for you to arrive where you were supposed to be. Which was in that room in the inn there at the start of your career. I suppose you are just old enough to start by now. And I suspect our celestial friends up here tumbled to this belatedly and tried to finish you off. It wouldn't have done them any good, as I shall shortly tell them." He began coughing again. They had climbed to where it was bitterly cold.

By this time, the world was a dark arch below them. Thasper could see the blush of the sun, beginning to show underneath the world. They climbed on. The light grew. The sun appeared, a huge brightness in the distance underneath. A dim memory came again to Thasper. He struggled to believe that none of this was true, and he did not succeed.

"How do you know all this?" he asked bluntly.

"Have you heard of a god called Ock?" Chrestomanci coughed. "He came to talk to me when you should have been the age you are now. He was worried—" He coughed again. "I shall have to save the rest of my breath for Heaven."

They climbed on, and the stars swam around them, until the stuff they were climbing changed and became solider. Soon they were climbing a dark ramp, which flushed pearly as they went upwards. Here, Chrestomanci let go of Thasper's arm and blew his nose on a gold-edged handkerchief, with an air of relief. The pearl of the ramp grew to silver and the silver to dazzling white. At length, they were walking on level whiteness, through hall after hall after hall.

The gods were gathered to meet them. None of them looked cordial.

"I fear we are not properly dressed," Chrestomanci murmured.

Thasper looked at the gods, and then at Chrestomanci, and squirmed with embarrassment. Fanciful and queer as Chrestomanci's garb was, it was still most obviously nightwear. The things on his feet were fur bedroom slippers. And there, looking like a piece of blue string around Chrestomanci's waist, was the turban Thasper should have been wearing. The gods were magnificent, in golden trousers and jeweled turbans, and got more so as they approached the greater gods. Thasper's eye was caught by a god in shining cloth of gold, who surprised him by beaming a friendly, almost anxious look at him. Opposite him was a huge liquid-looking figure draped in pearls and diamonds. This god swiftly, but quite definitely, winked. Thasper was too awed to react, but Chrestomanci calmly winked back.

At the end of the halls, upon a massive throne, towered the mighty figure of Great Zond, clothed in white and purple, with a crown on his head. Chrestomanci looked up at Zond and thoughtfully blew his nose. It was hardly respectful.

"For what reason do two mortals trespass in our halls?" Zond thundered coldly.

Chrestomanci sneezed. "Because of your own folly," he said. "You gods of Theare have had everything so well worked out for so long that you can't see beyond your own routine."

"I shall blast you for that," Zond announced.

"Not if any of you wish to survive," Chrestomanci said.

There was a long murmur of protest from the other gods. They wished to survive. They were trying to work out what Chrestomanci meant. Zond saw it as a threat to his authority and thought he had better be cautious. "Proceed," he said.

"One of your most efficient features," Chrestomanci said, "is that your prophecies always come true. So why, when a prophecy is unpleasant to you, do you think you can alter it? That, my good gods, is rank folly. Besides, no one can halt his own Dissolution, least of all you gods of Theare. But you forgot. You forgot you had deprived both yourselves and mankind of any kind of free will, by organizing yourselves so precisely. You pushed Thasper, the Sage of Dissolution, into my world, forgetting that there is still chance in my world. By chance, Thasper was discovered after only seven years. Lucky for Theare that he was. I shudder to think what might have happened if Thasper had remained three years old for all his allotted lifetime."

"That was my fault!" cried Imperion. "I take the blame." He turned to Thasper. "Forgive me," he said. "You are my own son."

Was this, Thasper wondered, what Alina meant by the gods blessing her womb? He had not thought it was more than a figure of speech. He looked at Imperion, blinking a little in the god's dazzle. He was not wholly impressed. A fine god, and an honest one, but Thasper could see he had a limited outlook. "Of course I forgive you," he said politely.

"It is also lucky," Chrestomanci said, "that none of you succeeded in killing the Sage. Thasper is a god's son. That means there can only ever be one of him, and because of your prophecy he has to be alive to preach Dissolution. You could have destroyed Theare. As it is, you have caused it to blur into a mass of cracks. Theare is too well organized to divide into two alternative worlds, like my world would. Instead, events have had to happen which could not have happened. Theare has cracked and warped, and you have all but brought about your own Dissolution."

"What can we do?" Zond said, aghast.

"There's only one thing you can do," Chrestomanci told him. "Let Thasper be. Let him preach Dissolution and stop trying to blow him up. That will bring about free will and a free future. Then either Theare will heal, or it will split, cleanly and painlessly, into two healthy new worlds."

"So we bring about our own downfall?" Zond asked mournfully.

"It was always inevitable," said Chrestomanci.

Zond sighed. "Very well. Thasper, son of Imperion, I reluctantly give you my blessing to go forth and preach Dissolution. Go in peace."

Thasper bowed. Then he stood there silent a long time. He did not notice Imperion and Ock both trying to attract his attention. The newspaper report had talked of the Sage as full of anguish and self-doubt. Now he knew why. He looked at Chrestomanci, who was blowing his nose again. "How can I preach Dissolution?" he said. "How can I not believe in the gods when I have seen them for myself?"

"That's a question you certainly should be asking," Chrestomanci croaked. "Go down to Theare and ask it." Thasper nodded and turned to go. Chrestomanci leaned towards him and said, from behind his handkerchief, "Ask yourself this too: Can the gods catch flu? I think I may have given it to all of them. Find out and let me know, there's a good chap."

SAKI was the pen name of an English writer and journalist named H. H. Munro. He was killed by a sniper's bullet during World War I. Some of his stories are funny. Some are chilling. Some are both.

There's a wild beast in the woods. Or there is a boy. Or perhaps . . .

GABRIEL-ERNEST

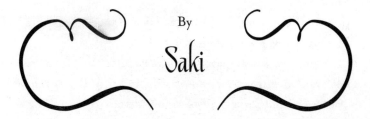

By
Saki

"THERE IS A WILD BEAST IN YOUR WOODS," said the artist Cunningham as he was being driven to the station. It was the only remark he had made during the drive, but as Van Cheele had talked incessantly his companion's silence had not been noticeable.

"A stray fox or two and some resident weasels. Nothing more formidable," said Van Cheele. The artist said nothing.

"What did you mean about a wild beast?" said Van Cheele later, when they were on the platform.

"Nothing. My imagination. Here is the train," said Cunningham. That afternoon Van Cheele went for one of his frequent rambles through his woodland property. He had a stuffed bittern in his study, and knew the names of quite a number of wild flowers, so his aunt had possibly some justification in describing him as a great naturalist. At any rate, he was a great walker. It was his custom to take mental notes of everything he saw during his walks, not so much for the purpose of assisting contemporary science as to provide topics for conversation afterwards. When the bluebells began to show themselves in flower he made a point of informing everyone of the fact; the season of the year might have warned his hearers of the likelihood of such an occurrence, but at least they felt that he was being absolutely frank with them.

What Van Cheele saw on this particular afternoon was, however, something far removed from his ordinary range of experience. On a shelf of smooth stone overhanging a deep pool in the hollow of an oak coppice a boy of about sixteen lay asprawl, drying his wet brown limbs luxuriously in the sun. His wet hair, parted by a recent dive, lay close to his head, and his light-brown eyes, so light that there was an almost tigerish gleam in them, were turned towards Van Cheele with a certain lazy watchfulness. It was an unexpected apparition, and Van Cheele found himself engaged in the novel process of thinking before he spoke. Where on earth could this wild-looking boy hail from? The miller's wife had lost a child some two months ago, supposed to have been swept away by the millrace, but that had been a mere baby, not a half-grown lad.

"What are you doing there?" he demanded.

"Obviously, sunning myself," replied the boy.

"Where do you live?"

"Here, in these woods."

"You can't live in the woods," said Van Cheele.

"They are very nice woods," said the boy, with a touch of patronage in his voice.

"But where do you sleep at night?"

"I don't sleep at night; that's my busiest time."

Van Cheele began to have an irritated feeling that he was grappling with a problem that was eluding him.

"What do you feed on?" he asked.

"Flesh," said the boy, and he pronounced the word with slow relish, as though he were tasting it.

"Flesh! What flesh?"

"Since it interests you, rabbits, wildfowl, hares, poultry, lambs in their season, children when I can get any; they're usually too well locked in at night, when I do most of my hunting. It's quite two months since I tasted child-flesh."

Ignoring the chaffing nature of the last remark Van Cheele tried to draw the boy on the subject of possible poaching operations.

"You're talking rather through your hat when you speak of feeding on hares." (Considering the nature of the boy's toilet the simile was hardly an apt one.) "Our hillside hares aren't easily caught."

"At night I hunt on four feet," was the somewhat cryptic response.

"I suppose you mean that you hunt with a dog?" hazarded Van Cheele.

The boy rolled slowly over onto his back, and laughed a weird low laugh, that was pleasantly like a chuckle and disagreeably like a snarl.

"I don't fancy any dog would be very anxious for my company, especially at night."

Van Cheele began to feel that there was something positively uncanny about the strange-eyed, strange-tongued youngster.

"I can't have you staying in these woods," he declared authoritatively.

"I fancy you'd rather have me here than in your house," said the boy.

The prospect of this wild, nude animal in Van Cheele's primly ordered house was certainly an alarming one.

"If you don't go I shall have to make you," said Van Cheele.

The boy turned like a flash, plunged into the pool, and in a moment had flung his wet and glistening body halfway up the bank where Van Cheele was standing. In an otter the movement would not have been remarkable; in a boy Van Cheele found it sufficiently startling. His foot slipped as he made an involuntary backward movement, and he found himself almost prostrate on the slippery weed-grown bank, with those tigerish yellow eyes not very far from his own. Almost instinctively he half raised his hand to his throat. The boy laughed again, a laugh in which the snarl had nearly driven out the chuckle, and then, with another of his astonishing lightning movements, plunged out of view into a yielding tangle of weed and fern.

"What an extraordinary wild animal!" said Van Cheele as he picked himself up. And then he recalled Cunningham's remark, "There is a wild beast in your woods."

Walking slowly homeward, Van Cheele began to turn over in his mind various local occurrences which might be traceable to the existence of this astonishing young savage.

Something had been thinning the game in the woods

lately, poultry had been missing from the farms, hares were growing unaccountably scarcer, and complaints had reached him of lambs being carried off bodily from the hills. Was it possible that this wild boy was really hunting the countryside in company with some clever poacher dog? He had spoken of hunting "four-footed" by night, but then, again, he had hinted strangely at no dog caring to come near him, "especially at night." It was certainly puzzling. And then, as Van Cheele ran his mind over the various depredations that had been committed during the last month or two, he came suddenly to a dead stop, alike in his walk and his speculations. The child missing from the mill two months ago—the accepted theory was that it had tumbled into the millrace and been swept away; but the mother had always declared she had heard a shriek on the hill side of the house, in the opposite direction from the water. It was unthinkable, of course, but he wished that the boy had not made that uncanny remark about child-flesh eaten two months ago. Such dreadful things should not be said even in fun.

Van Cheele, contrary to his usual wont, did not feel disposed to be communicative about his discovery in the wood. His position as a parish councillor and justice of the peace seemed somehow compromised by the fact that he was harboring a personality of such doubtful repute on his property; there was even a possibility that a heavy bill of damages for raided lambs and poultry might be laid at his door. At dinner that night he was unusually silent.

"Where's your voice gone to?" said his aunt. "One would think you had seen a wolf."

Van Cheele, who was not familiar with the old saying, thought the remark rather foolish; if he *had* seen a wolf on his property his tongue would have been extraordinarily busy with the subject.

At breakfast the next morning Van Cheele was conscious that his feeling of uneasiness regarding yesterday's episode had not wholly disappeared, and he resolved to go by train to the neighboring cathedral town, hunt up Cunningham, and learn from him what he had really seen that had prompted the remark about a wild beast in the woods. With this resolution taken, his usual cheerfulness partially returned, and he hummed a bright little melody as he sauntered to the morning room for his customary cigarette. As he entered the room the melody made way abruptly for a pious invocation. Gracefully asprawl on the ottoman, in an attitude of almost exaggerated repose, was the boy of the woods. He was drier than when Van Cheele had last seen him, but no other alteration was noticeable in his toilet.

"How dare you come here?" asked Van Cheele furiously.

"You told me I was not to stay in the woods," said the boy calmly.

"But not to come here. Supposing my aunt should see you!"

And with a view to minimizing that catastrophe Van

Cheele hastily obscured as much of his unwelcome guest as possible under the folds of a *Morning Post*. At that moment his aunt entered the room.

"This is a poor boy who has lost his way—and lost his memory. He doesn't know who he is or where he comes from," explained Van Cheele desperately, glancing apprehensively at the waif's face to see whether he was going to add inconvenient candor to his other savage propensities.

Miss Van Cheele was enormously interested.

"Perhaps his underlinen is marked," she suggested.

"He seems to have lost most of that, too," said Van Cheele, making frantic little grabs at the *Morning Post* to keep it in its place.

A naked homeless child appealed to Miss Van Cheele as warmly as a stray kitten or derelict puppy would have done.

"We must do all we can for him," she decided, and in a very short time a messenger, dispatched to the rectory, where a page boy was kept, had returned with a suit of pantry clothes, and the necessary accessories of shirt, shoes, collar, etc. Clothed, clean, and groomed, the boy lost none of his uncanniness in Van Cheele's eyes, but his aunt found him sweet.

"We must call him something till we know who he really is," she said. "Gabriel-Ernest, I think; those are nice suitable names."

Van Cheele agreed, but he privately doubted whether they were being grafted onto a nice suitable child. His misgivings were not diminished by the fact that his staid and elderly spaniel had bolted out of the house at the first incoming of the boy, and now obstinately remained shivering and yapping at the farther end of the orchard, while the canary, usually as vocally industrious as Van Cheele himself, had put itself on an allowance of frightened cheeps. More than ever he was resolved to consult Cunningham without loss of time.

As he drove off to the station, his aunt was arranging that Gabriel-Ernest should help her to entertain the infant members of her Sunday-school class at tea that afternoon.

Cunningham was not at first disposed to be communicative.

"My mother died of some brain trouble," he explained, "so you will understand why I am averse to dwelling on anything of an impossibly fantastic nature that I may see or think that I have seen."

"But what *did* you see?" persisted Van Cheele.

"What I thought I saw was something so extraordinary that no really sane man could dignify it with the credit of having actually happened. I was standing, the last evening I was with out, half hidden in the hedge growth by the orchard gate, watching the dying glow of the sunset. Suddenly I became aware of a naked boy—a bather from some neighboring pool, I took him to be—who was standing out on the bare hillside also watching the sunset. His pose was so suggestive of some wild faun of Pagan myth that I instantly wanted to engage him as a model, and in another moment I think I should have hailed him. But just then the sun dipped out of view, and all the orange and pink slid out of the landscape, leaving it cold and grey. And at the same moment an astounding thing happened—the boy vanished too!"

"What! vanished away into nothing?" asked Van Cheele excitedly.

"No; that is the dreadful part of it," answered the artist. "On the open hillside where the boy had been standing a second ago, stood a large wolf, blackish in color, with gleaming fangs and cruel, yellow eyes. You may think—"

But Van Cheele did not stop for anything as futile as thought. Already he was tearing at top speed towards the station. He dismissed the idea of a telegram. "Gabriel-Ernest is a werewolf" was a hopelessly inadequate effort at conveying the situation, and his aunt would think it was a code message to which he had omitted to give her the key. His one hope was that he might reach home before sundown. The cab which he chartered at the other end of the railway journey bore him with what seemed exasperating slowness along the country roads which were pink and mauve with the flush of the sinking sun. His aunt was putting away some unfinished jams and cake when he arrived.

"Where is Gabriel-Ernest?" he almost screamed.

"He is taking the little Toop child home," said his aunt. "It was getting so late, I thought it wasn't safe to let it go back alone. What a lovely sunset, isn't it?"

But Van Cheele, although not oblivious of the glow in

the western sky, did not stay to discuss its beauties. At a speed for which he was scarcely geared he raced along the narrow lane that led to the home of the Toops. On one side ran the swift current of the millstream; on the other rose the stretch of bare hillside. A dwindling rim of red sun showed still on the skyline, and the next turning must bring him in view of the ill-assorted couple he was pursuing. Then the color went suddenly out of things, and a grey light settled itself with a quick shiver over the landscape. Van Cheele heard a shrill wail of fear, and stopped running.

Nothing was ever seen again of the Toop child or Gabriel-Ernest, but the latter's discarded garments were found lying in the road, so it was assumed that the child had fallen into the water, and that the boy had stripped and jumped in, in a vain endeavor to save it. Van Cheele and some workmen who were nearby at the time testified to having heard a child scream loudly just near the spot where the clothes were found. Mrs. Toop, who had eleven other children, was decently resigned to her bereavement, but Miss Van Cheele sincerely mourned her lost foundling. It was on her initiative that a memorial brass was put up in the parish church to "Gabriel-Ernest, an unknown boy, who bravely sacrificed his life for another."

Van Cheele gave way to his aunt in most things, but he flatly refused to subscribe to the Gabriel-Ernest memorial.

8

E. NESBIT wrote her stories for children more than a hundred years ago. They range from the realistic to the magical. This is one of her few short stories that feels like a romp. And the cocka-toucan is a marvelous villain.

Primped and prodded into a too-tight dress, Matilda is sent to visit her ancient great-aunt Willoughby, but something goes wrong along the way. . . .

THE
COCKATOUCAN;
OR,
GREAT–AUNT
WILLOUGHBY

By

E. Nesbit

MATILDA'S EARS WERE RED AND SHINY. So were her cheeks. Her hands were red, too. This was because Pridmore had washed her. It was not the usual washing, which makes you clean and comfortable, but the "thorough good wash," which makes you burn and smart till you wish you could be like the poor little savages who do not know anything and run about bare in the sun, and only go into the water when they are hot.

Matilda wished she could have been born in a savage tribe, instead of in Brixton.

"Little savages," she said, "don't have their ears washed thoroughly, and they don't have new dresses that are prickly in the insides round their arms and cut them round the neck, do they, Pridmore?"

But Pridmore only said, "Stuff and nonsense"; and then she said: "Don't wriggle so, child, for goodness' sake." Pridmore was Matilda's nursemaid, and Matilda sometimes found her trying.

Matilda was quite right in believing that savage children do not wear frocks that hurt. It is also true that savage children are not overwashed, overbrushed, overcombed, gloved, booted, and hatted, and taken in an omnibus to

Streatham to see their Great-Aunt Willoughby. This was intended to be Matilda's fate. Her mother had arranged it. Pridmore had prepared her for it. Matilda, knowing resistance to be vain, had submitted to it.

But Destiny had not been consulted. And Destiny had plans of its own for Matilda.

When the last button of Matilda's boots had been fastened (the buttonhook always had a nasty temper, especially when it was hurried—and that day it bit a little piece of Matilda's leg quite spitefully), the wretched child was taken downstairs and put on a chair in the hall, to wait while Pridmore popped her own things on.

"I shan't be a minute," said Pridmore. Matilda knew better. She settled herself to wait, and swung her legs miserably. She had been to her Great-Aunt Willoughby's before, and she knew exactly what to expect. She would be asked about her lessons, and how many marks she had, and whether she had been a good girl. I can't think why grown-up people don't see how impertinent these questions are. Suppose you were to answer:

"I'm the top of my class, auntie, thank you, and I am very good. And now let us have a little talk about you, aunt, dear. How much money have you got, and have you been scolding the servants again, or have you tried to be good and patient, as a properly brought up aunt should be, eh, dear?"

Try this method with one of your aunts next time she begins asking you questions, and write and tell me what she says.

Matilda knew exactly what Aunt Willoughby's questions would be, and she knew how, when they were answered, her aunt would give her a small biscuit with caraway seeds in it, and then tell her to go with Pridmore and have her hands and face washed. Again!

Then she would be sent to walk in the garden; the garden had a gritty path, and geraniums and calceolarias and lobelias in the beds. You might not pick anything. There would be minced veal for dinner, with three-cornered bits of toast round the dish; and a tapioca pudding. Then the long afternoon with a book, a bound volume of *The Potterer's Saturday Night*, nasty small print, and all the stories about children who died young because they were too good for this world.

Matilda wriggled wretchedly. If she had been a little less uncomfortable she would have cried—but her new frock was too tight and prickly to let her forget it for a moment, even in tears.

When Pridmore came down at last she said, "Fie for shame, what a sulky face."

And Matilda said, "I'm not."

"Oh, yes, you are," said Pridmore—"you know you are—you don't appreciate your blessings."

"I wish it was *your* Aunt Willoughby," said Matilda.

"Nasty spiteful little thing," said Pridmore, and she shook Matilda.

Then Matilda tried to slap Pridmore, and the two went down the steps not at all pleased with each other.

They walked down the dull road to the dull omnibus, and Matilda was crying a little.

Now, Pridmore was a very careful person, though cross; but even the most careful persons make mistakes sometimes, and she must have taken the wrong omnibus or this story could never have happened, and where should we all have been then? This shows you that even mistakes are sometimes valuable, so do not be hard on grown-up people if they are wrong sometimes. You know, after all, it hardly ever happens.

It was a very bright green and gold omnibus, and inside the cushions were green and very soft. Matilda and her nursemaid had it all to themselves, and Matilda began to feel more comfortable, especially as she had wriggled till she had burst one of her shoulder seams and got more room for herself inside her frock.

So she said, "I'm sorry if I was cross, Priddy, dear."

Pridmore said, "So you ought to be," but she never said *she* was sorry for being cross, but you must not expect grown-up people to say that.

It was certainly the wrong omnibus—because instead of jolting slowly along dusty streets, it went quickly and smoothly down a green lane, with flowers in the hedges and green trees overhead. Matilda was so delighted that she sat quite still, a very rare thing with her. Pridmore was reading a penny story, called "The Vengeance of the Lady Constantia," so she did not notice anything.

"I don't care. I shan't tell her," said Matilda. "She'd

stop the bus as likely as not."

At last the bus stopped of its own accord. Pridmore put her story in her pocket and began to get out.

"Well, I never," she said, and got out very quickly and ran round to where the horses were. There were four of them. They were white horses with green harness, and their tails were very long indeed.

"Hi, young man," said Pridmore, to the omnibus driver, "you've brought us to the wrong place. This isn't Streatham Common, this isn't."

The driver was the most beautiful omnibus driver you ever saw. And his clothes were like him in beauty. He had white silk stockings and a ruffled silk shirt of white—and his coat and breeches were green and gold, so was the three-cornered hat which he lifted very politely when Pridmore spoke to him.

"I fear," he said, kindly, "that you must have taken, by some unfortunate misunderstanding, the wrong omnibus!"

"When does the next one go back?"

"The omnibus does not go back. It runs from Brixton here once a month, but it doesn't go back."

"But how does it get to Brixton again—to start again, I mean?" asked Matilda.

"We start a new one every time," said the driver, raising his three-cornered hat once more.

"And what becomes of the old ones?" Matilda asked.

"Ah," said the driver, smiling, "that depends. One

never knows beforehand, and things change so suddenly nowadays. Good morning. Thank you so much for your patronage. No—no—on no account, madam." He waved away the eightpence which Pridmore was trying to offer him for the fare from Brixton, and drove quickly off.

Then they looked round them. No—this was certainly *not* Streatham Common. The wrong omnibus had brought them to a strange village—the neatest, sweetest, reddest, greenest, cleanest, prettiest village in the world. The houses were grouped round a village green, on which children in pretty loose frocks or smocks were playing happily. Not a tight armhole was to be seen, or even imagined, in that happy spot. Matilda swelled herself out and burst three hooks and a bit more of the shoulder seams.

The shops seemed a little queer, Matilda thought. The names somehow did not match the things that were to be sold. For instance, where it said "Elias Grimes, tinsmith," there were loaves and buns in the window; and the shop that had "Baker" over the door was full of perambulators; the grocer and the wheelwright seemed to have changed names, or shops, or something; and Miss Scrimpling, dressmaker and milliner, had her shop window full of pork and sausage meat.

"What a funny, nice place," said Matilda. "I *am* glad we took the wrong omnibus."

A little boy in a yellow smock had come up close to them.

"I beg your pardon," he said, very politely, "but all

strangers are brought before the King at once. Please follow me."

"Well, of all the impudence!" said Pridmore. "Strangers, indeed! And who may you be, I should like to know?"

"I," said the little boy, bowing very low, "am the Prime Minister. I know I do not look it, but appearances are deceitful. It's only for a short time; I shall probably be myself again by tomorrow."

Pridmore muttered something which the little boy did not hear. Matilda caught a few words—"smacked," "bed," "bread and water"—familiar words, all of them.

"If it's a game," said Matilda to the boy, "I should like to play."

He frowned. "I advise you to come at once," he said, so sternly, that even Pridmore was a little frightened. "His Majesty's palace is in this direction." He walked away, and Matilda made a sudden jump, dragged her hand out of Pridmore's, and ran after him. So Pridmore had to follow, still grumbling.

The palace stood in a great green park, dotted with white-flowered maybushes. It was not at all like an English palace—St. James's or Buckingham Palace, for instance—because it was very beautiful and very clean. When they got in, they saw that the palace was hung with green silk and the footmen had green and gold liveries, and all the courtiers' clothes were the same colors.

Matilda and Pridmore had to wait a few moments while the King changed his scepter and put on a clean crown, and then they were shown into the audience chamber. The King came to meet them.

"It *is* kind of you to have come so far," he said. "Of *course* you'll stay at the palace?" He looked anxiously at Matilda.

"Are you *quite* comfortable, my dear?" he asked, doubt-fully.

Matilda was very truthful, for a girl.

"No," she said, "my frock cuts me round the arms."

"Ah," said he, "and you brought no luggage. Some of the Princess's frocks—her old ones perhaps. Yes, yes; this person—your maid, no doubt."

A loud laugh rang suddenly through the hall. The King looked uneasily round as though he expected something to happen. But nothing seemed likely to occur.

"Yes," said Matilda; "Pridmore is . . . Oh, dear."

For before her eyes she saw an awful change taking place in Pridmore. In an instant all that was left of the original Pridmore were the boots and the hem of her skirt—the top part of her had changed into painted iron and glass, and, even as Matilda looked, the bit of skirt that was left got flat and hard and square, the two feet turned into four feet, and they were iron feet, and there was no more Pridmore.

"Oh, my poor child," said the King; "your maid has turned into an Automatic Machine."

It was too true. The maid had turned into a machine such as those which you see in railway stations—greedy, grasping things, which take your pennies and give you back next to nothing in chocolate, and no change.

But there was no chocolate to be seen through the glass of the machine that had once been Pridmore. Only little rolls of paper.

The King silently handed some pennies to Matilda.

She dropped one in to the machine and pulled out the little drawer. There was a scroll of paper. Matilda opened it and read:

"Don't be tiresome."

She tried again. This time it was:

"If you don't give over I'll tell your ma first thing when she comes home."

The next was:

"Go along with you, do—always worrying."

So then Matilda *knew*.

"Yes," said the King, sadly, "I fear there's no doubt about it. Your maid has turned into an Automatic Nagging Machine. Never mind, my dear. She'll be all right tomorrow."

"I like her best like this, thank you," said Matilda, quickly. "I needn't put in any more pennies, you see."

"Oh! We mustn't be unkind and neglectful," said the King, gently, and he dropped in a penny himself. *He* got:

"You tiresome boy, you. Leave me be this minute."

"I can't help it then," said the King, wearily. "You've no idea how suddenly things change here. It's because—but I'll tell you all about it at tea. Go with nurse now, my dear, and see if any of the Princess's frocks will fit you."

Then a nice, kind, cuddly nurse led Matilda away to the

Princess's apartments, and took off the stiff frock that hurt, and put on a green silk gown as soft as birds' breasts, and Matilda kissed her for sheer joy at being so comfortable.

"And now, dearie," said the nurse, "you'd like to see the Princess, wouldn't you? Take care you don't hurt yourself with her. She's rather sharp."

Matilda did not understand this then. Afterwards she did.

The nurse took her through many marble corridors and up and down many marble steps, and at last they came to a garden full of white roses, and in the middle of it, on a green satin-covered eiderdown pillow as big as a feather bed, sat the Princess in a white gown.

She got up when Matilda came towards her, and it was like seeing a yard and a half of white tape stand up on one end and bow—a yard and a half of broad white tape, of course; but what is considered broad for tape is very narrow indeed for Princesses.

"How are you?" said Matilda, who had been taught manners.

"Very thin indeed, thank you," said the Princess. And she was. Her face was so white and thin that it looked as though it were made of oyster shell. Her hands were thin and white, and her fingers reminded Matilda of fish bones. Her hair and eyes were black, and Matilda thought she might have been pretty if she had been fatter. When she shook hands with Matilda her bony hand hurt, quite hard.

The Princess seemed pleased to see her visitor, and

invited her to sit with Her Highness on the satin cushion.

"I have to be very careful, or I should break," said she. "That's why the cushion's so soft, and I can't play many games for fear of accidents. Do you know any sitting-down games?"

The only thing Matilda could think of was "cat's cradle." So they played that with the Princess's green hair ribbon. Her fish-bony fingers were much cleverer at it than Matilda's little fat pink paws.

Matilda looked about her between the games and admired everything very much, and asked questions, of course. There was a very large bird chained to a perch in the middle of a very large cage. Indeed, the cage was so big that it took up all one side of the rose garden. The bird had a yellow crest like a cockatoo, and a very large bill like a toucan (if you don't know what a toucan is you do not deserve ever to go to the Zoological Gardens again).

"What is that bird?" asked Matilda.

"Oh," said the Princess, "that's my pet Cockatoucan. He's very valuable. If he were to die or be stolen, the Green Land would wither up and be like New Cross or Islington."

"How horrible," said Matilda, trembling.

"I've never been to those places, of course," said the Princess, shuddering, "but I hope I know my geography."

"All of it?" asked Matilda.

"Even the exports and imports," said the Princess. "Good-bye. I'm so thin I have to rest a good deal, or I should wear myself out. Nurse—take her away."

So nurse took her away to a wonderful room, where she amused herself till teatime with all the kinds of toys that you see and want in the shops when someone is buying you a box of bricks or a puzzle map—the kinds of toys you never get because they are so expensive.

Matilda had tea with the King. He was full of true politeness, and treated Matilda exactly as though she had been grown up; so that she was extremely happy and behaved beautifully.

The King told her all his troubles.

"You see," he began, "what a pretty place my Green Land was once. It has points even now; but things aren't what they used to be. It's that bird—that Cockatoucan. We daren't kill it or give it away, and every time it laughs something changes. Look at my Prime Minister. He was a six-foot man—and look at him now. I could lift him with one hand; and then your poor maid. It's all that bad bird."

"Why *does* it laugh?" asked Matilda.

"I can't think," said the King. "*I* don't see anything to laugh at."

"Can't you give it lessons or something nasty to make it miserable?"

"I have. I do. I assure you, my dear child, the lessons that bird has to swallow would choke a professor."

"Does it eat anything besides lessons?"

"Christmas pudding. But, there—what's the use of talking? That bird would laugh if it were fed on dog biscuits and senna tea."

His Majesty sighed and passed the buttered toast.

"You can't possibly," he went on, "have any idea of the kind of things that happen. The bird laughed one day at a Cabinet Council, and all my Ministers turned into little boys in yellow smocks. And we can't get any laws made till they come right again. It's not their fault—and I must keep their situation open for them, of course, poor things."

"Of course," said Matilda.

"There was the dragon, now," said the King. "When he came I offered the Princess's hand and half my kingdom to anyone who would kill him; it's an offer that's always made, you know."

"Yes," said Matilda.

"Well—a really respectable young Prince came along— and everyone turned out to see him fight the dragon; as much as ninepence each was paid for the front seats, I assure you, and the trumpets sounded, and the dragon came hurrying up. A trumpet is like a dinner bell to a dragon, you know. And the Prince drew his bright sword, and we all shouted, and then that wretched bird laughed, and the dragon turned into a pussycat, and the Prince killed it before he could stop himself. The populace was furious."

"What happened then?" asked Matilda.

"Well, I did what I could. I said, 'You shall marry the Princess, just the same.' So I brought the Prince home, and when we got there the Cockatoucan had just been laughing again, and the Princess had turned into a very old German governess. The Prince went home in a great hurry and an awful temper. The Princess was all right in a day or two. These are trying times, my dear."

"I am *so* sorry for you," said Matilda, going on with the preserved ginger.

"Well you may be," said the miserable monarch. "Why, if I were to try to tell you all that that bird has brought on my poor kingdom I should keep you up till long past your proper bedtime."

"*I* don't mind," said Matilda, kindly. "Do tell me some more."

"Why," the King went on, growing more and more agitated. "Why—at one titter from that revolting bird the long row of ancestors on my palace wall grew red-faced and vulgar; they began to drop their H's and to assert that their name was Smith, from Clapham Junction."

"How dreadful!"

"And once," the King went on, in a whisper, "it laughed so loudly that two Sundays came together, and next Thursday got lost and went prowling away and hid itself on the other side of Christmas. And now," he said, suddenly, "it's bedtime."

"Must I go?" asked Matilda.

"Yes, please," said the King. "I tell all strangers this tragic story because I always feel that perhaps some *stranger* might be clever enough to help me. You seem a very nice little girl: do you think *you* are clever?"

It is very nice even to be *asked* if you're clever. Your

Aunt Willoughby knows well enough that you're not. But Kings do say nice things. Matilda was very pleased.

"I don't *think* I'm clever," she was saying, quite honestly, when suddenly the sound of a hoarse laugh rang through the banqueting hall. Matilda put her hands to her head.

"Oh, dear," she cried. "I feel so different! Oh, wait a minute! Oh, whatever is it? Oh!"

She was silent for a moment. Then she looked at the King and said: "I was wrong, Your Majesty. I *am* clever, and I know it is not good for me to sit up late. Good night. Thank you so much for your nice party. In the morning I think I shall be clever enough to help you, unless the bird laughs me back into the other kind of Matilda."

But in the morning Matilda's head still felt strangely clear. Only, when she came down to breakfast, full of plans for helping the King, she found that the Cockatoucan must have laughed in the night, for the beautiful palace had turned into a butcher's shop, and the King, who was too wise to fight against fate, had tucked up his Royal robes, and was busy in the shop weighing out six ounces of the best mutton chops for a charwoman with a basket.

"I don't know how ever you can help me now," he said, despairing. "As long as the palace stays like this, it's no use trying to go on with being a King, or anything. I can only try to be a good butcher, and you shall keep the shop accounts, if you like, till that bird laughs me back into my palace again."

So the King settled down to business, respected by

his subjects, who had all, since the coming of the Cockatoucan, had their little ups and downs. And Matilda kept the books and wrote out the bills, and really they were both rather happy. Pridmore, disguised as the Automatic Machine, stood in the shop, and attracted many customers. They used to bring their children and make the poor innocents put their pennies in, and then read Pridmore's good advice. Some parents are so harsh. And the Princess sat in the back garden with the Cockatoucan, and Matilda played with her every afternoon. But one day, as the King was driving through another kingdom, the King of that kingdom looked out of his palace window and laughed as the cart went by, and shouted "Butcher." The Butcher-King did not mind this, because it was true, however rude. But when the other King called out, "What price cat's meat?" the King was very angry indeed, because the meat he sold was always of the best quality. When he told Matilda all about it, she said:

"Send the army to crush him."

So the King sent his army, and the enemy was crushed. The bird laughed the King back onto his throne, and laughed away the butcher's shop, just in time for His Majesty to proclaim a general holiday, and to organize a magnificent reception for the army. Matilda now helped the King to manage everything, and she wonderfully enjoyed the new and delightful feeling of being clever. So that she felt it was indeed too bad when the Cockatoucan laughed—just as the reception was beautifully arranged.

It laughed, and the general holiday turned into a new income tax; the magnificent reception changed itself to a Royal reprimand, and the army itself suddenly became a discontented Sunday-school treat, and had to be fed with buns and brought home in breaks, crying.

"Something *must* be done," said the King.

"Well," said Matilda, "I've been thinking. If you make me the Princess's governess, I'll see what I can do. I'm quite clever enough—"

"I must open Parliament to do that," said the King. "It's a constitutional change."

So he hurried off down the road to open Parliament. But the bird put its head on one side and laughed at him as he went by. He hurried on; but his beautiful crown grew large and brassy, and was set with cheap-colored glass in the worst possible taste; his robes turned from velvet and ermine into flannelette and rabbits' fur; his scepter grew twenty feet long, and extremely awkward to carry. But he persevered. His Royal blood was up.

"No bird," said he, "shall keep me from my duty and my Parliament."

But when he got there he was so agitated that he could not remember which was the right key to open Parliament with, and in the end he hampered the lock, and so could not open Parliament at all; and the members of Parliament went about making speeches in the roads, to the great hindrance of the traffic.

The poor King went home and burst into tears.

"Matilda," he said, "this is too much. You have always been a comfort to me. You stood by me when I was a butcher—you kept the books, you booked the orders, you ordered the stock. If you really are clever enough, now is the time to help me. If you won't, I'll give up the business—I'll leave off being a King—I'll go and be a butcher in the Camberwell New Road, and I will get another little girl to keep my books—not you."

This decided Matilda. She said: "Very well, Your Majesty—then give me leave to prowl at night. Perhaps I can find out what makes the Cockatoucan laugh. If I can do that, we can take care he never gets it—whatever it is."

"Ah," said the poor King, "if you could only do *that*!"

When Matilda went to bed that night she did not go to sleep: she lay and waited till all the palace was quiet, and then she crept softly, pussily, mousily, to the garden, where the Cockatoucan's cage was, and she hid behind a white rosebush, and looked, and listened. Nothing happened till it was grey dawn, and then it was only the Cockatoucan who woke up. But when the sun was round and red over the palace roof something came creeping, creeping, pussily, mousily, out of the palace. And it looked like a yard and a half of white tape creeping along, and it was the Princess herself.

She came quietly up to the cage and squeezed herself between the bars; they were very narrow bars, but a yard and a half of white tape can go through the bars of any birdcage *I* ever saw. And the Princess went up to the Cockatoucan and tickled him under his wings till he laughed aloud. Then, quick as thought, the Princess squeezed through the bars, and was back in her own room before the bird had finished laughing. And Matilda went back to bed. Next day all the sparrows had turned into cart horses; the roads were impassable.

That day, when she went as usual to play with the Princess, Matilda said to her, suddenly:

"Princess, what makes you so thin?"

The Princess caught Matilda's hand and pressed it with warmth.

"Matilda," she said, simply, "you have a noble heart! No one else has ever asked me that, though they tried to cure it. And I couldn't answer till I was asked, could I? It is a sad, a tragic tale. Matilda, I was once as fat as you are."

"I'm not so *very* fat," said Matilda.

"Well," said the Princess, impatiently, "I was quite fat enough, anyhow. And then I got thin."

"But how?"

"Because they would not let me have my favorite pudding every day."

"What a shame," said Matilda, "and what *is* your favorite pudding?"

"Bread and milk, of course, sprinkled with rose leaves, and with pear-drops in it."

Of course, Matilda went at once to the King, but while she was on her way the Cockatoucan happened to laugh, and when she reached the King he was in no condition for ordering dinner, for he had turned into a villa residence, replete with every modern improvement. Matilda only recognized him, as he stood sadly in the park, by the crown that stuck crookedly on one of the chimney pots, and the border of ermine along the garden path. So she ordered the Princess's favorite pudding on her own responsibility, and the whole Court had it every day for dinner till there was no single courtier but loathed the very sight of bread and milk, and there was hardly one who would not have run a mile rather than meet a pear-drop. Even Matilda herself got rather tired of it; though, being clever, she knew how good bread and milk is for you.

But the Princess got fatter and fatter, and rosier and rosier—her thread-paper gowns had to be let out and let out, till there were no more turnings-in to be let out—and then she had to wear her old ones that Matilda had been wearing, and then to get new ones. And as she got fatter she got kinder, till Matilda grew quite fond of her.

And the Cockatoucan had not laughed for a month.

When the Princess was as fat as any Princess ought to be, Matilda went to her one day and threw her arms round her and kissed her. The Princess kissed her back, and said:

"Very well. I *am* sorry, then. But I didn't want to say so. But now I will. And the Cockatoucan never laughs except when he's tickled. So there! He hates to laugh."

"And you won't do it again," said Matilda, "will you, dear?"

"No, of course not," said the Princess, very much

surprised. "Why should I? I was spiteful when I was thin, but now I'm fat again I want everyone to be happy."

"But how can anyone be happy," asked Matilda, severely, "when everyone is turned into something they weren't meant to be? There's your dear father—he's a desirable villa. The Prime Minister was a little boy, and he got back again, and now he's turned into a comic opera. Half the palace housemaids are breakers, dashing themselves against the palace crockery. The navy, to a man, are changed to French poodles, and the army to German sausages. Your favorite nurse is now a flourishing steam laundry; and I, alas, am too clever by half. Can't that horrible bird do anything to put us all right again?"

"No," said the Princess, dissolved in tears at this awful picture; "he told me once himself, that when he laughed he could only change one or two things at once, and then, as often as not, it turned out to be something he didn't expect. The only way to make everything come right again would be—but it can't be done! If we could only make him laugh on the wrong side of his mouth—that's the secret! He told me so; but I don't even know what it *is*, let alone being able to do it. Could *you* do it to him, Matilda?"

"No," said Matilda; "but let me whisper—he's listening—*Pridmore could!* She's often told me she'd do it to me. But she never has. Oh, Princess, I've got an idea!"

The two were whispering so low that the Cockatoucan could not hear, though he tried his hardest. Matilda and the Princess left him listening.

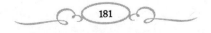

Presently he heard a sound of wheels. Four men came into the rose garden, wheeling a great red thing in a barrow. They set it down in front of the Cockatoucan, who danced on this perch with rage.

"Oh," he said, "if only someone would make me laugh—that horrible thing would be the one to change. I know it would. It would change into something much horrider than it is now. I feel it in all my feathers."

The Princess opened the cage door with the Prime Minister's key, which a tenor singer had found at the beginning of his music. It was also the key of the comic opera. She crept up behind the Cockatoucan and tickled him under both wings. He fixed his baleful eye on the red Automatic Machine and laughed long and loud, and he saw the red iron and glass change before his eyes into the form of Pridmore. Her cheeks were red with rage, and her eyes shone like glass with fury.

"Nice manners," said she; "what are *you* laughing at, I should like to know? I'll make you laugh on the wrong side of your mouth, my fine fellow!"

She sprang into the cage, and then and there, before the astonished Court, she shook that Cockatoucan till he really and truly did laugh on the wrong side of his mouth. It was a terrible sight to witness, and the sound of that wrong-sided laughter was horrible to hear.

But—instantly—all the things changed back, as if by magic, to what they had been before: the laundry became a nurse; the villa became a King; the other people were just what they had been before—and all Matilda's wonderful cleverness went out like the snuff of a candle.

The Cockatoucan himself fell in two—one half of him became a common ordinary toucan, such as you may have seen a hundred times at the zoo—unless you are unworthy to visit that happy place—and the other half became a weathercock, which, as you know, is always changing, and makes the wind change, too. So he has not quite lost his old power. Only, now that he is in halves, any power he may have has to be used without laughing. The poor, broken Cockatoucan, like King You-know-who in English history, has never, since that sad day, smiled again.

The grateful King sent an escort of the whole army—now no longer dressed in sausage skins, but in uniforms of dazzling beauty, with drums and banners—to see Matilda and Pridmore home. But Matilda was very sleepy; she had been clever for so long that she was quite tired out. It is, indeed, a very fatiguing thing, as no doubt you know. And the soldiers must have been sleepy, too, for one by one the whole army disappeared, and by the time Pridmore and Matilda reached home there was only one man in uniform left, and he was the policeman at the corner.

The next day Matilda began to talk to Pridmore about the Green Land, and the Cockatoucan, and the villa-residence King, but Pridmore only said:

"Pack of nonsense! Hold your tongue, do."

So, of course, Matilda understood that Pridmore did not wish to be reminded of the time when she was an

Automatic Nagging Machine, and at once, like a kind and polite little girl, she let the subject drop.

Matilda did not mention her adventures to the others at home, because she saw that they believed her to have spent the time with her Great-Aunt Willoughby.

And she knew if she had said that she has not been there, she would be sent at once, and she did not wish this.

She has often tried to get Pridmore to take the wrong omnibus again, which is the only way she knows of getting to the Green Land, but only once has she been successful, and then the omnibus did not go to the Green Land at all, but to the Elephant and Castle.

But no little girl ought to expect to go to the Green Land more than once in a lifetime. Many of us, indeed, are not even so fortunate as to go there once.

9

MARIA DAHVANA HEADLEY was once a non-fiction writer, and then she shifted her career and started making things up instead. I loved her recent novel, *Queen of Kings*, about a very scary Cleopatra. She was the assistant editor on this book and did everything that I couldn't do.

And here she tells a story about a Beast in a forest.

There's a Beast in the mini-forest, and everyone knows it, especially Angela, whose father hunts it full-time. She has no interest in anything to do with the Beast, until a collector arrives in town, attempting to use her as bait. . . .

MOVEABLE BEAST

By
Maria Dahvana Headley

IT'S LATE ON A THURSDAY AFTERNOON when I meet the guy who turns out to be the Beast collector. I'm not expecting anything life changing from anyone walking in the door of the Bastardville Dreamy Creamy. I got over Possibility when I was seven, right along with Santa Claus and Easter Bunny and Tooth Fairy. All I've got left is Suspicion.

Then Billy Beecham shows up at my job and changes everything. I work in an ice-cream shoppe. The two p's are on purpose. It looks like something out of a Norman Rockwell painting, but it's well known in these parts as the worst ice-cream shoppe in the history of the world. Not that the ice cream is bad. It comes from the same delivery truck that every other town's ice cream comes from. It's frozen. It's quiescent. The bad isn't in the ice cream. It's in the attitude. Just like every other ice-cream shoppe employee anywhere, I wear a pink smock and a visor, and I scoop as though my life depends on it. Then I hand over the ice cream, and say, "Have a miserable day."

Tourists get a huge charge out of it. They want me to say it again and again, but unless they order something else, it's not in my job description. On the day in question, the guy in question comes up to my counter and orders vanilla, which is already against my rules. Then he continues.

"I bet you have a nice smile," he says.

"Do you know how many people have died trying that?" I ask him, and adjust my visor. The answer is very zero.

"Only takes one," he says. "You look like you want to." I do not.

"Come on," he says. "It's been a hell of an afternoon, hunting out there in the mini-forest. I just need to see a pretty girl smile." He checks my name badge. "Angela. I'm Billy Beecham. I'm a Beast collector, with the—"

"Have a miserable day," I tell him, except that miserable is not the word I use. I use a rather more explosive word, a word we all know is a breach of protocol, but he's breaching too. Billy Beecham leans over the Plexiglas barrier, and tries to kiss me.

He's facedown in a tub of Peppy Ripple before I even know what I've done. Every girl in Bastardville takes a semester of self-defense in second grade. I hadn't realized the neck-pinch skill was still part of my physical vocabulary.

"What do you mean, Beast collector?" I ask him, but he doesn't answer. His face is covered in melt. His pith helmet—yes, he's wearing a pith helmet—has sprinkles stuck to the top. He grins, licks the ice cream from around his lips, and walks out of the Dreamy Creamy like he's done nothing wrong.

"There's only one Beast here," I yell after him. "And that Beast isn't collectible. Just so you know."

It's not my fault. I'm doing a good deed. I'm trying to save him. People are stupid sometimes.

"I'll see you later, Angela," the collector tosses over his shoulder. I'm apprehended by my supervisor, Phil, who drags me into the supply closet and says, "No swearing, Andrea. Bastardville is a family town."

Phil can't remember my name, even though he's my age, and has known me since kindergarten.

"All towns are family towns, Phil," I say.

"You're not a nice person," says Phil. "You shouldn't be around the ice cream." He backs out of the supply closet. "Stay in here and think about the error of your ways."

"I don't have to be a nice person," I tell Phil. "This isn't a nice place."

My town started about a hundred years ago as a Utopian community in a beautiful forest. The forest got littler, and we got bigger, and the whole Utopia thing began to melt down. By the time people realized that the woods were shrinking, we'd become a town surrounding a one-block by one-block mini-forest. But obviously, by that point, we'd figured some things out, and it was necessary to stay.

The Chamber of Commerce sent out a survey nine years ago in an attempt at attracting tourists, and that was when we renamed ourselves Bastardville. Second runner up was Awfulton, and third, the under-twenty-one favorite, was simply Suck. We weren't allowed to name ourselves any real swear words, because maps are G-rated. Now, we're visited by adventure backpackers, and the occasional Japanese vacationer. Some of them decide to stay. Some of them stay forever. The Beast stayed too.

Bastardville, USA: population 465, plus one Beast.

The mini-forest is the only place in town you can find any trees. Plant one elsewhere, it uproots and runs down Main Street and into the mini-forest. The Beast can be heard to roar from its confines every night. The whole thing is surrounded by houses on all sides.

We manage things.

At home, my Mother is, for the second time this week, baking cream pies and smashing them into her own face. The streets belong to the Mothers at night, and they like it that way. In the mornings they make eggs, and you want to think you'll never be poisoned, but you never really know for sure. My own Mother is no different. In Bastardville, you marry whomever the Mothers think you ought to marry. They get together, and draw names out of a hat. It's about that time for me. I'm sixteen, but my Mother hasn't done anything about it. I'm supposed to move forward into my role, but in truth? I want a different role.

I don't want to get married at all. If I thought I'd really have to, I'd walk into the mini-forest. I think the Beast might be preferable to Phil. Or anyone else I know. My Mother tried this too, but the Beast didn't take her, and so she married my Father. Now we're the only Family in Bastardville whose Father hunts the Beast full-time. My Father moved into the mini-forest about three years ago, with his pup tent and a few cans of tomatoes. He passed me a book called *Survivalism: A Primer*, shook my hand, and walked into the trees without once looking back. The Beast needs to be hunted. It doesn't feel satisfied unless it engages in conflict. Sometimes someone fully commits. Not women. Men only.

I don't see Billy Beecham again until Saturday night. My friends and I are doing our usual pack wander. Normally, we do a few laps around the mini-forest, and then crouch on the play equipment outside the grade school, and wait for something more to happen.

The Beast roars, but we pay it no attention. It's just talking to itself.

We're just at the point of looking for something to destroy, when Billy Beecham comes out of the mini-forest, wearing a suit. Glasses, tie, briefcase in his hand, and a huge smile on his face.

Nobody smiles in Bastardville. Our Beast, I will say it again, is nothing collectible. Why is the collector smiling? And why did the Beast roar? Maybe it was talking to Billy Beecham. But if it was, I don't know why the collector is smiling.

I can feel the blood boiling in my body, and so I take off running, leaving the rest of my group behind.

Sometime in the middle of the night, I worry about myself. What if I belong here?

The next day, I catch a glimpse of my Father. I haven't

seen him in months. Every other Father in Bastardville can be found next to their refrigerator at II P.M., staring forlornly into the condiments, sometimes dipping a finger in the mustard, or lapping at a jar of jam. Disgusting as that is, it'd be nice to know where my Father could be found at night. All the other Fathers attend their children's weddings. They get raving drunk at the reception. They're supposed to have at least one dance with their designated Mother, who is, in turn, supposed to trip in her high heels, and, as evening falls, go viciously at the Father with her handbag and her martini glass.

All Fathers except mine.

When I see my Father, he's standing on the edge of the mini-forest, at the same place where Billy Beecham emerged. He's staring into space. He has a red helium balloon in one hand, and in the other, a bag of fertilizer.

"Hey!" I say, but he takes off running.

It isn't fair that in this town of wrong, my family is wronger than everyone else's.

I run after him as fast as I can in my uniform's stupid little pink heels, but by the time my eyes adjust to the dark of the mini-forest, he's out of sight. I have, however much I don't want to think about this, a feeling. It's creepily possible my Father is in love with the Beast. Isn't that why people move out and leave their Families?

I can see the balloon bobbing, and I chase that, until there's a bellow, and a loud pop. Then there's nothing but dark. I've never been this far into the mini-forest before.

The bellows of the Beast are nothing you really want to hear. Particularly when you aren't wearing anything resembling stalking gear, you've never managed to read any of *Survivalism: A Primer*, and you are completely, idiotically alone.

The bellow happens again, all around me. I get ready to leave my Father to his Beast, but Billy Beecham appears, wearing a trench coat, and scraping a moss sample from one of the trees. There's another bellow, this one startled.

"Angela," he says, and winks, like it's a pleasant surprise to see me in the middle of a mini-forest.

"Leaving," I say. "You should too. The Beast is about to be on the move."

"Did you see it?" he asks.

"All the time," I say.

From somewhere nearby I hear my Father's voice, beginning to sing "Happy Birthday." I assume it's to himself. The Beast's birthday is anyone's guess. I guess you could figure it out, but you'd need a chain saw.

Could things be more pathetic? I straighten my uniform and walk out. In the direction I think is out, anyway. Which it isn't. That is, of course, implausible, because of the one-block-by-one-block factor. Nevertheless. I've gotten turned around. I feel like things are spinning. I feel like the trees are taller than they were. I note the fertilizer at their feet.

Billy Beecham is smiling at me when I return.

"Lost?" he says.

"What is it you do, anyway? You can't just be hunting

this one Beast," I ask, making the best of a bad situation.

"Collector," he says. "Began with butterflies, now assigned to beasts."

He pulls something out of his pocket. It keeps pulling and pulling like a magician's scarf. A net, but large enough to catch a whale in. Not big enough. Poor idiot.

"It's not like you'll catch the Beast," I tell him. "No one can. You'll end up living here on the edge, and you don't want to, believe me."

"How do you know?" asks Billy Beecham.

"No one *wants* to live here," I tell him. "We just do. We have to. We've been here a long time."

"Happy birthday to you," sings my Father from somewhere far away. I hear him blowing out his own candles, and the mini-forest gets as dark as a mini-forest surrounded by streetlamps can get. The mini-forest also gets larger. I feel it happening. Like it's taken a deep breath.

Billy Beecham grabs my hand, and takes off running, and I'm flying behind him like a streamer. He's making some sort of call with a whistle. A honk.

The Beast has never honked. My backyard borders the mini-forest, and if anyone's heard the voice of the Beast, it's me. The Beast roars.

Billy Beecham stops, and I crash into him. He's swinging his net around over his head. This is not what you do with our Beast. Our Beast is uncatchable.

"Here, Beast," he croons. "Beast, Beast, here, Beast. Does it need a virgin? You'll do."

I look at him. He doesn't even have the grace to blush.

"It doesn't need a virgin. It doesn't care about virgins."

"Not what I heard," Billy Beecham says, and resumes his clucking and net swinging. He has no idea how to call a Beast. I decide to show him.

How do you call this kind of Beast? It's the kind of Beast that responds to one hand clapping, and so I clap against a tree trunk. It's the kind of Beast that hears when a tree falls in the mini-forest and there's no one around. I feel it beginning to move. There is a tearing sound, and a racking sound.

It's not like our Beast doesn't have a history. It used to be a much bigger Beast.

It used to live in Scotland, and it came across the ocean on a ship it took over by talking to the planks. We keep it under control. That's why we're here, on all sides. Bastardville stands guard over our Beast. The last time it got loose, it took over half the Rocky Mountains and created a whole army of pines before we got it back.

Billy Beecham is staring at me.

"What?" I ask.

"Are you trying to poach my Beast?" he says.

I have already discovered that I don't like him. Forgive my momentary delusion. He belongs with his face in a tub of Peppy Ripple. He belongs here, in the mini-forest.

"It's not your Beast," I say. "It's its own Beast. We just keep it boundaried."

The Beast starts to walk. Billy Beecham sits down

abruptly, his face drained of color. I see my Father peering out from behind a tree, the bag of fertilizer still in his hand. He's grinning at me as the forest tilts and lifts us up. He gives me a thumbs-up. I've never seen fit to participate in this, but along with the neck-pinch skill, girls get some training early on in Beast Management. Maybe this is my calling. Maybe I'm a hunter. Maybe I'm a gatherer.

We're on the move. I think about the houses on the eastern border of the Beast. This is a bad little forest. It moves around. Those houses just went back up again, but thankfully, they're empty at present. The Beast tends to like to walk toward the sunrise. We've learned some things over the years. Mostly the Beast only moves a few feet, but today, it's really shaking. The birds that have been hanging out in the Beast's hair scream insulted screams and take off.

I can see a little bit, through the trees. We're way above the streetlamps now, and the Beast is maybe twenty feet in the air, walking on its taproots.

Billy Beecham's mouth is hanging open.

"You know what the Beast eats?" I ask him.

"I don't," Billy Beecham says. "Let me down." After a moment of looking at me, he increases his pitch to the high whine of someone being picked up against his will. "LET ME DOWN."

I feel a little bit of sympathy for him, but he is also the person who kissed me without an invitation. Collector. I don't like being collected any more than the Beast does.

Don't come in here, thinking you can collect Bastardville's Beast. Just be calm, go into the mini-forest, and let the Beast have a snack. You'd think people would learn.

Some people called us tree huggers here in Bastardville, back when we were Utopian. Some people called us weirdos, some people called us pagans, and we were those things too. We're part of an old tradition, Beast Managers, and this kind of Beast requires a lot of maintenance. It needs pruning and fertilizer. It needs exercise. It needs the occasional blood sacrifice. It's no big deal. That's what tourists and collectors are for.

I wrap Billy Beecham's net around my hand and sling it over him, using the neck-pinch skill. I wrap one end around a tree and tie a knot. I wave at my Father as I walk out of the clearing, so that the Beast can do its Beast thing.

"Are you going to let me be eaten?" Billy Beecham looks stunned.

"Don't you know that sometimes Beast collectors get collected?" I ask him.

"But you're a virgin."

"Virgins were never sacrifices," I say. "Not to this kind of Beast. Virgins are collaborators."

And the Beast moves like it hasn't moved in a hundred years. The Beast dances, and I turn my head as Billy Beecham sinks into the gaping maw of the mini-forest.

"Are you happy now?" I ask the Beast.

The Beast roars and slows its walk, dropping down into place only a little way from where it was crouching. After a moment, the birds return, and the breeze winds itself back into the Beast's twigs. The streetlamps come back on. The Mothers resume their night patrol of Bastardville's streets. My Father shakes a little more fertilizer on the Beast's roots, and the Beast sighs in satisfaction.

I lean back against one of the Beast's trees, and kick off my Dreamy Creamy high heels. I put my head back against the Beast, and listen to the Beast's giant heart beating.

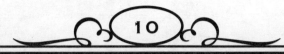

10

LARRY NIVEN is best known as a science-fiction writer. He created Ringworld, and many other futures. I learned a lot from him as a writer. He once wrote that writers should treasure their spelling mistakes, and when I typed Coraline instead of Caroline, I did. Is a horse an unnatural creature?

Time-traveling backward a thousand years in order to procure a long-extinct horse, Svetz is at a loss. He's never seen a horse before. This one looks almost right.. . . .

THE
FLIGHT OF THE
HORSE

Larry Niven

THE YEAR WAS 750 A.A. (*AnteAtomic*) or 1200 A.D. (*Anno Domini*), approximately. Hanville Svetz stepped out of the extension cage and looked about him.

To Svetz the atomic bomb was eleven hundred years old and the horse was a thousand years dead. It was his first trip into the past. His training didn't count; it had not included actual time travel, which cost several million commercials a shot. Svetz was groggy from the peculiar gravitational side effects of time travel. He was high on pre-industrial-age air, and drunk on his own sense of destiny; while at the same time he was not really convinced that he had *gone* anywhere. Or anywhen. Trade joke.

He was not carrying the anesthetic rifle. He had come to get a horse; he had not expected to meet one at the door. How big was a horse? Where were horses found? Consider what the Institute had had to go on: a few pictures in a salvaged children's book, and an old legend, not to be trusted, that the horse had once been used as a kind of animated vehicle!

In an empty land beneath an overcast sky, Svetz braced himself with one hand on the curved flank of the extension cage. His head was spinning. It took him several seconds to realize that he was looking at a horse.

It stood fifteen yards away, regarding Svetz with large intelligent brown eyes. It was much larger than he had expected. Further, the horse in the picture book had had a glossy brown pelt with a short mane, while the beast now facing Svetz was pure white, with a mane that flowed like a woman's long hair. There were other differences . . . but no matter, the beast matched the book too well to be anything but a horse.

To Svetz it seemed that the horse watched him, waited for him to realize what was happening. Then, while Svetz wasted more time wondering why he wasn't holding a rifle, the horse laughed, turned, and departed. It disappeared with astonishing speed.

Svetz began to shiver. Nobody had warned him that the horse might have been sentient! Yet the beast's mocking laugh had sounded far too human.

Now he knew. He was deep, deep in the past.

Not even the horse was as convincing as the emptiness the horse had left behind. No reaching apartment towers clawed the horizon. No contrails scratched the sky. The world was trees and flowers and rolling grassland, innocent of men.

The silence—it was as if Svetz had gone deaf. He had heard no sound since the laughter of the horse. In the year 1100 PostAtomic, such silence could have been found nowhere on Earth. Listening, Svetz knew at last that he had reached the British Isles before the coming of civilization. He had traveled in time.

The extension cage was the part of the time machine that did the traveling. It had its own air supply, and needed it while being pushed through time. But not here. Not before civilization's dawn—not when the air had never been polluted by fission wastes and the combustion of coal, hydrocarbons, tobaccos, wood, et al.

Now, retreating in panic from that world of the past to the world of the extension cage, Svetz nonetheless left the door open behind him.

He felt better inside the cage. Outside was an unexplored planet, made dangerous by ignorance. Inside the cage it was no different from a training mission. Svetz had spent hundreds of hours in a detailed mockup of this cage, with a computer running the dials. There had even been artificial gravity to simulate the peculiar side effects of motion in time.

By now the horse would have escaped. But he now knew its size, and he knew there were horses in the area. To business, then . . .

Svetz took the anesthetic rifle from where it was clamped to the wall. He loaded it with what he guessed was the right size of soluble crystalline anesthetic needle. The box held several different sizes, the smallest of which would knock a shrew harmlessly unconscious, the largest of which would do the same for an elephant. He slung the rifle and stood up.

The world turned grey. Svetz caught a wall clamp to stop himself from falling.

The cage had stopped moving twenty minutes ago. He shouldn't still be dizzy! —But it had been a long trip. Never before had the Institute for Temporal Research pushed a cage beyond zero PA. A long trip and a strange one, with gravity pulling Svetz's mass uniformly toward Svetz's navel . . .

When his head cleared, he turned to where other equipment was clamped to a wall. The flight stick was a lift field generator and power source built into five feet of pole, with a control ring at one end, a brush discharge at the other, and a bucket seat and seat belt in the middle. Compact even for Svetz's age, the flight stick was a spin-off from the spaceflight industries.

But it still weighed thirty pounds with the motor off. Getting it out of the clamps took all his strength. Svetz felt queasy, very queasy.

He bent to pick up the flight stick, and abruptly realized that he was about to faint.

He hit the door button and fainted.

"We don't know where on Earth you'll wind up," Ra Chen had told him. Ra Chen was the Director of the Institute for Temporal Research, a large round man with gross, exaggerated features and a permanent air of disapproval. "That's because we can't focus on a particular time of day— or on a particular year, for that matter. You won't appear underground or inside anything because of energy considerations. If you come out a thousand feet in the air, the cage won't fall; it'll settle slowly, using up energy with a profligate disregard for our budget. . . ."

And Svetz had dreamed that night, vividly. Over and over his extension cage appeared inside solid rock, exploded with a roar and a blinding flash.

"Officially the horse is for the Bureau of History," Ra Chen had said. "In practice it's for the Secretary-General, for his twenty-eighth birthday. Mentally he's about six years old, you know. The royal family's getting a bit inbred these days. We managed to send him a picture book we picked up in 130 PA, and now the lad wants a horse . . ."

Svetz had seen himself being shot for treason, for the crime of listening to such talk.

". . . Otherwise we'd never have gotten the appropriation for this trip. It's in a good cause. We'll do some cloning from the horse before we send the original to the UN. Then—well, genes are a code, and codes can be broken. Get us a male, and we'll make all the horses anyone could want."

But why would anyone want even one horse? Svetz had studied a computer duplicate of the child's picture book that an agent had pulled from a ruined house a thousand years ago. The horse did not impress him.

Ra Chen, however, terrified him.

"We've never sent anyone this far back," Ra Chen had told him the night before the mission, when it was too late to back out with honor. "Keep that in mind. If something goes wrong, don't count on the rule book. Don't count on your instruments. Use your head. Your head, Svetz. Gods know it's little enough to depend on . . ."

Svetz had not slept in the hours before departure.

"You're scared stiff," Ra Chen had commented just before Svetz entered the extension cage. "And you can hide it, Svetz. I think I'm the only one who's noticed. That's why I picked you, because you can be terrified and go ahead anyway. Don't come back without a horse. . . ."

The Director's voice grew louder. "Not without a horse, Svetz. Your *head*, Svetz, your HEAD . . ."

Svetz sat up convulsively. The air! Slow death if he didn't close the door! But the door was closed, and Svetz was sitting on the floor holding his head, which hurt.

The air system had been transplanted intact, complete with dials, from a martian sandboat. The dials read normally, of course, since the cage was sealed.

Svetz nerved himself to open the door. As the sweet, rich air of twelfth-century Britain rushed in, Svetz held his breath and watched the dials change. Presently he closed the door and waited, sweating, while the air system replaced the heady poison with its own safe, breathable mixture.

When next he left the extension cage, carrying the flight stick, Svetz was wearing another spin-off from the interstellar exploration industries. It was a balloon and he wore it over his head. It was also a selectively permeable membrane, intended to pass certain gases in and others out, to make a breathing-air mixture inside.

It was nearly invisible except at the rim. There, where light was refracted most severely, the balloon showed as a narrow golden circle enclosing Svetz's head. The effect was not unlike a halo as shown in medieval paintings. But Svetz didn't know about medieval paintings.

He wore also a simple white robe, undecorated, constricted at the waist, otherwise falling in loose folds. The Institute thought that such a garment was least likely to violate taboos of sex or custom. The trade kit dangled loose from his sash: a heat-and-pressure gadget, a pouch of corundum, small phials of additives for color.

Lastly he wore a hurt and baffled look. How was it that he could not breathe the clean air of his own past?

The air of the cage was the air of Svetz's time, and was nearly four percent carbon dioxide. The air of 750 Ante-Atomic held barely a tenth of that. Man was a rare animal here and now. He had breathed little air, he had destroyed few green forests, he had burnt scant fuel since the dawn of time.

But industrial civilization meant combustion. Combustion meant carbon dioxide thickening in the atmosphere many times faster than the green plants could turn it back to oxygen. Svetz was at the far end of two thousand years of adaptation to air rich in CO_2.

It takes a concentration of carbon dioxide to trigger

the autonomic nerves in the lymph glands in a man's left armpit. Svetz had fainted because he wasn't breathing.

So now he wore a balloon, and felt rejected.

He straddled the flight stick and twisted the control knob on the fore end. The stick lifted under him, and he wriggled into place on the bucket seat. He twisted the knob further.

He drifted upward like a toy balloon.

He floated over a lovely land, green and untenanted, beneath a pearl-grey sky empty of contrails. Presently he found a crumbling wall. He turned to follow it.

He would follow the wall until he found a settlement. If the old legend was true—and, Svetz reflected, the horse had certainly been *big* enough to drag a vehicle—then he would find horses wherever he found men.

Presently it became obvious that a road ran along the wall. There the dirt was flat and bare and consistently wide enough for a walking man; whereas elsewhere the land rose and dipped and tilted. Hard dirt did not a freeway make; but Svetz got the point.

He followed the road, floating at a height of ten meters.

There was a man in worn brown garments. Hooded and barefoot, he walked the road with patient exhaustion, propping himself with a staff. His back was to Svetz.

Svetz thought to dip toward him to ask concerning horses. He refrained. With no way to know where the cage would alight, he had learned no ancient languages at all.

He thought of the trade kit he carried, intended not

for communication, but instead of communication. It had never been field-tested. In any case it was not for casual encounters. The pouch of corundum was too small.

Svetz heard a yell from below. He looked down in time to see the man in brown running like the wind, his staff forgotten, his fatigue likewise.

"Something scared him," Svetz decided. But he could see nothing fearful. Something small but deadly, then.

The Institute estimated that man had exterminated more than a thousand species of mammal and bird and insect—some casually, some with malice—between now and the distant present. In this time and place there was no telling what might be a threat. Svetz shuddered. The brown man with the hairy face might well have run from a stinging thing destined to kill Hanville Svetz.

Impatiently Svetz upped the speed of his flight stick. The mission was taking far too long. Who would have guessed that centers of population would have been so far apart?

Half an hour later, shielded from the wind by a paraboloid force field, Svetz was streaking down the road at sixty miles per hour.

His luck had been incredibly bad. Wherever he had chanced across a human being, that person had been just leaving the vicinity. And he had found no centers of population.

Once he had noticed an unnatural stone outcropping high on a hill. No law of geology known to Svetz could have produced such an angular, flat-sided monstrosity. Curious, he had circled above it—and had abruptly realized that the thing was hollow, riddled with rectangular holes.

A dwelling for men? He didn't want to believe it. Living within the hollows of such a thing would be like living underground. But men tend to build at right angles, and this thing was *all* right angles.

Below the hollowed stone structure were rounded, hairy-looking hummocks of dried grass, each with a man-sized door. Obviously they must be nests for very large insects. Svetz had left that place quickly.

The road rounded a swelling green hill ahead of him. Svetz followed, slowing.

A hilltop spring sent a stream bubbling downhill to break the road. Something large was drinking at the stream.

Svetz jerked to a stop in midair. *Open water: deadly poison.* He would have been hard put to say which had startled him more: the horse, or the fact that it had just committed suicide.

The horse looked up and saw him.

It was the same horse. White as milk, with a flowing abundance of snowy mane and tail, it almost had to be the horse that had laughed at Svetz and run. Svetz recognized the malignance in its eyes, in the moment before it turned its back.

But how could it have arrived so fast?

Svetz was reaching for the gun when the situation turned upside down.

The girl was young, surely no more than sixteen. Her hair was long and dark and plaited in complex fashion. Her dress, of strangely stiff blue fabric, reached from her neck to her ankles. She was seated in the shadow of a tree, on dark cloth spread over the dark earth. Svetz had not noticed her, might never have noticed her . . .

But the horse walked up to her, folded its legs in alternate pairs, and laid its ferocious head in her lap.

The girl had not yet seen Svetz.

The horse obviously belonged to the girl. He could not simply shoot it and take it. It would have to be purchased . . . somehow.

He needed time to think! And there was no time, for the girl might look up at any moment. Baleful brown eyes watched him as he dithered . . .

He dared waste no more time searching the countryside for a wild horse. There was an uncertainty, a Finagle factor in the math of time travel. It manifested itself as an uncertainty in the energy of a returning extension cage, and it increased with time. Let Svetz linger too long, and he could be roasted alive in the returning cage.

Moreover, the horse had drunk open water. It would die, and soon, unless Svetz could return it to 1100 Post-Atomic. Thus the beast's removal from this time could not change the history of Svetz's own world. It was a good choice . . . if he could conquer his fear of the beast.

The horse was tame. Young and slight as she was, the girl had no trouble controlling it. What was there to fear?

But there was its natural weaponry . . . of which Ra
Chen's treacherous picture book had shown no sign.
Svetz surmised that later generations routinely removed it
before the animals were old enough to be dangerous. He
should have come a few centuries later . . .

And there was the look in its eye. The horse hated
Svetz, and it knew Svetz was afraid.

Could he shoot it from ambush?

No. The girl would worry if her pet collapsed without
reason. She would be unable to concentrate on what Svetz
was trying to tell her.

He would have to work with the animal watching him.
If the girl couldn't control it—or if he lost her trust—Svetz
had little doubt that the horse would kill him.

The horse looked up as Svetz approached, but made no
other move. The girl watched too, her eyes round with wonder. She called something that must have been a question.

Svetz smiled back and continued his approach. He was
a foot above the ground, and gliding at dead slow. Riding
the world's only flying machine, he looked impressive as all
hell, and knew it.

The girl did not smile back. She watched warily. Svetz
was within yards of her when she scrambled to her feet.

He stopped the flight stick at once and let it settle.
Smiling placatorially, he removed the heat-and-pressure
device from his sash. He moved with care. The girl was on
the verge of running.

The trade kit was a pouch of corundum, AI_2O_3, several phials of additives, and the heat-and-pressure gadget. Svetz poured corundum into the chamber, added a dash of chromic oxide, and used the plunger. The cylinder grew warm. Presently Svetz dropped a pigeon's-blood star ruby into his hand, rolled it in his fingers, held it to the sun. It was red as dark blood, with a blazing white six-pointed star.

It was almost too hot to hold.

Stupid! Svetz held his smile rigid. Ra Chen should have warned him! What would she think when she felt the gem's unnatural heat? What trickery would she suspect?

But he had to chance it. The trade kit was all he had.

He bent and rolled the gem to her across the damp ground.

She stooped to pick it up. One hand remained on the horse's neck, calming it. Svetz noticed the rings of yellow metal around her wrist; and he also noticed the dirt.

She held the gem high, looked into its deep red fire.

"Ooooh," she breathed. She smiled at Svetz in wonder and delight. Svetz smiled back, moved two steps nearer, and rolled her a yellow sapphire.

How had he twice chanced on the same horse? Svetz never knew. But he soon knew how it had arrived before him. . . .

He had given the girl three gems. He held three more in his hand while he beckoned her onto the flight stick. She shook her head; she would not go. Instead she mounted the animal.

She and the horse, they watched Svetz for his next move.

Svetz capitulated. He had expected the horse to follow the girl while the girl rode behind him on the flight stick. But if they both followed Svetz it would be the same.

The horse stayed to one side and a little behind Svetz's flight stick. It did not seem inconvenienced by the girl's weight. Why should it be? It must have been bred for the task. Svetz notched his speed higher, to find how fast he could conveniently move.

Faster he flew, and faster. The horse must have a limit. . . . He was up to eighty before he quit. The girl lay flat along the animal's back, hugging its neck to protect her face from the wind. But the horse ran on, daring Svetz with its eyes.

How to describe such motion? Svetz had never seen ballet. He knew how machinery moved, and this wasn't it. All he could think of was a man and a woman making love. Slippery-smooth rhythmic motion, absolute single-minded purpose, motion for the pleasure of motion. It was terrible in its beauty, the flight of the horse.

The word for such running must have died with the horse itself.

The horse would never have tired, but the girl did. She tugged on the animal's mane, and it stopped. Svetz gave her the jewels he held, made four more and gave her one.

She was crying from the wind, crying and smiling as she took the jewels. Was she smiling for the jewels, or for the joy of the ride? Exhausted, panting, she lay with her back against the warm, pulsing flank of the resting animal. Only her hand moved as she ran her fingers repeatedly through its silver mane. The horse watched Svetz with malevolent brown eyes.

The girl was homely. It wasn't just the jarring lack of makeup. There was evidence of vitamin starvation. She was short, less than five feet in height, and thin. There were marks of childhood disease. But happiness glowed behind her homely face, and it made her almost passable, as she clutched the corundum stones.

When she seemed rested, Svetz remounted. They went on.

He was almost out of corundum when they reached the extension cage. There it was that he ran into trouble.

The girl had been awed by Svetz's jewels, and by Svetz himself, possibly because of his height or his ability to fly. But the extension cage scared her. Svetz couldn't blame her. The side with the door in it was no trouble: just a seamless spherical mirror. But the other side blurred away in a direction men could not visualize. It had scared Svetz spitless the first time he saw the time machine in action.

He could buy the horse from her, shoot it here and pull it inside, using the flight stick to float it. But it would be so much easier if . . .

It was worth a try. Svetz used the rest of his corundum. Then he walked into the extension cage, leaving a trail of colored corundum beads behind him.

He had worried because the heat-and-pressure device would not produce facets. The stones all came out shaped like miniature hen's-eggs. But he was able to vary the color, using chromic oxide for red and ferric oxide for yellow and titanium for blue; and he could vary the pressure planes, to produce cat's-eyes or star gems at will. He left a trail of small stones, red and yellow and blue . . .

And the girl followed, frightened, but unable to resist the bait. By now she had nearly filled a handkerchief with the stones. The horse followed her into the extension cage.

Inside, she looked at the four stones in Svetz's hand: one of each color, red and yellow and light blue and black, the largest he could make. He pointed to the horse, then to the stones.

The girl agonized. Svetz perspired. She didn't want to give up the horse . . . and Svetz was out of corundum . . .

She nodded, one swift jerk of her chin. Quickly, before she could change her mind, Svetz poured the stones into her hand. She clutched the hoard to her bosom and ran out of the cage, sobbing.

The horse stood up to follow.

Svetz swung the rifle and shot it. A bead of blood appeared on the animal's neck. It shied back, then sighted on Svetz along its natural bayonet.

Poor kid, Svetz thought as he turned to the door. But she'd have lost the horse anyway. It had sucked polluted water from an open stream. Now he need only load the flight stick aboard . . .

Motion caught the corner of his eye.

A false assumption can be deadly. Svetz had not waited for the horse to fall. It was with something of a shock that he realized the truth. The beast wasn't about to fall. It was about to spear him like a cocktail shrimp.

He hit the door button and dodged.

Exquisitely graceful, exquisitely sharp, the spiral horn slammed into the closing door. The animal turned like white lightning in the confines of the cage, and again Svetz leapt for his life.

The point missed him by half an inch. It plunged past him and into the control board, through the plastic panel and into the wiring beneath.

Something sparkled and something sputtered.

The horse was taking careful aim, sighting along the spear in its forehead. Svetz did the only thing he could think of. He pulled the home-again lever.

The horse screamed as it went into free fall. The horn, intended for Svetz's navel, ripped past his ear and tore his breathing-balloon wide open.

Then gravity returned; but it was the peculiar gravity of an extension cage moving forward through time. Svetz and the horse were pulled against the padded walls. Svetz sighed in relief.

He sniffed again in disbelief. The smell was strong and strange, like nothing Svetz had ever smelled before. The animal's terrible horn must have damaged the air plant.

Very likely he was breathing poison. If the cage didn't return in time . . .

But would it return at all? It might be going anywhere, anywhen, the way that ivory horn had smashed through anonymous wiring. They might come out at the end of time, when even the black infrasuns gave not enough heat to sustain life.

There might not even be a future to return to. He had left the flight stick. How would it be used? What would they make of it, with its control handle at one end and the brush-style static discharge at the other and the saddle in the middle? Perhaps the girl would try to use it. He could visualize her against the night sky, in the light of a full moon . . . and how would that change history?

The horse seemed on the verge of apoplexy. Its sides heaved, its eyes rolled wildly. Probably it was the cabin air, thick with carbon dioxide. Again, it might be the poison the horse had sucked from an open stream.

Gravity died. Svetz and the horse tumbled in free fall, and the horse queasily tried to gore him.

Gravity returned, and Svetz, who was ready for it, landed on top. Someone was already opening the door.

Svetz took the distance in one bound. The horse followed, screaming with rage, intent on murder. Two men went flying as it charged out into the Institute control center.

"It doesn't take anesthetics!" Svetz shouted over his shoulder. The animal's agility was hampered here among the desks and lighted screens, and it was probably drunk on hyperventilation. It kept stumbling into desks and men. Svetz easily stayed ahead of the slashing horn.

A full panic was developing. . . .

"We couldn't have done it without Zeera," Ra Chen told him much later. "Your idiot tanj horse had the whole Center terrorized. All of a sudden it went completely tame, walked up to that frigid intern Zeera and let her lead it away."

"Did you get it to the hospital in time?"

Ra Chen nodded gloomily. Gloom was his favorite expression and was no indication of his true feelings. "We found over fifty unknown varieties of bacteria in the beast's bloodstream. Yet it hardly looked sick! It looked healthy as a . . . healthy as a . . . it must have tremendous stamina. We managed to save not only the horse, but most of the bacteria too, for the Zoo."

Svetz was sitting up in a hospital bed, with his arm up to the elbow in a diagnostician. There was always the chance that he too had located some long-extinct bacterium. He shifted uncomfortably, being careful not to move the wrong arm, and asked, "Did you ever find an anesthetic that worked?"

"Nope. Sorry about that, Svetz. We still don't know why your needles didn't work. The tanj horse is simply immune to tranks of any kind.

"Incidentally, there was nothing wrong with your air plant. You were smelling the horse."

"I wish I'd known that. I thought I was dying."

"It's driving the interns crazy, that smell. And we can't seem to get it out of the Center." Ra Chen sat down on the edge of the bed. "What bothers me is the horn on its forehead. The horse in the picture book had no horns."

"No, sir."

"Then it must be a different species. It's not really a horse, Svetz. We'll have to send you back. It'll break our budget, Svetz."

"I disagree, sir—"

"Don't be so tanj polite."

"Then don't be so tanj stupid, sir." Svetz was *not* going back for another horse. "People who kept tame horses must have developed the habit of cutting off the horn when the animal was a pup. Why not? We all saw how dangerous that horn is. Much too dangerous for a domestic animal."

"Then why does our horse have a horn?"

"That's why I thought it was wild, the first time I saw it. I suppose they didn't start cutting off horns until later in history."

Ra Chen nodded in gloomy satisfaction. "I thought so too. Our problem is that the Secretary-General is barely bright enough to notice that his horse has a horn, and the picture-book horse doesn't. He's bound to blame me."

"Mmm." Svetz wasn't sure what was expected of him.

"I'll have to have the horn amputated."

"Somebody's bound to notice the scar," said Svetz.

"Tanj it, you're right. I've got enemies at court. They'd

be only too happy to claim I'd mutilated the Secretary-General's pet." Ra Chen glared at Svetz. "All right, let's hear *your* idea."

Svetz was busy regretting. Why had he spoken? His vicious, beautiful horse, tamely docked of its killer horn . . . He had found the thought repulsive. His impulse had betrayed him. What could they do but remove the horn?

He had it. "Change the picture book, not the horse. A computer could duplicate the book in detail, but with a horn on every horse. Use the Institute computer, then wipe the tape afterward."

Morosely thoughtful, Ra Chen said, "That might work. I know someone who could switch the books." He looked up from under bushy black brows. "Of course, you'd have to keep your mouth shut."

"Yes, sir."

"Don't forget." Ra Chen got up. "When you get out of the diagnostician, you start a four-week vacation."

"I'm sending you back for one of these," Ra Chen told him four weeks later. He opened the bestiary. "We picked up the book in a public park around ten PostAtomic; left the kid who was holding it playing with a corundum egg."

Svetz examined the picture. "That's *ugly*. That's really ugly. You're trying to balance the horse, right? The horse was so beautiful, you've got to have one of these or the universe goes off balance."

Ra Chen closed his eyes in pain. "Just go get us the Gila monster, Svetz. The Secretary-General wants a Gila monster."

"How big is it?"

They both looked at the illustration. There was no way to tell.

"From the looks of it, we'd better use the *big* extension cage."

Svetz barely made it back that time. He was suffering from total exhaustion and extensive second-degree burns. The thing he brought back was thirty feet long, had vestigial batlike wings, breathed fire, and didn't look very much like the illustration; but it was as close as anything he'd found.

The Secretary-General loved it.

11

Two of my very favorite writers, growing up, were SAMUEL R. DELANY, who wrote books like *Nova* and *The Einstein Intersection*, which I loved even if I didn't understand them; and James Thurber, who wrote *The 13 Clocks*, which may be the best book in the world. Here Mr. Delany (Chip, to his friends) writes a story that may owe its inspiration to Thurber, but is very much his own tale. And what is inside the steamer trunk?

A very thin and very grey man arrives in a tavern with a large steamer trunk, which contains his "nearest and dearest friend." The man offers to pay for the assistance of the quick-witted Amos in procuring the cure his friend needs. Off Amos goes, questing for three shards of magical mirror. . . .

PRISMATICA

HOMMAGE À JAMES THURBER

By

Samuel R. Delany

ONE

ONCE THERE WAS A POOR MAN NAMED AMOS. He had nothing but his bright red hair, fast fingers, quick feet, and quicker wits. One grey evening when the rain rumbled in the clouds, about to fall, he came down the cobbled street toward Mariners' Tavern to play jackstraws with Billy Belay, the sailor with a wooden leg and a mouth full of stories that he chewed around and spit out all evening. Billy Belay would talk and drink and laugh and sometimes sing. Amos would sit quietly and listen and always won at jackstraws.

But this evening as Amos came into the tavern, Billy was quiet; and so was everyone else. Even Hidalga, the woman who owned the tavern and took no man's jabbering seriously, was leaning her elbows on the counter and listening with opened mouth.

The only man speaking was tall, thin, and grey. He wore a grey cape, grey gloves, grey boots, and his hair was grey. His voice sounded to Amos like wind over mouse fur, or sand ground into old velvet. The only thing about him not grey was a large black trunk beside him, high as his shoulder. Several rough and grimy sailors with cutlasses sat at his table—they were so dirty they were no color at all!

". . . and so," the soft grey voice went on, "I need someone clever and brave enough to help my nearest and dearest friend and me. It will be well worth someone's while."

"Who is your friend?" asked Amos. Though he had not heard the beginning of the story, the whole tavern seemed far too quiet for a Saturday night.

The grey man turned and raised grey eyebrows. "There is my friend, my nearest and dearest." He pointed to the trunk. From it came a low, muggy *Ulmphf.*

All the mouths that were hanging open about the tavern closed.

"What sort of help does he need?" asked Amos. "A doctor?"

The grey eyes widened, and all the mouths opened once more.

"You are talking of my nearest and dearest friend," said the grey voice, softly.

From across the room Billy Belay tried to make a sign for Amos to be quiet, but the grey man turned around, and the finger Billy had put to his lips went quickly into his mouth as if he were picking his teeth.

"Friendship is a rare thing these days," said Amos. "What sort of help do you and your friend need?"

"The question is: would you be willing to give it?" said the grey man.

"And the answer is: if it is worth my while," said Amos,

who really could think very quickly.

"Would it be worth all the pearls you could put in your pockets, all the gold you could carry in one hand, all the diamonds you could lift in the other, and all the emeralds you could haul up from a well in a brass kettle?"

"That is not much for true friendship," said Amos.

"If you saw a man living through the happiest moment of his life, would it be worth it then?"

"Perhaps it would," Amos admitted.

"Then you'll help my friend and me?"

"For all the pearls I can put in my pockets, all the gold I can carry in one hand, all the diamonds I can lift in the other, all the emeralds I can haul up from a well in a brass kettle, and a chance to see a man living through the happiest moment of his life—I'll help you!"

Billy Belay put his head down on the table and began to cry. Hidalga buried her face in her hands, and all the other people in the tavern turned away and began to look rather grey themselves.

"Then come with me," said the grey man, and the rough sailors with cutlasses rose about him and hoisted the trunk to their grimy shoulders—*Onvbpmf* came from the trunk—and the grey man flung out his cape, grabbed Amos by the hand, and ran out into the street.

In the sky the clouds swirled and bumped each other, trying to upset the rain.

Halfway down the cobbled street the grey man cried, "Halt!"

Everyone halted and put the trunk down on the sidewalk.

The grey man went over and picked up a tangerine-colored alley cat that had been searching for fish heads in a garbage pail. "Open the trunk," he said. One of the sailors took an iron key from his belt and opened the lock on the top of the trunk. The grey man took out his thin sword of grey steel and pried up the lid ever so slightly. Then he tossed the cat inside.

Immediately he let the lid drop, and the sailor with the iron key locked the lock on the top. From inside came the mew of a cat that ended with a deep, depressing *Elmblmpf.*

"I think," said Amos, who after all thought quickly and was quick to tell what he thought, "that everything is not quite right in there."

"Be quiet and help me," said the thin grey man, "or I shall put *you* in the trunk with my nearest and dearest."

For a moment Amos was just a little afraid.

TWO

Then they were on a ship, and all the boards were grey from having gone so long without paint. The grey man took Amos into his cabin, and they sat down on opposite sides of a table.

"Now," said the grey man, "here is a map."

"Where did you get it?" asked Amos.

"I stole it from my worse and worst enemy."

"What is it a map of?" Amos asked. He knew you should ask as many questions as possible when there were so many things you didn't know.

"It is a map of many places and many treasures, and I need someone to help me find them."

"Are these treasures the pearls and gold and diamonds and emeralds you told me about?"

"Nonsense," said the grey man. "I have more emeralds and diamonds and gold and pearls than I know what to do with," and he opened a closet door.

Amos stood blinking as jewels by the thousands fell out on the floor, glittering and gleaming, red, green, and yellow.

"Help me push them back in the closet," said the grey man. "They're so bright that if I look at them too long, I get a headache."

So they pushed the jewels back and leaned against the closet door till it closed.

Then they returned to the map.

"Then what *are* the treasures?" Amos asked, full of curiosity.

"The treasure is happiness, for me and my nearest and dearest friend."

"How do you intend to find it?"

"In a mirror," said the grey man. "In three mirrors, or rather, one mirror broken in three pieces."

"A broken mirror is bad luck," said Amos. "Who broke it?"

"A wizard so great and so old and so terrible that you and I need never worry about him."

"Does this map tell where the pieces are hidden?"

"Exactly," said the grey man. "Look, we are here."

"How can you tell?"

"The map says so," said the grey man. And sure enough, in large letters one corner of the map was marked HERE.

"Perhaps somewhere nearer than you think, up this one, and two leagues short of over there, the pieces are hidden."

"Your greatest happiness will be to look into this mirror?"

"It will be the greatest happiness of myself and of my nearest and dearest friend."

"Very well," said Amos. "When do we start?"

"When the dawn is foggy and the sun is hidden and the air is grey as grey can be."

"Very well," said Amos a second time. "Until then, I shall walk around and explore your ship."

"It will be tomorrow at four o'clock in the morning," said the grey man. "So don't stay up too late."

"Very well," said Amos a third time.

As Amos was about to leave, the grey man picked up a ruby that had fallen from the closet and not been put back. On the side of the trunk that now sat in the corner was a small triangular door that Amos had not seen. The grey man pulled it open, tossed in the ruby, and slammed it quickly: *Orghmflbfe*.

THREE

Outside, the clouds hung so low the top of the ship's tallest mast threatened to prick one open. The wind tossed about in Amos's red hair and scurried in and out of his rags. Sitting on the railing of the ship, a sailor was splicing a rope.

"Good evening," said Amos. "I'm exploring the ship, and I have very little time. I have to be up at four o'clock in the morning. So can you tell me what I must be sure to avoid because it would be so silly and uninteresting that I would learn nothing from it?"

The sailor frowned awhile, then said, "There is nothing at all interesting in the ship's brig."

"Thank you very much," said Amos, and walked on till he came to another sailor, whose feet were awash in soapsuds. The sailor was pushing a mop back and forth so hard that Amos decided he was trying to scrub the last bit of color off the grey boards. "Good evening to you too," said Amos. "I'm exploring the ship, and I have very little time since I'm to be up at four o'clock in the morning. I was told to avoid the brig. So could you point it out to me? I don't want to wander into it by accident."

The sailor leaned his chin on his mop handle awhile, then said, "If you want to avoid it, don't go down the second hatchway behind the wheelhouse."

"Thank you very much," said Amos, and hurried off to the wheelhouse. When he found the second hatchway, he went down very quickly and was just about to go to the barred cell when he saw the grimy sailor with the iron key—who must be the jailer as well, thought Amos.

"Good evening," Amos said. "How are you?"

"I'm fine, and how is yourself, and what are you doing down here?"

"I'm standing here, trying to be friendly," said Amos. "I was told there was nothing of interest down here. And since it is so dull, I thought I would keep you company."

The sailor fingered his key awhile, then said, "That is kind of you, I suppose."

"Yes, it is," said Amos. "What do they keep here that is so uninteresting everyone tells me to avoid it?"

"This is the ship's brig, and we keep prisoners here. What else should we keep?"

"That's a good question," said Amos. "What *do* you keep?"

The jailer fingered his key again, then said, "Nothing of interest at all."

Just then, behind the bars, Amos saw the pile of grubby grey blankets move. A corner fell away, and he saw just the edge of something as red as his own bright hair.

"I suppose, then," said Amos, "I've done well to avoid coming here." And he turned around and left. But that night, as the rain poured over the deck and the drum-drum-drumming of heavy drops lulled everyone on the ship to sleep, Amos hurried over the slippery boards under the dripping eaves of the wheelhouse to the second hatch-way, and went down. The lamps were low, the jailer was huddled asleep in a corner on a piece of grey canvas, but Amos went immediately to the bars and looked through.

More blankets had fallen away, and besides a red as bright as his own hair, he could see a green the color of parrot's feathers, a yellow as pale as Chinese mustard, and a blue as brilliant as the sky at eight o'clock in July. Have you ever watched someone asleep under a pile of blankets? You can see the blankets move up and down, up and down with breathing. That's how Amos knew this was a person. "*Pssst*," he said. "You colorful but uninteresting person, wake up and talk to me."

Then all the blankets fell away, and a man with more colors on him than Amos had ever seen sat up rubbing his eyes. His sleeves were green silk with blue and purple trimming. His cape was crimson with orange design. His shirt was gold with rainbow checks, and one boot was white and the other was black.

"Who are you?" asked the parti-colored prisoner.

"I am Amos, and I am here to see what makes you so uninteresting that everyone tells me to avoid you and covers you up with blankets."

"I am Jack, the Prince of the Far Rainbow, and I am a prisoner here."

"Neither one of those facts is so incredible compared to some of the strange things in this world," said Amos. "Why are you the Prince of the Far Rainbow, and why are you a prisoner?"

"Ah," said Jack, "the second question is easy to answer,

but the first is not so simple. I am a prisoner here because a skinny grey man stole a map from me and put me in the brig so I could not get it back from him. But why am I the Prince of the Far Rainbow? That is exactly the question asked me a year ago today by a wizard so great and so old and so terrible that you and I need never worry about him. I answered him, 'I am Prince because my father is King, and everyone knows I should be.' Then the wizard asked me, 'Why should you be Prince and not one of a dozen others? Are you fit to rule, can you judge fairly, can you resist temptation?' I had no idea what he meant, and again I answered, 'I am Prince because my father is King.' The wizard took a mirror and held it before me. 'What do you see?' he asked. 'I see myself, just as I should, the Prince of the Far Rainbow,' said I. Then the wizard grew furious and struck the mirror into three pieces and cried, 'Not until you look into this mirror whole again will you be Prince of the Far Rainbow, for a woman worthy of a prince is trapped behind the glass, and not till she is free can you rule in your own land.' There was an explosion, and when I woke up, I was without my crown, lying dressed as you see me now in a green meadow. In my pocket was a map that told me where all the pieces were hidden. Only it did not show me how to get back to the Far Rainbow. And still I do not know how to get home."

"I see, I see," said Amos. "How did the skinny grey man steal it from you, and what does he want with it?"

"Well," said Jack, "after I could not find my way home,

I decided I should try and find the pieces. So I began to search. The first person I met was the thin grey man, and with him was his large black trunk in which, he said, was his nearest and dearest friend. He said if I would work for him and carry his trunk, he would pay me a great deal of money with which I could buy a ship and continue my search. He told me that he himself would very much like to see a woman worthy of a prince. 'Especially,' he said, 'such a colorful prince as you.' I carried his trunk for many months, and at last he paid me a great deal of money with which I bought a ship. But then the skinny grey man stole my map, stole my ship, and put me here in the brig, and told me that he and his nearest and dearest friend would find the mirror all for themselves."

"What could he want with a woman worthy of a prince such as you?" asked Amos.

"I don't even like to think about it," said Jack. "Once he asked me to unzip the leather flap at the end of the trunk and stick my head in to see how his nearest and dearest friend was getting along. But I would not because I had seen him catch a beautiful blue bird with red feathers round its neck and stick it through the same zipper, and all there was was an uncomfortable sound from the trunk, something like *Orulmhf*."

"Oh, yes," said Amos. "I know the sound. I do not like to think what he would do with a woman worthy of a prince such as you either." Yet Amos found himself thinking of it. "His lack of friendship for you certainly doesn't speak well of his friendship for his nearest and dearest."

Jack nodded.

"Why doesn't he get the mirror himself, instead of asking me?" Amos wanted to know.

"Did you look at where the pieces were hidden?" asked Jack.

"I remember that one is two leagues short of over there, the second is up this one, and the third is somewhere nearer than you think."

"That's right," said Jack. "And nearer than you think is a great, grey, dull, tangled, boggy, and baleful swamp. The first piece is at the bottom of a luminous pool in the center. But it is so grey there that the grey man would blend completely in with the scenery and never get out again. Up this one is a mountain so high that the North Wind lives in a cave there. The second piece of the mirror is on the highest peak of that mountain. But it is so windy there, and the grey man is so thin, he would be blown away before he was halfway to the top. Two leagues short of over there, where the third piece is, there stretches a garden of violent colors and rich perfumes where black butterflies glisten on the rims of pink marble fountains, and bright vines weave in and about. The only thing white in the garden is a silver-white unicorn who guards the last piece of the mirror. Perhaps the grey man could get that piece himself, but he will not want to, I know, for lots of bright colors give him a headache."

"Then it says something for his endurance that he was

able to put up with your glittering clothes for so long," said Amos. "Anyway, I don't think it's fair of our grey friend to get your mirror with your map. You should at least have a chance at it. Let me see, the first place we are going is somewhere nearer than you think."

"In the swamp, then," said Jack.

"Would you like to come with me," asked Amos, "and get the piece yourself?"

"Of course," said Jack. "But how?"

"I have a plan," said Amos, who could think very quickly when he had to. "Simply do as I say." Amos began to whisper through the bars. Behind them the jailer snored on his piece of canvas.

FOUR

At four o'clock the next morning when the dawn was foggy and the sun was hidden and the air was grey as grey could be, the ship pulled up to the shore of a great, grey, dull, tangled, boggy, and baleful swamp.

"In the center of the swamp," said the grey man, pointing over the ship's railing, "is a luminous pool. At the bottom of the pool is a piece of mirror. Can you be back with it by lunch?"

"I think so," said Amos. "But that *is* terribly grey. I might blend into the scenery so completely I could never get out again."

"With your red hair?" asked the grey man.

"My red hair," said Amos, "is only on the top of my head. My clothes are ragged and dirty and will probably turn grey in no time with all that mist. Are there any bright-colored clothes on the ship, glittering with gold and gleaming with silk?"

"There is my closet full of jewels," said the grey man. "Wear as many as you want."

"They would weigh me down," said Amos, "and I could not be back for lunch. No, I need a suit of clothes that is bright and brilliant enough to keep me from losing myself in all that. For if I *do* lose myself, *you* will never have your mirror."

So the grey man turned to one of his sailors and said, "You know where you can get him such a suit."

As the man started to go, Amos said, "It seems a shame to take someone's clothes away, especially since I might not come back anyway. Give my rags to whoever owns the suit to keep for me until I return." Amos jumped out of his rags and handed them to the sailor, who trotted off toward the wheelhouse. Minutes later he was back with a bright costume: the sleeves were green silk with blue and purple trimming, the cape was crimson with orange design, the shirt was gold with rainbow checks, and sitting on top of it all was one white boot and one black.

"These are what I need," said Amos, putting on the clothes quickly, for he was beginning to get chilly standing in his underwear. Then he climbed over the edge of the boat into the swamp. He was so bright and colorful that nobody saw the figure in dirty rags run quickly behind them to the far end of the ship and also climb over into the swamp. Had the figure been Amos—it was wearing Amos's rags—the red hair might have attracted some attention, but Jack's hair, for all his colorful costume, was a very ordinary brown.

The grey man looked after Amos until he disappeared. Then he put his hand on his forehead, which was beginning to throb a little, and leaned against the black trunk, which had been carried to the deck.

Glumphvmr came from the trunk.

"Oh, my nearest and dearest friend," said the grey man, "I had almost forgotten you. Forgive me." He took from his pocket an envelope, and from the envelope he took a large, fluttering moth. "This flew in my window last night," he said. The wings were pale blue, with brown bands on the edges, and the undersides were flecked with spots of gold. He pushed in a long metal flap at the side of the trunk, very like a mail slot, and slid the moth inside.

Fuffle came from the trunk, and the grey man smiled.

In the swamp, Amos waited until the prince had found him. "Did you have any trouble?" Amos asked.

"Not at all," laughed Jack. "They didn't even notice that the jailer was gone." For what they had done last night, after we left them, was to take the jailer's key, free the prince, and tie up the jailer and put him in the cell under all the grey blankets. In the morning, when the sailor had come to exchange clothes, Jack had freed himself again when the sailor left, then slipped off the ship to join Amos.

"Now let us find your luminous pool," said Amos, "so we can be back by lunch."

"Together they started through the marsh and muck. "You know," said Amos, stopping once to look at a grey spiderweb that spread from the limb of a tree above them to a vine creeping on the ground, "this place isn't so grey after all. Look closely."

And in each drop of water on each strand of the web, the light was broken up as if through a tiny prism into blues and yellows and reds. As they looked, Jack sighed. "These are the colors of the Far Rainbow," he said.

He said no more, but Amos felt very sorry for him. They went quickly now toward the center of the swamp. "No, it isn't completely grey," said Jack. On a stump beside them a green-grey lizard blinked a red eye at them, a golden hornet buzzed above their heads, and a snake that was grey on top rolled out of their way and showed an orange belly.

"And look at that!" cried Amos.

Ahead through the tall grey tree trunks, silvery light rose in the mist.

"The luminous pool!" cried the prince, and they ran forward.

Sure enough, they found themselves on the edge of a round, silvery pool. Across from them, large frogs croaked, and one or two bubbles broke the surface. Together Amos and Jack looked into the water.

Perhaps they expected to see the mirror glittering in the weeds and pebbles at the bottom of the pool; perhaps they expected their own reflections. But they saw neither. Instead, the face of a beautiful girl looked up at them from below the surface.

Jack and Amos frowned. The girl laughed, and the water bubbled.

"Who are you?" asked Amos.

In return, from the bubbles they heard, "Who are you?"

"I am Jack, Prince of the Far Rainbow," said Jack, "and this is Amos."

"I am a woman worthy of a prince," said the face in the water, "and my name is Lea."

Now Amos asked, "Why are you worthy of a prince? And how did you get where you are?"

"Ah," said Lea, "the second question is easy to answer, but the first is not so simple. For that is the same question asked me a year and a day ago by a wizard so great and so old and so terrible that you and I need never worry about him."

"What did you say to him?" asked Jack.

"I told him I could speak all the languages of men, that I was brave and strong and beautiful, and could govern beside any man. He said I was proud, and that my pride was good. But then he saw how I looked in mirrors at my own face, and he said that I was vain, and my vanity was bad, and that it would keep me apart from the prince I was worthy of. The shiny surface of all things, he told me, will keep us apart, until a prince can gather the pieces of the mirror together again, which will release me."

"Then I am the prince to save you," said Jack.

"Are you indeed?" asked Lea, smiling. "A piece of the mirror I am trapped in lies at the bottom of this pool. Once I myself dived from a rock into the blue ocean to retrieve the pearl of white fire I wear on my forehead now. That was the deepest dive ever heard of by man or woman, and this pool is ten feet deeper than that. Will you still try?"

"I will try and perhaps die trying," said Jack, "but I can do no more and no less." Then Jack filled his lungs and dove headlong into the pool.

Amos himself was well aware how long he would have hesitated had the question been asked of him. As the seconds passed, he began to fear for Jack's life, and wished he had had a chance to figure some other way to get the mirror out. One minute passed; perhaps they could have tricked the girl into bringing it up herself. Two minutes— they could have tied a string to the leg of a frog and sent him down to do the searching. Three minutes—there was not a bubble on the water, and Amos surprised himself by deciding the only thing to do was to jump in and at least try to save the prince. But there was a splash at his feet!

Jack's head emerged, and a moment later his hand holding the large fragment of a broken mirror came into sight. Amos was so delighted he jumped up and down. The prince swam to shore, and Amos helped him out. Then they leaned the mirror against a tree and rested for a while. "It's well I wore these rags of yours," said Jack, "and not my own clothes, for the weeds would have caught in my cloak and the boots would have pulled me down and I would have never come up. Thank you, Amos."

"It's a very little thing to thank me for," Amos said. "But we had better start back if we want to be at the ship in time for lunch."

So they started back and by noon had nearly reached the ship. Then the prince left the mirror with Amos and darted on ahead to get back to the cell. Then Amos walked out to the boat with the broken glass.

"Well," he called up to the thin grey man, who sat on the top of the trunk, waiting, "here is your mirror from the bottom of the luminous pool."

The grey man was so happy he jumped from the trunk, turned a cartwheel, then fell to wheezing and coughing and had to be slapped on the back several times.

"Good for you," he said when Amos had climbed onto the deck and given him the glass. "Now come have lunch with me, but for heaven's sake get out of that circus tent before I get another headache."

So Amos took off the prince's clothes and the sailor took them to the brig and returned with Amos's rags. When he had dressed and was about to go in with the grey man to lunch, his sleeve brushed the grey man's arm. The grey man stopped and frowned so deeply his face became almost black. "These clothes are wet, and the ones you wore were dry."

"So they are," said Amos. "What do you make of that?"

The grey man scowled and contemplated and cogitated, but could not make anything of it. At last he said, "Never mind. Come and eat."

The sailors carried the black trunk below with them, and Amos and his host ate a heavy and hearty meal. The grey man speared all the radishes from the salad on his knife and flipped them into a funnel he had stuck in a round opening in the trunk: *Fulrmp, Melrulf, Ulfmphgrumf!*

FIVE

"When do I go after the next piece?" Amos asked when they had finished.

"Tomorrow evening when the sunset is golden and the sky is turquoise and the rocks are stained red in the setting sun," said the grey man. "I shall watch the whole proceedings with sunglasses."

"I think that's a good idea," said Amos. "You won't get such a headache."

That night Amos again went to the brig. No one had missed the jailer yet. So there was no guard at all.

"How is our friend doing?" Amos asked the prince,

pointing to the bundle of blankets in the corner.

"Well enough," said Jack. "I gave him food and water when they brought me some. I think he's asleep now."

"Good," said Amos. "So one-third of your magic mirror has been found. Tomorrow evening I go off for the second piece. Would you like to come with me?"

"I certainly would," said Jack. "But tomorrow evening it will not be so easy; for there will be no mist to hide me."

"Then we'll work it so you won't have to hide," said Amos. "If I remember you right, the second piece is on the top of a windy mountain so high the North Wind lives in a cave there."

"That's right," said Jack.

"Very *well* then, I have a plan." Again Amos began to whisper through the bars, and Jack smiled and nodded.

They sailed all that night and all the next day, and toward evening they pulled in to a rocky shore where just a few hundred yards away a mountain rose high and higher into the clear twilight.

The sailors gathered on the deck of the ship just as the sun began to set, and the grey man put one grey gloved hand on Amos's shoulder and pointed to the mountain with his other.

"There, among the windy peaks, is the cave of the North Wind. Even higher, on the highest and windiest peak, is the second fragment of the mirror. It is a long, dangerous, and treacherous climb. Shall I expect you back for breakfast?"

"Certainly," said Amos. "Fried eggs, if you please, once over lightly, and plenty of hot sausages."

"I will tell the cook," said the grey man.

"Good," said Amos. "Oh, but one more thing. You say it is windy there. I shall need a good supply of rope, then, and perhaps you can spare a man to go with me. A rope is not much good if there is a person only on one end. If I have someone with me, I can hold him if he blows off, and he can do the same for me." Amos turned to the sailors. "What about that man there? He has a rope and is well muffled against the wind."

"Take whom you like," said the grey man, "so long as you bring back my mirror." The well-muffled sailor with the coil of rope on his shoulder stepped forward with Amos. Had the grey man not been wearing his sunglasses against the sunset, he might have noticed something familiar about the sailor, who kept looking at the mountain and would not look back. But as it was, he suspected nothing.

Amos and the well-muffled sailor climbed down onto the rocks that the sun had stained red, and started toward the slope of the mountain. Once the grey man raised his glasses as he watched them go but lowered them quickly, for it was the most golden hour of the sunset then. The sun sank, and he could not see them anymore. Even so, he stood at the rail a long time, till a sound in the darkness roused him from his reverie: *Blmvghm!*

. . .

Amos and Jack climbed long and hard through the evening. When darkness fell, at first they thought they would have to stop, but the clear stars made a mist over the jagged rocks, and a little later the moon rose. After that it was much easier going. Shortly the wind began. First a breeze merely tugged at their collars. Then rougher gusts began to nip their fingers. At last buffets of wind flattened them against the rock one moment, then tried to jerk them loose the next. The rope was very useful indeed, and neither one complained. They simply went on climbing, steadily through the hours. Once Jack paused a moment to look back over his shoulder at the silver sea and said something that Amos couldn't hear.

"What did you say?" cried Amos above the howl.

"I said," the prince cried back, "look at the moon!"

Now Amos looked over his shoulder too and saw that the white disk was going slowly down.

They began again, climbing faster than ever, but in another hour the bottom of the moon had already sunk below the edge of the ocean. At last they gained a fair-sized ledge where the wind was not so strong. Above, there seemed no way to go any higher.

Jack gazed out at the moon and sighed. "If it were daylight, I wonder if I could I see all the way to the Far Rainbow from here."

"You might," said Amos. But though his heart was with Jack, he still felt a good spirit was important to keep up. "But we might see it a lot more clearly from the top of this mountain." But as he said it, the last light of the moon winked out. Now even the stars were gone, and the blackness about them was complete. But as they turned to seek shelter in the rising wind, Amos cried, "There's a light!"

"Where's a light?" cried Jack.

"Glowing behind those rocks," cried Amos.

An orange glow outlined the top of a craggy boulder, and they hurried toward it over the crumbly ledge. When they climbed the rock, they saw that the light came from behind another wall of stone farther away, and they scrambled toward it, pebbles and bits of ice rolling under their hands. Behind the wall they saw that the light was even stronger above another ridge, and they did their best to climb it without falling who-knows-how-many hundreds of feet to the foot of the mountain. At last they pulled themselves onto the ledge and leaned against the side, panting. Far ahead of them, orange flames flickered brightly and there was light on each face. For all the cold wind, their foreheads were still shiny with the sweat of the effort.

"Come on," said Amos, "just a little way. . . ."

And from half a dozen directions they heard: *Come on, just a little . . . just a little way . . . little way . . .*

They stared at each other and Jack jumped up. "Why, we must be in the cave of . . ."

And echoing back they heard ". . . *must be in the cave . . . in the cave of . . . cave of . . .*

". . . the North Wind," whispered Amos.

They started forward again toward the fires. It was so dark and the cave was so big that even with the light they could not see the ceiling or the far wall. The fires themselves burned in huge scooped-out basins of stone. They had been put there for a warning, because just beyond them the floor of the cave dropped away and there was only darkness.

"I wonder if she's at home," whispered Jack.

Then before them was a rushing and a rumbling and a rolling like thunder, and from the blackness a voice said, "I am the North Wind, and I am very much at home."

A blast of air sent the fires reeling in the basins, and the sailor's cap that Jack wore flew back into the darkness.

"Are you really the North Wind?" Amos asked.

"Yes, I am really the North Wind," came the thunderous voice. "Now you tell me who you are before I blow you into little pieces and scatter them over the whole wide world."

"I am Amos, and this is Jack, Prince of the Far Rainbow," said Amos. "We wandered into your cave by accident and meant nothing impolite. But the moon went down, so we had to stop climbing, and we saw your light."

"Where were you climbing to?"

Now Jack said, "To the top of the mountain where there is a piece of a mirror."

"Yes," said the North Wind, "there is a mirror there. A wizard so great and so old and so terrible that you and I never need worry about him placed it there a year and a day ago. I blew him there myself in return for a favor he did me a million years past, for it was he who made this cave for me by artful and devious magic."

"We have come to take the mirror back," said Jack.

The North Wind laughed so loudly that Amos and the prince had to hold on to the walls to keep from blowing away. "It is so high and so cold up there that you will never reach it," said the Wind. "Even the wizard had to ask my help to put it there."

"Then," called Amos, "you could help us get there too?"

The North Wind was silent a whole minute. Then she asked, "Why should I? The wizard built my cave for me. What have you done to deserve such help?"

"Nothing yet," said Amos. "But we can help you if you help us."

"How can you help me?" asked the Wind.

"Well," said Amos, "like this. You say you are really the North Wind. How can you prove it?"

"How can you prove you are really you?" returned the Wind.

"Easily," said Amos. "I have red hair, I have freckles, I am five feet, seven inches tall, and I have brown eyes. All you need do is go to Hidalga who owns the Mariners' Tavern and ask her who has red hair, is so tall, with such eyes, and she will tell you, 'It is my own darling Amos.' And Hidalga's word should be proof enough for anybody. Now, what do you look like?"

"What do I look like?" demanded the North Wind.

"Yes, describe yourself to me."

"I'm big and I'm cold and I'm blustery—"

"That's what you feel like," said Amos. "Not what you look like. I want to know how I would recognize you if I saw you walking quietly down the street toward me when you were not working."

"I'm freezing and I'm icy and I'm chilling—"

"Again, that's not what you look like; it's what you feel like."

The North Wind rumbled to herself for a while and at last confessed: "But no one has seen the wind."

"So I had heard," said Amos. "But haven't you ever looked into a mirror?"

"Alas," sighed the North Wind, "mirrors are always kept inside people's houses where I am never invited. So I never had a chance to look in one. Besides, I have been too busy."

"Well," said Amos, "if you help get us to the top of the mountain, we will let you look into the fragment of the mirror." Then he added, "Which is more than your friend the wizard did, apparently." Jack gave Amos a little kick, for it is not a good thing to insult a wizard so great and so old and so terrible as all that, even if you or I don't have to worry about him.

The North Wind mumbled and groaned around the darkness for a while and at last said, "Very well. Climb on my shoulders, and I shall carry you up to the highest peak of this mountain. When I have looked into your mirror, I will carry you down again to where you may descend the rest of the way by yourselves."

Amos and Jack were happy as they had ever been, and the North Wind roared to the edge of the ledge, and they climbed on her back, one on each shoulder. They held themselves tight by her long, thick hair, and the Wind's great wings filled the cave with such a roaring that the fires, had they not been maintained by magic, would have been blown out. The sound of the great wing feathers clashing against one another was like steel against bronze.

The North Wind rose up in her cave and sped toward the opening that was so high they could not see the top and so wide they could not see the far wall, and her leaf-matted hair brushed the ceiling, and her long, ragged toenails scraped the floor, and the tips of her wings sent boulders crashing from either side as she leapt into the black. They circled so high they cleared the clouds, and once again the stars were like diamonds dusting the velvet night. She flew so long that at last the sun began to shoot spears of gold across the horizon; and when the ball of the sun had rolled halfway over the edge of the sea, she settled one foot on a crag to the left, her other foot on the pinnacle to the right, and bent down and set them on the tallest peak in the middle.

"Now where is the mirror?" asked Amos, looking around.

The dawning sun splashed the snow and ice with silver.

"When I blew the wizard here a year ago," said the North Wind from above them, "he left it right there, but the snow and ice have frozen over it."

Amos and the prince began to brush the snow from a lump on the ground, and beneath the white covering was pure and glittering ice. It was a very large lump, nearly as large as the black trunk of the skinny grey man.

"It must be in the center of this chunk of ice," said Jack. As they stared at the shiny, frozen hunk, something moved inside it, and they saw it was the form of lovely Lea, who had appeared to them in the pool.

She smiled at them and said, "I am glad you have come for the second piece of the mirror, but it is buried in this frozen shard of ice. Once, when I was a girl, I chopped through a chunk of ice to get to an earring my mother had dropped the night before in a winter dance. That block of ice was the coldest and hardest ice any man or woman had ever seen. This block is ten degrees colder. Can you chop through it?"

"I can try," said Jack, "or perhaps die trying. But I can do no more and no less." And he took the small pickax they had used to help them climb the mountain.

"Will you be finished before breakfast time?" asked Amos, glancing at the sun.

"Of course before breakfast," said the prince, and fell to chopping. The ice chips flew around him, and he worked up such a sweat that in all the cold he still had to take off his shirt. He worked so hard that in one hour he had laid open the chunk, and there, sticking out, was the broken fragment of mirror. Tired but smiling, the prince lifted it from the ice and handed it to Amos. Then he went to pick up his shirt and coat.

"All right, North Wind," cried Amos. "Take a look at yourself."

"Stand so that the sun is in your eyes," said the North Wind, towering over Amos, "because I do not want anyone else to see before I have."

So Amos and Jack stood with the sun in their eyes, and the great blustering North Wind squatted down to look at herself in the mirror. She must have been pleased with what she saw, because she gave a long, loud laugh that nearly blew them from the peak. Then she leapt a mile into the air, turned over three times, then swooped down upon them, grabbing them up and setting them on her shoulders. Amos and Jack clung to her long, thick hair as the Wind began to fly down the mountain. The Wind cried out in a windy voice: "Now I shall tell all the leaves and whisper to all the waves who I am and what I look like, so they can chatter about it among themselves in autumn and rise and doff their caps to me before a winter storm." The North Wind was happier than she had ever been since the wizard first made her cave.

It gets light on the top of a mountain well before it does at the foot, and this mountain was so high that when they reached the bottom the sun was nowhere in sight, and they had a good half hour until breakfast time.

"You run and get back in your cell," said Amos, "and when I have given you enough time, I shall return and eat my eggs and sausages."

So the prince ran down the rocks to the shore and snuck onto the ship, and Amos waited for the sun to come up. When it did, he started back.

SIX

But, at the boat, all had not gone according to Amos's plan during the night. The grey man, still puzzling over Amos's wet clothes—and at last he began to inquire whom Amos had solicited from the sailors to go with him—had gone to the brig himself.

In the brig he saw immediately that there was no jailer and then that there was no prisoner. Furious, he rushed into the cell and began to tear apart the bundle of blankets in the corner. And out of the blankets rolled the jailer, bound and gagged and dressed in the colorful costume of the Prince of the Far Rainbow. For it was the jailer's clothes that Jack had worn when he had gone with Amos to the mountain.

When the gag came off, the story came out, and the part of the story the jailer had slept through, the grey man could guess for himself. So he untied the jailer and called the sailors and made plans for Amos's and the prince's return. The last thing the grey man did was take the beautiful costume back to his cabin where the black trunk was waiting.

When Amos came up to the ship with the mirror under his arm, he called, "Here's your mirror. Where are my eggs and sausages?"

"Sizzling hot and waiting," said the grey man, lifting his sunglasses. "Where is the sailor you took to help you?"

"Alas," said Amos, "he was blown away in the wind." He climbed up the ladder and handed the grey man the mirror. "Now we only have a third to go, if I remember right. When do I start looking for that?"

"This afternoon when the sun is its highest and hottest," said the grey man.

"Don't I get a chance to rest?" asked Amos. "I have been climbing up and down mountains all night."

"You may take a nap," said the grey man. "But come and have breakfast first." The grey man put his arm around Amos's shoulder and took him down to his cabin where the cook brought them a big, steaming platter of sausages and eggs.

"You have done very well," said the grey man, pointing to the wall where he had hung the first two pieces of mirror together. Now they could make out what the shape of the third would be. "And if you get the last one, you will have done very well indeed."

"I can almost feel the weight of those diamonds and emeralds and gold and pearls right now," said Amos.

"Can you really?" asked the grey man. He pulled a piece of green silk from his pocket, went to the black box, and stuffed it into a small square door: *Orlmnb!*

"Where is the third mirror hidden?" asked Amos.

"Two leagues short of over there is a garden of violent colors and rich perfume, where black butterflies glisten on the rims of pink marble fountains, and the only thing white in it is a silver-white unicorn who guards the third piece of the mirror."

"Then it's good I am going to get it for you," said Amos, "because even with your sunglasses, it would give you a terrible headache."

"Curses," said the grey man, "but you're right." He took from his pocket a strip of crimson cloth with orange design, went to the trunk, and lowered it through a small round hole in the top. As the last of it dropped from sight, the trunk went *Mlpbgrm!*

"I am very anxious to see you at the happiest moment of your life," said Amos. "But you still haven't told me what you and your nearest and dearest friend expect to find in the mirror."

"Haven't I?" said the grey man. He reached under the table and took out a white leather boot, went to the trunk, lifted the lid, and tossed it in.

Org! This sound was not from the trunk; it was Amos swallowing his last piece of sausage much too fast. He and the grey man looked at one another, and neither said anything. The only sound was from the trunk: *Grublmeumplefrmp . . . hic!*

"Well," said Amos at last, "I think I'll go outside and walk around the deck a bit."

"Nonsense," said the grey man, smoothing his grey gloves over his wrists. "If you're going to be up this afternoon, you'd better go to sleep right now."

"Believe me, a little air would make me sleep much better."

"Believe *me*," said the grey man, "I have put a little something in your eggs and sausages that will make you sleep much better than all the air in the world."

Suddenly Amos felt his eyes grow heavy, his head grow light, and he slipped down in his chair.

When Amos woke up, he was lying on the floor of the ship's brig inside the cell, and Jack, in his underwear—for the sailors had jumped on him when he came back in the morning and given the jailer back his clothes—was trying to wake him up.

"What happened to you?" Amos asked, and Jack told him.

"What happened to you?" asked Jack, and Amos told him.

"Then we have been found out, and all is lost," said the prince. "For it is noon already, and the sun is at its highest and hottest. The boat has docked two leagues short of over there, and the grey man must be about to go for the third mirror himself."

"May his head split into a thousand pieces," and Amos, "with the pain."

"Pipe down in there," said the jailer. "I'm trying to sleep." And he spread out his piece of grey canvas and lay down.

Outside the water lapped at the ship, and after a moment Jack said, "A river runs by the castle of the Far Rainbow, and when you go down into the garden, you can hear the water against the wall just like that."

"Now don't be sad," said Amos. "We need all our wits about us."

From somewhere there was the sound of knocking.

"Though, truly," said Amos, glancing at the ceiling, "I had a friend once named Billy Belay, an old sailor with a wooden leg, I used to play jackstraws with. When he would go upstairs to his room in the Mariners' Tavern, you could hear him walking overhead just like that."

That knocking came again.

"Only that isn't above us," said Jack. "It's below."

They looked at the floor. Then Jack got down on his hands and knees and looked under the cot. "There's a trapdoor there," he whispered to Amos, "and somebody's knocking."

"A trapdoor in the *bottom* of a ship?" asked Amos.

"We won't question it," said Jack, "we'll just open it."

They grabbed the ring and pulled the door back. Through the opening there was only the green surface of the water. Then, below the surface, Lea appeared.

"What are you doing here?" whispered Amos.

"I've come to help you," she said. "You have gotten

two-thirds of the broken mirror. Now you must get the last piece."

"How did you get here?" asked Jack.

"Only the shiny surface of things keeps us apart," said Lea. "Now if you dive through here, you can swim out from under the boat."

"And once we get out from under the boat," said Amos, "we can climb back in."

"Why should we do that?" asked Jack.

"I have a plan," said Amos.

"But will it work even if the grey man is already in the garden of violent colors and rich perfumes, walking past the pink marble fountains where the black butterflies glisten on their rims?" asked Jack.

"It will work as long as the silver-white unicorn guards the fragment of the mirror," said Amos, "and the grey man doesn't have his hands on it. Now dive."

The prince dove, and Amos dove after him.

"Will you pipe down in there," called the jailer without opening his eyes.

In the garden the grey man, with sunglasses tightly over his eyes and an umbrella above his head, was indeed walking through violent colors and rich perfumes, past pink marble fountains where black butterflies glistened. It was hot; he was dripping with perspiration, and his head was in agony.

He had walked a long time, and even through his dark

glasses he could make out the green and red blossoms, the purple fruit on the branches, the orange melons on the vines. The most annoying thing of all, however, were the swarms of golden gnats that buzzed about him. He would beat them away with the umbrella, but they came right back again.

After what seemed a long, long time, he saw a flicker of silver white, and coming closer, he saw it was a unicorn. It stood in the little clearing, blinking. Just behind the unicorn was the last piece of the mirror.

"Well it's about time," said the grey man, and began walking toward it. But as soon as he stepped into the clearing, the unicorn snorted and struck his front feet against the ground, one after the other.

"I'll just get it quickly without any fuss," said the grey man. But when he stepped forward, the unicorn also stepped forward, and the grey man found the sharp point of the unicorn's horn against the grey cloth of his shirt, right where it covered his bellybutton.

"I'll have to go around it then," said the grey man. But when he moved to the right, the unicorn moved to the right; and when he moved to the left, the unicorn did the same.

From the mirror there was a laugh.

The grey man peered across the unicorn's shoulder, and in the piece of glass he saw not his own reflection but the face of a young woman. "I'm afraid," she said cheerfully, "that you shall never be able to pick up the mirror unless the unicorn lets you, for it was placed here by a wizard so great and so old and so terrible that you and I need never worry about him."

"Then what must I do to make this stubborn animal let me by? Tell me quickly because I am in a hurry and have a headache."

"You must prove yourself worthy," said Lea.

"How do I do that?"

"You must show how clever you are," said Lea. "When I was free of this mirror, my teacher, in order to see how well I had learned my lessons, asked me three questions. I answered all three, and these three questions were harder than any questions ever heard by man or woman. I am going to ask you three questions that are ten times as hard, and if you answer them correctly, you may pick up the mirror."

"Ask me," said the grey man.

"First," said Lea, "who is standing just behind your left shoulder?"

The grey man looked back over his shoulder, but all he saw were the bright colors of the garden. "Nobody," he said.

"Second," said Lea, "who is standing just behind your right shoulder?"

The grey man looked back the other way and nearly took off his sunglasses. Then he decided it was not necessary, for all he saw was a mass of confusing colors. "Nobody," he said.

"Third," said Lea, "what are they going to do to you?"

"There is nobody there, and they are going to do nothing," said the grey man.

"You have gotten all three questions wrong," said Lea sadly.

Then somebody grabbed the grey man by the right arm, and somebody grabbed him by the left, and they pulled him down on his back, rolled him over on his stomach, and tied his hands behind him. One picked him up by the shoulders and the other by the feet, and they only paused long enough to get the mirror from the clearing, which the unicorn let them have gladly, for there was no doubt that they could have answered Lea's questions.

For one of the two was Amos, wearing the top half of the costume of the Prince of the Far Rainbow, minus a little green patch from the sleeve and a strip from the crimson cape; he had stood behind some bushes so the grey man could not see his less colorful pants. The other was Prince Jack himself, wearing the bottom of the costume, minus the white leather boot; he had stood behind a low-hanging branch so the grey man had not been able to see him from the waist up.

With the mirror safe—nor did they forget the grey man's umbrella and sunglasses—they carried him back to the ship. Amos's plan had apparently worked; they had managed to climb back in the ship and get the costume from the grey man's cabin without being seen and then sneak off after him into the garden.

But here luck turned against them, for no sooner had

they reached the shore again when the sailors descended on them. The jailer had at last woken up and, finding his captives gone, had organized a searching party, which set out just as Amos and the prince reached the boat.

"Crisscross, cross, and double-cross!" cried the grey man triumphantly as once more Amos and Jack were led to the brig.

The trapdoor had been nailed firmly shut this time, and even Amos could not think of a plan.

"Cast off for the greyest and gloomiest island on the map," cried the grey man.

"Cast off!" cried the sailors.

"And do not disturb me till we get there," said the skinny grey man. "I have had a bad day today, and my head is killing me."

The grey man took the third piece of mirror to his cabin, but he was too ill to fit the fragments together. So he put the last piece on top of the trunk, swallowed several aspirins, and lay down.

SEVEN

On the greyest, gloomiest island on the map is a large grey gloomy castle. Stone steps lead up from the shore to the castle entrance. This was the skinny grey man's gloomy grey home. On the following grey afternoon, the ship pulled up to the bottom of the steps, and the grey man, leading two bound figures, walked up to the door.

Later, in the castle hall, Amos and the prince stood bound by the back wall. The grey man chuckled to himself as he hung up the two-thirds completed mirror. The final third was on the table.

"At last it is about to happen," said the grey man. "But first, Amos, you must have your reward for helping me so much."

He led Amos, still tied, to a small door in the wall. "In there is my jewel garden. I have more jewels than any man in the world. Ugh! They give me a headache. Go quickly, take your reward, and when you come back, I shall show you a man living through the happiest moment of his life. Then I will put you *and* your jewels into the trunk with my nearest and dearest friend."

With the tip of his thin grey sword he cut Amos's ropes, thrusting him into the jewel garden and closing the small door firmly behind him.

It was a sad Amos who wandered through those bright piles of precious gems that glittered and gleamed about. The walls were much too high to climb and they went all the way around. Being a clever man, Amos knew there were some situations in which it was a waste of wit to try and fig-ure a way out. So, sadly, he picked up a small wheelbarrow lying on top of a hill of rubies and began to fill his pockets with pearls. When he had hauled up a cauldron full of gold from the well in the middle of the garden, he put all his reward in the wheelbarrow, went back to the small door, and knocked.

The door opened, and, with the wheelbarrow, Amos was yanked through and bound again. The grey man marched him back to the prince's side and wheeled the barrow to the middle of the room.

"In just a moment," said the thin grey man, "you will see a man living through the happiest moment of his life. But first I must make sure my nearest and dearest friend can see, too." He went to the large black trunk, which seemed even blacker and larger, and stood it on its side; then with the great iron key he opened it almost halfway so that it faced toward the mirror. But from where Amos and Jack were, they could not see into it at all.

The grey man took the last piece of the mirror, went to the wall, and fitted it in place, saying, "The one thing I have always wanted more than anything else, for myself, for my nearest and dearest friend, is a woman worthy of a prince."

Immediately there was thunder, and light shot from the restored glass. The grey man stepped back, and from the mirror stepped the beautiful and worthy Lea.

"Oh, happiness!" laughed the thin grey man. "She is grey too!"

For Lea was cloaked in grey from head to foot. But almost before the words were out, she loosed her grey cloak, and it fell about her feet.

"Oh, horrors!" cried the thin grey man, and stepped back again.

Under her cloak she wore a scarlet cape with flaming rubies that glittered in the lightning. Now she loosed her scarlet cape, and that too fell to the floor.

"Oh, misery!" screamed the grey man, and stepped back once more.

For beneath her scarlet cape was a veil of green satin, and topazes flashed yellow along the hem. Now she threw the veil back from her shoulders.

"Oh, ultimate depression!" shrieked the thin grey man, and stepped back again, for the dress beneath the veil was silver with trimmings of gold, and her bodice was blue silk set with sapphires.

The last step took the thin grey man right into the open trunk. He cried out, stumbled, the trunk overturned on its side, and the lid fell to with a clap.

There wasn't any sound at all.

"I had rather hoped we might have avoided that," said Lea as she came over to untie Jack and Amos. "But there is nothing we can do now. I can never thank you enough for gathering the mirror and releasing me."

"Nor can we thank you," said Amos, "for helping us do it."

"Now," said Jack, rubbing his wrists, "I can look at myself again and see why I am Prince of the Far Rainbow."

He and Lea walked to the mirror and looked at their reflections.

"Why," said Jack, "I am a prince because I am worthy to be a prince, and with me is a woman worthy to be a princess."

In the gilded frame now was no longer their reflection,

but a rolling land of green and yellow meadows, with red and white houses, and far off a golden castle against a blue sky.

"That's the land of the Far Rainbow!" cried Jack. "We could almost step through into it!" And he began to go forward.

"What about me?" cried Amos. "How do I get home?"

"The same way we do," said Lea. "When we are gone, look into the mirror and you will see your home too."

"And that?" asked Amos, pointing to the trunk.

"What about it?" said Jack.

"Well, what's in it?"

"Look and see," said Lea.

"I'm afraid to," said Amos. "It has said such dreadful and terrible things."

"You, afraid?" laughed Jack. "You, who rescued me three times from the brig, braved the grey swamp, and rode the back of the North Wind!"

But Lea asked gently, "What did it say? I have studied the languages of men, and perhaps I can help. What did it say?"

"Oh, awful things," said Amos, "like *onvbpmf* and *elmblmpf* and *orghmflbfe*."

"That means," said Lea, "'I was put in this trunk by a wizard so great and so old and so terrible that you and I need never worry about him.'"

"And it said *glumphvmr* and *fuffle* and *fulrmp*," Amos told her.

"That means," said Lea, "'I was put here to be the nearest and dearest friend to all those grim, grey people who cheat everybody they meet and who can enjoy nothing colorful in the world.'"

"Then it said *orlmnb* and *mlpbgrm* and *gruglmeumplefrmp—hic!*"

"Loosely translated," said Lea: "'One's duty is often a difficult thing to do with the cheerfulness, good nature, and diligence that others expect of us; nevertheless . . .'"

"And when the thin grey man fell into the trunk," said Amos, "it didn't make any sound at all."

"Which," said Lea, "can be stated as: 'I've done it.' Roughly speaking."

"Go see what's in the trunk," said Jack. "It's probably not so terrible after all."

"If you say so," said Amos. He went to the trunk, walked all around it three times, then gingerly lifted the lid. He didn't see anything, so he lifted it farther. When he still didn't see anything, he opened it all the way. "Why, there's nothing in—" he began. But then something caught his eye at the very bottom of the trunk, and he reached in and picked it up.

It was a short, triangular bar of glass.

"A prism!" said Amos. "Isn't that amazing. That's the most amazing thing I ever heard of."

But then he was alone in the castle hall. Jack and Lea had already left. Amos ran to the mirror just in time to see them walking away across the green and yellow meadows to the golden castle. Lea leaned her head on Jack's shoulder, and the prince turned to kiss her raven hair, and Amos thought: "Now there are *two* people living through the happiest moment of their lives."

Then the picture changed, and he was looking down a familiar seaside cobbled street, wet with rain. A storm had just ended, and the clouds were breaking apart. Down the block the sign of the Mariners' Tavern swung in the breeze.

Amos ran to get his wheelbarrow, put the prism on top, and wheeled it to the mirror. Then, just in case, he went back and locked the trunk tightly.

Someone opened the door of the Mariners' Tavern and called inside, "Why is everybody so glum this evening when there's a beautiful rainbow looped across the world?"

"It's Amos!" cried Hidalga, running from behind the counter.

"It *is* Amos!" cried Billy Belay, thumping after her on his wooden leg.

Everyone else in the tavern came running outside too. Sure enough it was Amos, and sure enough a rainbow looped above them to the far horizons.

"Where have you been?" cried Hidalga. "We all thought you were dead."

"You wouldn't believe me if I told you," said Amos, "for you are always saying you take no man's jabbering seriously."

"Any man who can walk out of a tavern one night with

nothing and come back in a week with that"—and she pointed to the wheelbarrow full of gold and jewels—"is a man to be taken seriously."

"Then marry me," said Amos, "for I always thought you had uncommonly good sense in matters of whom to believe and whom not to. Your last words have proved you worthy of my opinion."

"I certainly shall," said Hidalga, "for I always thought you an uncommonly clever man. Your return with this wheelbarrow has proved *you* worthy of *my* opinion."

"I thought you were dead too," said Billy Belay, "after you ran out of here with that thin grey man and his big black trunk. He told us terrible stories of the places he intended to go. And you just up and went with him without having heard anything but the reward."

"There are times," said Amos, "when it is better to know only the reward and not the dangers."

"And this was obviously such a time," said Hidalga, "for you are back now, and we are to be married."

"Well, come in, then," said Billy, "and play me a game of jackstraws, and you can tell us all about it."

They went back into the tavern, wheeling the barrow before them.

"What is this?" asked Hidalga as they stepped inside. She picked up the glass prism from the top of the barrow.

"That," said Amos, "is the other end of the Far Rainbow."

"The other end of the rainbow?" asked Hidalga.

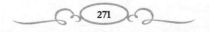

"Over there," said Amos, pointing back out the door, "is that end. And over there is this end," and he pointed out the front window, "and right here is the other end."

Then he showed her how a white light shining through it would break apart and fill her hands with all the colors she could think of.

"Isn't that amazing," said Hidalga. "That's the most amazing thing I ever heard of."

"That's exactly what I said," Amos told her, and they were both very happy, for they were both clever enough to know that when a husband and wife agree about such things, it means a long and happy marriage is ahead.

12

MEGAN KURASHIGE is a dancer who sometimes writes. I wish she would write more, but that
would mean she would dance less. Here she shows
us some unnatural creatures made by hand.

There's a strange collection in the Museum of
Natural History, an exhibit of rogue taxidermy,
hoaxes created by the enterprising to fool people
into believing in monsters. Or are they hoaxes?

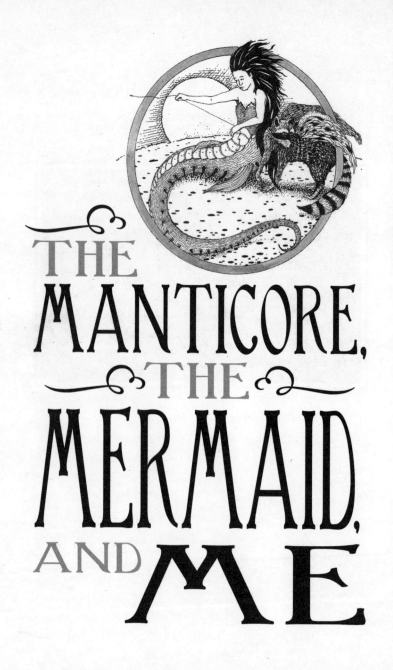

THE
MANTICORE,
THE
MERMAID,
AND ME

By
Megan Kurashige

IT WAS A HOT, BLUE DAY IN AUGUST when Matthew and I went to the Museum of Natural History for the air-conditioning. I wanted to go to the movies, but Matthew's mother had told him, at breakfast, that she was cleaning up another scandal in the Zoological Gallery. There was even an article in the paper about it. Matthew had cut it out before he got on the train and we began our argument while he was trying to retrieve the piece of newsprint from his back pocket.

"It's cheaper than the movies," he said. "I've got my mom's pass, so it'll be free, actually. It's air-conditioned. We can stay all day."

I made a face. Once, when we went to the beach, Matthew spent the whole afternoon crouched by a single tide pool and, while I walked up and down the sand, slowly burning, he watched a tiny crab eat its way through the arm of a dead starfish. It was like watching a horror movie in slow motion, but Matthew thought it was the most interesting thing in the world.

"The movies are air-conditioned," I said.

"Yeah, but we'll only be there for an hour and a half. Two at the most."

The train's ventilation system had given up, and the air was piling into a thick, damp haze. By the time Matthew rescued the newspaper article from his pocket, the paper was limp and so wrinkled that he had to stretch it across his knee before I could see what it was.

UNNATURAL SPECIMEN SMUGGLED INTO MUSEUM, it said. Beneath the headline, a grainy, black-and-white photograph showed a stuffed raccoon with a pair of soft, gray wings folded over its back. The photograph had been taken through glass and the photographer's reflection partially obscured the subject, but the raccoon's face was clearly visible, its lips flared in an artificial snarl. A caption under the raccoon's feet called it "an audacious hoax."

"Where's the article?" I asked.

"I just cut out the picture. That's the interesting part. My mom says they got the article wrong anyway. It wasn't actually in any of the exhibits, just glued on the wall next to one. Don't you want to see it?"

"Not really." The museum was the kind of place that tracked cold little fingerprints down the back of my neck. Quiet spaces full of dead things, all posed like they were happy to be that way. "And didn't your mom say that they got rid of it already?"

"But we have her pass. We can go in the back and have a look around. Besides, it's my turn to choose." He took the pass out of his pocket and tapped it against his nose, still sunburned from the weekend before, when I made him spend hours at a carnival so we could ride the Ferris wheel at sunset.

"Fine," I said. I had made a mistake the weekend before and kissed him while we were pressed together in our gondola, surrounded by a red-and-orange sky, and I wasn't going to make the same mistake again. We sat across from each other in the train with our knees pulled up so they wouldn't touch. I crossed my arms and Matthew laughed, leaning in so close that I could see an eyelash that had come loose and was hanging askew on the top of his cheek.

The museum was cool and full of shade and, after coming in from the street where the sunlight reflected off the pavement, my eyes couldn't decide where to look.

"Let's go straight there," Matthew said. He already knew the way. We sped past cases of dried insects pinned to canvas, down a hall decorated with topographical maps, through a dim room of enormous brown bones, and across a rotunda lined with dioramas. Groups of people trundled in front and behind us, all heading the same way. The kids were all shouting the same thing.

"The raccoon!"

"The raccoon!"

They crowded the doorway of the Zoological Gallery, pushing their way into air that had a mothball tinge, a dusty, faintly chemical prickle that crawled up noses and into brains.

"The raccoon!"

Matthew laughed and grabbed my hand. We slid along the crowd's edges, around a corner, and into a small room that could have been a closet, emptied of everything except a pair of Australian platypuses, displayed with a nest of eggs, and a stumpy man whose green hat had a clump of feathers tucked under the brim like a fisherman's lure.

"Anybody there?" the man asked.

"Nobody," Matthew said. "Except for us."

"Good." The man lifted a piece of white card out of a paper bag. He lifted a stick of glue. He coated one side of the card with the glue, making lavish swoops and curves, and then flipped it over, pressing it down on the plaque that described the *Platypus, or Ornithorhynchus anatinus*, and smoothing it out with his fingers.

"You can't do that," I said. The glue bulged around the sides of the card and the man smeared it with his thumb.

"Why not?" the man asked. "Don't you ever get tired of looking at things the way they are?"

Matthew pointed his two fingers at me, like a gun. He was always telling me the same thing.

"You can't do that," I said, "because someone else did all the work to figure out what those things are, and to name them, and to write it down so everyone else can know what they're looking at. And now you're messing it up." I pushed Matthew in the shoulder and the gun wavered, wilted, fell away.

"You could at least read it," Matthew said.

I read the card. The print was very small.

THE STORY OF JENNY HANIVER

A long time ago, there was a girl named Jenny Haniver who lived at the edge of the sea. She lived with her mother, who was old and blind, and with nobody else. Jenny could sail, and she could fish, and her eyes were the same color as the sea.

At some point, a man fell in love with Jenny. They would have married and lived to be happy and old. They would have had children and grandchildren and, on their last day, sailed out of life together.

But before that could happen, the man was swept out by a wave. He would have drowned, but Jenny was an excellent swimmer and she saved him. Afterwards, she died.

Jenny's mother wrapped her daughter's body in silvery fish. She sewed them together with hair that she tore from her own head. She popped their eyes with a silver pin and whispered secret words into their fishy ears.

Jenny Haniver swam away without saying goodbye. The man watched until she disappeared, and he watched for many days after that, but she was something else, something new, and she never came back.

I looked at the platypuses again when I finished reading. The man had replaced one of them with a shriveled, dry thing that had a bulbous head, a narrow, bony chest, and a brittle fish tail the color of dust. Next to it, the platypus looked just as strange, a creature sewn up from different parts.

"This is Mr. Jabricot," Matthew said. "He works with my mom."

Mr. Jabricot pressed his chin into his chest. He clasped his hands together and bent his head over them, smiling as if he were taking a bow. "Your mother is an excellent woman," he said. "A woman of unimpeachable character. It's to her credit that she would never suspect any of her employees of doing something like this. Not you though. You would tip a place upside down before settling for something as easy as that." He turned to me and held out his hand. I took it, but instead of folding his palm and shaking, he tapped the backs of my fingers with his thumb. "Clever. Moderately pretty. Pragmatic. Did you like the story?"

"No," I said. I wasn't in the mood for sad endings, not then. I waited for Matthew to notice that the conversation was getting strange, that it might be a nice time to leave, that we were loitering in a small room with a man who had just defaced a museum exhibit with some paper and glue and a thing that, in the best light, would still look like a fish stranded in the desert; but Matthew was looking at the thing next to the platypus, checking it for seams.

"It's a sad one, I know," Mr. Jabricot said. "But, most stories are if you follow them long enough. Do you know what we call a Jenny Haniver these days?"

I pictured a girl, once dead, swimming off in a new skin made of fish, also once dead. She flicked her tail, buoyant, seaworthy. "A monster?"

"No, not a monster," Mr. Jabricot said. He rubbed the tips of his fingers together, as if he were trying to feel the quality of his thoughts. "Sometimes it's close, but not exactly. A Jenny Haniver, in this modern era, is what we call the art of the rogue taxidermist. A special creature summoned from the skins of animals that are plainer and more likely. Bits of monkey, bits of fish, all you have to do is suggest and people will build their own loop of possibility where mermaids chase after ships and sing to drowning sailors."

"We should go," Matthew said. He whistled, blowing air across the back of my neck. It was supposed to be a signal, secret code for when we couldn't talk, but Matthew was always changing the rules about what things meant. "My mom's picking us up."

We sat on the train. It was still hot. Matthew cradled the Jenny Haniver in his lap. Crisp, bright sunlight fell through the windows and broke across the fake creature, picking out its pinched, desiccated face and crumbling tail.

I couldn't believe he took it.

"Easy," he said. "I held it behind me and when we walked out, I held it in front of me."

"But, why?" I asked.

He wanted to see how it was made. He wanted to find all the seams and split them open, pry off the draping and reveal whatever it was hiding. Mr. Jabricot, he said, was a genius and Matthew didn't understand a half, a quarter even, of the things he did. He held out the creature while he talked and I took it because otherwise he would wave it around, dragging eyes to our corner where I balanced a piece of stolen loot across my knees, surprised by its lightness and clean perfection. If there were seams, they were invisible. Up close, the thing looked like no one could possibly have made it. It looked more dead than dead.

"Don't take it apart," I said.

Matthew stopped talking. We both stared at the creature, beautiful and dry and impossible. "I won't do it today," he said. "And we'll have to keep it at your house. If my mom finds it, something bad will happen."

"She'll find out about Mr. Jabricot."

"She'll ban us from the museum."

"She'll ground you."

"She'll say I'm a bad influence."

"She won't let us be friends."

We ran out of bad things before we got to my stop.

My parents didn't notice the Jenny Haniver. I carried it to my room while Mom was in the kitchen and Dad flipped from one version to the next of the evening news. We had a nice dinner: pasta and ice cream, a conversation about plumbing and neighbors that drifted past me, stuffed with people I didn't really know.

"How's Matthew?" Mom asked. She reserved washing the dishes for time to talk about things she thought were important. She scrubbed tomato sauce off a plate.

"He's fine." I stacked glasses.

"You've known each other for a while."

"Yep." I wiped a bowl dry and thought about the creature tucked under my bed and the way Matthew had looked at it, like it was the sort of thing he saw every day, like he knew how the pieces went together. Old hat. The usual.

"Well," Mom said. She turned on the garbage disposal and let it roar through the kitchen. "I hope you guys are having a nice time."

In the middle of the night, the creature woke me up. I could feel it lying there, under my bed, sending woozy thoughts of upside-down waves and vast, wet shadows with rows of sharp teeth seeping up through the mattress and into my sleep. I got out from under the covers and bent over until my knees touched the floor.

"Go to sleep," I said.

I climbed back into bed and felt really dumb.

In the middle of a dream, one that involved the underside of waves and shadows with teeth, I carried the creature to the bathroom. It needed water, it told me. I shut the door, turned on the light, and filled the bathtub.

Not too cold, it said.

And I said, please?

It splashed water on me when I dropped it in, a pale shape that sunk and then darted sideways, growing fatter and more graceful as it made circles around the tub. Its scales were sleek silver gray, its body streaked and dabbed with black from the top of its head to the tips of its pliable, swishing fins. As it swam, the black drifted up and became a cloud of swaying hair. The creature rolled over in the tub and spouted water at me from newly plump cheeks.

This, it said, is the equivalent of laughing. At you. You should see your face.

In the middle of a dream, one in which I was wiping water off my face, Jenny Haniver draped her arms over the side of the tub and asked me if I believed in monsters.

"There are so many different kinds," she said. "You have the ones that look like what we are, like me, and then you have the other ones. It's hard to decide which are more dangerous. I guess you could make an argument either way." She lifted one arm off the tub and held it up as if she were admiring the softness of her skin. Then she reached out, pinched a few strands of my hair, and tore them off my head.

"Ow!" I said. This was more than I signed up for. I was going to kill Matthew, if I ever saw him again. I was going to throw him from the Ferris wheel, have him eaten by crabs, feed him to the platypus, turn him in to the museum, turn him in to his mother, leave him alone—all alone—with a dried-out bit of fish and bit of monkey, freshly reconstituted into a beautiful monster.

Jenny Haniver took something thin and sharp from her

own hair. A needle, curved at one end and straight at the other. She threaded it with a strand of my hair and pointed to her side where a split had appeared, a seam bursting open even though there was nothing coming through.

"It wears out," she said. "That's a good thing to remember."

When I woke up, the bathtub was empty. It smelled like fish and there was a clump of long, black hair caught around the opening of the drain. Puddles dotted the floor. I cleaned everything up before my parents could get out of bed.

Matthew's voice flew out of the phone and hit me in the ear. "You have to get over here! Mr. Jabricot has something new that he's going to try. He says we can be there. We can help. We can be the first people to see it. Do you even know how amazing that is?" I could hear him breathing hard into the phone, blowing big, whistling breaths down the line at me. I was pretty sure this wasn't secret code for anything, except for the fact that Matthew, if left unattended, would collapse from the thrill.

"What about the Jenny Haniver?" I asked. How do you tell your friend that his stolen treasure walked itself out while you were sleeping? Or dragged itself out, on two arms and a flopping, shredding tail? How are you supposed to tell anyone something like that?

"Don't worry about it. Mr. Jabricot knows everything. He thinks we're hilarious." Matthew laughed and I could hear someone else laughing behind him. "Come on. Hurry up."

How are you supposed to talk to the person who you used to think was your best friend in the world? "Sure," I said.

Mr. Jabricot let me in through a plain door on the back side of the museum. It opened onto a bland corridor and I followed Mr. Jabricot into it, past doors that were mostly closed. He was wearing his green hat again and a brown tweed jacket with felt patches over the elbows. He looked like a teacher or a librarian and, for some reason, the similarity made me want to laugh.

"So," he said, "Jenny Haniver. What do you think about her story now?"

"It's the same thing," I said. "She gets sewn up. She turns into a monster. She leaves."

"I think you're lacking some inspiration." Mr. Jabricot made two scolding clicks at the back of his throat. "Or, you're lying. The moral of the story is: you can't see anything unless you look at it inside another skin. Your friend can't figure that one out, but I assume you're smarter than he is." He patted my shoulder.

I decided that I had been lying, but hadn't realized it until he made me consider the possibility. I was about to apologize, but Mr. Jabricot opened the door at the end of the hall. The room inside was cold and smelled of plaster, chemicals, and the sharp, uncomfortable scent of strong disinfectant. There were shelves full of tools and bottles and boxes piled with soft scraps that looked like fur. Matthew was sitting on the edge of a long table, poking through a tray of mismatched glass eyes.

"This is Mr. Jabricot's office. My mom never comes here. She says it's creepy." Matthew held a flat gold eye with a slotted pupil up to his face. "I think it's the most gorgeous room in the world. Every time I come here, I feel like the excitement is going to punch me in the face."

I sat on the table next to him. Mr. Jabricot moved around the room, returning boxes to shelves and sweeping a dry paintbrush across the bared surfaces. Fur and dust drifted to the floor.

"You really work here?" I asked.

"Of course. I take care of the collection. Patch up moth damage, reset loose eyes, paint on the stripes and dapples when they start to fade. Everything else, I squeeze in around the edges."

"Like the Jenny Haniver?" I asked. "And the raccoon?" I wondered if the raccoon had been put away in a storage room, or thrown away, or if it were somewhere outside, prowling the halls on nimble, dark-nailed feet.

"Yes," Mr. Jabricot said. "And this new thing I'm working on. The one I was hoping to show you." He moved toward a cabinet at the side of the room, but Matthew was off the table and ahead of him, pulling the doors open and gathering in his arms a mound of sable, a sliding, ruddy pile of fur that fell in sheets to the floor and ended in something that dragged and clattered. He held it up to me and then spun around, sliding his arms in, ducking his head under, and coming up again, dressed in a fur coat.

"It's a manticore," he said. He smiled so hard that his face went shiny where it stretched over his cheeks and his chin.

He just looked like Matthew in a fur coat. A fur coat with one set of paws dangling from the cuffs and another flopped on the floor. It had a sad, crooked tail with a spike tied to the end of it and a fluffy collar that rose all the way to his ears.

"You look silly," I said. Matthew rolled his eyes.

"A manticore," Mr. Jabricot said, "has the body of a lion, the head of a man, and the tail of a dragon." He held up a needle, curved at one end and straight at the other, and threaded it with a strand of something long and dark. Matthew held up his own needle and they began stitching him up, one from the top and one from the bottom.

"It has a terrible voice, like a dozen trumpets," Matthew said. "It has a mouth full of teeth, three rows of them, like a shark." As they stitched, the coat shrank. It clung to his back, wrapped around his legs, and pulled his shoulders over so he was bent, then kneeling, then standing on four paws. The claws scraped the floor.

They stitched and stitched. I told them to stop.

Stop, I said. It's stupid, whatever you're doing. I don't believe it, I said. Why is that tail lashing? I can't believe how stupid I was to come. I'm going to close my eyes and when I open them, I won't be here, you won't be here, none of this will have happened.

They didn't hear me.

A manticore's voice sounds exactly like a dozen trumpets, if a dozen trumpets were playing twelve different jazz scores and all the musicians were deaf and stranded at different points in time.

I opened my eyes.

The manticore was standing on Mr. Jabricot. Its claws pierced the brown tweed of Mr. Jabricot's coat and its tail swung in an arc that shrank the world down to nothing but the poisonous spike tracing the edge of it. The manticore knocked Mr. Jabricot's hat from his head, and I could see that the top of Mr. Jabricot's head was balding, a circle of tender, shiny flesh ringed by short hair as plain as the coat of a mouse.

"Oh no," Mr. Jabricot said. "Oh no oh no oh no."

The manticore's mouth was full of teeth, three yellowing rows of them, and it ground them together as it studied all the soft and delicate parts of the man lying beneath its claws. The twelve trumpets screamed and Mr. Jabricot covered his ears.

The teeth looked terrible shoved into Matthew's face. They stretched his mouth so wide that his lips couldn't close over them. They crowded his nose and pressed his chin back to accommodate their three rows, turning Matthew's face into a different shape. It wouldn't have been able to laugh, or smile, or twist its lips up at one corner over something it found more interesting than anything else in the room. It didn't look like Matthew at all.

"Spit those out," I said. I reached out and grabbed the manticore's fur. I pulled it toward me, or maybe it pulled me toward it. I couldn't be sure because Mr. Jabricot struggled up from the floor and ran from the room. He was sobbing; I could hear it underneath the trumpets screaming and doors slamming and the voices of people coming down through the halls. I worked my fingers into a seam, already wearing out and pulling apart. I ripped it and the manticore bit my arm.

"Stop that," I said. The manticore ignored me, so I ignored the teeth sinking into my arm, the smell of blood, and the aching, blinding pain, and found another seam and ripped that one too. The manticore was unraveling now. Its fur peeled off in long strips. Its teeth fell out, one by one. It let go of my arm and ran for the door, howling in a brassy voice that sounded less and less like a roar.

My arm was bleeding, so I sewed it up. There were needles in a cupboard and I used a piece of hair from my own head. It hurt more than I thought it would, but less than having a manticore's teeth stuck in your arm. It healed in a week and when my mom asked what happened, I said I had been scratched by a cat.

"Do you need an antibiotic?" she asked.

I told her that I didn't think so. It wasn't anything dangerous and, besides, it was almost healed.

. . .

Matthew was grounded. They found him in a closet in the museum, asleep in the wreckage of a very expensive specimen, a half-lion, half-tiger skin that Mr. Jabricot had been commissioned to mount as part of a display on rare hybrids of the world. His mom made a formal apology to the museum board and tried to quit her job out of embarrassment, but they begged her to come back, with the condition that Matthew would never go into the museum again.

I haven't decided what I am going to say to him yet. I think he still might be my best friend.

The scar on my arm is very faint and narrow. It's about the width of a piece of hair and curves three times between my shoulder and my elbow. Sometimes, on hot and quiet afternoons, I'll go outside alone and look at it in the sun.

On the rare occasion, I sing.

A trumpet, just one, sounds sweet when it finds the right tune. If you're lucky, a monster does too.

13

The second werewolf story in this book. If I love werewolves (and I do) it is because I read this story, with its professor, magician, Nazi spies, and Hollywood film actress, at an age where such things left lasting impressions. It is a very silly story by a very good writer and editor, ANTHONY BOUCHER.

Professor Wolfe Wolf, unlucky in love, is drowning his sorrows in a bar, when he meets a magician, who informs him that he's not destined to be a professor, but a werewolf. Detectives, spies, brainy secretaries . . . Things, needless to say, do not go at all according to plan.

THE
COMPLEAT
WEREWOLF

By

Anthony Boucher

THE PROFESSOR GLANCED AT THE NOTE:

Don't be silly — Gloria.

Wolfe Wolf crumpled the sheet of paper into a yellow ball and hurled it out the window into the sunshine of the bright campus spring. He made several choice and profane remarks in fluent Middle High German.

Emily looked up from typing the proposed budget for the departmental library. "I'm afraid I didn't understand that, Professor Wolf. I'm weak on Middle High."

"Just improvising," said Wolf, and sent a copy of the *Journal of English and Germanic Philology* to follow the telegram.

Emily rose from the typewriter. "There's something the matter. Did the committee reject your monograph on Hager?"

"That monumental contribution to human knowledge? *Oh*, no. Nothing so important as that."

"But you're so upset—"

"The office wife!" Wolf snorted. "And pretty damned polyandrous at that, with the whole department on your hands. Go away."

Emily's dark little face lit up with a flame of righteous anger that removed any trace of plainness. "Don't talk to me like that, Mr. Wolf. I'm simply trying to help you. And it isn't the whole department. It's—"

Professor Wolf picked up an inkwell, looked after the telegram and the *Journal,* then set the glass pot down again. "No. There are better ways of going to pieces. Sorrows drown easier than they smash. Get Herbrecht to take my two o'clock, will you?"

"Where are you going?"

"To hell in sectors. So long."

"Wait. Maybe I can help you. Remember when the dean jumped you for serving drinks to students? Maybe I can—"

Wolf stood in the doorway and extended one arm impressively, pointing with that curious index which was as long as the middle finger. "Madam, academically you are indispensable. You are the prop and stay of the existence of this department. But at the moment this department can go to hell, where it will doubtless continue to need your invaluable services."

"But don't you see—" Emily's voice shook. "No. Of course not. You wouldn't see. You're just a man—no, not even a man. You're just Professor Wolf. You're Woof-woof."

Wolf staggered. "I'm what?"

"Woof-woof. That's what everybody calls you because your name's Wolfe Wolf. All your students, everybody. But you wouldn't notice a thing like that. Oh, no. Woof-woof, that's what you are."

"This," said Wolfe Wolf, "is the crowning blow. My heart is breaking, my world is shattered, I've got to walk a mile from the campus to find a bar; but all this isn't enough. I've got to be called Woof-woof. Goodbye!"

He turned, and in the doorway caromed into a vast and yielding bulk, which gave out with a noise that might have been either a greeting of "Wolf!" or more probably an inevitable grunt of "Oof!"

Wolf backed into the room and admitted Professor Fearing, paunch, pince-nez, cane, and all. The older man waddled over to his desk, plumped himself down, and exhaled a long breath. "My dear boy," he gasped. "Such impetuosity."

"Sorry, Oscar."

"Ah, youth—" Professor Fearing fumbled about for a handkerchief, found none, and proceeded to polish his pince-nez on his somewhat stringy necktie. "But why such haste to depart? And why is Emily crying?"

"Is she?"

"You see?" said Emily hopelessly, and muttered "Woof-woof" into her damp handkerchief.

"And why do copies of the JEGP fly about my head as I harmlessly cross the campus? Do we have teleportation on our hands?"

"Sorry," Wolf repeated curtly. "Temper. Couldn't stand that ridiculous argument of Glocke's. Goodbye."

"One moment." Professor Fearing fished into one of his unnumbered handkerchiefless pockets and produced a sheet of yellow paper. "I believe this is yours?"

Wolf snatched at it and quickly converted it into confetti.

Fearing chuckled. "How well I remember when Gloria was a student here! I was thinking of it only last night when I saw her in *Moonbeams and Melody*. How she did upset this whole department! Heavens, my boy, if I'd been a younger man myself—"

"I'm going. You'll see about Herbrecht, Emily?"

Emily sniffled and nodded.

"Come, Wolfe." Fearing's voice had grown more serious. "I didn't mean to plague you. But you mustn't take these things too hard. There are better ways of finding consolation than in losing your temper or getting drunk."

"Who said anything about—"

"Did you need to say it? No, my boy, if you were to— You're not a religious man, are you?"

"Good God, no," said Wolf contradictorily.

"If only you were . . . If I might make a suggestion, Wolfe, why don't you come over to the temple tonight? We're having very special services. They might take your mind off Glo—off your troubles."

"Thanks, no. I've always meant to visit your temple— I've heard the damnedest rumors about it—but not tonight. Some other time."

"Tonight would be especially interesting."

"Why? What's so special of a feast day about April thirtieth?"

Fearing shook his gray head. "It is shocking how ignorant a scholar can be outside of his chosen field . . . But you know the place, Wolfe; I'll hope to see you there tonight."

"Thanks. But my troubles don't need any supernatural solutions. A couple of zombies will do nicely, and I do *not* mean serviceable stiffs. Goodbye, Oscar." He was halfway through the door before he added as an afterthought, "'Bye, Emily."

"Such rashness," Fearing murmured. "Such impetuosity. Youth is a wonderful thing to enjoy, is it not, Emily?"

Emily said nothing, but plunged into typing the proposed budget as though all the fiends of hell were after her, as indeed many of them were.

The sun was setting, and Wolf's tragic account of his troubles had laid an egg, too. The bartender had polished every glass in the joint and still the repetitive tale kept pouring forth. He was torn between a boredom new even in his experience and a professional admiration for a customer who could consume zombies indefinitely.

"Did I tell you about the time she flunked the midterm?" Wolf demanded truculently.

"Only three times," said the bartender.

"All right, then; I'll tell you. Yunnerstand, I don't do things like this. Profeshical ethons, that's what's I've got. But this was different. This wasn't like somebody that doesn't know just because she doesn't know; this was a girl that didn't know because she wasn't the kind of girl that has to know the kind of things a girl has to know if she's the kind of girl that ought to know that kind of things. Yunnerstand?"

The bartender cast a calculating glance at the plump little man who sat alone at the end of the deserted bar, carefully nursing his gin-and-tonic.

"She made me see that. She made me see lossa things and I can still see the things she made me see the things. It wasn't just like a professor falls for a coed, yunnerstand? This was different. This was wunnaful. This was like a whole new life, like."

The bartender sidled down to the end of the bar. "Brother," he whispered softly. The little man with the odd beard looked up from his gin-and-tonic. "Yes, colleague?"

"I listen to that potted professor another five minutes, I'm going to start smashing up the joint. How's about slipping down there and standing in for me, huh?"

The little man looked Wolf over and fixed his gaze especially on the hand that clenched the tall zombie glass. "Gladly, colleague." He nodded.

The bartender sighed a gust of relief.

"She was Youth," Wolf was saying intently to where the bartender had stood. "But it wasn't just that. This was different. She was Life and Excitement and Joy and Ecstasy and stuff. Yunner—" He broke off and stared at the empty space. "*Uh-mazing!*" he observed. "Right before my very eyes. *Uh-mazing!*"

"You were saying, colleague?" the plump little man prompted from the adjacent stool.

Wolf turned. "So there you are. Did I tell you about the time I went to her house to check her term paper?"

"No. But I have a feeling you will."

"Howja know? Well, this night—"

The little man drank slowly; but his glass was empty by the time Wolf had finished the account of an evening of pointlessly tentative flirtation. Other customers were drifting in, and the bar was now about a third full.

"—and ever since then—" Wolf broke off sharply. "That isn't you," he objected.

"I think it is, colleague."

"But you're a bartender and *you* aren't a bartender."

"No. I'm a magician."

"Oh. That explains it. Now, like I was telling you— Hey! Your bald is beard."

"I beg your pardon?"

"Your bald is beard. Just like your head. It's all jussa fringe running around."

"I like it that way."

"And your glass is empty."

"That's all right too."

"Oh, no it isn't. It isn't every night you get to drink with a man that proposed to Gloria Garton and got turned down. This is an occasion for celebration." Wolf thumped loudly on the bar and held up his first two fingers.

The little man regarded their equal length. "No," he

said softly. "I think I'd better not. I know my capacity. If I have another—well, things might start happening."

"Lettemappen!"

"No. Please, colleague. I'd rather—"

The bartender brought the drinks. "Go on, brother," he whispered. "Keep him quiet. I'll do you a favor sometime."

Reluctantly the little man sipped at his fresh gin-and-tonic.

The professor took a gulp of his nth zombie. "My name's Woof-woof," he proclaimed. "Lots of people call me Wolfe Wolf. They think that's funny. But it's really Woof-woof. Wazoors?"

The other paused a moment to decipher that Arabic-sounding word, then said, "Mine's Ozymandias the Great."

"That's a funny name."

"I told you, I'm a magician. Only I haven't worked for a long time. Theatrical managers are peculiar, colleague. They don't want a real magician. They won't even let me show 'em my best stuff. Why, I remember one night in Darjeeling—"

"Glad to meet you, Mr. . . . . Mr.—"

"You can call me Ozzy. Most people do."

"Glad to meet you, Ozzy. Now, about this girl. This Gloria. Yunnerstand, donya?"

"Sure, colleague."

"She thinks being a professor of German is nothing. She wants something glamorous. She says if I was an actor, now, or a G-man— Yunnerstand?"

Ozymandias the Great nodded.

"Awright, then! So yunnerstand. Fine. But whatd-dayou want to keep talking about it for? Yunnerstand. That's that. To hell with it."

Ozymandias's round and fringed face brightened. "Sure," he said, and added recklessly, "Let's drink to that."

They clinked glasses and drank. Wolf carelessly tossed off a toast in Old Low Frankish, with an unpardonable error in the use of the genitive.

The two men next to them began singing "My Wild Irish Rose," but trailed off disconsolately. "What we need," said the one with the derby, "is a tenor."

"What I need," Wolf muttered, "is a cigarette."

"Sure," said Ozymandias the Great. The bartender was drawing beer directly in front of them. Ozymandias reached across the bar, removed a lighted cigarette from the barkeep's ear, and handed it to his companion.

"Where'd that come from?"

"I don't quite know. All I know is how to get them. I told you I was a magician."

"Oh. I see. Pressajijijation."

"No. Not a prestidigitator; I said a magician. Oh, blast it! I've done it again. More than one gin-and-tonic and I start showing off."

"I don't believe you," said Wolf flatly. "No such thing as magicians. That's just as silly as Oscar Fearing and his temple and what's so special about April thirtieth anyway?"

The bearded man frowned. "Please, colleague. Let's forget it."

"No. I don't believe you. You pressajijijated that ciga-rette. You didn't magic it." His voice began to rise. "You're a fake."

"Please, brother," the barkeep whispered. "Keep him quiet."

"All right," said Ozymandias wearily. "I'll show you something that can't be prestidigitation." The couple adjoining had begun to sing again. "They need a tenor. All right; listen!"

And the sweetest, most ineffably Irish tenor ever heard joined in on the duet. The singers didn't worry about the source; they simply accepted the new voice gladly and were spurred on to their very best, with the result that the bar knew the finest harmony it had heard since the night the Glee Club was suspended en masse.

Wolf looked impressed, but shook his head. "That's not magic either. That's ventrocolism."

"As a matter of strict fact, that was a street singer who was killed in the Easter Rebellion. Fine fellow, too; never heard a better voice, unless it was that night in Darjeeling when—"

"Fake!" said Wolfe Wolf loudly and belligerently.

Ozymandias once more contemplated that long index finger. He looked at the professor's dark brows that met in a straight line over his nose. He picked his companion's limpish hand off the bar and scrutinized the palm. The growth of hair was not marked, but it was perceptible.

The magician chortled. "And you sneer at magic!"

"Whasso funny about me sneering at magic?"

Ozymandias lowered his voice. "Because, my fine furry friend, you are a werewolf."

The Irish martyr had begun "Rose of Tralee," and the two mortals were joining in valiantly.

"I'm what?"

"A werewolf."

"But there isn't any such thing. Any fool knows that."

"Fools," said Ozymandias, "know a great deal which the wise do not. There are werewolves. There always have been, and quite probably always will be." He spoke as calmly and assuredly as though he were mentioning that the earth was round. "And there are three infallible physical signs: the meeting of eyebrows, the long index finger, the hairy palms. You have all three. And even your name is an indication. Family names do not come from nowhere. Every Smith has an ancestor somewhere who was a smith. Every Fisher comes from a family that once fished. And your name is Wolf."

The statement was so quiet, so plausible, that Wolf faltered.

"But a werewolf is a man that changes into a wolf. I've never done that. Honest I haven't."

"A mammal," said Ozymandias, "is an animal that bears its young alive and suckles them. A virgin is nonetheless a mammal. Because you have never changed does not make you any the less a werewolf."

"But a werewolf—" Suddenly Wolf's eyes lit up. "A werewolf! But that's even better than a G-man! Now I can show Gloria!"

"What on earth do you mean, colleague?"

Wolf was climbing down from his stool. The intense excitement of this brilliant new idea seemed to have sobered him. He grabbed the little man by the sleeve. "Come on. We're going to find a nice quiet place. And you're going to prove you're a magician."

"But how?"

"You're going to show me how to change!"

Ozymandias finished his gin-and-tonic, and with it drowned his last regretful hesitation. "Colleague," he announced, "you're on!"

Professor Oscar Fearing, standing behind the curiously carved lectern of the Temple of the Dark Truth, concluded the reading of the prayer with mumbling sonority. "And on this night of all nights, in the name of the black light that glows in the darkness, we give thanks!" He closed the parchment-bound book and faced the small congregation, calling out with fierce intensity, "Who wishes to give his thanks to the Lower Lord?"

A cushioned dowager rose. "I give thanks!" she shrilled excitedly. "My Ming Choy was sick, even unto death. I took of her blood and offered it to the Lower Lord, and he had mercy and restored her to me!"

Behind the altar an electrician checked his switches and spat disgustedly. "Bugs! Every last one of 'em!"

The man who was struggling into a grotesque and horrible costume paused and shrugged. "They pay good money. What's it to us if they're bugs?"

A tall, thin old man had risen uncertainly to his feet. "I give thanks!" he cried. "I give thanks to the Lower Lord that I have finished my great work. My protective screen against magnetic bombs is a tried and proven success, to the glory of our country and science and the Lord."

"Crackpot," the electrician muttered.

The man in costume peered around the altar. "Crackpot, hell! That's Chiswick from the physics department. Think of a man like that falling for this stuff! And listen to him: he's even telling about the government's plans for installation. You know, I'll bet you one of these fifth columnists could pick up something around here."

There was silence in the temple when the congregation had finished its thanksgiving. Professor Fearing leaned over the lectern and spoke quietly and impressively. "As you know, brothers in Darkness, tonight is May Eve, the thirtieth of April, the night consecrated by the Church to that martyr missionary St. Walpurgis, and by us to other and deeper purposes. It is on this night, and this night only, that we may directly give our thanks to the Lower Lord himself. Not in wanton orgy and obscenity, as the Middle Ages misconceived his desires, but in praise and in the deep, dark joy that issues forth from Blackness."

"Hold your hats, boys," said the man in the costume. "Here I go again."

"*Eka!*" Fearing thundered. "*Dva tri chatur! Pancha! Shassapta! Ashta nava dasha ekadasha!*" He paused. There was always the danger that at this moment some scholar in this university town might recognize that the invocation, though perfect Sanskrit, consisted solely of the numbers from one to eleven. But no one stirred, and he launched forth in more apposite Latin: "*Per vota nostra ipse nunc surgat nobis dicatus Baal Zebub!*"

"Baal Zebub!" the congregation chorused.

"Cue," said the electrician, and pulled a switch.

The lights flickered and went out. Lightning played across the sanctuary. Suddenly out of the darkness came a sharp bark, a yelp of pain, and a long-drawn howl of triumph.

A blue light now began to glow dimly. In its faint reflection, the electrician was amazed to see his costumed friend at his side, nursing his bleeding hand.

"What the hell—" the electrician whispered.

"Hanged if I know. I go out there on cue, all ready to make my terrifying appearance, and what happens? Great big hell of a dog up and nips my hand. Why didn't they tell me they'd switched the script?"

In the glow of the blue light the congregation reverently contemplated the plump little man with the fringe of beard and the splendid gray wolf that stood beside him. "Hail, O Lower Lord!" resounded the chorus, drowning out one spinster's murmur of "But my *dear*, I swear he was *much* handsomer last year."

"Colleagues!" said Ozymandias the Great, and there was utter silence, a dread hush awaiting the momentous words of the Lower Lord. Ozymandias took one step forward, placed his tongue carefully between his lips, uttered the ripest, juiciest raspberry of his career, and vanished, wolf and all.

Wolfe Wolf opened his eyes and shut them again hastily. He had never expected the quiet and sedate Berkeley Inn to install centrifugal rooms. It wasn't fair. He lay in darkness, waiting for the whirling to stop and trying to reconstruct the past night.

He remembered the bar all right, and the zombies. And the bartender. Very sympathetic chap that, up until he suddenly changed into a little man with a fringe of beard. That was where things began getting strange. There was something about a cigarette and an Irish tenor and a werewolf. Fantastic idea, that. Any fool knows—

Wolf sat up suddenly. He *was* the werewolf. He threw back the bedclothes and stared down at his legs. Then he sighed relief. They were long legs. They were hairy enough. They were brown from much tennis. But they were indisputably human.

He got up, resolutely stifling his qualms, and began to pick up the clothing that was scattered nonchalantly about the floor. A crew of gnomes was excavating his skull, but he hoped they might go away if he didn't pay too much attention to them. One thing was certain: he was going to be good from now on. Gloria or no Gloria, heartbreak or no heartbreak, drowning your sorrows wasn't good enough. If you felt like this and could imagine you'd been a werewolf—

But why should he have imagined it in such detail? So many fragmentary memories seemed to come back as he dressed. Going up Strawberry Canyon with the fringed beard, finding a desolate and isolated spot for magic, learning the words—

Hell, he could even remember the words. The word that changed you and the one that changed you back.

Had he made up those words, too, in his drunken imaginings? And had he made up what he could only barely recall—the wonderful, magical freedom of changing, the single, sharp pang of alteration and then the boundless happiness of being lithe and fleet and free?

He surveyed himself in the mirror. Save for the unwonted wrinkles in his conservative single-breasted gray suit, he looked exactly what he was: a quiet academician; a little better built, a little more impulsive, a little more romantic than most, perhaps, but still just that—Professor Wolf.

The rest was nonsense. But there was, that impulsive side of him suggested, only one way of proving the fact. And that was to say The Word.

"All right," said Wolfe Wolf to his reflection. "I'll show you." And he said it.

The pang was sharper and stronger than he'd remembered.

Alcohol numbs you to pain. It tore him for a moment with an anguish like the descriptions of childbirth. Then it was gone, and he flexed his limbs in happy amazement. But he was not a lithe, fleet, free beast. He was a helplessly trapped wolf, irrevocably entangled in a conservative single-breasted gray suit.

He tried to rise and walk, but the long sleeves and legs tripped him over flat on his muzzle. He kicked with his paws, trying to tear his way out, and then stopped. Werewolf or no werewolf, he was likewise still Professor Wolf, and this suit had cost thirty-five dollars. There must be some cheaper way of securing freedom than tearing the suit to shreds.

He used several good, round Low German expletives. This was a complication that wasn't in any of the werewolf legends he'd ever read. There, people just—*boom!*—became wolves or—*bang!*—became men again. When they were men, they wore clothes; when they were wolves, they wore fur. Just like Hyperman becoming Bark Lent again on top of the Empire State Building and finding his street clothes right there. Most misleading. He began to remember now how Ozymandias the Great had made him strip before teaching him the words—

The words! That was it. All he had to do was say the word that changed you back—*Absarka!*—and he'd be a man again, comfortably fitted inside his suit. Then he could strip and play what games he wished. You see? Reason solves all. "*Absarka!*" he said.

Or thought he said. He went through all the proper mental processes for saying *Absarka!* but all that came out of his muzzle was a sort of clicking whine. And he was still a conservatively dressed and helpless wolf.

This was worse than the clothes problem. If he could be released only by saying *Absarka!* and if, being a wolf, he could say nothing, why, there he was. Indefinitely. He could go find Ozzy and ask—but how could a wolf wrapped up in a gray suit get safely out of a hotel and set out hunting for an unknown address?

He was trapped. He was lost. He was—"*Absarka!*"

Professor Wolfe Wolf stood up in his grievously rumpled gray suit and beamed on the beard-fringed face of Ozymandias the Great.

"You see, colleague," the little magician explained, "I figured you'd want to try it again as soon as you got up, and I knew darned well you'd have your troubles. Thought I'd come over and straighten things out for you."

Wolf lit a cigarette in silence and handed the pack to Ozymandias. "When you came in just now," he said at last, "what did you see?"

"You as a wolf."

"Then it really—I actually—"

"Sure. You're a full-fledged werewolf, all right."

Wolf sat down on the rumpled bed. "I guess," he ventured slowly, "I've got to believe it. And if I believe that—but it means I've got to believe everything I've always scorned. I've got to believe in gods and devils and hells and—"

"You needn't be so pluralistic. But there is a God." Ozymandias said this as calmly and convincingly as he had stated last night that there were werewolves.

"And if there's a God, then I've got a soul?"

"Sure."

"And if I'm a werewolf—hey!"

"What's the trouble, colleague?"

"All right, Ozzy. You know everything. Tell me this: Am I damned?"

"For what? Just for being a werewolf? Shucks, no; let me explain. There's two kinds of werewolves. There's the cursed kind that can't help themselves, that just go turning into wolves without any say in the matter; and there's the voluntary kind like you. Now, most of the voluntary kind are damned, sure, because they're wicked men who lust for blood and eat innocent people. But they aren't damnably wicked because they're werewolves; they became werewolves because they are damnably wicked. Now, you changed yourself just for the hell of it and because it looked like a good way to impress a gal; that's an innocent-enough motive, and being a werewolf doesn't make it any less so. Werewolves don't have to be monsters; it's just that we hear about only the ones that are."

"But how can I be voluntary when you told me I was a werewolf before I ever changed?"

"Not everybody can change. It's like being able to roll

your tongue or wiggle your ears. You can, or you can't; and that's that. And as with those abilities, there's probably a genetic factor involved, though nobody's done any serious research on it. You were a werewolf *in posse;* now you're one *in esse*."

"Then it's all right? I can be a werewolf just for having fun, and it's safe?"

"Absolutely."

Wolf chortled. "Will I show Gloria! Dull and unglamorous indeed! Anybody can marry an actor or a G-man; but a werewolf—"

"Your children probably will be, too," said Ozymandias cheerfully.

Wolf shut his eyes dreamily, then opened them with a start. "You know what?"

"What?"

"I haven't got a hangover anymore! This is marvelous. This is— Why, this is practical. At last the perfect hangover cure. Shuffle yourself into a wolf and back and— Oh, that reminds me. How do I get back?"

"Absarka."

"I know. But when I'm a wolf I can't say it."

"That," said Ozymandias sadly, "is the curse of being a white magician. You keep having to use the second-best form of spells, because the best would be black. Sure, a black-magic werebeast can turn himself back whenever he wants to. I remember in Darjeeling—"

"But how about me?"

"That's the trouble. You have to have somebody to say *Absarka!* for you. That's what I did last night, or do you remember? After we broke up the party at your friend's temple . . . tell you what. I'm retired now, and I've got enough to live on modestly because I can always magic up little . . . Are you going to take up werewolfing seriously?"

"For a while, anyway. Till I get Gloria."

"Then why shouldn't I come and live here in your hotel? Then I'll always be handy to *Absarka!* you. After you get the girl, you can teach her."

Wolf extended his hand. "Noble of you. Shake." And then his eye caught his wristwatch. "Good Lord! I've missed two classes this morning. Werewolfing's all very well, but a man's got to work for his living."

"Most men." Ozymandias calmly reached his hand into the air and plucked a coin. He looked at it ruefully. It was a gold moidore. "Hang these spirits; I simply cannot explain to them about gold being illegal."

From Los Angeles, Wolf thought, with the habitual contempt of the Northern Californian as he surveyed the careless sport coat and the bright-yellow shirt of his visitor.

This young man rose politely as the professor entered the office. His green eyes gleamed cordially and his red hair glowed in the spring sunlight. "Professor Wolf?" he asked.

Wolf glanced impatiently at his desk. "Yes."

"O'Breen's the name. I'd like to talk to you a minute."

"My office hours are from three to four Tuesdays and Thursdays. I'm afraid I'm rather busy now."

"This isn't faculty business. And it's important." The young man's attitude was affable and casual, but he managed nonetheless to convey a sense of urgency that piqued Wolf's curiosity. The all-important letter to Gloria had waited while he took two classes; it could wait another five minutes.

"Very well, Mr. O'Breen."

"And alone, if you please."

Wolf himself hadn't noticed that Emily was in the room. He now turned to the secretary and said, "All right. If you don't mind, Emily—"

Emily shrugged and went out.

"Now, sir. What is this important and secret business?"

"Just a question or two. To start with, how well do you know Gloria Garton?"

Wolf paused. You could hardly say, "Young man, I am about to repropose to her in view of my becoming a were-wolf." Instead he simply said—the truth, if not the whole truth—"She was a pupil of mine a few years ago."

"I said *do*, not *did*. How well do you know her now?"

"And why should I bother to answer such a question?"

The young man handed over a card. Wolf read:

FERGUS O'BREEN
PRIVATE INQUIRY AGENT
LICENSED BY THE STATE OF CALIFORNIA

Wolf smiled. "And what does this mean? Divorce evidence? Isn't that the usual field of private inquiry agents?"

"Miss Garton isn't married, as you probably know very well. I'm just asking if you've been in touch with her much lately."

"And I'm simply asking why you should want to know."

O'Breen rose and began to pace around the office. "We don't seem to be getting very far, do we? I'm to take it that you refuse to state the nature of your relations with Gloria Garton?"

"I see no reason why I should do otherwise." Wolf was beginning to be annoyed.

To his surprise, the detective relaxed into a broad grin. "Okay. Let it ride. Tell me about your department. How long have the various faculty members been here?"

"Instructors and all?"

"Just the professors."

"I've been here for seven years. All the others at least a good ten, probably more. If you want exact figures, you can probably get them from the dean, unless, as I hope"— Wolf smiled cordially—"he throws you out flat on your red pate."

O'Breen laughed. "Professor, I think we could get on. One more question, and you can do some pate-tossing yourself. Are you an American citizen?"

"Of course."

"And the rest of the department?"

"All of them. And now would you have the common decency to give me some explanation of this fantastic far-rago of questions?"

"No," said O'Breen casually. "Goodbye, professor." His alert green eyes had been roaming about the room, sharply noticing everything. Now, as he left, they rested on Wolf's long index finger, moved up to his heavy meeting eyebrows, and returned to the finger. There was a suspicion of a startled realization in those eyes as he left the office.

But that was nonsense, Wolf told himself. A private detective, no matter how shrewd his eyes, no matter how apparently meaningless his inquiries, would surely be the last man on earth to notice the signs of lycanthropy. Funny. "Werewolf" was a word you could accept. You could say, "I'm a werewolf," and it was all right. But say "I am a lycan-thrope" and your flesh crawled. Odd. Possibly material for a paper on the influence of etymology on connotation for one of the learned periodicals.

But, hell! Wolfe Wolf was no longer primarily a scholar.

He was a werewolf now, a white-magic werewolf, a werewolf-for-fun; and fun he was going to have. He lit his pipe, stared at the blank paper on his desk, and tried desperately to draft a letter to Gloria. It should hint at just enough to fascinate her and hold her interest until he could go south when the term ended and reveal to her the whole wonderful new truth. It—

Professor Oscar Fearing grunted his ponderous way into the office. "Good afternoon, Wolfe. Hard at it, my boy?"

"Afternoon," Wolf replied distractedly, and continued to stare at the paper.

"Great events coming, eh? Are you looking forward to seeing the glorious Gloria?"

Wolf started. "How—what do you mean?"

Fearing handed him a folded newspaper. "You hadn't heard?"

Wolf read with growing amazement and delight:

GLORIA GARTON TO ARRIVE FRIDAY
Local Girl Returns to Berkeley

As part of the most spectacular talent hunt since the search for Scarlett O'Hara, Gloria Garton, glamorous Metropolis starlet, will visit Berkeley Friday. Friday afternoon at the Campus Theater, Berkeley canines will have their chance to compete in the nationwide quest for a dog to play Tookah the wolf dog in the great Metropolis epic "Fangs of the Forest," and Gloria Garton herself will be present at the auditions.

"I owe so much to Berkeley," Miss Garton said. "It will mean so much to me to see the campus and the city again." Miss Garton has the starring human role in "Fangs of the Forest."

Miss Garton was a student at the University of California when she received her first chance in films. She is a member of Mask and Dagger, honorary dramatic society, and Rho Rho Rho sorority.

. . .

Wolfe Wolf glowed. This was perfect. No need now to wait till term was over. He could see Gloria now and claim her in all his wolfish vigor. Friday—today was Wednesday; that gave him two nights to practice and perfect the technique of werewolfry. And then—

He noticed the dejected look on the older professor's face, and a small remorse smote him. "How did things go last night, Oscar?" he asked sympathetically. "How were your big Walpurgis Night services?"

Fearing regarded him oddly. "You know that now? Yesterday April thirtieth meant nothing to you."

"I got curious and looked it up. But how did it go?"

"Well enough," Fearing lied feebly. "Do you know, Wolfe," he demanded after a moment's silence, "what is the real curse of every man interested in the occult?"

"No. What?"

"That true power is never enough. Enough for your-self, perhaps, but never enough for others. So that no matter what your true abilities, you must forge on beyond them into charlatanry to convince the others. Look at St. Germain. Look at Francis Stuart. Look at Cagliostro. But the worst tragedy is the next stage: when you realize that your powers were greater than you supposed and that the charlatanry was needless. When you realize that you have no notion of the extent of your powers. Then—"

"Then, Oscar?"

"Then, my boy, you are a badly frightened man."

Wolf wanted to say something consoling. He wanted to say, "Look, Oscar. It was just me. Go back to your half-hearted charlatanry and be happy." But he couldn't do that. Only Ozzy could know the truth of that splendid gray wolf. Only Ozzy and Gloria.

The moon was bright on that hidden spot in the canyon. The night was still. And Wolfe Wolf had a severe case of stage fright. Now that it came to the real thing—for this morning's clothes-complicated fiasco hardly counted and last night he could not truly remember—he was afraid to plunge cleanly into wolfdom and anxious to stall and talk as long as possible.

"Do you think," he asked the magician nervously, "that I could teach Gloria to change, too?"

Ozymandias pondered. "Maybe, colleague. It'd depend. She might have the natural ability, and she might not. And, of course, there's no telling what she might change into."

"You mean she wouldn't necessarily be a wolf?"

"Of course not. The people who can change, change into all sorts of things. And every folk knows best the kind that most interests it. We've got an English and Central European tradition, so we know mostly about werewolves. But take Scandinavia and you'll hear chiefly about were-bears, only they call 'em berserkers. And Orientals, now, they're apt to know about weretigers. Trouble is, we've thought so much about *werewolves* that that's all we know the signs for; I wouldn't know how to spot a weretiger just off-hand."

"Then there's no telling what might happen if I taught her The Word?"

"Not the least. Of course, there's some werethings that just aren't much use being. Take like being a wereant. You change and somebody steps on you and that's that. Or like a fella I knew once in Madagascar. Taught him The Word, and know what? Hanged if he wasn't a werediplodo-cus. Shattered the whole house into little pieces when he changed and damned near trampled me under hoof before I could say *Absarka!* He decided not to make a career of it. Or then there was that time in Darjeeling . . . but, look, colleague, are you going to stand around here naked all night?"

"No," said Wolf. "I'm going to change now. You'll take my clothes back to the hotel?"

"Sure. They'll be there for you. And I've put a very small spell on the night clerk, just enough for him not to notice wolves wandering in. Oh, and by the way—anything missing from your room?"

"Not that I noticed. Why?"

"Because I thought I saw somebody come out of it this afternoon. Couldn't be sure, but I think he came from there. Young fella with red hair and Hollywood clothes."

Wolfe Wolf frowned. That didn't make sense. Pointless questions from a detective were bad enough, but searching your hotel room . . . But what were detectives to a full-fledged werewolf? He grinned, nodded a friendly goodbye to Ozymandias the Great, and said The Word.

The pain wasn't so sharp as this morning, though still quite bad enough. But it passed almost at once, and his whole body filled with a sense of limitless freedom. He lifted his snout and sniffed deep at the keen freshness of this night air. A whole new realm of pleasure opened up for him through this acute new nose alone. He wagged his tail amicably at Ozzy and set off up the canyon on a long, easy lope.

For hours, loping was enough—simply and purely enjoying one's wolfness was the finest pleasure one could ask. Wolf left the canyon and turned up into the hills, past the Big C and on into noble wildness that seemed far remote from all campus civilization. His brave new legs were stanch and tireless, his wind seemingly inexhaustible. Every turning brought fresh and vivid scents of soil and leaves and air, and life was shimmering and beautiful.

But a few hours of this, and Wolf realized that he was damned lonely. All this grand exhilaration was very well, but if his mate Gloria were loping by his side . . . And what fun was it to be something as splendid as a wolf if no one admired you? He began to want people, and he turned back to the city.

Berkeley goes to bed early. The streets were deserted. Here and there a light burned in a rooming house where some solid grind was plodding on his almost-due term paper. Wolf had done that himself. He couldn't laugh in this shape, but his tail twitched with amusement at the thought.

He paused along the tree-lined street. There was a fresh human scent here, though the street seemed empty. Then he heard a soft whimpering, and trotted off toward the noise.

Behind the shrubbery fronting an apartment house sat a disconsolate two-year-old, shivering in his sunsuit and obviously lost for hours on hours. Wolf put a paw on the child's shoulder and shook him gently.

The boy looked around and was not in the least afraid. "He'o," he said, brightening up.

Wolf growled a cordial greeting, and wagged his tail and pawed at the ground to indicate that he'd take the lost infant wherever it wanted to go.

The child stood up and wiped away its tears with a dirty fist which left wide black smudges. "Tootootootoo!" he said.

Games, thought Wolf. He wants to play choo-choo. He took the child by the sleeve and tugged gently.

"Tootootootoo!" the boy repeated firmly. "Die way."

The sound of a railway whistle, to be sure, does die away; but this seemed a poetic expression for such a toddler, Wolf thought, and then abruptly would have snapped his fingers if he'd had them. The child was saying "2222 Dwight Way," having been carefully brought up to tell his address when lost. Wolf glanced up at the street sign.

Bowditch and Hillegas; 2222 Dwight would be just a couple of blocks.

Wolf tried to nod his head, but the muscles didn't seem to work that way. Instead he wagged his tail in what he hoped indicated comprehension, and started off leading the child.

The infant beamed and said, "Nice woof-woof."

For an instant Wolf felt like a spy suddenly addressed by his right name, then realized that if some say "bow-wow" others might well say "woof-woof."

He led the child for two blocks without event. It felt good, having an innocent human being like this. There was something about children; he hoped Gloria felt the same. He wondered what would happen if he could teach this confiding infant The Word. It would be swell to have a pup that would—

He paused. His nose twitched and the hair on the back of his neck rose. Ahead of them stood a dog: a huge mongrel, seemingly a mixture of St. Bernard and husky. But the growl that issued from his throat indicated that carrying brandy kegs or rushing serum was not for him. He was a bandit, an outlaw, an enemy of man and dog. And they had to pass him.

Wolf had no desire to fight. He was as big as this monster and certainly, with his human brain, much cleverer; but scars from a dogfight would not look well on the human body of Professor Wolf, and there was, moreover, the danger of hurting the toddler in the fracas. It would be

ANTHONY BOUCHER

wiser to cross the street. But before he could steer the child that way, the mongrel brute had charged at them, yapping and snarling.

Wolf placed himself in front of the boy, poised and ready to leap in defense. The scar problem was secondary to the fact that this baby had trusted him. He was ready to face this cur and teach him a lesson, at whatever cost to his own human body. But halfway to him the huge dog stopped. His growls died away to a piteous whimper. His great flanks trembled in the moonlight. His tail curled craven between his legs. And abruptly he turned and fled.

The child crowed delightedly. "Bad woof-woof go away." He put his little arms around Wolf's neck. "*Nice* woof-woof." Then he straightened up and said insistently, "Tootootootoo. Die way," and Wolf led on, his strong wolf's heart pounding as it had never pounded at the embrace of a woman.

"Tootootootoo" was a small frame house set back from the street in a large yard. The lights were still on, and even from the sidewalk Wolf could hear a woman's shrill voice.

"—since five o'clock this afternoon, and you've got to find him, Officer. You simply must. We've hunted all over the neighborhood and—"

Wolf stood up against the wall on his hind legs and rang the doorbell with his front right paw.

"Oh! Maybe that's somebody now. The neighbors said they'd— Come, Officer, and let's see— Oh!"

At the same moment Wolf barked politely, the toddler

yelled "Mamma!" and his thin and worn-looking young mother let out a scream—half delight at finding her child and half terror of this large gray canine shape that loomed behind him. She snatched up the infant protectively and turned to the large man in uniform. "Officer! Look! That big dreadful thing! It stole my Robby!"

"No," Robby protested firmly. "Nice woof-woof."

The officer laughed. "The lad's probably right, ma'am. It *is* a nice woof-woof. Found your boy wandering around and helped him home. You haven't maybe got a bone for him?"

"Let that big, nasty brute into my home? Never! Come on, Robby."

"Want my nice woof-woof."

"I'll woof-woof you, staying out till all hours and giving your father and me the fright of our lives. Just wait till your father sees you, young man; he'll— Oh, good night, Officer!"

And she shut the door on the yowls of Robby.

The policeman patted Wolf's head. "Never mind about the bone, Rover. She didn't so much as offer me a glass of beer, either. My, you're a husky specimen, aren't you, boy?

"Look almost like a wolf. Who do you belong to, and what are you doing wandering about alone? Huh?" He turned on his flash and bent over to look at the nonexistent collar.

He straightened up and whistled. "No license. Rover, that's bad. You know what I ought to do? I ought to turn you in. If you weren't a hero that just got cheated out of his bone, I'd— Hell, I ought to do it, anyway. Laws are laws, even for heroes. Come on, Rover. We're going for a walk."

Wolf thought quickly. The pound was the last place on earth he wanted to wind up. Even Ozzy would never think of looking for him there. Nobody'd claim him, nobody'd say *Absarka!* and in the end a dose of chloroform . . . He wrenched loose from the officer's grasp on his hair and with one prodigious leap cleared the yard, landed on the sidewalk, and started hell for leather up the street. But the instant he was out of the officer's sight he stopped dead and slipped behind a hedge.

He scented the policeman's approach even before he heard it. The man was running with the lumbering haste of two hundred pounds. But opposite the hedge, he too stopped. For a moment Wolf wondered if his ruse had failed; but the officer had paused only to scratch his head and mutter, "Say! There's something screwy here. *Who rang that doorbell?* The kid couldn't reach it, and the dog— Oh, well," he concluded. "Nuts," and seemed to find in that monosyllabic summation the solution to all his problems.

As his footsteps and smell died away, Wolf became aware of another scent. He had only just identified it as cat when someone said, "You're were, aren't you?"

Wolf started up, lips drawn back and muscles tense. There was nothing human in sight, but someone had spoken to him. Unthinkingly, he tried to say, "Where are you?" but all that came out was a growl.

"Right behind you. Here in the shadows. You can scent me, can't you?"

"But you're a cat," Wolf thought in his snarls. "And you're talking."

"Of course. But I'm not talking human language. It's just your brain that takes it that way. If you had your human body, you'd think I was just going *meowrr.* But you are were, aren't you?"

"How do you . . . why do you think so?"

"Because you didn't try to jump me, as any normal dog would have. And besides, unless Confucius taught me all wrong, you're a wolf, not a dog; and we don't have wolves around here unless they're were."

"How do you know all this? Are you—"

"Oh, no. I'm just a cat. But I used to live next door to a werechow named Confucius. He taught me things."

Wolf was amazed. "You mean he was a man who changed to chow and stayed that way? Lived as a pet?"

"Certainly. This was back at the worst of the depression. He said a dog was more apt to be fed and looked after than a man. I thought it was a smart idea."

"But how terrible! Could a man so debase himself as—"

"Men don't debase themselves. They debase each other. That's the way of most weres. Some change to keep from being debased, others to do a little more effective debasing. Which are you?"

"Why, you see, I—"

"*Sh!* Look. This is going to be fun. Holdup."

Wolf peered around the hedge. A well-dressed, middle-aged man was walking along briskly, apparently enjoying a night constitutional. Behind him moved a thin, silent figure. Even as Wolf watched, the figure caught up with him and whispered harshly, "Up with 'em, buddy!"

The quiet pomposity of the stroller melted away. He was ashen and aspen as the figure slipped a hand around into his breast pocket and removed an impressive wallet.

And what, thought Wolf, was the good of his fine, vigorous body if it merely crouched behind hedges as a spectator? In one fine bound, to the shocked amazement of the were-wise cat, he had crossed the hedge and landed with his forepaws full in the figure's face. It went over backward with him on top, and then there came a loud noise, a flash of light, and a frightful sharp smell. For a moment Wolf felt an acute pang in his shoulder, like the jab of a long needle, and then the pain was gone.

But his momentary recoil had been enough to let the figure get to its feet. "Missed you, huh?" it muttered. "Let's see how you like a slug in the belly, you interfering—" and he applied an epithet that would have been a purely literal description if Wolf had not been were.

There were three quick shots in succession even as Wolf sprang. For a second he experienced the most acute stomachache of his life. Then he landed again. The figure's head hit the concrete sidewalk and he was still.

Lights were leaping into brightness everywhere. Among all the confused noises, Wolf could hear the shrill complaints of Robby's mother, and among all the compounded smells, he could distinguish the scent of the policeman who had wanted to impound him. That meant getting the hell out, and quick.

The city meant trouble, Wolf decided as he loped off. He could endure loneliness while he practiced his wolfry, until he had Gloria. Though just as a precaution he must arrange with Ozzy about a plausible-looking collar, and—

The most astounding realization yet suddenly struck him! He had received four bullets, three of them square in the stomach, and he hadn't a wound to show for it! Being a werewolf certainly offered its practical advantages. Think of what a criminal could do with such bulletproofing. Or— but no. He was a werewolf for fun, and that was that.

But even for a werewolf, being shot, though relatively painless, is tiring. A great deal of nervous energy is absorbed in the magical and instantaneous knitting of those wounds. And when Wolfe Wolf reached the peace and calm of the uncivilized hills, he no longer felt like reveling in freedom. Instead he stretched out to his full length, nuzzled his head down between his forepaws and slept.

"Now the essence of magic," said Heliophagus of Smyrna, "is deceit; and that deceit is of two kinds. By magic, the magician deceives others; but magic deceives the magician himself."

So far the lycanthropic magic of Wolfe Wolf had worked smoothly and pleasantly, but now it was to show him the

ANTHONY BOUCHER

second trickery that lurks behind every magic trick. And the first step was that he slept.

He woke in confusion. His dreams had been human—and of Gloria—despite the body in which he dreamed them, and it took several full minutes for him to reconstruct just how he happened to be in that body. For a moment in the dream, even the episode in which he and Gloria had been eating blueberry waffles on a roller coaster seemed more sanely plausible than the reality.

But he readjusted quickly, and glanced up at the sky. The sun looked as though it had been up at least an hour, which meant in May that the time was somewhere between six and seven. Today was Thursday, which meant that he was saddled with an eight-o'clock class. That left plenty of time to change back, shave, dress, breakfast, and resume the normal life of Professor Wolf—which was, after all, important if he intended to support a wife.

He tried, as he trotted through the streets, to look as tame and unwolflike as possible, and apparently succeeded. No one paid him any mind save children, who wanted to play, and dogs, who began by snarling and ended by cowering away terrified. His friend the cat might be curiously tolerant of weres, but not so dogs.

He trotted up the steps of the Berkeley Inn confidently. The clerk was under a slight spell and would not notice wolves. There was nothing to do but rouse Ozzy, be *Absarka!'d,* and—

"Hey! Where are you going? Get out of here! Shoo!"

It was the clerk, a stanch and brawny young man, who straddled the stairway and vigorously waved him off.

"No dogs in here! Go on now. Scoot!"

Quite obviously this man was under no spell, and equally obviously there was no way of getting up that staircase short of using a wolf's strength to tear the clerk apart. For a second, Wolf hesitated. He had to get changed back. It would be a damnable pity to use his powers to injure another human being. If only he had not slept, and arrived before this unmagicked day clerk came on duty; but necessity knows no—

Then the solution hit him. Wolf turned and loped off just as the clerk hurled an ashtray at him. Bullets may be relatively painless, but even a werewolf's rump, he learned promptly, is sensitive to flying glass.

The solution was foolproof. The only trouble was that it meant an hour's wait, and he was hungry. Damnably hungry. He found himself even displaying a certain shocking interest in the plump occupant of a baby carriage. You do get different appetites with a different body. He could understand how some originally well-intentioned werewolves might in time become monsters. But he was stronger in will, and much smarter. His stomach could hold out until this plan worked.

The janitor had already opened the front door of Wheeler Hall, but the building was deserted. Wolf had no trouble reaching the second floor unnoticed or finding his class-room. He had a little more trouble holding the chalk between his teeth and a slight tendency to gag on the dust; but by balancing his forepaws on the eraser trough, he could manage quite nicely. It took three springs to catch the ring of the chart in his teeth, but once that was pulled down there was nothing to do but crouch under the desk and pray that he would not starve quite to death.

The students of German 31B, as they assembled reluc-tantly for their eight-o'clock, were a little puzzled at being confronted by a chart dealing with the influence of the gold standard on world economy, but they decided simply that the janitor had been forgetful.

The wolf under the desk listened unseen to their gath-ering murmurs, overheard that cute blonde in the front row make dates with three different men for that same night, and finally decided that enough had assembled to make his chances plausible. He slipped out from under the desk far enough to reach the ring of the chart, tugged at it, and let go.

The chart flew up with a rolling crash. The students broke off their chatter, looked up at the blackboard, and beheld in a huge and shaky scrawl the mysterious letters

ABSARKA

It worked. With enough people, it was an almost math-ematical certainty that one of them in his puzzlement—for the race of subtitle readers, though handicapped by the talkies, still exists—would read the mysterious word aloud. It was the much-bedated blonde who did it.

"*Absarka*," she said wonderingly.

And there was Professor Wolfe Wolf, beaming cordially at his class.

The only flaw was this: he had forgotten that he was only a werewolf, and not Hyperman. His clothes were still at the Berkeley Inn, and here on the lecture platform he was stark naked.

Two of his best pupils screamed and one fainted. The blonde only giggled appreciatively.

Emily was incredulous but pitying.

Professor Fearing was sympathetic but reserved.

The chairman of the department was cool.

The dean of letters was chilly.

The president of the university was frigid.

Wolfe Wolf was unemployed.

And Heliophagus of Smyrna was right. "The essence of magic is deceit."

"But what can I do?" Wolf moaned into his zombie glass. "I'm stuck. I'm stymied. Gloria arrives in Berkeley tomorrow, and here I am—nothing. Nothing but a futile, worthless werewolf. You can't support a wife on that. You can't raise a family. You can't— Hell, you can't even propose . . . I want another. Sure you won't have one?"

Ozymandias the Great shook his round, fringed head. "The last time I took two drinks I started all this. I've got to behave if I want to stop it. But you're an able-bodied, strapping young man; surely, colleague, you can get work?"

"Where? All I'm trained for is academic work, and this scandal has put the kibosh on that forever. What university is going to hire a man who showed up naked in front of his class without even the excuse of being drunk? And supposing I try something else—say one of these jobs in defense that all my students seem to be getting—I'd have to give references, say something about what I'd been doing with my thirty-odd years. And once these references were checked—Ozzy, I'm a lost man."

"Never despair, colleague. I've learned that magic gets you into some tight squeezes, but there's always a way of getting out. Now, take that time in Darjeeling—"

"But what can I do? I'll wind up like Confucius the werechow and live off charity, if you'll find me somebody who wants a pet wolf."

"You know," Ozymandias reflected, "you may have something there, colleague."

"Nuts! That was a joke. I can at least retain my self-respect, even if I go on relief doing it. And I'll bet they don't like naked men on relief, either."

"No. I don't mean just being a pet wolf. But look at it this way: What are your assets? You have only two outstanding abilities. One of them is to teach German, and that is now completely out."

"Check."

"And the other is to change yourself into a wolf. All right, colleague. There must be some commercial possibilities in that. Let's look into them."

"Nonsense."

"Not quite. For every kind of merchandise there's a market. The trick is to find it. And you, colleague, are going to be the first practical commercial werewolf on record."

"I could— They say Ripley's Odditorium pays good money. Supposing I changed six times a day regular for delighted audiences?"

Ozymandias shook his head sorrowfully. "It's no good. People don't want to see real magic. It makes 'em uncomfortable—starts 'em wondering what else might be loose in the world. They've got to feel sure it's all done with mirrors. I know. I had to quit vaudeville because I wasn't smart enough at faking it; all I could do was the real thing."

"I could be a Seeing Eye dog, maybe?"

"They have to be female."

"When I'm changed I can understand animal language. Maybe I could be a dog trainer and—No, that's out. I forgot: they're scared to death of me.''

But Ozymandias's pale blue eyes had lit up at the suggestion. "Colleague, you're warm. Oh, are you warm! Tell me: Why did you say your fabulous Gloria was coming to Berkeley?"

"Publicity for a talent hunt."

"For what?"

"A dog to star in *Fangs of the Forest.*"

"And what kind of a dog?"

"A—" Wolf's eyes widened and his jaw sagged. "A wolf dog," he said softly.

And the two men looked at each other with a wild surmise—silent, beside a bar in Berkeley.

"It's all the fault of that damned Disney dog," the trainer complained. "Pluto does anything. Everything. So our poor mutts are expected to do likewise. Listen to that dope! 'The dog should come into the room, give one paw to the baby, indicate that he recognizes the hero in his Eskimo disguise, go over to the table, find the bone, and clap his paws gleefully!' Now, who's got a set of signals to cover stuff like that? Pluto!" He snorted.

Gloria Garton said, "Oh." By that one sound she managed to convey that she sympathized deeply, that the trainer was a nice-looking young man whom she'd just as soon see again, and that no dog star was going to steal *Fangs of the Forest* from her. She adjusted her skirt slightly, leaned back, and made the plain wooden chair on the bare theater stage seem more than ever like a throne.

"All right." The man in the violet beret waved away the last unsuccessful applicant and read from a card: "'Dog: Wopsy. Owner: Mrs. Channing Galbraith. Trainer: Luther Newby.' Bring it in."

An assistant scurried offstage, and there was a sound of whines and whimpers as a door opened.

"What's got into those dogs today?" the man in the violet beret demanded. "They all seem scared to death and beyond."

"I think," said Fergus O'Breen, "that it's that big, gray wolf dog. Somehow, the others just don't like him."

Gloria Garton lowered her bepurpled lids and cast a queenly stare of suspicion on the young detective. There was nothing wrong with his being there. His sister was head of publicity for Metropolis, and he'd handled several confidential cases for the studio; even one for her, that time her chauffeur had decided to try his hand at blackmail. Fergus O'Breen was a Metropolis fixture; but still it bothered her.

The assistant brought in Mrs. Galbraith's Wopsy. The man in the violet beret took one look and screamed. The scream bounced back from every wall of the theater in the ensuing minute of silence. At last he found words. "A wolf dog! Tookah is the greatest role ever written for a wolf dog! And what do they bring us? A terrier, yet! So if we wanted a terrier we could cast Asta!"

"But if you'd only let us show you—" Wopsy's tall young trainer started to protest.

"Get out!" the man in the violet beret shrieked. "Get out before I lose my temper!"

Wopsy and her trainer slunk off.

"In El Paso," the casting director lamented, "they

bring me a Mexican hairless. In St. Louis it's a Pekinese yet! And if I do find a wolf dog, it sits in a corner and waits for somebody to bring it a sled to pull."

"Maybe," said Fergus, "you should try a real wolf."

"Wolf, *schmolf!* We'll end up wrapping John Barrymore in a wolfskin." He picked up the next card. "'Dog: Yoggoth. Owner and trainer: Mr. O. Z. Manders.' Bring it in."

The whining noise offstage ceased as Yoggoth was brought out to be tested. The man in the violet beret hardly glanced at the fringe-bearded owner and trainer. He had eyes only for that splendid gray wolf. "If you can only act . . ." he prayed, with the same fervor with which many a man has thought. "If you could only cook . . ."

He pulled the beret to an even more unlikely angle and snapped, "All right, Mr. Manders. The dog should come into the room, give one paw to the baby, indicate that he recognizes the hero in his Eskimo disguise, go over to the table, find the bone, and clap his paws joyfully. Baby here, hero here, table here. Got that?"

Mr. Manders looked at his wolf dog and repeated, "Got that?"

Yoggoth wagged his tail.

"Very well, colleague," said Mr. Manders. "Do it."

Yoggoth did it.

The violet beret sailed into the flies, on the wings of its owner's triumphal scream of joy. "He did it!" he kept burbling. "He did it!"

"Of course, colleague," said Mr. Manders calmly.

The trainer who hated Pluto had a face as blank as a vampire's mirror. Fergus O'Breen was speechless with wonderment. Even Gloria Garton permitted surprise and interest to cross her regal mask.

"You mean he can do anything?" gurgled the man who used to have a violet beret.

"Anything," said Mr. Manders.

"Can he— Let's see, in the dance-hall sequence . . . can he knock a man down, roll him over, and frisk his back pocket?"

Even before Mr. Manders could say, "Of course," Yoggoth had demonstrated, using Fergus O'Breen as a convenient dummy.

"Peace!" the casting director sighed. "Peace . . . Charley!" he yelled to his assistant. "Send 'em all away. No more tryouts. We've found Tookah! It's wonderful."

The trainer stepped up to Mr. Manders. "It's more than that, sir. It's positively superhuman. I'll swear I couldn't detect the slightest signal, and for such complicated operations, too. Tell me, Mr. Manders, what system do you use?"

Mr. Manders made a Hoople-ish *kaff-kaff* noise. "Professional secret, you understand, young man. I'm planning on opening a school when I retire, but obviously until then—"

"Of course, sir. I understand. But I've never seen anything like it in all my born days."

"I wonder," Fergus O'Breen observed abstractly from

the floor, "if your marvel dog can get off of people, too?"

Mr. Manders stifled a grin. "Of course! Yoggoth!"

Fergus picked himself up and dusted from his clothes the grime of the stage, which is the most clinging grime on earth. "I'd swear," he muttered, "that beast of yours enjoyed that."

"No hard feelings, I trust, Mr.—"

"O'Breen. None at all. In fact, I'd suggest a little celebration in honor of this great event. I know you can't buy a drink this near the campus, so I brought along a bottle just in case."

"Oh," said Gloria Garton, implying that carousals were ordinarily beneath her; that this, however, was a special occasion; and that possibly there was something to be said for the green-eyed detective after all.

This was all too easy, Wolfe Wolf-Yoggoth kept thinking. There was a catch to it somewhere. This was certainly the ideal solution to the problem of how to earn money as a werewolf. Bring an understanding of human speech and instructions into a fine animal body, and you are the answer to a director's prayer. It was perfect as long as it lasted; and if *Fangs of the Forest* was a smash hit, there were bound to be other Yoggoth pictures. Look at Rin-Tin-Tin. But it was too easy. . . .

His ears caught a familiar "Oh," and his attention reverted to Gloria. This "Oh" had meant that she really shouldn't have another drink, but since liquor didn't affect her anyway and this was a special occasion, she might as well.

She was even more beautiful than he had remembered. Her golden hair was shoulder-length now, and flowed with such rippling perfection that it was all he could do to keep from reaching out a paw to it. Her body had ripened, too; was even more warm and promising than his memories of her. And in his new shape he found her greatest charm in something he had not been able to appreciate fully as a human being: the deep, heady scent of her flesh.

"To *Fangs of the Forest*!" Fergus O'Breen was toasting. "And may that pretty-boy hero of yours get a worse mauling than I did."

Wolf-Yoggoth grinned to himself. That had been fun. That'd teach the detective to go crawling around hotel rooms.

"And while we're celebrating, colleagues," said Ozymandias the Great, "why should we neglect our star? Here, Yoggoth."

And he held out the bottle.

"He drinks, yet!" the casting director exclaimed delightedly.

"Sure. He was weaned on it."

Wolf took a sizable gulp. It felt good. Warm and rich—almost the way Gloria smelled.

"But how about you, Mr. Manders?" the detective insisted for the fifth time. "It's your celebration really. The

ANTHONY BOUCHER

poor beast won't get the four-figure checks from Metropolis. And you've taken only one drink."

"Never take two, colleague. I know my danger point. Two drinks in me and things start happening."

"More should happen yet than training miracle dogs? Go on, O'Breen. Make him drink. We should see what happens."

Fergus took another long drink himself. "Go on. There's another bottle in the car, and I've gone far enough to be resolved not to leave here sober. And I don't want sober companions, either." His green eyes were already beginning to glow with a new wildness.

"No, thank you, colleague."

Gloria Garton left her throne, walked over to the plump man, and stood close, her soft hand resting on his arm. "Oh," she said, implying that dogs were dogs, but still that the party was unquestionably in her honor and his refusal to drink was a personal insult.

Ozymandias the Great looked at Gloria, sighed, shrugged, resigned himself to fate, and drank.

"Have you trained many dogs?" the casting director asked.

"Sorry, colleague. This is my first."

"All the more wonderful! But what's your profession otherwise?"

"Well, you see, I'm a magician."

"Oh," said Gloria Garton, implying delight, and went so far as to add, "I have a friend who does black magic."

"I'm afraid, ma'am, mine's simply white. That's tricky enough. With the black you're in for some real dangers."

"Hold on!" Fergus interposed. "You mean really a magician? Not just presti . . . sleight of hand?"

"Of course, colleague."

"Good theater," said the casting director. "Never let 'em see the mirrors."

"Uh-huh," Fergus nodded. "But look, Mr. Manders. What can you do, for instance?"

"Well, I can change—"

Yoggoth barked loudly.

"Oh, no," Ozymandias covered hastily, "that's really a little beyond me. But I can—"

"Can you do the Indian rope trick?" Gloria asked languidly. "My friend says that's terribly hard."

"Hard? Why, ma'am, there's nothing to it. I can remember that time in Darjeeling—"

Fergus took another long drink. "I," he announced defiantly, "want to see the Indian rope trick. I have met people who've met people who've met people who've seen it, but that's as close as I ever get. And I don't believe it."

"But, colleague, it's so simple."

"I don't believe it."

Ozymandias the Great drew himself up to his full lack of height. "Colleague, you are about to see it!" Yoggoth tugged warningly at his coattails. "Leave me alone, Wolf. An aspersion has been cast!"

Fergus returned from the wings dragging a soiled

length of rope. "This do?"

"Admirably."

"What goes?" the casting director demanded.

"Shh!" said Gloria. "Oh—"

She beamed worshipfully on Ozymandias, whose chest swelled to the point of threatening the security of his buttons. "Ladies and gentlemen!" he announced, in the manner of one prepared to fill a vast amphitheater with his voice. "You are about to behold Ozymandias the Great in the Indian Rope Trick! Of course," he added conversationally, "I haven't got a small boy to chop into mincemeat, unless perhaps one of you— No? Well, we'll try it without. Not quite so impressive, though. And will you stop yapping, Wolf?"

"I thought his name was Yogi," said Fergus.

"Yoggoth. But since he's part wolf on his mother's side—Now, quiet, all of you!"

He had been coiling the rope as he spoke. Now he placed the coil in the center of the stage, where it lurked like a threatening rattler. He stood beside it and deftly, professionally, went through a series of passes and mumblings so rapidly that even the superhumanly sharp eyes and ears of Wolf-Yoggoth could not follow them.

The end of the rope detached itself from the coil, reared in the air, turned for a moment like a head uncertain where to strike, then shot straight up until all the rope was uncoiled. The lower end rested a good inch above the stage.

Gloria gasped. The casting director drank hurriedly. Fergus, for some reason, stared curiously at the wolf.

"And now, ladies and gentlemen—oh, hang it, I do wish I had a boy to carve—Ozymandias the Great will ascend this rope into that land which only the users of the rope may know. Onward and upward! Be right back," he added reassuringly to Wolf.

His plump hands grasped the rope above his head and gave a little jerk. His knees swung up and clasped about the hempen pillar. And up he went, like a monkey on a stick, up and up and up—until suddenly he was gone.

Just gone. That was all there was to it. Gloria was beyond even saying "Oh." The casting director sat his beautiful flannels down on the filthy floor and gaped. Fergus swore softly and melodiously. And Wolf felt a premonitory prickling in his spine.

The stage door opened, admitting two men in denim pants and work shirts. "Hey!" said the first. "Where do you think you are?"

"We're from Metropolis Pictures," the casting director started to explain, scrambling to his feet.

"I don't care if you're from Washington, we gotta clear this stage. There's movies here tonight. Come on, Joe, help me get 'em out. And that pooch, too."

"You can't, Fred," said Joe reverently, and pointed. His voice sank to an awed whisper. "That's Gloria Garton—"

"So it is. Hi, Miss Garton. Cripes, wasn't that last one of yours a stinkeroo!"

"Your public, darling," Fergus murmured.

"Come on!" Fred shouted. "Out of here. We gotta clean up. And you, Joe! Strike that rope!"

Before Fergus could move, before Wolf could leap to the rescue, the efficient stagehand had struck the rope and was coiling it up.

Wolf stared up into the flies. There was nothing up there. Nothing at all. Someplace beyond the end of that rope was the only man on earth he could trust to say *Absarka!* for him; and the way down was cut off forever.

Wolfe Wolf sprawled on the floor of Gloria Garton's boudoir and watched that vision of volupty change into her most fetching negligee.

The situation was perfect. It was the fulfillment of all his dearest dreams. The only flaw was that he was still in a wolf's body.

Gloria turned, leaned over, and chucked him under the snout. "Wuzzum a cute wolf dog, wuzzum?"

Wolf could not restrain a snarl.

"Doesn't um like Gloria to talk baby talk? Um was a naughty wolf, yes, um was."

It was torture. Here you are in your best-beloved's hotel room, all her beauty revealed to your hungry eyes, and she talks baby talk to you! Wolf had been happy at first when Gloria suggested that she might take over the care of her costar pending the reappearance of his trainer—for none of them was quite willing to admit that "Mr. O. Z.

Manders" might truly and definitely have vanished—but he was beginning to realize that the situation might bring on more torment than pleasure.

"Wolves are funny," Gloria observed. She was more talkative when alone, with no need to be cryptically fascinating. "I knew a Wolfe once, only that was his name. He was a man. And he was a funny one."

Wolf felt his heart beating fast under his gray fur. To hear his own name on Gloria's warm lips . . . but before she could go on to tell her pet how funny Wolfe was, her maid rapped on the door.

"A Mr. O'Breen to see you, madam."

"Tell him to go 'way."

"He says it's important, and he does look, madam, as though he might make trouble."

"Oh, all right." Gloria rose and wrapped her negligee more respectably about her. "Come on, Yog— No, that's a silly name. I'm going to call you Wolfie. That's cute. Come on, Wolfie, and protect me from the big, bad detective."

Fergus O'Breen was pacing the sitting room with a certain vicious deliberateness in his strides. He broke off and stood still as Gloria and the wolf entered.

"So?" he observed tersely. "Reinforcements?"

"Will I need them?" Gloria cooed.

"Look, light of my love life." The glint in the green eyes was cold and deadly. "You've been playing games, and whatever their nature, there's one thing they're not. And that's cricket."

Gloria gave him a languid smile. "You're amusing, Fergus."

"Thanks. I doubt, however, if your activities are."

"You're still a little boy playing cops and robbers. And what boogeyman are you after now?"

"Ha-ha," said Fergus politely. "And you know the answer to that question better than I do. That's why I'm here."

Wolf was puzzled. This conversation meant nothing to him. And yet he sensed a tension of danger in the air as clearly as though he could smell it.

"Go on," Gloria snapped impatiently. "And remember how dearly Metropolis Pictures will thank you for annoying one of its best box-office attractions."

"Some things, my sweeting, are more important than pictures, though you mightn't think it where you come from. One of them is a certain federation of forty-eight units. Another is an abstract concept called democracy."

"And so?"

"And so I want to ask you one question: Why did you come to Berkeley?"

"For publicity on *Fangs*, of course. It was your sister's idea."

"You've gone temperamental and turned down better ones. Why leap at this?"

"You don't haunt publicity stunts yourself, Fergus. Why are *you* here?"

Fergus was pacing again. "And why was your first act in

Berkeley a visit to the office of the German department?"

"Isn't that natural enough? I used to be a student here."

"Majoring in dramatics, and you didn't go near the Little Theater. Why the German department?" He paused and stood straight in front of her, fixing her with his green gaze.

Gloria assumed the attitude of a captured queen defying the barbarian conqueror. "Very well. If you must know—I went to the German department to see the man I love."

Wolf held his breath, and tried to keep his tail from thrashing.

"Yes," she went on impassionedly, "you strip the last veil from me, and force me to confess to you what he alone should have heard first. This man proposed to me by mail. I foolishly rejected his proposal. But I thought and thought—and at last I knew. When I came to Berkeley I had to see him—"

"And did you?"

"The little mouse of a secretary told me he wasn't there. But I shall see him yet. And when I do—"

Fergus bowed stiffly. "My congratulations to you both, my sweeting. And the name of this more than fortunate gentleman?"

"Professor Wolfe Wolf."

"Who is doubtless the individual referred to in this?" He whipped a piece of paper from his sport coat and thrust it at Gloria. She paled and was silent. But Wolfe Wolf did not wait for her to reply. He did not care. He knew the solution to his problem now, and he was streaking unobserved for her boudoir.

Gloria Garton entered the boudoir a minute later, a shaken and wretched woman. She unstoppered one of the delicate perfume bottles on her dresser and poured herself a stiff tot of whiskey. Then her eyebrows lifted in surprise as she stared at her mirror. Scrawlingly lettered across the glass in her own deep-crimson lipstick was the mysterious word

ABSARKA

Frowning, she said it aloud. "*Absarka—*"

From behind a screen stepped Professor Wolfe Wolf, incongruously wrapped in one of Gloria's lushest dressing robes.

"Gloria dearest—" he cried.

"Wolfe!" she exclaimed. "What on earth are you doing here in my room?"

"I love you. I've always loved you since you couldn't tell a strong from a weak verb. And now that I know that you love me—"

"This is terrible. Please get out of here!"

"Gloria—"

"Get out of here, or I'll sic my dog on you. Wolfie— Here, nice Wolfie!"

"I'm sorry, Gloria. But Wolfie won't answer you."

"Oh, you beast! Have you hurt Wolfie? Have you—"

"I wouldn't touch a hair on his pelt. Because, you see, Gloria darling, I am Wolfie."

"What on earth do you—" Gloria stared around the room. It was undeniable that there was no trace of the presence of a wolf dog. And here was a man dressed only in one of her robes and no sign of his own clothes. And after that funny little man and the rope . . .

"You thought I was drab and dull," Wolf went on. "You thought I'd sunk into an academic rut. You'd sooner have an actor or a G-man. But I, Gloria, am something more exciting than you've ever dreamed of. There's not another soul on earth I'd tell this to, but I, Gloria, am a werewolf."

Gloria gasped. "That isn't possible! But it does all fit in. What I heard about you on campus, and your friend with the funny beard and how he vanished, and, of course, it explains how you did tricks that any real dog couldn't possibly do—"

"Don't you believe me, darling?"

Gloria rose from the dresser chair and went into his arms. "I believe you, dear. And it's wonderful! I'll bet there's not another woman in all Hollywood that was ever married to a werewolf!"

"Then you will—"

"But of course, dear. We can work it out beautifully. We'll hire a stooge to be your trainer on the lot. You can work daytimes, and come home at night and I'll say that word for you. It'll be perfect."

"Gloria . . ." Wolf murmured with tender reverence.

"One thing, dear. Just a little thing. Would you do Gloria a favor?"

"Anything!"

"Show me how you change. Change for me now. Then I'll change you back right away."

Wolf said The Word. He was in such ecstatic bliss that he hardly felt the pang this time. He capered about the room with all the litheness of his fine wolfish legs, and ended up before Gloria, wagging his tail and looking for approval.

Gloria patted his head. "Good boy, Wolfie. And now, darling, you can just damned well stay that way."

Wolf let out a yelp of amazement.

"You heard me, Wolfie. You're staying that way. You didn't happen to believe any of that guff I was feeding the detective, did you? Love you? I should waste my time! But this way you can be very useful to me. With your trainer gone, I can take charge of you and pick up an extra thousand a week or so. I won't mind that. And Professor Wolfe Wolf will have vanished forever, which fits right in with my plans."

Wolf snarled.

"Now, don't try to get nasty, Wolfie darling. Um wouldn't threaten ums darling Gloria, would ums? Remember what I can do for you. I'm the only person that can turn you into a man again. You wouldn't dare teach anyone else that. You wouldn't dare let people know what you really are. An ignorant person would kill you. A smart one would have you locked up as a lunatic."

Wolf still advanced threateningly.

"Oh, no. You can't hurt me. Because all I'd have to do would be to say the word on the mirror. Then you wouldn't be a dangerous wolf anymore. You'd just be a man here in my room, and I'd scream. And after what happened on the campus yesterday, how long do you think you'd stay out of the madhouse?"

Wolf backed away and let his tail droop.

"You see, Wolfie darling? Gloria has ums just where she wants ums. And ums is damned well going to be a good boy."

There was a rap on the boudoir door, and Gloria called, "Come in."

"A gentleman to see you, madam," the maid announced. "A Professor Fearing."

Gloria smiled her best cruel and queenly smile. "Come along, Wolfie. This may interest you."

Professor Oscar Fearing, overflowing one of the graceful chairs of the sitting room, beamed benevolently as Gloria and the wolf entered. "Ah, my dear! A new pet. Touching."

"And what a pet, Oscar. Wait till you hear."

Professor Fearing buffed his pince-nez against his sleeve. "And wait, my dear, until you hear all that I have learned. Chiswick has perfected his protective screen against magnetic bombs, and the official trial is set for next week. And Farnsworth has all but completed his researches on a new process for obtaining osmium. Gas warfare may start any day, and the power that can command a plentiful supply of—"

"Fine, Oscar," Gloria broke in. "But we can go over all this later. We've got other worries right now."

"What do you mean, my dear?"

"Have you run onto a redheaded young Irishman in a yellow shirt?"

"No, I— Why, yes. I did see such an individual leaving the office yesterday. I believe he had been to see Wolfe."

"He's on to us. He's a detective from Los Angeles, and he's tracking us down. Someplace he got hold of a scrap of record that should have been destroyed. He knows I'm in it, and he knows I'm tied up with somebody here in the German department."

Professor Fearing scrutinized his pince-nez, approved of their cleanness, and set them on his nose. "Not so much excitement, my dear. No hysteria. Let us approach this calmly. Does he know about the Temple of the Dark Truth?"

"Not yet. Nor about you. He just knows it's somebody in the department."

"Then what could be simpler? You have heard of the strange conduct of Wolfe Wolf?"

"Have I!" Gloria laughed harshly.

"Everyone knows of Wolfe's infatuation with you.

Throw the blame onto him. It should be easy to clear yourself and make you appear an innocent tool. Direct all attention to him and the organization will be safe. The Temple of the Dark Truth can go its mystic way and extract even more invaluable information from weary scientists who need the emotional release of a false religion."

"That's what I've tried to do. I gave O'Breen a long song and dance about my devotion to Wolfe, so obviously phony he'd be bound to think it was a cover-up for something else. And I think he bit. But the situation's a damned sight trickier than you guess. Do you know where Wolfe Wolf is?"

"No one knows. After the president . . . ah . . . rebuked him, he seems to have vanished."

Gloria laughed again. "He's right here. In this room."

"My dear! Secret panels and such? You take your espionage too seriously. Where?"

"There!"

Professor Fearing gaped. "Are you serious?"

"As serious as you are about the future of Fascism. That is Wolfe Wolf."

Fearing approached the wolf incredulously and extended his hand.

"He might bite," Gloria warned him a second too late.

Fearing stared at his bleeding hand. "That, at least," he observed, "is undeniably true." And he raised his foot to deliver a sharp kick.

"No, Oscar! Don't! Leave him alone. And you'll have to take my word for it—it's way too complicated. But the wolf is Wolfe Wolf, and I've got him absolutely under control. He's perfectly in our hands. We'll switch suspicion to him, and I'll keep him this way while Fergus and his friends the G-men go off hotfoot on his trail."

"My dear!" Fearing ejaculated. "You're mad. You're more hopelessly mad than the devout members of the temple." He took off his pince-nez and stared again at the wolf. "And yet Tuesday night— Tell me one thing: From whom did you get this . . . this wolf dog?"

"From a funny plump little man with a fringy beard."

Fearing gasped. Obviously he remembered the furor in the temple, and the wolf and the fringe-beard. "Very well, my dear. I believe you. Don't ask me why, but I believe you. And now—"

"Now, it's all set, isn't it? We keep him here helpless, and we use him to—"

"The wolf as scapegoat. Yes. Very pretty."

"Oh! One thing—" She was suddenly frightened.

Wolfe Wolf was considering the possibilities of a sudden attack on Fearing. He could probably get out of the room before Gloria could say *Absarka!* But after that? Whom could he trust to restore him? Especially if G-men were to be set on his trail . . .

"What is it?" Fearing asked.

"That secretary. That little mouse in the department office. She knows it was you I asked for, not Wolf. Fergus can't have talked to her yet, because he swallowed my story; but he will. He's thorough."

"Hm-m-m. Then, in that case—"

"Yes, Oscar?"

"She must be attended to." Professor Oscar Fearing beamed genially and reached for the phone.

Wolf acted instantly, on inspiration and impulse. His teeth were strong, quite strong enough to jerk the phone cord from the wall. That took only a second, and in the next second he was out of the room and into the hall before Gloria could open her mouth to speak that word that would convert him from a powerful and dangerous wolf to a futile man.

There were shrill screams and a shout or two of "Mad dog!" as he dashed through the hotel lobby, but he paid no heed to them. The main thing was to reach Emily's house before she could be "attended to." Her evidence was essential. That could swing the balance, show Fergus and his G-men where the true guilt lay. And, besides, he admitted to himself, Emily was a damned nice kid. . . .

His rate of collision was about one point six six per block, and the curses heaped upon him, if theologically valid, would have been more than enough to damn him forever. But he was making time, and that was all that counted. He dashed through traffic signals, cut into the path of trucks, swerved from under streetcars, and once even leaped over a stalled car that was obstructing him. Everything was going fine, he was halfway there, when two hundred pounds of human flesh landed on him in a flying tackle.

He looked up through the brilliant lighting effects of smashing his head on the sidewalk and saw his old nemesis, the policeman who had been cheated of his beer.

"So, Rover!" said the officer. "Got you at last, did I? Now we'll see if you'll wear a proper license tag. Didn't know I used to play football, did you?"

The officer's grip on his hair was painfully tight. A gleeful crowd was gathering and heckling the policeman with fantastic advice.

"Get along, boys," he admonished. "This is a private matter between me and Rover here. Come on," and he tugged even harder.

Wolf left a large tuft of fur and skin in the officer's grasp and felt the blood ooze out of the bare patch on his neck. He heard a ripe oath and a pistol shot simultaneously, and felt the needlelike sting through his shoulder. The awestruck crowd thawed before him. Two more bullets hied after him, but he was gone, leaving the most dazed policeman in Berkeley.

"I hit him," the officer kept muttering blankly. "I hit the—"

Wolfe Wolf coursed along Dwight Way. Two more blocks and he'd be at the little bungalow that Emily shared with a teaching assistant in something or other. Ripping out that telephone had stopped Fearing only momentarily; the orders would have been given by now; the henchmen would be on their way. But he was almost there. . . .

"He'o!" a child's light voice called to him. "Nice woof-woof come back!"

Across the street was the modest frame dwelling of Robby and his shrewish mother. The child had been playing on the sidewalk. Now he saw his idol and deliverer and started across the street at a lurching toddle. "Nice woof-woof!" he kept calling. "Wait for Robby!"

Wolf kept on. This was no time for playing games with even the most delightful of cubs. And then he saw the car. It was an ancient jalopy, plastered with wisecracks even older than itself; and the high school youth driving was obviously showing his girlfriend how it could make time on this deserted residential street. The girl was a cute dish, and who could be bothered watching out for children?

Robby was directly in front of the car. Wolf leaped straight as a bullet. His trajectory carried him so close to the car that he could feel the heat of the radiator on his flank. His forepaws struck Robby and thrust him out of danger. They fell to the ground together, just as the car ground over the last of Wolf's caudel vertebrae.

The cute dish screamed. "Homer! Did we hit them?"

Homer said nothing, and the jalopy zoomed on.

Robby's screams were louder. "You hurt me!! You hurt me! *Baaaaad* woof-woof!"

His mother appeared on the porch and joined in with her own howls of rage. The cacophony was terrific. Wolf let out one wailing yelp of his own, to make it perfect and to lament his crushed tail, and dashed on. This was no time to clear up misunderstandings.

But the two delays had been enough. Robby and the policeman had proved the perfect unwitting tools of Oscar Fearing. As Wolf approached Emily's little bungalow, he saw a gray sedan drive off. In the rear was a small, slim girl, and she was struggling.

Even a werewolf's lithe speed cannot equal that of a motorcar. After a block of pursuit, Wolf gave up and sat back on his haunches panting. It felt funny, he thought even in that tense moment, not to be able to sweat, to have to open your mouth and stick out your tongue and . . .

"Trouble?" inquired a solicitous voice.

This time, Wolf recognized the cat. "Heavens, yes," he assented wholeheartedly. "More than you ever dreamed of."

"Food shortage?" the cat asked. "But that toddler back there is nice and plump."

"Shut up," Wolf snarled.

"Sorry; I was just judging from what Confucius told me about werewolves. You don't mean to tell me that you're an altruistic were?"

"I guess I am. I know werewolves are supposed to go around slaughtering, but right now I've got to save a life."

"You expect me to believe that?"

"It's the truth."

"Ah," the cat reflected philosophically. "Truth is a dark and deceitful thing."

Wolfe Wolf was on his feet. "Thanks," he barked. "You've done it."

"Done what?"

"See you later." And Wolf was off at top speed for the Temple of the Dark Truth.

That was the best chance. That was Fearing's headquarters. The odds were at least even that when it wasn't being used for services it was the hangout of his ring, especially since the consulate had been closed in San Francisco. Again the wild running and leaping, the narrow escapes; and where Wolf had not taken these too seriously before, he knew now that he might be immune to bullets, but certainly not to being run over. His tail still stung and ached tormentingly. But he had to get there. He had to clear his own reputation, he kept reminding himself; but what he really thought was, I have to save Emily.

A block from the temple he heard the crackle of gunfire. Pistol shots and, he'd swear, machine guns, too. He couldn't figure what it meant, but he pressed on. Then a bright-yellow roadster passed him and a vivid flash came from its window. Instinctively he ducked. You might be immune to bullets, but you still didn't just stand still for them.

The roadster was gone and he was about to follow when a glint of bright metal caught his eye. The bullet that had missed him had hit a brick wall and ricocheted back onto the sidewalk. It glittered there in front of him—pure silver!

This, he realized abruptly, meant the end of his

immunity. Fearing had believed Gloria's story, and with his smattering of occult lore he had known the successful counterweapon. A bullet, from now on, might mean no more needle sting, but instant death.

And so Wolfe Wolf went straight on.

He approached the temple cautiously, lurking behind shrubbery. And he was not the only lurker. Before the temple, crouching in the shelter of a car every window of which was shattered, were Fergus O'Breen and a moon-faced giant. Each held an automatic, and they were taking pot shots at the steeple.

Wolf's keen lupine hearing could catch their words even above the firing. "Gabe's around back," Moonface was explaining. "But it's no use. Know what that damned steeple is? It's a revolving machine-gun turret. They've been ready for something like this. Only two men in there, far as we can tell, but that turret covers all the approaches."

"Only two?" Fergus muttered.

"And the girl. They brought a girl here with them. If she's still alive."

Fergus took careful aim at the steeple, fired, and ducked back behind the car as a bullet missed him by milli-meters. "Missed him again! By all the kings that ever ruled Tara, Moon, there's got to be a way in there. How about tear gas?"

Moon snorted. "Think you can reach the firing gap in that armored turret at this angle?"

"That girl . . ." said Fergus.

Wolf waited no longer. As he sprang forward, the gunner noticed him and shifted his fire. It was like a needle
shower in which all the spray is solid steel. Wolf's nerves
ached with the pain of reknitting. But at least machine
guns apparently didn't fire silver.

The front door was locked, but the force of his drive
carried him through and added a throbbing ache in his
shoulder to his other comforts. The lower-floor guard, a
pasty-faced individual with a jutting Adam's apple, sprang
up, pistol in hand. Behind him, in the midst of the lit-
ter of the cult, ceremonial robes, incense burners, curious
books, even a Ouija board, lay Emily.

Pasty-face fired. The bullet struck Wolf full in the chest
and for an instant he expected death. But this, too, was
lead, and he jumped forward. It was not his usual powerful
leap. His strength was almost spent by now. He needed to
lie on cool earth and let his nerves knit. And this spring
was only enough to grapple with his foe, not to throw him.

The man reversed his useless automatic and brought
its butt thudding down on the beast's skull. Wolf reeled
back, lost his balance, and fell to the floor. For a moment
he could not rise. The temptation was so strong just to lie
there and . . .

The girl moved. Her bound hands grasped a corner of
the Ouija board. Somehow, she stumbled to her rope-tied
feet and raised her arms. Just as Pasty-face rushed for the
prostrate wolf, she brought the heavy board down.

Wolf was on his feet now. There was an instant of

temptation. His eyes fixed themselves to the jut of that Adam's apple, and his long tongue licked his jowls. Then he heard the machine-gun fire from the turret, and tore himself from Pasty-face's unconscious form.

Ladders are hard on a wolf, damned near impossible. But if you use your jaws to grasp the rung above you and pull up, it can be done. He was halfway up the ladder when the gunner heard him. The firing stopped, and Wolf heard a rich German oath in what he automatically recognized as an East Prussian dialect with possible Lithuanian influences. Then he saw the man himself, a broken-nosed blond, staring down the ladder well.

The other man's bullets had been lead. So this must be the one with the silver. But it was too late to turn back now. Wolf bit the next rung and hauled up as the bullet struck his snout and stung through. The blond's eyes widened as he fired again and Wolf climbed another rung. After the third shot he withdrew precipitately from the opening.

Shots still sounded from below, but the gunner did not return them. He stood frozen against the wall of the turret watching in horror as the wolf emerged from the well. Wolf halted and tried to get his breath. He was dead with fatigue and stress, but this man must be vanquished.

The blond raised his pistol, sighted carefully, and fired once more. He stood for one terrible instant, gazing at this deathless wolf and knowing from his grandmother's stories what it must be. Then deliberately he clamped his teeth on the muzzle of the automatic and fired again.

Wolf had not yet eaten in his wolf's body, but food must have been transferred from the human stomach to the lupine. There was at least enough for him to be extensively sick.

Getting down the ladder was impossible. He jumped. He had never heard anything about a wolf's landing on its feet, but it seemed to work. He dragged his weary and bruised body along to where Emily sat by the still unconscious Pasty-face, his discarded pistol in her hand. She wavered as the wolf approached her, as though uncertain yet as to whether he was friend or foe.

Time was short. With the machine gun silenced, Fergus and his companions would be invading the temple at any minute. Wolf hurriedly nosed about and found the planchette of the Ouija board. He pushed the heart-shaped bit of wood onto the board and began to shove it around with his paw.

Emily watched, intent and puzzled. "A," she said aloud. "B—S—"

Wolf finished the word and edged around so that he stood directly beside one of the ceremonial robes. "Are you trying to say something?" Emily frowned.

Wolf wagged his tail in vehement affirmation and began again.

"A—" Emily repeated. "B—S—A—R—"

He could already hear approaching footsteps.

"—K—A— What on earth does that mean? *Absarka—*"

Ex-professor Wolfe Wolf hastily wrapped his naked

human body in the cloak of the Dark Truth. Before either he or Emily knew quite what was happening, he had folded her in his arms, kissed her in a most thorough expression of gratitude, and fainted.

Even Wolf's human nose could tell, when he awakened, that he was in a hospital. His body was still limp and exhausted. The bare patch on his neck, where the policeman had pulled out the hair, still stung, and there was a lump where the butt of the automatic had connected. His tail, or where his tail had been, sent twinges through him if he moved. But the sheets were cool and he was at rest and Emily was safe.

"I don't know how you got in there, Mr. Wolf, or what you did; but I want you to know you've done your country a signal service." It was the moonfaced giant speaking.

Fergus O'Breen was sitting beside the bed too. "Congratulations, Wolf. And I don't know if the doctor would approve, but here."

Wolfe Wolf drank the whiskey gratefully and looked a question at the huge man.

"This is Moon Lafferty," said Fergus. "FBI man. He's been helping me track down this ring of spies ever since I first got wind of them."

"You got them—all?" Wolf asked.

"Picked up Fearing and Garton at the hotel," Lafferty rumbled.

"But how— I thought—"

"You thought we were out for you?" Fergus answered. "That was Garton's idea, but I didn't quite tumble. You see, I'd already talked to your secretary. I knew it was Fearing she'd wanted to see. And when I asked around about Fearing, and learned of the temple and the defense researches of some of its members, the whole picture cleared up."

"Wonderful work, Mr. Wolf," said Lafferty. "Any time we can do anything for you— And how you got into that machine-gun turret— Well, O'Breen, I'll see you later. Got to check up on the rest of this roundup. Pleasant convalescence to you, Wolf."

Fergus waited until the G-man had left the room. Then he leaned over the bed and asked confidentially, "How about it, Wolf? Going back to your acting career?"

Wolf gasped. "What acting career?"

"Still going to play Tookah? If Metropolis makes *Fangs* with Miss Garton in a federal prison."

Wolf fumbled for words. "What sort of nonsense—"

"Come on, Wolf. It's pretty clear I know that much. Might as well tell me the whole story."

Still dazed, Wolf told it. "But how in heaven's name did you know it?" he concluded.

Fergus grinned. "Look. Dorothy Sayers said someplace that in a detective story the supernatural may be introduced only to be dispelled. Sure, that's swell. Only in real life there come times when it won't be dispelled. And this was one. There was too damned much. There were your eyebrows and fingers, there were the obviously real magical powers of your friend, there were the tricks which no dog could possibly do without signals, there was the way the other dogs whimpered and cringed—I'm pretty hardheaded, Wolf, but I'm Irish. I'll string along only so far with the materialistic, but too much coincidence is too much."

"Fearing believed it too," Wolf reflected. "But one thing that worries me: if they used a silver bullet on me once, why were all the rest of them lead? Why was I safe from then on?"

"Well," said Fergus, "I'll tell you. Because it wasn't 'they' who fired the silver bullet. You see, Wolf, up till the last minute I thought you were on 'their' side. I somehow didn't associate good will with a werewolf. So I got a mold from a gunsmith and paid a visit to a jeweler and—I'm damned glad I missed," he added sincerely.

"*You're* glad!"

"But look. Previous question stands. Are you going back to acting? Because if not, I've got a suggestion."

"Which is?"

"You say you fretted about how to be a practical, commercial werewolf. All right. You're strong and fast. You can terrify people even to commit suicide. You can overhear conversations that no human being could get in on. You're invulnerable to bullets. Can you tell me better qualifications for a G-man?"

Wolf goggled. "Me? A G-man?"

"Moon's been telling me how badly they need new men. They've changed the qualifications lately so that your language knowledge'll do instead of the law or accounting they used to require. And after what you did today, there won't be any trouble about a little academic scandal in your past. Moon's pretty sold on you."

Wolf was speechless. Only three days ago he had been in torment because he was not an actor or a G-man. Now—

"Think it over," said Fergus.

"I will. Indeed I will. Oh, and one other thing. Has there been any trace of Ozzy?"

"Nary a sign."

"I like that man. I've got to try to find him and—"

"If he's the magician I think he is, he's staying up there only because he's decided he likes it."

"I don't know. Magic's tricky. Heavens knows I've learned that. I'm going to try to do my damnedest for that fringe-bearded old colleague."

"Wish you luck. Shall I send in your other guest?"

"Who's that?"

"Your secretary. Here on business, no doubt."

Fergus disappeared discreetly as he admitted Emily. She walked over to the bed and took Wolf's hand. His eyes drank in her quiet, charming simplicity, and his mind wondered what freak of belated adolescence had made him succumb to the blatant glamour of Gloria.

They were silent for a long time. Then at once they both said, "How can I thank you? You saved my life."

Wolf laughed. "Let's not argue. Let's say we saved our life."

"You mean that?" Emily asked gravely.

Wolf pressed her hand. "Aren't you tired of being an office wife?"

In the bazaar of Darjeeling, Chulundra Lingasuta stared at his rope in numb amazement. Young Ali had climbed up only five minutes ago, but now as he descended he was a hundred pounds heavier and wore a curious fringe of beard.

14

NALO HOPKINSON is a Caribbean writer of horror, myth, magic, and science fiction, and is equally as good at whatever she chooses to write. Here's a contemporary story that feels like an old myth.

Gilla swallowed a cherry pit, and now her mouth is full of startling words she'd never normally speak. In the old stories of the saints, trees take root through flesh, but in this one, a gift from a tree transforms into teeth.

THE
SMILE
ON THE
FACE

By

Nalo Hopkinson

"There was a young lady..."

"Geez, who gives a hoot what a . . . what? What is a laidly worm, anyway?" Gilla muttered. She was curled up on the couch, school library book on her knees.

"Mm?" said her mother, peering at the computer monitor. She made a noise of impatience and hit a key on the keyboard a few times.

"Nothing, Mum. Just I don't know what this book's talking about." Boring old school assignment. Gilla wanted to go and get ready for Patricia's party, but Mum had said she should finish her reading first.

"Did you say, 'laidly worm'?" her mother asked. Her fingers were clicking away at the keyboard again now. Gilla wished she could type that quickly. But that would mean practising, and she wasn't about to do any more of that than she had to.

"Yeah."

"It's a type of dragon."

"So why don't they just call it that?"

"It's a special type. It doesn't have wings, so it just crawls along the ground. Its skin oozes all the time. Guess that protects it when it crawls, like a slug's slime."

"Yuck, Mum!"

Gilla's mother smiled, even as she was writing. "Well, you wanted to know."

"No, I didn't. I just have to know, for school."

"A laidly worm's always ravenous and it makes a noise like a cow in gastric distress."

Gilla giggled. Her mother stopped typing and finally looked at her. "You know, I guess you could think of it as a larval dragon. Maybe it eats and eats so it'll have enough energy to moult into the flying kind. What a cool idea. I'll have to look into it." She turned back to her work. "Why do you have to know about it? What're you reading?"

"This lady in the story? Some guy wanted to marry her, but she didn't like him, so he put her in his dungeon . . ."

". . . and came after her one night in the form of a laidly worm to eat her," Gilla's mother finished. "You're learning about Margaret of Antioch?"

Gilla boggled at her. "Saint Margaret, yeah. How'd you know?"

"How?" Her mother swivelled the rickety steno chair round to face Gilla and grinned, brushing a tangle of dreadlocks back from her face. "Sweetie, this is your mother, remember? The professor of African and Middle Eastern studies?"

"Oh." And her point? Gilla could tell that her face had that "huh?" look. Mum probably could see it too, 'cause she said:

"Gilla, Antioch was in ancient Turkey. In the Middle East?"

"Oh yeah, right. Mum, can I get micro-braids?"

Now it was her mum looking like, huh? "What in the world are those, Gilla?"

Well, at least she was interested. It wasn't a "no" straight off the bat. "These tiny braid extensions, right? Maybe only four or five strands per braid. And they're straight, not like . . . Anyway, Kashy says that the hairdressing salon across from school does them. They braid the extensions right into your own hair, any colour you want, as long as you want them to be, and they can style them just like that. Kashy says it only takes a few hours, and you can wear them in for six weeks."

Her mum came over, put her warm palms gently on either side of Gilla's face and looked seriously into her eyes. Gilla hated when she did that, like she was still a little kid. "You want to tame your hair," her mother said. Self-consciously, Gilla pulled away from her mum's hands, smoothed back the cloudy mass that she'd tied out of the way with a bandanna so that she could do her homework without getting hair in her eyes, in her mouth, up her nose. Her mum continued, "You want hair that lies down and plays dead, and you want to pay a lot of money for it, and you want to do it every six weeks."

Gilla pulled her face away. The book slid off her knee to the floor. "Mum, why do you always have to make every-thing sound so horrible?" Some of her hair had slipped out of the bandanna; it always did. Gilla could see three or four black sprigs of it dancing at the edge of her vision, tickling her forehead. She untied the bandanna and furiously retied it, capturing as much of the bushy mess as she could and binding it tightly with the cloth.

Her mother just shook her head at her. "Gilla, stop being such a drama queen. How much do micro-braids cost?"

Gilla was ashamed to tell her now, but she named a figure, a few bucks less than the sign in the salon window had said. Her mother just raised one eyebrow at her.

"That, my girl, is three months of your allowance."

Well, yeah. She'd been hoping that Mum and Dad would pay for the braids. Guess not.

"Tell you what, Gilla; you save up for it, then you can have them."

Gilla grinned.

"But," her mother continued, "you have to continue buying your bus tickets while you're saving."

Gilla stopped grinning.

"Don't look so glum. If you make your own lunch to take every day, it shouldn't be so bad. Now, finish reading the rest of the story."

And Mum was back at her computer again, tap-tap-tap. Gilla pouted at her back but didn't say anything, 'cause really, she was kind of pleased. She was going to get micro-braids! She hated soggy, made-the-night-before sandwiches, but it'd be worth it. She ignored the little voice in her mind that was saying, "every six weeks?" and went back to her reading.

"Euw, gross."

"Now what?" her mother asked.

"This guy? This, like, laidly worm guy thing? It *eats* Saint Margaret, and then she's in his stomach; like, *inside* him! and she prays to Jesus, and she's sooo holy that the wooden cross around her neck turns back into a tree, and it puts its roots into the ground *through* the dragon guy thing, and its branches bust him open and he dies, and out she comes!"

"Presto bingo," her mum laughs. "Instant patron saint of childbirth!"

"Why?" But Gilla thought about that one a little bit, and she figured she might know why. "Never mind, don't tell me. So they made her a saint because she killed the dragon guy thing?"

"Well yes, they sainted her eventually, after a bunch of people tortured and executed her for refusing to marry that man. She was a convert to Christianity, and she said she'd refused him because he wasn't a Christian. But Gilla, some people think that she wasn't a Christian anymore either, at least not by the end."

"Huh?" Gilla wondered when Kashy would show up. It was almost time for the party to start.

"That thing about the wooden cross turning back into a living tree? That's not a very Christian symbol, that sprouting tree. A dead tree made into the shape of a cross, yes. But not a living, magical tree. That's a pagan symbol.

Maybe Margaret of Antioch was the one who commanded the piece of wood around her neck to sprout again. Maybe the story is telling us that when Christianity failed her, she claimed her power as a wood witch. Darling, I think that Margaret of Antioch was a hamadryad."

"Jeez, Mum; a cobra?" That much they had learned in school. Gilla knew the word *hamadryad*.

Her mother laughed. "Yeah, a king cobra is a type of hamadryad, but I'm talking about the original meaning. A hamadryad was a female spirit whose soul resided in a tree. A druid is a man, a tree wizard. A hamadryad is a woman; a tree witch, I guess you could say. But where druids lived outside of trees and learned everything they could about them, a hamadryad doesn't need a class to learn about it. She just *is* a tree."

Creepy. Gilla glanced out the window to where black branches beckoned, clothed obscenely in tiny spring leaves. She didn't want to talk about trees.

The doorbell rang. "Oh," said Gilla. "That must be Kashy!" She sprang up to get the door, throwing her textbook aside again.

There was a young lady of Niger...

"It kind of creaks sometimes, y'know?" Gilla enquired of Kashy's reflection in the mirror.

In response, Kashy just tugged harder at Gilla's hair. "Hold still, girl. Lemme see what I can do with this. And shut up with that weirdness. You're always going on about that tree. Creeps me out."

Gilla sighed, resigned, and leaned back in the chair. "Okay. Only don't pull it too tight, okay? Gives me a head-ache." When Kashy had a makeover jones on her, there was nothing to do but submit and hope you could wash the goop off your face and unstick your hair from the mousse before you had to go outdoors and risk scaring the pigeons. That last experiment of Kashy's with the "natural" lipstick had been such a disaster. Gilla had been left looking as though she'd been eating fried chicken and had forgotten to wash the grease off her mouth. It had been months ago, but Foster was still giggling over it.

Gilla crossed her arms. Then she checked out the mir-ror and saw how that looked, how it made her breasts puff out. She remembered Roger in the schoolyard, pointing at her the first day back at school in September and bel-lowing, "Boobies!" She put her arms on the rests of the chair instead. She sucked her stomach in and took a quick glance in the mirror to see if that made her look slimmer. Fat chance. Really fat. It did make her breasts jut again, though; oh, goody. She couldn't win. She sighed once more and slumped a little in the chair, smushing both bust and belly into a lumpy mass.

"And straighten up, okay?" Kashy said. "I can't reach the front of your head with you sitting hunched over like that." Kashy's hands were busy, sectioning Gilla's thick black hair into four and twisting each section into plaits.

"That tree," Gilla replied. "The one in the front yard."

Kashy just rolled her perfectly made-up eyes. "Okay, so tell me again about that wormy old cherry tree."

"I don't like it. I'm trying to sleep at night, and all I can hear is it creaking and groaning and . . . *talking* to itself all night!"

"Talking!" Kashy giggled. "So now it's talking to you?"

"Yes. Swaying. Its branches rubbing against each other. Muttering and whispering at me, night after night. I hate that tree. I've always hated it. I wish Mum or Dad would cut it down." Gilla sighed. Since she'd started ninth grade two years ago, Gilla sighed a lot. That's when her body, already sprouting with puberty, had laid down fat pads on her chest, belly and thighs. When her high, round butt had gotten rounder. When her budding breasts had swelled even bigger than her mother's. And when she'd started hearing the tree at night.

"What's it say?" Kashy asked. Her angular brown face stared curiously at Gilla in the mirror.

Gilla looked at Kashy, how she had every hair in place, how her shoulders were slim and how the contours of the tight sweater showed off her friend's tiny, pointy breasts. Gilla and Kashy used to be able to wear each other's clothes, until two years ago.

"Don't make fun of me, Kashy."

"I'm not." Kashy's voice was serious; the look on her face, too. "I know it's been bothering you. What do you hear the tree saying?"

"It . . . it talks about the itchy places it can't reach, where its bark has gone knotty. It talks about the taste of soil, all gritty and brown. It says it likes the feeling of worms sliding in and amongst its roots in the wet, dark earth."

"Gah! You're making this up, Gilla!"

"I'm not!" Gilla stormed out of her chair, pulling her hair out of Kashy's hands. "If you're not going to believe me, then don't ask, okay?"

"Okay, okay, I believe you!" Kashy shrugged her shoulders, threw her palms skyward in a gesture of defeat. "Slimy old worms feel good, just"—she reached out and slid her hands briskly up and down Gilla's bare arms—"rubbing up against you!" And she laughed, that perfect Kashy laugh, like tiny, friendly bells.

Gilla found herself laughing too. "Well, that's what it says!"

"All right, girl. What else does it say?"

At first Gilla didn't answer. She was too busy shaking her hair free of the plaits, puffing it up with her hands into a kinky black cloud. "I'm just going to wear it like this to the party, okay? I'll tie it back with my bandanna and let it poof out behind me. That's the easiest thing." *I'm never going to look like you, Kashy. Not anymore.* In the upper grades at school, everybody who hung out together looked alike. The skinny glam girls hung with the skinny glam girls. The goth guys and girls hung out in back of the school and shared clove cigarettes and black lipstick. The fat girls clumped together. How long would Kashy stay tight with her? Turning so she couldn't see her own plump, gravid body in the mirror, she dared to look at her friend. Kashy was biting her bottom lip, looking contrite.

"I'm sorry," she said. "I shouldn't have laughed at you."

"It's okay." Gilla took a cotton ball from off the dresser, doused it in cold cream, started scraping the makeup off her face. She figured she'd keep the eyeliner on. At least she had pretty eyes, big and brown and sparkly. She muttered at Kashy, "It says it likes stretching and growing, reaching for the light."

Who went for a ride...

"Bye, Mum!" Gilla and Kashy surged out the front door. Gilla closed it behind her, then, standing on her doorstep with her friend, took a deep breath and turned to face the cherry tree. Half its branches were dead. The remaining twisted ones made a mockery of the tree's spring finery of new green leaves. It crouched on the front lawn, gnarling at them. It stood between them and the curb, and the walkway was super long. They'd have to walk under the tree's grasping branches the whole way.

The sun was slowly diving down the sky, casting a soft orange light on everything. Daylean, Dad called it; that time between the two worlds of day and night when anything could happen. Usually Gilla liked this time of day best. Today she scowled at the cherry tree and told Kashy, "Mum says women used to live in the trees."

"What, like, in tree houses? Your mum says the weird-est things, Gilla."

"No. They used to be the spirits of the trees. When the trees died, so did they."

"Well, this one's almost dead, and it can't get you. And you're going to have to walk past it to reach the street, and I know you want to go to that party, so take my hand and come on."

Gilla held tight to her friend's firm, confident hand. She could feel the clammy dampness of her own palm. "Okay," Kashy said, "on three, we're gonna run all the way to the curb, all right? One, two, three!"

And they were off, screeching and giggling, Gilla doing her best to stay upright in her new wedgies, the first thing even close to high heels that her parents had ever let her wear. Gilla risked a glance sideways. Kashy looked grace-ful and coltish. Her breasts didn't bounce. Gilla put on her broadest smile, screeched extra loud to let the world know how much fun she was having, and galumphed her way to streetside. As she and Kashy drew level with the tree, she felt the tiniest "bonk" on her head. She couldn't brush whatever it was off right away, 'cause she needed her hands to keep her balance. Laughing desperately from all this funfunfun, she ran. They made it safely to the curb. Kashy bent, panting, to catch her breath. For all that she looked so trim, she had no wind at all. Gilla swam twice a week and was on the volleyball team, and that little run had barely even given her a glow. She started searching with her hands for whatever had fallen in her hair.

It was smooth, roundish. It had a stem. She pulled it out and looked at it. A perfect cherry. So soon? She could have sworn that the tree hadn't even blossomed yet. "Hah!" she yelled at the witchy old tree. She brandished the cherry at it. "A peace offering? So you admit defeat, huh?" In elation at having gotten past the tree, she forgot who in the story had been eater and who eaten. "Well, you can't eat me, cause I'm gonna eat YOU!" And she popped the cherry into her mouth, bursting its sweet roundness between her teeth. The first cherry of the season. It tasted wonderful, until a hearty slap on her shoulder made her gulp.

"Hey, girl," Foster's voice said. "You look great! You too, of course, Kashy."

Gilla didn't answer. She put horrified hands to her mouth. Foster, big old goofy Foster with his twinkly eyes and his too-baggy sweatshirt, gently took the shoulder that he'd slapped so carelessly seconds before. "You okay, Gilla?"

Kashy looked on in concern.

Gilla swallowed. Found her voice. "Damn it, Foster! You made me swallow it!"

Seeing that she was all right, Foster grinned his silly grin. "And you know what Roger says about girls who swallow!"

"No, man; you made me swallow the cherry pit!" Oh, God; what was going to happen now?

"Ooh, scary," Foster said. "It's gonna grow into a tree

inside you, and then you'll be sooorry!" He made cartoon monster fingers in Gilla's face and mugged at her. Kashy burst out laughing. Gilla too. Lightly, she slapped Foster's hands away. Yeah, it was only an old tree.

"C'mon," she said. "Let's go to this party already."

They went and grabbed their bikes out of her parents' garage. It was a challenge riding in those wedge heels, but at least she was wearing pants, unlike Kashy, who seemed to have perfected how to ride in a tight skirt with her knees decently together, as she perfected everything to do with her appearance. Gilla did her best to look dignified without dumping the bike.

"I can't wait to start driving lessons," Kashy complained. "I'm getting all sweaty. I'm going to have to do my makeup all over again when I get to Patricia's place." She perched on her bike like a princess in her carriage, and neither Gilla nor Foster could persuade her to move any faster than a crawl. Gilla swore that if Kashy could, she would have ridden sidesaddle in her little skirt.

All the way there, Foster, Gilla and Kashy argued over what type of cobra a hamadryad was. Gilla was sure she remembered one thing; hamadryads had inflatable hoods just below their heads. She tried to ignore how the ride was making the back of her neck sticky. The underside of the triangular mass of her hair was glued uncomfortably to her skin.

Who went for a ride on a tiger...

．　．　．

They could hear music coming from Patricia's house. The three of them locked their bikes to the fence and headed inside. Gilla surreptitiously tugged the hem of her blouse down over her hips. But Kashy'd known her too long. Her eyes followed the movement of Gilla's hands, and she sighed. "I wish I had a butt like yours," Kashy said.

"What? You crazy?"

"Naw, man. Look how nice your pants fit you. Mine always sag in the behind."

Foster chuckled. "Yeah, sometimes I wish I had a butt like Gilla's too."

Gilla looked at him, baffled. Beneath those baggy pants Foster always wore, he had a fine behind; strong and shapely. She'd seen him in swim trunks.

Foster made grabbing motions at the air. "Wish I had it right here, warm and solid in between these two hands."

Kashy hooted. Gilla reached up and swatted Foster on the back of the head. He ducked, grinning. All three of them were laughing as they stepped into the house.

After the coolness of the spring air outside, the first step into the warmth and artificial lighting of Patricia's place was a shock. "Hey there, folks," said Patricia's dad. "Welcome. Let me just take your jackets, and you head right on in to the living room."

"Jeez," Gilla muttered to Foster once they'd handed off their jackets. "The 'rents aren't going to hang around, are they? That'd be such a total drag."

In the living room were some of their friends from school, lounging on the chairs and the floor, laughing and talking and drinking bright red punch out of plastic glasses. Everybody was on their best behaviour, since Patricia's parents were still around. Boring. Gilla elbowed Foster once they were out of Mr. Bright's earshot. "Try not to be too obvious about ogling Tanya, okay? She's been making goo-goo eyes at you all term."

He put a hand to his chest, looked mock innocent. "Who, me?" He gave a wave of his hand and went off to say hi to some of his buddies.

Patricia's mother was serving around mini patties on a tray. She wore stretch pants that made her big butt look bigger than ever when she bent over to offer the tray, and even through her heavy sweatshirt Gilla could make out where her large breasts didn't quite fit into her bra but exploded up over the top of it. Oh, hell. Gilla'd forgotten to check how she looked in her new blouse. She'd have to get to the bathroom soon. Betcha a bunch of the other girls were already lined up outside it, waiting to fix their hair, their makeup, readjust their pantyhose, renew their "natural" lipstick.

Patricia, looking awkward but sweet in a little flowered dress, grinned at them and beckoned them over. Gilla smoothed her hair back, sucked her gut in, and started to head over towards her, picking her way carefully in her wedgies.

She nearly toppled as a hand grabbed her ankle. "Hey,

big girl. Mind where you put that foot. Wouldn't want you to step on my leg and break it."

Gilla felt her face heat with embarrassment. She yanked her leg out of Roger's grip and lost her balance. Kashy had to steady her. Roger chuckled. "Getting a little top-heavy there, Gilla?" he said. His buddies Karl and Haygood, lounging near him, snickered.

Karl was obviously trying to look up Kashy's skirt. Kashy smoothed it down over her thighs, glared at him and led the way to where Patricia was sitting. "Come on, girl," she whispered to Gilla. "The best thing is to ignore them."

Cannot ignore them all your days. Gilla smiled her too-bright smile, hugged Patricia and kissed her cheek. "Mum and Dad are going soon," Patricia whispered at them. "They promised me."

"They'd better," Kashy said.

"God, I know," Patricia groaned. "They'd better not embarrass me like this too much longer." She went to greet some new arrivals.

Gilla perched on the couch with Kashy, trying to find a position that didn't make her tummy bulge, trying to keep her mind on the small talk. Where was Foster? Oh, in the corner. Tanya was sitting way close to him, tugging at her necklace and smiling deeply into his eyes. Foster had his "I'm such a stud" smile on.

Mr. Bright came in with a tray of drinks. He pecked his chubby wife on the lips as she went by. He turned and contemplated her when her back was to him. He was smiling when he turned back. The smile lingered happily on his face long after the kiss was over.

Are you any less than she? Well, she certainly was, thank heaven. With any luck, it'd be a few years before she was as round as Mrs. Bright. And what was this "less than she" business, anyway? Who talked like that? Gilla took a glass of punch from Mr. Bright's tray and sucked it down, trying to pay attention to Jahanara and Kashy talking about whether 14-karat gold was better for necklaces than 18-karat.

"Mum," said Patricia from over by the door. "Dad?"

Her mother laughed nervously. "Yes, we're going, we're going. You have the phone number at the Hamptons' house?"

"Yesss, Mum," Patricia hissed. "See you later, okay?" She grabbed their coats from the hallway closet, all but bustled them out the door.

"We'll be back by two A.M.!" her dad yelled over his shoulder. Everyone sat still until they heard that lovely noise, the sound of the car starting up and driving off down the street.

Foster got up, took the CD out of the stereo player. Thank God. Any more of that kiddie pop, and Gilla'd thought she'd probably barf. Foster grinned around to everyone, produced another CD from his chest pocket and put it into the CD player. A jungle mix started up. People cheered and started dancing. Patricia turned out all the lights but the one in the hallway.

And now Gilla needed to pee. Which meant she had to pass the clot of people stuck all over Roger again. Well, she really needed to check on that blouse, anyway. She'd just make sure she was far from Roger's grasping hands. She stood, tugged at the hem of her blouse so it was covering her bum again. *Reach those shoulders tall too, strong one. Stretch now.* When had she started talking to herself like that? But it was good advice. She fluffed up her hair, drew herself up straight and walked with as much dignity as she could in the direction of the bathroom.

Roger and Gilla had been the first in their class to hit puberty. Roger's voice had deepened into a raspy bass, and his shoulders, chest and arms had broadened with muscle. He'd shot up about a foot in the past few months, it seemed. He sauntered rather than walked and he always seemed to be braying an opinion on everything, the more insulting the better. Gilla flicked a glance at him. In one huge hand he had a paper napkin which he'd piled with three patties, two huge slices of black rum cake and a couple of slices of ham. He was pushing the food into his mouth as he brayed some boasty something at his buddies. He seemed barely aware of his own chewing and swallowing. Probably took a lot of feeding to keep that growing body going. He was handsome, though. Had a broad baby face with nice full lips and the beginnings of a goatee. People were willing to hang with him just in hopes that he would pay attention to them, so why did he need to spend his time making Gilla's life miserable?

Oops. Shouldn't even have thought it, 'cause now he'd noticed her noticing. He caught and held her gaze, and still looking at her, leaned over and murmured something at the knot of people gathered around him. The group burst out laughing. "No, really?" said Clarissa in a high, witchy voice. Gilla put her head down and surged out of the room, not stopping until she was up the stairs to the second floor and inside the bathroom. She stayed in there for as long as she dared.

When she came out, Clarissa was in the second-floor hallway. Gilla said, "Bathroom's free now."

"Did you really let them do that to you?"

"Huh?" In confusion, Gilla met Clarissa's eyes. Clarissa's cheeks were flushed and she had a bright, knowing look on her face.

"Roger told us. How you let him suck on your . . ." Clarissa bit on her bottom lip. Her cheeks got even pinker. "Then you let Haygood do it too. Don't you, like, feel like a total slut now?"

"But I didn't . . ."

"Oh, come on, Gilla. We all saw how you were looking at Roger."

Liar! Can such a liar live? The thought hissed through Gilla, strong as someone whispering in her ear.

"You know," Clarissa said, "you're even kinda pretty. If you just lost some weight, you wouldn't have to throw yourself at all those guys like that."

Gilla felt her face go hot. Her mouth filled with saliva.

She was suddenly very aware of little things: the bite of her bra into her skin, where it was trying to contain her fat, swingy breasts; the hard, lumpy memory of the cherry pit slipping down her throat; the bristly triangular hedge of her hair, bobbing at the base of her neck and swelling to cover her ears. Her mouth fell open, but no words came out.

"He doesn't even really like you, you know." Clarissa smirked at her and sauntered past her into the bathroom.

She couldn't, she mustn't still be there when Clarissa got out of the bathroom. In the awkward wedge heels, she clattered her way down the stairs like an elephant, her mind a jumble. Once in the downstairs hallway, she didn't head back towards the happy, warm sound of laughter and music in the living room, but shoved her way out the front door.

It was even darker out there, despite the porch light being on. Foster was out on the porch, leaning against the railing and whispering with someone. Tanya, shivering in the short sundress she was wearing, was staring wide-eyed at Foster and hanging on every word. "And then," Foster said, gesturing with his long arms, "I grabbed the ball from him, and I . . ." He turned, saw Gilla. "Hey girl, what's up?"

Tanya looked at her like she was the insurance salesman who'd interrupted her dinner.

"I, Foster," stammered Gilla. "What's *calumny* mean?"

"Huh?" He pushed himself upright, looking concerned. "'Scuse me, Tanya, okay?"

"All right," Tanya said sulkily. She went inside.

Gilla stood in the cold, shivering. *That liar! He has no right!*

Foster asked again, "What's up?"

"Calumny. What's it mean?" she repeated.

"I dunno. Why?"

"I think it means a lie, a really bad one." *He and his toadies. If you find a nest of vipers, should you not root it out?* "It just came to me, you know?" Her thoughts were whipping and thrashing in the storm in her head. *We never gave them our favor!*

Foster came and put a hand on her shoulder, looked into her eyes. "Gilla, who's telling lies? You gonna tell me what's going on?"

The warmth of her friend's palm through the cloth of her blouse brought her back to herself. "Damn, it's cold out here!"

Something funny happened to Foster's face. He hesitated, then opened his arms to her. "Here," he said.

Blinking with surprise, Gilla stepped into the hug. She stopped shivering. They stood there for a few seconds, Gilla wondering what, what? Should she put her arms around him too? Were they still just friends? Was he just warming her up because she was cold? Did he like her? Well of course he liked her, he hung out with her and Kashy during lunch period at school almost every day. Lots of the guys gave him the gears for that. But did he like her like *that*? Did she want him to? *By your own choice, never by another's.* What was she supposed to do now? And what was with all these weird things she seemed to be thinking all of a sudden?

"Um, Gilla?"

"Yeah?"

"Could you get off my foot now?"

The laughter that bubbled from her tasted like cherries in the back of her throat. She stepped off poor Foster's abused toes, leaned her head into his shoulder, giggling. "Oh, Foster. Why didn't you just say I was hurting you?"

Foster was giggling too, his voice high with embarrassment. "I didn't know what to say, or what was the right thing to do, or what."

"You and me both."

"I haven't held too many girls like that before. I mean, only when I'm sure they want me to."

Now Gilla backed up so she could look at him better. "Really? What about Tanya?"

He looked sheepish, and kind of sullen. "Yeah, I bet she'd like that. She's nice, you know? Only . . ."

"Only what?" Gilla sat on the rail beside Foster.

"She just kinda sits there, like a sponge. I talk and I talk, and she just soaks it all up. She doesn't say anything interesting back, she doesn't tell me about anything she does, she just wants me to entertain her. Saniya was like that too, and Kristen," he said, naming a couple of his short-lived school romances. "I like girls, you know? A lot. I just want one with a brain in her head. You and

Kashy got more going on than that, right? More fun hanging with you guys."

"So?" said Gilla, wondering what she was going to say.
"So what?"

"So what about Kashy?" She stumbled over her friend's
name, because what she was really thinking was, *What about
me?* Did she even like Foster like that?

"Oh, look," drawled a way too familiar voice. "It's the
faggot and the fat girl."

Roger, Karl and Haygood had just come lumbering
out of the house. Haygood snickered. Gilla froze.

"Oh, give it up, Roger," Foster drawled back. He
lounged against the railing again. "It's so freaking tired.
Every time you don't know what to say—which, my friend,
is often—you call somebody 'faggot.'"

Haygood and Karl, their grins uncertain, glanced
from Roger to Foster and back again. Foster got an evil
smile, put a considering finger to his chin. "You ever hear
of the pot calling the kettle black?"

At that, Karl and Haygood started to howl with laughter. Roger growled. That was the only way to describe the
sound coming out of his mouth. Karl and Foster touched
their fists together. "Good one, man. Good one," Karl
said. Foster grinned at him.

But Roger elbowed past Karl and stood chest to chest
with Foster, his arms crossed in front of him, almost like
he was afraid to let his body touch Foster's. Roger glared
at Foster, who stayed lounging calmly on the railing with a

smirk on his face, looking Roger straight in the face. "And you know both our mothers ugly like duppy too, so you can't come at me with that one either. You know that's true, man; you know it."

Before he had even finished speaking, Haygood and Karl had cracked up laughing. Then, to Gilla's amazement, Roger's lips started to twitch. He grinned, slapped Foster on the back, shook his hand. "A'ight man, a'ight," said Roger. "You got me." Foster grinned, mock-punched Roger on the shoulder.

"We're going out back for a smoke," Haygood said. "You coming, Foster?"

"Yeah man, yeah. Gilla, catch you later, okay?" The four of them slouched off together, Roger trailing a little. Just before they rounded the corner of the house, Roger looked back at Gilla. He pursed his lips together and smooched at her silently. Then they were gone. Gilla stood there, hugging herself, cold again.

She crept back inside. The lights were all off, except for a couple of candles over by the stereo. Someone had moved the dinner table with the food on it over there too, to clear the floor. A knot of people were dancing right in the centre of the living room. There was Clarissa, with Jim. Clarissa was jigging about, trying to look cool. Bet she didn't even know she wasn't on the beat. "Rock on," Gilla whispered.

The television was on, the sound inaudible over the music. A few people huddled on the floor around it, watching a skinny blonde chick drop-kick bad guys. The blue light from the TV flickered over their faces like cold flame.

On the couches all around the room, couples were necking. Gilla tried to make out Kashy's form, but it was too dark to really see if she was there. Gilla scouted the room out until she spied an empty lone chair. She went and perched on it, bobbed her head to the music and tapped her foot, pretending to have a good time.

She sighed. Sometimes she hated parties. She wanted to go and get a slice of that black rum cake. It was her favourite. But people would see her eating. She slouched protectively over her belly and stared across the room at the television. The programme had changed. Now it was an old-time movie or something, with guys and girls on a beach. Their bathing suits were in this ancient style, and the girls' hair, my God. One of them wore hers in this weird puffy 'do. To Gilla's eye, she looked a little chunky, too. How had she gotten a part in this movie? The actors started dancing on the beach, this bizarre kind of shimmy thing. The people watching the television started pointing and laughing. Gilla heard Hussain's voice say, "No, don't change the channel! That's Frankie Avalon and Annette Funicello!" Yeah, Hussain would know crap like that.

"Gilla, move your butt over! Make some room!" It was Kashy, shoving her hips onto the same chair that Gilla was on. Gilla giggled and shifted over for her. They each cotched on the chair, not quite fitting. "Guess what?" Kashy said. "Remi just asked me out!"

Remi was *fine*; he was just Kashy's height when she was in heels, lean and broad-shouldered with big brown eyes, strong hands, and those smooth East-African looks. The knot that had been in Gilla's throat all night got harder. She swallowed around it and made her mouth smile. But she never got to mumble insincere congratulations to her friend, because just then . . .

They came back . . .

Roger strode in with his posse, all laughing so loudly that Gilla could hear them over the music. Foster shot Gilla a grin that made her toes feel all warm. Kashy looked at her funny, a slight smile on her face. Roger went and stood smirking at the television. On the screen, the chunky chick and the funny-looking guy in the old-fashioned bathing suits and haircuts were playing Postman in a phone booth with their friends. Postman! Stupid kid game.

They came back . . .
They came back from the ride . . .

Gilla wondered how she'd gotten herself into this. Roger had grabbed Clarissa, hugged her tight to him, announced that he wanted to play Postman, and in two twos Clarissa and Roger's servile friends had put the lights on and herded everybody into an old-fashioned game of Postman. Girls in the living room, guys stationed in closets all over the house, and Clarissa and Hussain playing . . .

"Postman!" yelled Hussain. "I've got a message for Kashy!" He was enjoying the hell out of this. That was a neat plan Hussain had come up with to avoid kissing any girls. Gilla had a hunch that females weren't his type.

"It's Remi!" Kashy whispered. She sprang to her feet. "I bet it's Remi!" She glowed at Gilla, and followed Hussain off to find her "message" in some closet or bathroom somewhere and neck with him.

Left sitting hunched over on the hard chair, Gilla glared at their departing backs. She thought about how Roger's friends fell over themselves to do anything he said, and tried to figure out where she'd learned the word "servile." The voice no longer seemed like a different voice in her head now, just her own. But it knew words she didn't know, things she'd never experienced, like how it felt to unfurl your leaves to the bright taste of the sun, and the empty screaming space in the air as a sister died, her bark and pith chopped through to make ships or firewood.

"That's some craziness," she muttered to herself.

"Postman!" chirped Clarissa. Her eyes sparkled and her colour was high. Yeah, bet she'd been off lipping at some "messages" of her own. *Lipping.* Now there was another weird word. "Postman for Gilla!" said Clarissa.

Gilla's heart started to thunk like an axe chopping through wood. She stood. "What . . . ?"

Clarissa smirked at her. "Postman for you, hot stuff. You coming, or not?" And then she was off up the stairs and into the depths of Mr. and Mrs. Bright's house.

Who could it be? Who wanted to kiss her? Gilla felt tiny dots of clammy sweat spring out under her eyes. Maybe Remi? No, no. He liked Kashy. Maybe, please, maybe Foster?

Clarissa was leading her on a winding route. They passed a hallway closet. Muffled chuckles and thumps came from inside. "No, wait," murmured a male voice. "Let *me* take it off." Then they went by the bathroom. The giggles that wriggled out from under the bathroom door came from two female voices.

"There is no time so sap-sweet as the spring bacchanalia," Gilla heard herself saying.

Clarissa just kept walking. "You are *so* weird," she said over her shoulder.

They passed a closed bedroom door. Then came to another bedroom. Its door was closed, too, but Clarissa just slammed it open. "Postman!" she yelled.

The wriggling on the bed resolved itself into Patricia Bright and Haygood, entwined. Gilla didn't know where to look. At least their clothes were still on, sort of. Patricia looked up from under Haygood's armpit with a self-satisfied smile. "Jeez, I'm having an intimate birthday moment here."

"Sorry," said Clarissa, sounding not the least bit sorry, "but Gilla's got a date." She pointed towards the closet door. "Have a gooood time, killa Gilla," Clarissa told her. Haygood snickered.

Gilla felt cold. "In there?" she asked Clarissa.

"Yup," Clarissa chirruped. "Your special treat." She turned on her heel and headed out the bedroom door, yelling, "Who needs the Postman?"

"You gonna be okay, Gilla?" Patricia asked. She looked concerned.

"Yeah, I'll be fine. Who's in there?"

Patricia smiled. "That's half the fun, silly: not knowing."

Haygood just leered at her. Gilla made a face at him.

"Go on and enjoy yourself, Gilla," Patricia said. "If you need help, you can always let us know, okay?"

"Okay." Gilla was rooted where she stood. Patricia and Haygood were kissing again, ignoring her.

She could go back into the living room. She didn't have to do this. But . . . who? Remembering the warm cloak of Foster's arms around her, heavy as a carpet of fall leaves, Gilla found herself walking towards the closet. She pulled the door open, tried to peer in. A hand reached out and yanked her inside.

With the lady inside . . .

Hangers reached like twigs in the dark to catch in Gilla's hair. Clothing tangled her in it. A heavy body pushed her back against a wall. Blind, Gilla reached her arms out, tried to feel who it was. Strong hands pushed hers away, started squeezing her breasts, her belly. "Fat girl . . ." oozed a voice.

Roger. Gilla hissed, fought. He was so strong! His face was on hers now, his lips at her lips. The awful thing was, his breath tasted lovely. Unable to do anything else, she turned her mouth away from his. That put his mouth right at her ear. With warm, damp breath he said, "You know you want it, Gilla. Come on. Just relax." The words crawled into her ears. His laugh was mocking.

And the smile on the face...

Gilla's hair bristled at the base of her neck. She pushed at Roger, tried to knee him in the groin, but he just shoved her legs apart and laughed. "Girl, you know this is the only way a thick girl like you is going to get any play. You know it."

She knew it. She was only good for this. Thighs too heavy—*Must not a trunk be strong to bear the weight?*—belly too round—*Should the fruits of the tree be sere and wasted, then?*—hair too nappy—*A well-leafed tree is a healthy tree.* The words, her own words, whirled around and around in her head. What? What?

Simply this: you must fight those who would make free with you. Win or lose, you must fight.

A taste like summer cherries rose in Gilla's mouth again. Kashy envied her shape, her strength.

The back of Gilla's neck tingled. The sensation unfurled down her spine. She gathered power from the core of her, from that muscled, padded belly, and elbowed Roger high in the stomach. "No!" she roared, a fiery breath. The wind *whuffed* out of Roger. He tumbled back against the opposite wall, slid bonelessly down to the ground. Gilla fell onto her hands and knees, solidly centred on all fours. Her toes, her fingers flexed. She wasn't surprised to feel her limbs flesh themselves into four knotted appendages, backwards-crooked and strong as wood. She'd sprouted claws, too. She tapped them impatiently.

"Oh, God," moaned Roger. He tried to pull his feet up against his body, farther away from her. "Gilla, what the hell? Is that you?"

Foster had liked holding her. He found her beautiful. With a tickling ripple, the thought clothed Gilla in scales, head to toe. When she looked down at her new dragon feet, she could see the scales twinkling, cherry-red. She lashed her new tail, sending clothing and hangers flying. Roger whimpered, "I'm sorry."

Testing out her bunchy, branchy limbs, Gilla took an experimental step closer to Roger. He began to sob.

And you? asked the deep, fruity voice in her mind. *What say you of you?*

Gilla considered, licking her lips. Roger smelled like meat. *I think I'm all those things that Kashy and Foster like about me. I'm a good friend.*

Yes.

I'm pretty. No, I'm beautiful.

Yes.

I'm good to hold.

Yes.

I bike hard.

Yes.

I run like the wind.

Yes.

I use my brain—well, sometimes.

(A smile to the voice this time.) *Yes.*

I use my lungs.

Yes!

Gilla inhaled a deep breath of musty closet and Roger's fear-sweat. Her sigh made her chest creak like tall trees in a gentle breeze, and she felt her ribs unfurling into batlike wings. They filled the remaining closet space. "Please," whispered Roger. "Please."

"Hey, Rog?" called Haygood. "You must be having a real good time in there, if you're begging for more."

"Please, what?!" roared Gilla. At the nape of her neck, her hamadryad hood flared open. She exhaled a hot wind. Her breath smelled like cherry pie, which made her giggle. She was having a good time, even if Roger wasn't.

The giggles erupted as small gouts of flame. One of them lit the hem of Roger's sweater. "Please don't!" he yelled, beating out the fire with his hands. "God, Gilla; stop!"

Patricia's voice came from beyond the door. "That doesn't sound too good," she said to Haygood. "Hey, Gil?" she shouted. "You okay in there?".

Roger scrabbled to his feet. "Whaddya mean, is *Gilla* okay? Get me out of here! She's turned into some kind of monster!" He started banging on the inside of the closet door.

A polyester dress was beginning to char. No biggie. Gilla flapped it out with a wing. But it *was* getting close in the closet, and Haygood and Patricia were yanking on the door. Gilla swung her head towards it. Roger cringed. Gilla ignored him. She nosed the door open and stepped outside. Roger pushed past her. "Oh God, Haygood; get her off me!"

Haygood's shirt was off, his jeans zipper not done up all the way. His lips looked swollen. He peered suspiciously at Gilla. "Why?" he asked Roger. "What's she doing?"

Patricia was still wriggling her dress down over her hips. Her hair was a mess. "Yeah," she said to Roger, "what's the big problem? You didn't hurt her, did you?" She turned to Gilla, put a hand on her scaly left foreshoulder. "You okay, girl?"

What in the world was going on? Why weren't they scared? "Uh," replied Gilla. "I dunno. How do I look?"

Patricia frowned. "Same as ever," she said, just as Kashy and Foster burst into the room.

"We heard yelling," Kashy said, panting. "What's up? Roger, you been bugging Gilla again?"

Foster took Gilla's paw. "Did he trick you into the closet with him?"

"Why's everyone tripping?" Roger was nearly screeching. "Can't you see? She's some kind of dragon, or something!"

That was the last straw. Gilla started to laugh. Great belly laughs that started from her middle and came guffawing through her snout. Good thing there was no fire this time, cause Gilla didn't know if she could have stopped it. She laughed so hard that the cherry pit she'd swallowed came back up. "Urp," she said, spitting it into her hand. Her hand. She was back to normal now.

She grinned at Roger. He goggled. "How'd you do that?" he demanded.

Gilla ignored him. Her schoolmates had started coming into the room from all over the house to see what the racket was. "Yeah, he tricked me," Gilla said, so they could all hear. "Roger tricked me into the closet, and then he stuck his hand down my bra."

"What a creep," muttered Clarissa's boyfriend Jim.

Foster stepped up to Roger, glaring. "What is your problem, man?" Roger stuck his chest out and tried to glare back, but he couldn't meet Foster's eyes. He kept sneaking nervous peeks around Foster at Gilla.

Clarissa snickered at Gilla. "So what's the big deal? You do it with him all the time, anyway."

Oh, enough of this ill-favoured chit. Weirdly, the voice felt like it was coming from Gilla's palm now. The hand where she held the cherry pit. But it still sounded and felt like her own thoughts. Gilla stalked over to Clarissa. "You don't believe that Roger attacked me?"

Clarissa made a face of disgust. "I believe that you're so fat and ugly that you'll go with anybody, 'cause nobody would have you."

"That's dumb," said Kashy. "How could she go with

anybody, if nobody would have her?"

"I'll have her," said Foster. He looked shyly at Gilla. Then his face flushed. "I mean, I'd like, I mean . . ." No one could hear the end of the sentence, because they were laughing so hard. Except Roger, Karl and Haygood.

Gilla put her arms around Foster, afraid still that she'd misunderstood. But he hugged back, hard. Gilla felt all warm. Foster was such a goof. "Clarissa," said Gilla, "if something bad ever happens to you and nobody will believe your side of the story, you can talk to me. Because I know what it's like."

Clarissa reddened. Roger swore and stomped out of the room. Haygood and Karl followed him.

Gilla regarded the cherry pit in the palm of her hand. Considered. Then she put it in her mouth again and swallowed it down.

"Why'd you do that?" Foster asked.

"Just felt like it."

"A tree'll grow inside you," he teased.

Gilla chuckled. "I wish. Hey, I never did get a real Postman message." She nodded towards the closet. "D'you wanna?"

Foster ducked his head, took her hand. "Yeah."

Gilla led the way, grinning.

They came back from the ride
With the lady inside,
And a smile on the face of the tiger.

15

Of course, bicycles aren't unnatural creatures. And nor are paper clips. So what, in this story by master short-story writer AVRAM DAVIDSON, do two bike-shop owners have to be afraid of?

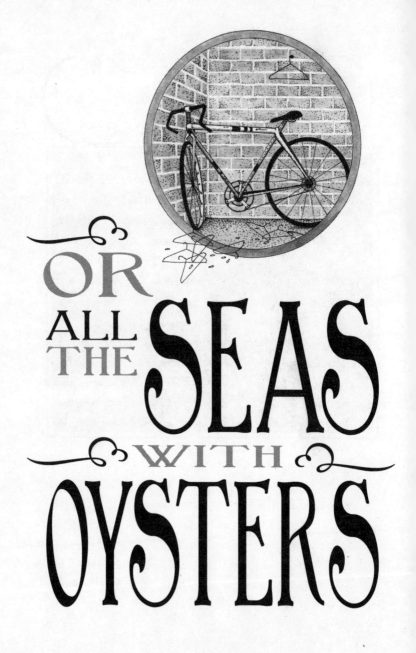

OR
ALL
THE
SEAS
WITH
OYSTERS

By

Avram Davidson

WHEN THE MAN CAME IN TO THE F & O BIKE SHOP, Oscar greeted him with a hearty "Hi, there!" Then, as he looked closer at the middle-aged visitor with the eyeglasses and business suit, his forehead creased and he began to snap his thick fingers.

"Oh, say, I know you," he muttered. "Mr.—um—name's on the tip of my tongue, doggone it . . ." Oscar was a barrel-chested fellow. He had orange hair.

"Why, sure you do," the man said. There was a Lion's emblem in his lapel. "Remember, you sold me a girl's bicycle with gears, for my daughter? We got to talking about that red French racing bike your partner was working on—"

Oscar slapped his big hand down on the cash register. He raised his head and rolled his eyes up. "Mr. Whatney!" Mr. Whatney beamed. "Oh, *sure*. Gee, how could I forget? And we went across the street afterward and had a couple a' beers. Well, how you *been*, Mr. Whatney? I guess the bike—it was an English model, wasn't it? Yeah. It must of given satisfaction or you would of been back, huh?"

Mr. Whatney said the bicycle was fine, just fine. Then he said, "I understand there's been a change, though. You're all by yourself now. Your partner . . ."

Oscar looked down, pushed his lower lip out, nodded. "You heard, huh? Ee-up. I'm all by myself now. Over three months now."

The partnership had come to an end three months ago, but it had been faltering long before then. Ferd liked books, long-playing records, and high-level conversation. Oscar liked beer, bowling, and women. Any women. Anytime.

The shop was located near the park; it did a big trade in renting bicycles to picnickers. If a woman was barely old enough to be *called* a woman, and not quite old enough to be called an *old* woman, or if she was anywhere in between, and if she was alone, Oscar would ask, "How does that machine feel to you? All right?"

"Why . . . I guess so."

Taking another bicycle, Oscar would say, "Well, I'll just ride along a little bit with you, to make sure. Be right back, Ferd." Ferd always nodded gloomily. He knew that Oscar would not be right back. Later, Oscar would say, "Hope you made out in the shop as good as I did in the park."

"Leaving me all alone here all that time," Ferd grumbled.

And Oscar usually flared up. "Okay, then, next time *you* go and leave *me* stay here. See if I begrudge you a little fun." But he knew, of course, that Ferd—tall, thin, popeyed Ferd—would never go. "Do you good," Oscar said, slapping his sternum. "Put hair on your chest."

Ferd muttered that he had all the hair on his chest

that he needed. He would glance down covertly at his lower arms; they were thick with long black hair, though his upper arms were slick and white. It was already like that when he was in high school, and some of the others would laugh at him—call him "Ferdie the Birdie." They knew it bothered him, but they did it anyway. How was it possible—he wondered then; he still did now—for people deliberately to hurt someone else who hadn't hurt them? How was it possible?

He worried over other things. All the time.

"The Communists—" He shook his head over the newspaper. Oscar offered an advice about the Communists in two short words. Or it might be capital punishment. "Oh, what a terrible thing if an innocent man was to be executed," Ferd moaned. Oscar said that was the guy's tough luck.

"Hand me that tire iron," Oscar said.

And Ferd worried even about other people's minor concerns. Like the time the couple came in with the tandem and the baby basket on it. Free air was all they took; then the woman decided to change the diaper and one of the safety pins broke.

"Why are there never any safety pins?" the woman fretted, rummaging here and rummaging there. "There are *never* any safety pins."

Ferd made sympathetic noises, went to see if he had any; but, though he was sure there'd been some in the office, he couldn't find them. So they drove off with one side of the diaper tied in a clumsy knot.

At lunch, Ferd said it was too bad about the safety pins. Oscar dug his teeth into a sandwich, tugged, tore, chewed, swallowed. Ferd liked to experiment with sandwich spreads—the one he liked most was cream cheese, olives, anchovy, and avocado, mashed up with a little mayonnaise—but Oscar always had the same pink luncheon meat.

"It must be difficult with a baby." Ferd nibbled. "Not just traveling, but raising it."

Oscar said, "Jeez, there's drugstores in every block, and if you can't read, you can at least reckernize them."

"Drugstores? Oh, to buy safety pins, you mean."

"Yeah. Safety pins."

"But . . . you know . . . it's true . . . there's never any safety pins when you look."

Oscar uncapped his beer, rinsed the first mouthful around. "Aha! Always plenny of clothes hangers, though. Throw 'em out every month, next month same closet's full of 'em again. Now whatcha wanna do in your spare time, you invent a device which it'll make safety pins outa clothes hangers."

Ferd nodded abstractedly. "But in my spare time I'm working on the French racer . . ." It was a beautiful machine, light, low slung, swift, red and shining. You felt like a bird when you rode it. But, good as it was, Ferd knew he could make it better. He showed it to everybody who came in the place until his interest slackened.

Nature was his latest hobby, or, rather, reading about nature. Some kids had wandered by from the park one day with tin cans in which they had put salamanders and toads, and they proudly showed them to Ferd. After that, the work on the red racer slowed down and he spent his spare time on natural history books.

"Mimicry!" he cried to Oscar. "A wonderful thing!"

Oscar looked up interestedly from the bowling scores in the paper. "I seen Edie Adams on TV the other night, doing her imitation of Marilyn Monroe. Boy, oh, boy."

Ferd was irritated, shook his head. "Not that kind of mimicry. I mean how insects and arachnids will mimic the shapes of leaves and twigs and so on, to escape being eaten by birds or other insects and arachnids."

A scowl of disbelief passed over Oscar's heavy face. "You mean they change their *shapes*? What you giving me?"

"Oh, it's true. Sometimes the mimicry is for aggressive purposes, though—like a South-African turtle that looks like a rock and so the fish swim up to it and then it catches them. Or that spider in Sumatra. When it lies on its back, it looks like a bird dropping. Catches butterflies that way."

Oscar laughed, a disgusted and incredulous noise. It died away as he turned back to the bowling scores. One hand groped at his pocket, came away, scratched absently at the orange thicket under the shirt, then went patting his hip pocket.

"Where's that pencil?" he muttered, got up, stomped into the office, pulled open drawers. His loud cry of

"Hey!" brought Ferd into the tiny room.

"What's the matter?" Ferd asked.

Oscar pointed to a drawer. "Remember that time you claimed there were no safety pins here? Look—whole gah-damn drawer is full of 'em."

Ferd stared, scratched his head, said feebly that he was certain he'd looked there before . . .

A contralto voice from outside asked, "Anybody here?"

Oscar at once forgot the desk and its contents, called, "Be right with you," and was gone. Ferd followed him slowly.

There was a young woman in the shop, a rather massively built young woman, with muscular calves and a deep chest. She was pointing out the seat of her bicycle to Oscar, who was saying "Uh-huh" and looking more at her than at anything else. "It's just a little too far forward ("Uh-huh"), as you can see. A wrench is all I need ("Uh-huh"). It was silly of me to forget my tools."

Oscar repeated, "Uh-huh" automatically, then snapped to. "Fix it in a jiffy," he said, and—despite her insistence that she could do it herself—he did fix it. Though not quite in a jiffy. He refused money. He prolonged the conversation as long as he could.

"Well, thank *you*," the young woman said. "And now I've got to go."

"That machine feel all right to you now?"

"Perfectly. Thanks—"

"Tell you what, I'll just ride along with you a little bit, just—"

Pear-shaped notes of laughter lifted the young woman's bosom. "Oh, you couldn't keep up with me! My machine is a *racer!*"

The moment he saw Oscar's eye flit to the corner, Ferd knew what he had in mind. He stepped forward.

His cry of "No" was drowned out by his partner's loud, "Well, I guess this racer here can keep up with yours!"

The young woman giggled richly, said, well, they would see about that, and was off. Oscar, ignoring Ferd's outstretched hand, jumped on the French bike and was gone. Ferd stood in the doorway, watching the two figures, hunched over their handlebars, vanish down the road into the park. He went slowly back inside.

It was almost evening before Oscar returned, sweaty but smiling. Smiling broadly. "Hey, what a babe!" he cried. He wagged his head, he whistled, he made gestures, noises like escaping steam. "Boy, oh, boy, what an afternoon!"

"Give me the bike," Ferd demanded.

Oscar said, yeah, sure; turned it over to him and went to wash. Ferd looked at the machine. The red enamel was covered with dust; there was mud spattered and dirt and bits of dried grass. It seemed soiled—degraded. He had felt like a swift bird when he rode it . . .

Oscar came out wet and beaming. He gave a cry of dismay, ran over.

"Stand away," said Ferd, gesturing with the knife. He slashed the tires, the seat and seat cover, again and again.

"You crazy?" Oscar yelled. "You outa your mind? Ferd, no, don't, Ferd—"

Ferd cut the spokes, bent them, twisted them. He took the heaviest hammer and pounded the frame into shape-lessness, and then he kept on pounding till his breath was gasping.

"You're not only crazy," Oscar said bitterly, "you're rotten jealous. You can go to hell." He stomped away.

Ferd, feeling sick and stiff, locked up, went slowly home. He had no taste for reading, turned out the light and fell into bed, where he lay awake for hours, listening to the rustling noises of the night and thinking hot, twisted thoughts.

They didn't speak to each other for days after that, except for the necessities of the work. The wreckage of the French racer lay behind the shop. For about two weeks, neither wanted to go out back where he'd have to see it.

One morning Ferd arrived to be greeted by his partner, who began to shake his head in astonishment even before he started speaking. "How did you *do* it, how did you *do* it, Ferd? Jeez, what a beautiful job—I gotta hand it to you—no more hard feelings, huh, Ferd?"

Ferd took his hand. "Sure, sure. But what are you talking about?"

Oscar led him out back. There was the red racer, all in one piece, not a mark or scratch on it, its enamel bright as ever. Ferd gaped. He squatted down and examined it. It *was* his machine. Every change, every improvement he had made, was there.

He straightened up slowly. "Regeneration . . ."

"Huh? What say?" Oscar asked. Then, "Hey, kiddo, you're all white. Whad you do, stay up all night and didn't get no sleep? Come on in and siddown. But I still don't see how you done it."

Inside, Ferd sat down. He wet his lips. He said, "Oscar—listen—"

"Yeah?"

"Oscar. You know what regeneration is? No? Listen. Some kinds of lizards, you grab them by the tail, the tail breaks off and they grow a new one. If a lobster loses a claw, it regenerates another one. Some kinds of worms—and hydras and starfish—you cut them into pieces, each piece will grow back the missing parts. Salamanders can regenerate lost hands, and frogs can grow legs back."

"No kidding, Ferd. But, uh, I mean: nature. Very interesting. But to get back to the bike now—how'd you manage to fix it so good?"

"I never touched it. It regenerated. Like a newt. Or a lobster."

Oscar considered this. He lowered his head, looked up at Ferd from under his eyebrows. "Well, now, Ferd . . . look . . . how come all broke bikes don't do that?"

"This isn't an ordinary bike. I mean it isn't a real bike." Catching Oscar's look, he shouted, "Well, it's *true*!"

The shout changed Oscar's attitude from bafflement to incredulity. He got up. "So for the sake of argument, let's say all that stuff about the bugs and the eels or whatever the hell you were talking about is true. But they're alive. A bike ain't." He looked down triumphantly.

Ferd shook his leg from side to side, looked at it. "A crystal isn't, either, but a broken crystal can regenerate itself if the conditions are right. Oscar, go see if the safety pins are still in the desk. Please, Oscar?"

He listened as Oscar, muttering, pulled the desk drawers out, rummaged in them, slammed them shut, tramped back.

"Naa," he said. "All gone. Like that lady said that time, and you said, there never are any safety pins when you want 'em. They disap—Ferd? What're—"

Ferd jerked open the closet door, jumped back as a shoal of clothes hangers clattered out.

"And like *you* say," Ferd said with a twist of his mouth, "on the other hand, there are always plenty of clothes hangers. There weren't any here before."

Oscar shrugged. "I don't see what you're getting at. But anybody could of got in here and took the pins and left the hangers. *I* could of—but I didn't. Or *you* could of. Maybe—" He narrowed his eyes. "Maybe you walked in your sleep and done it. You better see a doctor. Jeez, you look rotten."

Ferd went back and sat down, put his head in his hands. "I *feel* rotten. I'm scared, Oscar. Scared of what?" He breathed noisily. "I'll tell you. Like I explained before, about how things that live in the wild places, they mimic other things there. Twigs, leaves . . . toads that look like rocks. Well, suppose there are . . . things . . . that live in people places. Cities. Houses. These things could imitate—well, other kinds of things you find in people places—"

"*People* places, for crise sake!"

"Maybe they're a different kind of life-form. Maybe they get their nourishment out of the elements in the air. You know what safety pins are—these other kinds of them? Oscar, the safety pins are the pupa forms and then they, like, *hatch*. Into the larval forms. Which look just like coat hangers. They feel like them, even, but they're not. Oscar, they're not, not really, not really, not . . ."

He began to cry into his hands. Oscar looked at him. He shook his head.

After a minute, Ferd controlled himself somewhat. He snuffled. "All these bicycles the cops find, and they hold them waiting for owners to show up, and then we buy them at the sale because no owners show up because there aren't any, and the same with the ones the kids are always trying to sell us, and they say they just found them, and they really did because they were never made in a factory. They grew. They grow. You smash them and throw them away, they regenerate."

Oscar turned to someone who wasn't there and waggled his head. "Hoo, boy," he said. Then, to Ferd: "You mean one day there's a safety pin and the next day instead there's a coat hanger?"

Ferd said, "One day there's a cocoon; the next day there's a moth. One day there's an egg; the next day there's a chicken. But with . . . these it doesn't happen in the open daytime where you can see it. But at night, Oscar—at night you can *hear* it happening. All the little noises in the night-time, Oscar—"

Oscar said, "Then how come we ain't up to our belly button in bikes? If I had a bike for every coat hanger—"

But Ferd had considered that, too. If every codfish egg, he explained, or every oyster spawn grew to maturity, a man could walk across the ocean on the backs of all the codfish or oysters there'd be. So many died, so many were eaten by predatory creatures, that nature had to produce a maximum in order to allow a minimum to arrive at maturity. And Oscar's question was, then who, uh, eats the, uh, coat hangers?

Ferd's eyes focused through wall, buildings, park, more buildings, to the horizon. "You got to get the picture. I'm not talking about real pins or hangers. I got a name for the others—false friends, I call them. In high-school French, we had to watch out for French words that looked like English words, but really were different. *Faux amis*, they call them. False friends. Pseudo-pins. Pseudo-hangers . . . Who eats them? I don't know for sure. Pseudo-vacuum cleaners, maybe?"

His partner, with a loud groan, slapped his hands against his thighs. He said, "Ferd, Ferd, for crise sake. You know what's the trouble with you? You talk about oysters, but you forgot what they're good for. You forgot there's two kinds of people in the world. Close up them books, them bug books and French books. Get out, mingle, meet people. Soak up some brew. You know what? The next time Norma—that's this broad's name with the racing bike—the next time she comes here, *you* take the red racer and *you* go out in the woods with her. I won't mind. And I don't think she will, either. Not *too* much."

But Ferd said no. "I never want to touch the red racer again. I'm afraid of it."

At this, Oscar pulled him to his feet, dragged him protestingly out to the back and forced him to get on the French machine. "Only way to conquer your fear of it!"

Ferd started off, white-faced, wobbling. And in a moment was on the ground, rolling and thrashing, screaming.

Oscar pulled him away from the machine.

"It threw me!" Ferd yelled. "It tried to kill me! Look—blood!"

His partner said it was a bump that threw him—it was his own fear. The blood? A broken spoke. Grazed his cheek. And he insisted Ferd get on the bicycle again, to conquer his fear.

But Ferd had grown hysterical. He shouted that no man was safe—that mankind had to be warned. It took Oscar a long time to pacify him and to get him to go home and into bed.

. . .

He didn't tell all this to Mr. Whatney, of course. He merely said that his partner had gotten fed up with the bicycle business.

"It don't pay to worry and try to change the world," he pointed out. "I always say take things the way they are. If you can't lick 'em, join 'em."

Mr. Whatney said that was his philosophy, exactly. He asked how things were, since.

"Well . . . not *too* bad. I'm engaged, you know. Name's Norma. Crazy about bicycles. Everything considered, things aren't bad at all. More work, yes, but I can do things all my own way, so . . ."

Mr. Whatney nodded. He glanced around the shop. "I see they're still making drop-frame bikes," he said, "though, with so many women wearing slacks, I wonder they bother."

Oscar said, "Well, I dunno. I kinda like it that way. Ever stop to think that bicycles are like people? I mean, of all the machines in the world, only bikes come male and female."

Mr. Whatney gave a little giggle, said that was *right*, he had never thought of it like that before. Then Oscar asked if Mr. Whatney had anything in particular in mind—not that he wasn't always welcome.

"Well, I wanted to look over what you've got. My boy's birthday is coming up—"

Oscar nodded sagely. "Now here's a job," he said, "which you can't get it in any other place but here. Specialty of the house. Combines the best features of the French racer and the American standard, but it's made right here, and it comes in three models—Junior, Intermediate, and Regular. Beautiful, ain't it?"

Mr. Whatney observed that, say, that might be just the ticket. "By the way," he asked, "what's become of the French racer, the red one, used to be here?"

Oscar's face twitched. Then it grew bland and innocent and he leaned over and nudged his customer.

"Oh, *that* one. Old Frenchy? Why, I put *him* out to stud!"

And they laughed and they laughed, and after they told a few more stories they concluded the sale, and they had a few beers and they laughed some more. And then they said what a shame it was about poor Ferd, poor old Ferd, who had been found in his own closet with an unraveled coat hanger coiled tightly around his neck.

16

PETER S. BEAGLE has been one of the premiere fantasists in America for fifty years. His book *The Last Unicorn* is a classic. I thought we would finish with the most natural of all unnatural creatures. For Death is nothing but natural. Even when she's a lady.

For years Lady Neville has thrown the finest parties to entertain the finest people, and she's bored with all of them. There's one person she's never met though . . .

COME LADY DEATH

By
Peter S. Beagle

THIS ALL HAPPENED IN ENGLAND a long time ago, when that George who spoke English with a heavy German accent and hated his sons was King. At that time there lived in London a lady who had nothing to do but give parties. Her name was Flora, Lady Neville, and she was a widow and very old. She lived in a great house not far from Buckingham Palace, and she had so many servants that she could not possibly remember all their names; indeed, there were some she had never even seen. She had more food than she could eat, more gowns that she could ever wear; she had wine in her cellars that no one would drink in her lifetime, and her private vaults were filled with great works of art that she did not know she owned. She spent the last years of her life giving parties and balls to which the greatest lords of England—and sometimes the King himself—came, and she was known as the wisest and wittiest woman in all London.

But in time her own parties began to bore her, and though she invited the most famous people in the land and hired the greatest jugglers and acrobats and dancers and magicians to entertain them, still she found her parties duller and duller. Listening to court gossip, which she had always loved, made her yawn. The most marvelous music, the most exciting feats of magic put her to sleep. Watching a beautiful young couple dance by her made her feel sad, and she hated to feel sad.

And so, one summer afternoon she called her closest friends around her and said to them, "More and more I find that my parties entertain everyone but me. The secret of my long life is that nothing has ever been dull for me. For all my life, I have been interested in everything I saw and been anxious to see more. But I cannot stand to be bored, and I will not go to parties at which I expect to be bored, especially if they are my own. Therefore, to my next ball I shall invite the one guest I am sure no one, not even myself, could possibly find boring. My friends, the guest of honor at my next party shall be Death himself."

A young poet thought that this was a wonderful idea, but the rest of her friends were terrified and drew back from her. They did not want to die, they pleaded with her. Death would come for them when he was ready; why should she invite him before the appointed hour, which would arrive soon enough? But Lady Neville said, "Precisely. If Death has planned to take any of us on the night of my party, he will come whether he is invited or not. But if none of us are to die, then I think it would be charming to have Death among us—perhaps even to perform some little trick if he is in a good humor. And think of being able to say that we had been to a party with Death! All of London will envy us, all of England."

The idea began to please her friends, but a young lord, very new to London, suggested timidly, "Death is so busy. Suppose he has work to do and cannot accept your invitation?"

"No one has ever refused an invitation of mine," said Lady Neville, "not even the King." And the young lord was not invited to her party.

She sat down then and there and wrote out the invitation. There was some dispute among her friends as to how they should address Death. "His Lordship Death" seemed to place him only on the level of a viscount or a baron. "His Grace Death" met with more acceptance, but Lady Neville said it sounded hypocritical. And to refer to Death as "His Majesty" was to make him the equal of the King of England, which even Lady Neville would not dare to do. It was finally decided that all should speak of him as "His Eminence Death," which pleased nearly everyone.

Captain Compson, known both as England's most dashing cavalry officer and most elegant rake, remarked next, "That's all very well, but how is the invitation to reach Death? Does anyone here know where he lives?"

"Death undoubtedly lives in London," said Lady Neville, "like everyone else of any importance, though he probably goes to Deauville for the summer. Actually, Death must live fairly near my own house. This is much the best section of London, and you could hardly expect a person of Death's importance to live anywhere else. When I stop to think of it, it's really rather strange that we haven't met before now, on the street."

Most of her friends agreed with her, but the poet, whose name was David Lorimond, cried out, "No, my lady, you are wrong! Death lives among the poor. Death lives in the foulest, darkest alleys of this city, in some vile, rat-ridden hovel that smells of—" He stopped here, partly because Lady Neville had indicated her displeasure, and partly because he had never been inside such a hut or thought of wondering what it smelled like. "Death lives among the poor," he went on, "and comes to visit them every day, for he is their only friend."

Lady Neville answered him as coldly as she had spoken to the young lord. "He may be forced to deal with them, David, but I hardly think that he seeks them out as companions. I am certain that it is as difficult for him to think of the poor as individuals as it is for me. Death is, after all, a nobleman."

There was no real argument among the lords and ladies that Death lived in a neighborhood at least as good as their own, but none of them seemed to know the name of Death's street, and no one had ever seen Death's house.

"If there were a war," Captain Compson said, "Death would be easy to find. I have seen him, you known, even spoken to him, but he has never answered me."

"Quite proper," said Lady Neville. "Death must always speak first. You are not a very correct person, Captain." But she smiled at him, as all women did.

Then an idea came to her. "My hairdresser has a sick

child, I understand," she said. "He was telling me about it yesterday, sounding most dull and hopeless. I will send for him and give him the invitation, and he in his turn can give it to Death when he comes to take the brat. A bit unconventional, I admit, but I see no other way."

"If he refuses?" asked a lord who had just been married.

"Why should he?" asked Lady Neville.

Again, it was the poet who exclaimed amidst the general approval that this was a cruel and wicked thing to do. But he fell silent when Lady Neville innocently asked him, "Why, David?"

So the hairdresser was sent for, and when he stood before them, smiling nervously and twisting his hands to be in the same room with so many great lords, Lady Neville told him the errand that was required of him. And she was right, as she usually was, for he made no refusal. He merely took the invitation in his hand and asked to be excused.

He did not return for two days, but when he did he presented himself to Lady Neville without being sent for and handed her a small white envelope. Saying, "how very nice of you, thank you very much," she opened it and found therein a plain calling card with nothing on it except these words: *Death will be pleased to attend Lady Neville's ball.*

"Death gave you this?" she asked the hairdresser eagerly. "What was he like?" But the hairdresser stood still, looking past her, and said nothing, and she, not really waiting for an answer, called a dozen servants to her and told them to run and summon her friends. As she paced up and down the room waiting for them, she asked again, "What is Death like?" The hairdresser did not reply.

When her friends came they passed the little card excitedly from hand to hand, until it had gotten quite smudged and bent from their fingers. But they all admitted that, beyond its message, there was nothing particularly unusual about it. It was neither hot nor cold to the touch, and what little odor clung to it was rather pleasant. Everyone said that it was a very familiar smell, but no one could give it a name. The poet said that it reminded him of lilacs but not exactly.

It was Captain Compson, however, who pointed out the one thing that no one else had noticed. "Look at the handwriting itself," he said. "Have you ever seen anything more graceful? The letters seem as light as birds. I think we have wasted our time speaking of Death as His This and His That. A woman wrote this note."

Then there was an uproar and a great babble, and the card had to be handed around again so that everyone could exclaim, "Yes, by God!" over it. The voice of the poet rose out of the hubbub saying, "It is very natural, when you come to think of it. After all, the French say *la mort*. Lady Death. I should much prefer Death to be a woman."

"Death rides a great black horse," said Captain Compson firmly, "and wears armor of the same color. Death is very tall, taller than anyone. It was no woman I saw on the battlefield, striking right and left like any soldier. Perhaps the hairdresser wrote it himself, or the hairdresser's wife."

But the hairdresser refused to speak, though they gathered around him and begged him to say who had given him the note. At first they promised him all sorts of rewards, and later they threatened to do terrible things to him. "Did you write this card?" he was asked, and "Who wrote it, then? Was it a living woman? Was it really Death? Did Death say anything to you? How did you know it was Death? Is Death a woman? Are you trying to make fools of us all?"

Not a word from the hairdresser, not one word, and finally Lady Neville called her servants to have him whipped and thrown into the street. He did not look at her as they took him away, or utter a sound.

Silencing her friends with a wave of her hand, Lady Neville said, "The ball will take place two weeks from tonight. Let Death come as Death pleases, whether as man or woman or strange, sexless creature." She smiled calmly. "Death may well be a woman," she said. "I am less certain of Death's form than I was, but I am also less frightened of Death. I am too old to be afraid of anything that can use a quill pen to write me a letter. Go home now, and as you make your preparations for the ball, see that you speak of it to your servants, that they may spread the news all over London. Let it be known that on this one night no one in the world will die, for Death will be dancing at Lady Neville's ball."

For the next two weeks Lady Neville's great house shook and groaned and creaked like an old tree in a gale as the servants hammered and scrubbed, polished and painted, making ready for the ball. Lady Neville had always been very proud of her house, but as the ball drew near she began to be afraid that it would not be nearly grand enough for Death, who was surely accustomed to visiting in the homes of richer, mightier people than herself. Fearing the scorn of Death, she worked night and day supervising her servants' preparations. Curtains and carpets had to be cleaned, gold work and silverware polished until they gleamed by themselves in the dark. The grand staircase that rushed down into the ballroom like a waterfall was washed and rubbed so often that it was almost impossible to walk on it without slipping. As for the ballroom itself, it took thirty-two servants working at once to clean it properly, not counting those who were polishing the glass chandelier that was taller than a man and the fourteen smaller lamps. And when they were done she made them do it all over, not because she saw any dust or dirt anywhere, but because she was sure that Death would.

As for herself, she chose her finest gown and saw to its laundering personally. She called in another hairdresser and had him put up her hair in the style of an earlier time, wanting to show Death that she was a woman who enjoyed her age and did not find it necessary to ape the young and beautiful. All the day of the ball she sat before her mirror, not making herself up much beyond the normal touches of rouge and eye shadow and fine rice powder, but staring at the lean old face she had been born with, wondering how it would appear to Death. Her steward asked her to approve his wine selection, but she sent him away and stayed at her mirror until it was time to dress and go downstairs to meet her guests.

Everyone arrived early. When she looked out of a window, Lady Neville saw that the driveway of her home was choked with carriages and fine horses. "It all looks like a great funeral procession," she said. The footman cried the names of her guests to the echoing ballroom. "Captain Henry Compson, His Majesty's Household Cavalry! Mr. David Lorimond! Lord and Lady Torrance!" (They were the youngest couple there, having been married only three months before.) "Sir Roger Harbison! The Contessa della Candini!" Lady Neville permitted them all to kiss her hand and made them welcome.

She had engaged the finest musicians she could find to play for the dancing, but though they began to play at her signal not one couple stepped out on the floor, nor did one young lord approach her to request the honor of the first dance, as was proper. They milled together, shining and murmuring, their eyes fixed on the ballroom door. Every time they heard a carriage clatter up the driveway, they seemed to flinch a little and draw closer together; every time the footman announced the arrival of another guest, they all sighed softly and swayed a little on their feet with relief.

"Why did they come to my party if they were afraid?" Lady Neville muttered scornfully to herself. "I am not afraid of meeting Death. I ask only that Death may be impressed by the magnificence of my house and the flavor of my wines. I will die sooner than anyone here, but I am not afraid."

Certain that Death would not arrive until midnight, she moved among her guests, attempting to calm them, not with her words, which she knew they would not hear, but with the tone of her voice as if they were so many frightened horses. But little by little, she herself was infected by their nervousness; whenever she sat down she stood up again immediately, she tasted a dozen glasses of wine without finishing any of them, and she glanced constantly at her jeweled watch, at first wanting to hurry the midnight along and end the waiting, later scratching at the watch face with her forefinger, as if she would push away the night and drag the sun backward in the sky. When midnight came, she was standing with the rest of them, breathing through her mouth, shifting from foot to foot, listening for the sound of carriage wheels turning in gravel.

When the clock began to strike midnight, everyone, even Lady Neville and the brave Captain Compson, gave one startled little cry and then was silent again, listening to the tolling of the clock. The smaller clocks upstairs began to chime. Lady Neville's ears hurt. She caught sight of herself in the ballroom mirror, one gray face turned up toward the ceiling as if she were gasping for air, and she thought, "Death will be a woman, a hideous, filthy old crone as tall and strong as a man. And the most terrible thing of all will be that she will have my face." All the clocks stopped striking, and Lady Neville closed her eyes.

She opened them again only when she heard the whispering around her take on a different tone, one in which fear was fused with relief and a certain chagrin. For no new carriage stood in the driveway. Death had not come.

The noise grew slowly louder; here and there people were beginning to laugh. Near her, Lady Neville heard young Lord Torrance say to his wife, "There, my darling, I told you there was nothing to be afraid of. It was all a joke."

I am ruined, Lady Neville thought. The laughter was increasing; it pounded against her ears in strokes, like the chiming of the clocks. *I wanted to give a ball so grand that those who were not invited would be shamed in front of the whole city, and this is my reward. I am ruined, and I deserve it.*

Turning to the poet Lorimond, she said, "Dance with me, David." She signaled to the musicians, who at once began to play. When Lorimond hesitated, she said, "Dance with me now. You will not have another chance. I shall never give a party again."

Lorimond bowed and led her out onto the dance floor. The guests parted for them, and the laughter died down for a moment, but Lady Neville knew that it would soon begin again. *Well, let them laugh*, she thought. *I did not fear Death when they were all trembling. Why should I fear their laughter?* But she could feel a stinging at the thin lids of her eyes, and she closed them once more as she began to dance with Lorimond.

And then, quite suddenly, all the carriage horses outside the house whinnied loudly, just once, as the guests had cried out at midnight. There were a great many horses, and their one salute was so loud that everyone in the room became instantly silent. They heard the heavy steps of the footman as he went to open the door, and they shivered as if they felt the cool breeze that drifted into the house. Then they heard a light voice saying, "Am I late? Oh, I am so sorry. The horses were tired," and before the footman could reenter to announce her, a lovely young girl in a white dress stepped gracefully into the ballroom doorway and stood there smiling.

She could not have been more than nineteen. Her hair was yellow, and she wore it long. It fell thickly upon her bare shoulders that gleamed warmly through it, two limestone islands rising out of a dark golden sea. Her face was wide at the forehead and cheekbones, and narrow at the chin, and her skin was so clear that many of the ladies there—Lady Neville among them—touched their own faces wonderingly, and instantly drew their hands away as though their own skin had rasped their fingers. Her mouth was pale, where the mouths of other women were red and orange and even purple. Her eyebrows, thicker and straighter than was fashionable, met over dark, calm eyes that were set so deep in her young face and were so black, so uncompromisingly black, that the middle-aged wife of a middle-aged lord murmured, "Touch of the gypsy there, I think."

"Or something worse," suggested her husband's mistress.

"Be silent!" Lady Neville spoke louder than she had intended, and the girl turned to look at her. She smiled, and Lady Neville tried to smile back, but her mouth seemed very stiff. "Welcome," she said. "Welcome, my lady Death."

A sigh rustled among the lords and ladies as the girl took the old woman's hand and curtsied to her, sinking and rising in one motion, like a wave. "You are Lady Neville," she said. "Thank you so much for inviting me." Her accent was as faint and as almost familiar as her perfume.

"Please excuse me for being late," she said earnestly. "I had to come from a long way off, and my horses are so tired."

"The groom will rub them down," Lady Neville said, "and feed them if you wish."

"Oh, no," the girl answered quickly. "Tell him not to go near the horses, please. They are not really horses, and they are very fierce."

She accepted a glass of wine from a servant and drank it slowly, sighing softly and contentedly. "What good wine," she said. "And what a beautiful house you have."

"Thank you," said Lady Neville. Without turning, she could feel every woman in the room envying her, sensing it as she could always sense the approach of rain.

"I wish I lived here," Death said in her low, sweet voice. "I will, one day."

Then, seeing Lady Neville become as still as if she had

turned to ice, she put her hand on the old woman's arm and said, "Oh, I'm sorry, I'm so sorry. I am so cruel, but I never mean to be. Please forgive me, Lady Neville. I am not used to company, and I do such stupid things. Please forgive me."

Her hand felt as light and warm on Lady Neville's arm as the hand of any other young girl, and her eyes were so appealing that Lady Neville replied, "You have said nothing wrong. While you are my guest, my house is yours."

"Thank you," said Death, and she smiled so radiantly that the musicians began to play quite by themselves, with no sign from Lady Neville. She would have stopped them, but Death said, "Oh, what lovely music! Let them play, please."

So the musicians played a gavotte, and Death, unabashed by eyes that stared at her in greedy terror, sang softly to herself without words, lifted her white gown slightly with both hands, and made hesitant little patting steps with her small feet. "I have not danced in so long," she said wistfully. "I'm quite sure I've forgotten how."

She was shy; she would not look up to embarrass the young lords, not one of whom stepped forward to dance with her. Lady Neville felt a flood of shame and sympathy, emotions she thought had withered in her years ago. *Is she to be humiliated at my own ball?* she thought angrily. *It is because she is Death; if she were the ugliest, foulest hag in all the world they would clamor to dance with her, because they are gentlemen and they know what is expected of them. But no gentleman will dance with Death, no matter how beautiful she is.* She glanced sideways at David Lorimond. His face was so flushed, and his hands were clasped so tightly as he stared at Death that his fingers were like glass, but when Lady Neville touched his arm he did not turn, and when she hissed, "David!" he pretended not to hear her.

Then Captain Compson, gray haired and handsome in his uniform, stepped out of the crowd and bowed gracefully before Death. "If I may have the honor," he said.

"Captain Compson," said Death, smiling. She put her arm in his. "I was hoping you would ask me."

This brought a frown from the older women, who did not consider it a proper thing to say, but for that Death cared not a rap. Captain Compson led her to the center of the floor, and there they danced. Death was curiously graceless at first—she was too anxious to please her partner, and she seemed to have no notion of rhythm. The captain himself moved with the mixture of dignity and humor that Lady Neville had never seen in another man, but when he looked at her over Death's shoulder, she saw something that no one else appeared to notice: that his face and eyes were immobile with fear, and that, though he offered Death his hand with easy gallantry, he flinched slightly when she took it. And yet he danced as well as Lady Neville had ever seen him.

Ah, that's what comes of having a reputation to maintain, she thought. *Captain Compson too must do what is expected of him. I hope someone else will dance with her soon.*

But no one did. Little by little, other couples overcame

their fear and slipped hurriedly out on the floor when Death was looking the other way, but nobody sought to relieve Captain Compson of his beautiful partner. They danced every dance together. In time, some of the men present began to look at her with more appreciation than terror, but when she returned their glances and smiled at them, they clung to their partners as if a cold wind were threatening to blow them away.

One of the few who stared at her frankly and with pleasure was young Lord Torrance, who usually danced only with his wife. Another was the poet Lorimond. Dancing with Lady Neville, he remarked to her, "If she is Death, what do these frightened fools think they are? If she is ugliness, what must they be? I hate their fear. It is obscene."

Death and Captain danced past them at that moment, and they heard him say to her, "But if that was truly you that I saw in the battle, how can you have changed so? How can you have become so lovely?"

Death's laughter was gay and soft. "I thought that among so many beautiful people it might be better to be beautiful. I was afraid of frightening everyone and spoiling the party."

"They all thought she would be ugly," said Lorimond to Lady Neville. "I—I knew she would be beautiful."

"Then why have you not danced with her" Lady Neville asked him. "Are you also afraid?"

"No, oh, no," the poet answered quickly and passionately. "I will ask her to dance very soon. I only want to look at her a little longer."

. . .

The musicians played on and on. The dancing wore away the night as slowly as falling water wears down a cliff. It seemed to Lady Neville that no night had ever endured longer, and yet she was neither tired nor bored. She danced with every man there, except with Lord Torrance, who was dancing with his wife as if they had just met that night, and, of course, with Captain Compson. Once he lifted his hand and touched Death's golden hair very lightly. He was a striking man still, a fit partner for so beautiful a girl, but Lady Neville looked at his face each time she passed him and realized that he was older than anyone knew.

Death herself seemed younger than the youngest there. No woman at the ball danced better than she now, though it was hard for Lady Neville to remember at what point her awkwardness had given way to the liquid sweetness of her movements. She smiled and called to everyone who caught her eye—and she knew them all by name; she sang constantly, making up words to the dance tunes, nonsense words, sounds without meaning, and yet everyone strained to hear her soft voice without knowing why. And when, during a waltz, she caught up the trailing end of her gown to give her more freedom as she danced, she seemed to Lady Neville to move like a little sailing boat over a still evening sea.

Lady Neville heard Lady Torrance arguing angrily with the Contessa della Candini. "I don't care if she is Death, she's no older than I am, she can't be!"

"Nonsense," said the Contessa, who could not afford to be generous to any other woman. "She is twenty-eight, thirty, if she is an hour. And that dress, that bridal gown she wears—really!"

"Vile," said the woman who had come to the ball as Captain Compson's freely acknowledged mistress. "Tasteless. But one should know better than to expect taste from Death, I suppose." Lady Torrance looked as if she were going to cry.

"They are jealous of Death," Lady Neville said to herself. "How strange. I am not jealous of her, not in the least. And I do not fear her at all." She was very proud of herself.

Then, as unbidden as they had begun to play, the musicians stopped. They began to put away their instruments. In the sudden shrill silence, Death pulled away from Captain Compson and ran to look out of one of the tall windows, pushing the curtains apart with both hands. "Look!" she said, with her back turned to them. "Come and look. The night is almost gone."

The summer sky was still dark, and the eastern horizon was only a shade lighter than the rest of the sky, but the stars had vanished and the trees near the house were gradually becoming distinct. Death pressed her face against the window and said, so softly that the other guests could barely hear her, "I must go now."

"No," Lady Neville said, and was not immediately aware that she had spoken. "You must stay a while longer. The ball was in your honor. Please stay."

Death held out both hands to her, and Lady Neville came and took them in her own. "I've had a wonderful time," she said gently. "You cannot possibly imagine how it feels to be actually invited to such a ball as this, because you have given them and gone to them all your life. One is like another to you, but for me it is different. Do you understand me?" Lady Neville nodded silently. "I will remember this night forever," Death said.

"Stay," Captain Compson said. "Stay just a little longer." He put his hand on Death's shoulder, and she smiled and leaned her cheek against it. "Dear Captain Compson," she said. "My first real gallant. Aren't you tired of me yet?"

"Never," he said. "Please stay."

"Stay," said Lorimond, and he too seemed about to touch her. "Stay. I want to talk to you. I want to look at you. I will dance with you if you stay."

"How many followers I have," Death said in wonder. She stretched one hand toward Lorimond, but he drew back from her and then flushed in shame. "A soldier and a poet. How wonderful it is to be a woman. But why did you not speak to me earlier, both of you? Now it is too late. I must go."

"Please, stay," Lady Torrance whispered. She held on to her husband's hand for courage. "We think you are so beautiful, both of us do."

"Gracious Lady Torrance," the girl said kindly. She turned back to the window, touched it lightly, and it flew open. The cold raw air rushed into the ballroom, fresh with rain but already smelling faintly of the London streets over which it had passed. They heard birdsong and the strange, harsh nickering of Death's horses.

"Do you want me to stay?" she asked. The question was put, not to Lady Neville, nor to Captain Compson, nor to any of her admirers, but to the Contessa della Candini, who stood well back from them all, hugging her flowers to herself and humming a little song of irritation. She did not in the least want Death to stay, but she was afraid that all the other women would think her envious of Death's beauty, and so she said, "Yes. Of course I do."

"Ah," said Death. She was almost whispering. "And you," she said to another woman, "do you want me to stay? Do you want me to be one of your friends?"

"Yes," said the woman, "because you are beautiful and a true lady."

"And you," said Death to a man, "and you," to a woman, "and you," to another man, "do you want me to stay?" And they all answered, "Yes, Lady Death, we do."

"Do you want me, then?" she cried at last to all of them. "Do you want me to live among you and to be one of you, and not to be Death anymore? Do you want me to visit your houses and come to all your parties? Do you want me to ride horses like yours instead of mine, do you want me to wear the kind of dresses you wear, and say the things you would say? Would one of you marry me, and would the rest of you dance at my wedding and bring gifts to my children? Is that what you want?"

"Yes," said Lady Neville. "Stay here, stay with me, stay with us."

Death's voice, without becoming louder, had become clearer and older; too old a voice, thought Lady Neville, for such a young girl. "Be sure," said Death. "Be sure of what you want, be very sure. Do all of you want me to stay? For if one of you says to me, no, go away, then I must leave at once and never return. Be sure. Do you all want me?"

And everyone there cried with one voice, "Yes! Yes, you must stay with us. You are so beautiful that we cannot let you go."

"We are tired," said Captain Compson.

"We are blind," said Lorimond, adding, "especially to poetry."

"We are afraid," said Lord Torrance quietly, and his wife took his arm and said, "Both of us."

"We are dull and stupid," said Lady Neville, "and growing old uselessly. Stay with us, Lady Death."

And then Death smiled sweetly and radiantly and took a step forward, and it was as though she had come down among them from a great height. "Very well," she said. "I will stay with you. I will be Death no more. I will be a woman."

The room was full of a deep sigh, although no one was seen to open his mouth. No one moved, for the golden-haired girl was Death still, and her horses still whinnied for her outside. No one could look at her for long, although she was the most beautiful girl anyone there had ever seen.

"There is a price to pay," she said. "There is always a price. Some one of you must become Death in my place, for there must forever be Death in the world. Will anyone choose? Will anyone here become Death of his own free will? For only thus can I become a human girl."

No one spoke, no one spoke at all. But they backed slowly away from her, like waves slipping back down a beach to the sea when you try to catch them. The Contessa della Candini and her friends would have crept quietly out of the door, but Death smiled at them and they stood where they were. Captain Compson opened his mouth as though he were going to declare himself, but he said nothing. Lady Neville did not move.

"No one," said Death. She touched a flower with her finger, and it seemed to crouch and flex itself like a pleased cat. "No one at all," she said. "Then I must choose, and that is just, for that is the way that I became Death. I never wanted to be Death, and it makes me so happy that you want me to become one of yourselves. I have searched a long time for people who would want me. Now I have only to choose someone to replace me and it is done. I will choose very carefully."

"Oh, we were so foolish," Lady Neville said to herself. "We were so foolish." But she said nothing aloud; she merely clasped her hands and stared at the young girl, thinking vaguely that if she had had a daughter she would have been greatly pleased if she resembled the Lady Death.

"The Contessa della Candini," said Death thoughtfully,

and that woman gave a little squeak of terror because she could not draw her breath for a scream. But Death laughed and said, "No, that would be silly." She said nothing more, but for a long time after that the Contessa burned with humiliation at not having been chosen to be Death.

"Not Captain Compson," murmured Death, "because he is too kind to become Death, and because it would be too cruel to him. He wants to die so badly." The expression on the captain's face did not change, but his hands began to tremble.

"Not Lorimond," the girl continued, "because he knows so little about life, and because I like him." The poet flushed, and turned white, and then turned pink again. He made as if to kneel clumsily on one knee, but instead he pulled himself erect and stood as much like Captain Compson as he could.

"Not the Torrances," said Death, "never Lord and Lady Torrance, for both of them care too much about another person to take any pride in being Death." But she hesitated over Lady Torrance for awhile, staring at her out of her dark and curious eyes. "I was your age when I became Death," she said at last. "I wonder what it will be like to be your age again. I have been Death for so long." Lady Torrance shivered and did not speak.

And at last Death said quietly, "Lady Neville."

"I am here," Lady Neville answered.

"I think you are the only one," said Death. "I choose you, Lady Neville."

Again Lady Neville heard every guest sigh softly, and although her back was to them all she knew that they were sighing in relief that neither themselves nor anyone dear to themselves had been chose. Lady Torrance gave a little cry of protest, but Lady Neville knew that she would have cried out at whatever choice Death made. She heard herself say calmly, "I am honored. But was there no one more worthy than I?"

"Not one," said Death. "There is no one quite so weary of being human, no one who knows better how meaningless it is to be alone. And there is no one else here with the power to treat life"—and she smiled sweetly and cruelly—"the life of your hairdresser's child, for instance, as the meaningless thing it is. Death has a heart, but it is forever an empty heart, and I think, Lady Neville, that your heart is like a dry riverbed, like a seashell. You will be very content as Death, more so than I, for I was very young when I became Death."

She came toward Lady Neville, light and swaying, her deep eyes wide and full of the light of the red morning sun that was beginning to rise. The guests at the ball moved back from her, although she did not look at them, but Lady Neville clenched her hands tightly and watched Death come toward her with her little dancing steps. "We must kiss each other," Death said. "That is the way I became death." She shook her head delightedly, so that her soft hair swirled about her shoulders. "Quickly, quickly," she said. "Oh, I cannot wait to be human again."

"You may not like it," Lady Neville said. She felt very calm, though she could hear her old heart pounding in her chest and feel it in the tips of her fingers. "You may not like it after a while," she said.

"Perhaps not." Death's smile was very close to her now. "I will not be as beautiful as I am, and perhaps people will not love me as much as they do now. But I will be human for a while, and at last I will die. I have done my penance."

"What penance?" the old woman asked the beautiful girl. "What was it you did? Why did you become Death?"

"I don't remember," said the Lady Death. "And you too will forget in time." She was smaller than Lady Neville, and so much younger. In her white dress she might have been the daughter that Lady Neville had never had, who would have been with her always and held her mother's head lightly in the crook of her arm when she felt old and sad. Now she lifted her head to kiss Lady Neville's cheek, and as she did so she whispered in her ear, "You will still be beautiful when I am ugly. Be kind to me then."

Behind Lady Neville the handsome gentlemen and ladies murmured and sighed, fluttering like moths in their evening dress, in their elegant gowns. "I promise," she said, and then she pursed her dry lips to kiss the soft, sweet-smelling cheek of the young Lady Death.

CREATURE CONTRIBUTORS

BEAGLE, Peter S. (1939–) is the author of *The Last Unicorn*, and more than twenty-five other books, both fiction and nonfiction. He's also a poet, screenwriter, and songwriter, and the winner of a World Fantasy Award for Lifetime Achievement in 2011.

"Come Lady Death" was first published in 1963.

BOUCHER, Anthony, aka William Anthony Parker White, aka H. H. Holmes, (1911–1968) was a science-fiction author, respected literary critic, and writer of mysteries and short stories. He was also the first English translator of Jorge Luis Borges, the author of numerous radio plays, and a founder of the *Magazine of Fantasy and Science Fiction*.

"The Compleat Werewolf" was first published in 1942.

DAVIDSON, Avram (1923–1993) was the author of dozens of short stories and novels. He wrote everything from space opera to science fiction to detective novels, along with a series of alternate history novels about the medieval magician Vergil Magus (derived from Virgil).

"Or All the Seas with Oysters" was first published in 1958.

DELANY, Samuel R. (1942–) is an author, professor, and critic. He's written a number of award-winning books in a variety of genres, including science fiction, fantasy, memoir, and criticism, the first (*The Jewels of Aptor*) published when he was twenty. He is a member of the Science Fiction Hall of Fame.

"Prismatica" was first published in 1977.

GAIMAN, Neil (1960–) is the author of many novels and short stories, including *Coraline* and *The Graveyard Book*, as well as screenplays, graphic novels, songs, and television scripts. He's the winner of a Newbery Medal.

"Sunbird" was first published in 2005.

HEADLEY, Maria Dahvana (1977–) is the author of *The Year of Yes: A Memoir,* and the historical fantasy novel, *Queen of Kings,* as well as many short stories and plays.

"Moveable Beast" was first published in this anthology.

HOPKINSON, Nalo (1960–) is the World Fantasy Award–winning author of four novels (*Brown Girl in the Ring, Midnight Robber, The Salt Roads, The New Moon's Arms*), a short-story collection (*Skin Folk*), and editor of several anthologies.

"The Smile on the Face" was first published in 2004.

JONES, Diana Wynne (1934–2011) was the British science-fiction and fantasy author responsible for, among many other things, the novel *Howl's Moving Castle* and the Chrestomanci series. She won a World Fantasy Award for Lifetime Achievement in 2011.

"The Sage of Theare" was first published in 1982.

KURASHIGE, Megan (1983–) is a professional dancer and writer. She and her sister, Shannon Kurashige, collaborate on wild and quixotic dance projects under the name Sharp & Fine in San Francisco. Her fiction and poetry have previously appeared in *Sybil's Garage*, *Strange Horizons*, and *Electric Velocipede*.

"The Manticore, The Mermaid, and Me" was first published in this anthology.

NESBIT, E., aka Edith Nesbit, (1858–1924) was the author of more than sixty books for children, most famously *The Railway Children*, along with many short stories and poems.

"The Cockatoucan" was first published in 1900.

NIVEN, Larry (1938–) is the author of many works of science fiction and fantasy, including the novel *Ringworld*. He's also a humorist, particularly known for the Superman spoof "Man of Steel, Woman of Kleenex."

"Flight of the Horse" was first published in 1969, under the variant title "Get a Horse!"

OKORAFOR, Nnedi (1974–) is the author of three young-adult novels, two children's books, and the 2010 World Fantasy Award–winning novel *Who Fears Death*.

"Ozioma the Wicked" was first published in this anthology.

SAKI, aka H. H. Munro, (1870–1916) was born in British Burma (now Myanmar), and worked in England for most of his life. He wrote political sketches, plays, a novel, and a quantity of short stories, many of which deal with the notion of feral adolescence.

"Gabriel-Ernest," Saki's werewolf plus Lost Boy tale, was first published in 1909.

STOCKTON, Frank R. (1834–1902) was an American writer and humorist particularly known for his children's fairy tales. He was, for years, a wood engraver, and then a newspaper journalist. Interestingly, his fable *The Lady or the Tiger*—neither fairy tale nor humorous, is his most famous work and a classroom staple.

"The Griffin and the Minor Canon" was first published in 1885.

WILSON, Gahan (1930–) is an American author, cartoonist, and illustrator best known for his cartoons depicting horror-fantasy scenarios. His work has been seen in publications ranging from *The New Yorker* to *National Lampoon*.

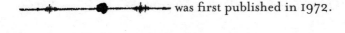 was first published in 1972.

YU, E. Lily (1990–) was born in Oregon and raised in New Jersey. Her stories have appeared in *Kenyon Review Online, Clarkesworld,* and *The Best Science Fiction and Fantasy of the Year*. She received the 2012 John W. Campbell Award for Best New Writer.

"The Cartographer Wasps and the Anarchist Bees" was first published in 2011.

CREATURE ILLUSTRATOR

MORROW-CRIBBS, Briony (1982–) is a fine artist who has also illustrated two *New York Times* bestsellers: *Wicked Plants: The Weed That Killed Lincoln's Mother and Other Botanical Atrocities* and *Wicked Bugs: The Louse That Conquered Napoleon's Army and Other Diabolical Insects*. Currently Briony teaches etching at the University of Wisconsin–Madison.
www.brionymorrow-cribbs.com